P9-CDI-988

LIBERTY

Also by Stephen Coonts

Liberty
America
Combat (Ed)
Cuba
Fortunes of War
Hong Kong
Flight of the Intruder
The Minotaur
Under Siege
The Red Horseman
The Intruders
Final Flight
The Cannibal Queen (non-fiction)
War in the Air (non-fiction)

LIBERTY

Stephen Coonts

First published in Great Britain in 2002 by Orion Books
an imprint of The Orion Publishing Group
Orion House, 5 Upper St Martin's Lane, London WC2H 9EA

A CIP catalogue record for this book is available from the British Library

ISBN (hardback) 0 75284 631 0
ISBN (trade paperback) 0 75284 632 9

Printed and bound in Britain by
Clays Ltd, St Ives plc

This book is dedicated to everyone who believes in political and religious freedom—Liberty—wherever they may be.

ACKNOWLEDGMENTS

This story was developed and written in the twelve months following the September 11, 2001, attacks on New York and Washington, D.C., by suicidal religious fanatics who again proved, if more proof were needed, the vulnerability of the civilization and economy that feeds, clothes, and houses the six billion people marooned on this small planet.

The author's editor at St. Martin's Press, the indomitable Charles Spicer, and the author's wife, Deborah Buell Coonts, were instrumental in the development of the plot. Gilbert "Gil" Pascal assisted with numerous technical points and suggested one of the main plot twists. Ross Statham shed valuable light on the world of computers and the Internet. Tom and Kay Harper assisted with the descriptions of Cairo. Dr. Matt Cooper provided valuable information on the effects of the drug ketamine. The author is deeply in their debt.

This novel is a work of fiction. As usual, the author is solely responsible for the story, characters, incidents, and dialogue contained herein.

PROLOGUE

The night was sinister. In the vast grassy steppe of central Asia there were no towns, no villages, no isolated farmhouses with electricity to power a light that would break the great darkness. Overhead, twenty thousand feet of clouds blocked the light from moon and stars, absorbed all of it and left the Earth with nothing.

Two vehicles drove along a crumbling asphalt road, an old Ford van without windows and a two-axle truck with an enclosed cargo compartment. Their headlights were the only sign of life in the night. Beside the road was a large fence of woven wire topped with three strands of barbed wire. Occasionally, small rusted metal signs were attached to the wire, their Cyrillic lettering all but illegible.

Several hours after dark the van and truck topped a gentle rise, and their drivers saw a light in the distance. As they approached they could see it was a naked bulb mounted high on a pole beside a gate, a break in the wire. Beside the gate was a guard shack. Four armed men, soldiers, lounged near the gate, two seated, two leaning against the gate itself, a metal pole that blocked the entrance.

The van and truck turned off the highway and came to a stop by the gate. A man got out of the passenger seat of the van and approached the guard shack. He spoke to one of the guards. In a moment an officer came out of the wooden frame building. He shined a flashlight into the front seat of the van, examined the driver's face, then walked around behind the van and gestured at the rear doors.

The man beside him opened the doors, allowed the officer to look inside with the flashlight. Four men holding assault rifles were sitting on the floor. Several dark canvas bags were visible in the crowded vehicle, as well as sacks that might contain food and a variety of water containers.

After the officer had inspected the truck, including its cargo compartment, he walked back to the guard shack and went inside, leaving the passenger standing amid the soldiers.

Through the windows the officer could be seen placing a telephone call. His men stood near the gate, their weapons in their hands, staring at the dark, dirty van and its patchy paint.

When the officer hung up the telephone, he stepped to the door of the building, motioned to the soldiers. They opened the gate and waved at the driver of the van.

The vehicles left the lonely guard shack and its light behind. The road wound up a gentle ridge out of the valley, topped the crest, and continued across the steppe.

Fifteen minutes later they reached a fenced compound festooned with lights. An armed guard waved them through the gate as they approached. They drove past two idling tanks. The men in the turrets watched them, spoke into mouthpieces that hung from their headsets. A soldier directed the vehicles to halt near a well-lit one-story building with small windows. A dozen armed soldiers in battle dress were arrayed in front of this building and across the street.

Four people were seated inside at a long table in the main room, three army officers and a woman dressed in a well-cut dark suit. The woman was smoking. Assault rifles lay on the table in front of the army officers.

"I am Ashruf," the passenger from the van said in Russian. He glanced at each of the soldiers, measuring them perhaps, yet his eyes lingered on the woman, who was slender, with long black hair, and appeared to be about thirty years of age.

One of the soldiers spoke. "General Petrov." He glanced at his watch. "You're late."

"We didn't want to cross the border until dark." Ashruf gestured upward. "Satellites."

"They can see nothing under all these clouds," General Petrov muttered. He was wrong about that, but he didn't know it. Petrov was a fleshy man of medium height, with close-cropped gray hair. He nodded toward an ovoid shape strapped to a wooden pallet in the corner of the room. "There it is. Do you want to inspect it?"

"There were supposed to be four."

"There are hundreds. After we see the color of your money, you may pick any four you like."

Ashruf walked over to the shape, bent to examine it. He was a fit man, slightly above medium height, with a short, trimmed beard. He was dressed in slacks, sandals, a loose shirt, and wore a turban.

Even though the room was brightly lit, Ashruf removed a flashlight from his pocket and examined every square inch of the object on the pallet.

General Petrov came over to Ashruf, squatted. "Are you satisfied?"

Ashruf glanced at him, then continued with his inspection. Finally he stood, walked to the door, and went out.

When he returned he carried a shiny aluminum case. He brought it over to the pallet, set it on the wooden floor, and opened it. After flipping some switches, he removed a wand from his pocket and plugged the cord into the box. He waved the wand over the metal shape as he examined the gauges of his instrument. He turned off the power to the instrument, unplugged the wand, closed the cover and hoisted it.

"I am satisfied," he said.

"Good," said Petrov. "Now we shall inspect the money. Bring it in and put it on the table."

Ashruf and three of his men carried in duffel bags. They dumped the contents on the table, United States currency, bundles of hundred-dollar bills, fifty to a bundle. The army officers and the civilians picked up random bundles and began counting.

While this was going on Ashruf and his men stood and watched.

The woman, whose name was Anna Modin, chose a random bundle and tore it apart. She spread the currency on the table, then picked up a leather bag from the floor beside her chair and set it on the table. Opening it, she removed a black light and a magnifying glass mounted on a small light table. She used these tools to examine the bills, one by one.

When she finished she gathered up the bills, counted them, snapped a rubber band around them, then dived deep in the pile for another bundle. After tearing it apart, she began inspecting random bills.

"It's all real," Ashruf remarked to Petrov, who paid no attention. He continued to count bills within the bundles.

When Modin put away her equipment, the soldiers carefully arranged the bundles in stacks, then counted them. General Petrov announced, "Two million dollars. Does everyone agree?"

They all did. A gesture from Petrov caused the officers to begin placing the stacks of currency in the duffel bags.

"So," Petrov said, addressing Ashruf, "do you want this one, or do you want to choose all four at random?"

Ashruf took his time, apparently making up his mind. "We will take this one and three more."

"Each of them weighs about a hundred kilos. Six men can handle one."

Ashruf nodded again, once.

"Use your people," Petrov said.

The armed Russians watched as Ashruf and his colleagues, which was everyone from the van and truck, arranged themselves around the pallet. At Ashruf's command, they hoisted it off the ground, then worked it through the door and out to the truck. With much huffing and puffing, they lifted the pallet and its shape high enough to slide it into the bed of the cargo compartment. Then they climbed into the truck and shoved mightily until they got the pallet into one corner, where they secured it with ropes.

With Ashruf and his men in their truck following along behind, Petrov climbed into a truck loaded with armed soldiers and led the way into the darkness. They drove for several miles, passed through several more high fences, and entered an area containing long rows of earthen mounds. Finally the lead truck stopped and the soldiers piled out of the back. They directed the driver of the following truck to park in front of the steel double doors. One of the soldiers used a key to open the lock, then two men opened the doors and turned on lights inside the mound.

Several dozen pallets were stored within. An ovoid shape was strapped to each with metal straps. Beside each one a steel rod protruded from the ground, one with a wire that led to the metal fittings on the rear of each shape.

"Take your pick," Petrov said.

The shapes were painted white, yet on some of them a fungus had begun to grow. Ashruf scraped at the fungus with a fingernail, removing the flora and the white paint underneath. His flashlight beam revealed rust spots on the steel skins.

He used the device in the aluminum case. After checking eight or nine of the objects, he selected three that seemed to have the least amount of surface corrosion. As Ashruf and his men disconnected the grounding wires, General Petrov remarked, "If I were you, I'd be careful with those warheads while they are ungrounded. The detonators are in the high explosive. If you let electromagnetic energy build up on one of those things, it's conceivable you raghead sons of bitches and a whole lot of your friends are going to find yourself instantly in hell with Mohammed."

Ashruf ignored the general. Speaking Arabic, he arranged his men around the first pallet, hoisted it carefully, and carried it to the truck. When they had that warhead secured, they returned to the magazine for another.

The entire operation took about half an hour.

Anna Modin was standing outside the one-story building in the compound area when the party returned from the magazines. Ashruf stayed in the cab beside the truck driver while his colleagues climbed down from the back of the truck, locked the cargo door, and entered the van. With General Petrov and Modin watching, the van followed the truck out of the compound past the tanks and headed for the main gate.

"A profitable evening, General," Anna Modin said. "Two million American dollars. Congratulations."

"You have earned your ten thousand," Petrov said as he watched the taillights of the van and Ashruf's truck cross the low ridge beyond the compound gate. When the lights disappeared from view, he suggested, "Let's drink to our good fortune."

"Did you recognize him?" Petrov asked, meaning Ashruf.

"Oh, yes," Anna Modin said. "The name he uses most often is Frouq al-Zuair. He's Egyptian, I think. He may be Palestinian or Saudi. He is wanted by the Israelis and the Egyptians. Bombs are his specialty, yet as I recall, the Egyptians want him for hacking some tourists to death with a machete. Infidels, you know."

"He has friends with money," Petrov said. He was a practical man.

"You would have done the world a favor," Anna mused, "if you had just shot them and kept their money."

"And the evening would have been just as profitable," Petrov said, grinning. "Alas, Anna Mikhailova, you don't understand the intricacies of capitalism and international trade. Killing customers is bad for business. Zuair and his friends may return someday with more millions."

"Someday," Anna Modin said hopefully, and followed General Petrov toward his office.

CHAPTER ONE

The tall, lean man walked out the entrance of the United Nations building in Manhattan and paused at the top of the main staircase to extract a cigarette from a metal case. He wore a dark gray suit of an expensive cut and a deep blue silk tie. Over that he wore a well-tailored wool coat. He lit his cigarette, snapped the lighter shut, and descended the staircase.

He joined the throngs on the sidewalk and walked purposefully, taking no more note of his fellow pedestrians than any other New Yorker. He turned westward on East Forty-sixth Street, which was one-way eastbound and choked with traffic, as usual. Striding along with the pace of a man who has a destination but is not late, he crossed Second, Third, Lexington and Park Avenues, and turned north on Madison.

On Forty-eighth, he turned west again. Crossing Fifth Avenue, he took no notice of the crowds or people in front of the plaza at Rockefeller Center, but walked steadily through them, ditched his cigarette at the door of the NBC building—he was on his third by then—and went inside. Seven minutes later he was on the Rockefeller Center subway platform. He stepped aboard a southbound F train just before the doors closed and grabbed a bar near the door. The train got under way immediately.

As the train roared through darkness, the tall man casually examined the faces of his fellow passengers, then stood at ease holding the metal bar. He watched with no apparent interest as people got on and off the train at each stop.

In Brooklyn he exited the train, climbed to the street and immediately went back down into the subway station. In minutes he was aboard another F train heading north, back into Manhattan.

This time he exited the train at Grand Street in Little Italy. Up on the sidewalk, he began walking south. An hour later the tall man passed the entrance of the Staten Island Ferry and walked into Battery Park. Several times he checked his watch.

Once he stopped and lit another cigarette, then sat on a bench overlooking New York Harbor. After fifteen minutes of this, he went back toward the ferry pier and began walking north on Broadway. Three blocks later he caught a northbound taxi.

"Seventy-ninth and Riverside Drive, please."

Broadway was a crawl. The taxi driver, a man from the Middle East, mouthed common obscenities at every stoplight. North of Times Square the cab made better time.

After he left the taxi, the tall man walked toward the Hudson River. Soon he was strolling the River Walk. He turned onto the pedestrian pier that jutted into the river and walked behind several dozen people standing against the railing facing south. Many had cameras and were shooting pictures of the skyline to the south where the twin towers of the World Trade Center had stood.

At the end of the pier were several benches, all empty save one. Four men, two of them policemen in uniform, were turning strollers and tourists away from the bench area, but the tall man walked by them without a word. The middle-aged man seated on the bench was wearing jeans, tennis shoes, a faded ski jacket, and wraparound sunglasses that hid his eyes. He had a rolled-up newspaper in his hand. He glanced at the tall man as he approached.

"Good morning, Jake," the tall man said.

"Hello, Ilin."

"I'm clean, I presume."

"Ever since the Rockefeller Center subway station."

The tall man nodded. His name was Janos Ilin, and he was a senior officer in the SVR (*Sluzhba Vneshnei Razvedki*), the Russian Foreign Intelligence Service, which was the bureaucratic successor to the foreign intelligence arm—the First Chief Directorate—of the Soviet-era KGB. The man in jeans was Rear Admiral Jake Grafton of the United States Navy. He appeared to be in his late forties, had short, thinning hair combed straight back, and a nose that was a size too large for his face. He looked reasonably fit, with a fading tan that suggested he spent time in the sun on a regular basis.

"Poor tradecraft, meeting in the open like this," Jake said. Ilin had picked the meeting place.

Ilin grinned. "Sometimes the best places are in plain sight."

Ilin stood examining the surroundings. After a minute spent looking south at the southern end of Manhattan, he ran his eyes along the shoreline, the people on the pier, then turned to watch the boats going up and down the Hudson. "That atrocity," he said, gesturing toward the southern end of Manhattan, "would never have happened in Russia."

Jake Grafton made a noncommittal noise.

"I know what you are thinking," Ilin continued, after a glance at the American. "You are thinking that we would never have given several dozen Arabs the free run of the country, to do whatever they had the money to do, and that is true. But that is not the critical factor. Bin Laden, al-Qaeda, the Islamic Jihad—all those religious fascists know that if they ever pull a stunt like that—" he gestured to the south "—in Russia, we will hunt them to the ends of the earth and execute them wherever we find them. We will exterminate the lot of them. To the very last man."

"The same way the KGB murdered Hafizullah Amin in Kabul?" Jake asked. In 1979 KGB special forces disguised in Afghan uniforms assaulted the presidential palace and assassinated the president of Afghanistan, his family, and entourage. Moscow's handpicked successor asked for Soviet help, which fortunately was immediately at hand since the Red Army had already invaded.

"Precisely. But you Americans don't do things the Russian way." Ilin got out his cigarette case and lit one.

"Thank God. You killed a million Afghanis and lost what, about thirty thousand of your own in Afghanistan?"

"As I recall, you killed four million Vietnamese and lost fifty-eight thousand Americans in your little brushfire war."

"I served that one up, I suppose." Jake sighed. "Two men followed you to Rockefeller Center. Apparently Russians. Someone over there doesn't trust you."

"Touché," Janos Ilin said. His lips formed the trace of a smile. "Can you describe them?"

Jake reached under his jacket and produced two photos. He handed them to Ilin, who glanced at each one, then passed them back. "I know them. Thanks for coming today."

"Why me?" Jake Grafton asked as he pocketed the photos.

Yesterday Ilin had telephoned Callie Grafton at the Graftons' apartment in Roslyn, Virginia, and asked for Jake's office telephone number. Since she knew Ilin—he had worked with her husband the previous year—she gave it to him. Then he telephoned the FBI/CIA Joint Antiterrorism Task Force at CIA headquarters in Langley and asked for Grafton by name. The call came from a pay telephone in New York City. When Grafton came on the line, Ilin asked to meet him in New York the following day. They had set up the meet. Grafton had arranged to have agents monitor Ilin's progress around New York to ensure he wasn't followed. If he had been, Grafton would not have been waiting on the pier.

"I heard you were the senior military liaison officer to the FBI/CIA antiterrorism task force. I know you, so . . ."

"I don't think that's classified information, but I don't recall anyone doing a press release on my new assignment."

A trace of a smile crossed Ilin's face. "The fact that I know is my credential. Let's reserve that topic for a few minutes."

Jake took off his sunglasses, folded them carefully, and put them in a shirt pocket inside his jacket. His eyes, Ilin noticed, were gray and hard as he scrutinized the Russian's face. "So what are you doing in New York? Servicing a mole?"

"I came to see you."

"Did the Center send you?"

"No."

Ilin stepped to the railing facing south, which he leaned on. Jake Grafton joined him. A police helicopter buzzed down the river and jets could be heard going into Newark and Teterboro. Contrails could be seen in the blue sky overhead. Ilin watched them a moment as he finished his cigarette, then tossed the butt into the river.

"Islamic terrorists can be placed in three general categories," Ilin said conversationally. "The foot soldiers are recruited from refugee camps and poor villages throughout the Arab world. These young men are ignorant, usually illiterate, and know little or nothing of the Western world. They are the shock troops and suicide commandos who smite the Israelis and murder tourists in the Arab world. They speak only Arabic. They blend in quite well in Arab society, but are essentially unable to function outside of it. These are the troops that bin Laden and his ilk train as Islamic warriors in Afghanistan and Libya and Iraq."

Grafton nodded.

"The second category, if you will, are Arabs with better educations, usually literate, some even possess a technical skill. The fundamentalists actively recruit these people, appeal to their religious sensitivities, wish to convert them to their perverted view of Islam. Since these people have often lived outside the Arab world they can move freely in Western society. These people are dangerous. They are the ones who hijacked the airliners that crashed into the World Trade Center and the Pentagon. By the way, the plane that hit the Pentagon was supposed to crash the White House. The one that crashed in Pennsylvania was supposed to hit the Capitol Building."

"Umm," Jake said. He knew all of this, of course, but Ilin had gone to a lot of trouble to arrange this meeting and he was willing to listen to what he had to say.

"The third category of terrorists can be thought of as generals. Bin Laden and his chief lieutenants, financiers, bankers, technical advisers, and so forth. These people are Muslims. For whatever reason, terrorism appeals to their ethnic and religious view of the world."

Ilin paused and glanced around him, almost an automatic gesture.

"And there is a fourth category. Few of these people are Arabs, few are Muslims. They see profit in terrorism. Some of them take pleasure in the pain the terrorists inflict, for every reason under the sun. These people are enemies of America, enemies of Western civilization. I came today to talk to you about several people in this category."

"This fourth group," Jake mused. "Are any of them Russians?"

"Russians, Germans, French, Egyptians, Japanese, Chinese, Hindu, you name it. America is the big boy in the world—many people have grievances, real and imagined."

"Hate is a powerful emotion," Jake muttered.

"One of America's many enemies is a Russian general named Petrov. He doesn't hate America, he loves money. A few weeks ago he sold four missile warheads for two million dollars."

"To whom?"

"They call themselves the Sword of Islam. Petrov is in charge of a base near Rubtsovsk. The man who led the team that picked up the weapons was Frouq al-Zuair, a man who has been knocking around the Middle East causing random mayhem for many years. He hacked some tourists to death in Egypt and evaded the roundup of extremists by escaping to Iraq. Who his friends are, where they are, I don't know.

In fact, I am not supposed to know about Petrov or Zuair or the weapons."

"But you do know?"

"A little, yes."

"Is it true? Or fiction that you are supposed to pass along?"

"True, I think. Although one can never be absolutely sure. And honestly, the Center doesn't know I am telling this to you."

"How'd you hear of it?" Grafton was shoulder to shoulder with Ilin.

"That I can't tell you. Suffice it to say that I believe the information is credible. I know of Petrov. He's capable of a stunt like that. I'm passing it to the American government to do with as they see fit. For what it's worth, most of our senior politicians don't know of this matter and would not admit it happened even if they did know. They can't afford a rupture with the United States."

"Are you saying we can't use this information?"

"Your government shouldn't brace Moscow on it. They'll deny it. And don't let my government know where you heard it. I'm a dead man if it gets back to them."

"I'll do the best I can."

"So we get around to your question about how I knew you had been assigned to the antiterrorism task force. We have a mole in the CIA."

"Jesus," Jake muttered, shaking his head.

"His name is Richard Doyle. Don't let him see anything with my name on it."

"What if we arrest him?"

"That's up to you. As long as he doesn't learn that I betrayed him."

"We may use him to feed you disinformation. There's a spy term for that, though I have forgotten it."

"Richard Doyle is a traitor," Janos Ilin said softly. "He signed his death warrant when he agreed to spy for the communists fifteen years ago. He's been living on borrowed time ever since."

"Fifteen years?" Jake was horrified.

Ilin took out his thin metal case, opened it and extracted another cigarette. He played with it in his fingers. His hands, Jake noted, were steady.

"Fifteen years . . . and now he gets the chop."

"Unfortunately, Mr. Doyle must be sacrificed for a larger cause."

"Who made that decision?"

"I did," Ilin said without inflection. "A man must take responsibility for the world in which he lives. If he doesn't, someone will do it for him, someone like bin Laden, Lenin, Stalin, Hitler, Mao. . . . Murderous fanatics are always ready to purge us of our ills." He shrugged. "I happen to believe that the planet is better off with civilization than without it. This tired old rock doesn't need six billion starving people marooned on it."

"And you? Are you a traitor?"

"Label me any way you wish." Ilin grinned savagely. "I don't want to read about four two-hundred-kiloton nuclear explosions devastating the only superpower left in the world. Russia needs a few friends."

"Where are the weapons now?"

"I don't know. They could be anywhere on the planet," Ilin said, and puffed slowly and lazily. Airplanes came and went overhead. The late-winter breeze was out of the west and carried the smell of the Hudson.

"What kind of information is the SVR getting from Doyle?"

"That's an interesting question," Ilin said, brightening perceptibly. "I don't see all of the Doyle material, but one listens, makes guesses, surmises. Doyle is quite a source. Almost too good. I got the impression that his control and the Center have wondered at times if perhaps he was a double agent, yet his information has been good. From across a surprisingly large spectrum of the intelligence world."

"He's getting intelligence from someone else inside our government?"

"He's remarkably well informed."

"Any guesses where some of this other stuff is coming from?"

"Somewhere in the FBI, I would imagine. Counterintelligence."

"Want to give me a sample or two?"

"No."

"The Sword of Islam," Jake mused. "I've heard of them. Rumor has it they were involved with something called the Manhattan Project, but we assumed it was that." He pointed toward the southern skyline.

"That would be a dangerous assumption," Ilin said. "Four tactical nukes, warheads for long-range, stand-off antiship missiles. Fleet killers. Each packs roughly twenty times the yield of the weapons you used on Hiroshima and Nagasaki. Easily transported. If competent technicians get their hands on them, they could be used as portable bombs."

"Handy."

"Quite. I would imagine each warhead would weigh about a hundred kilos, and be, perhaps, a little larger than a soccer ball. As some wit pointed out years ago, the terrorists could disguise them as cocaine and bring them in through the Miami airport."

"Any other thoughts?"

"Don't assume that the target is America. Oh, certainly, America is the great Satan and all that, but the real target is Western civilization."

He smacked his hands together. "This web of airplanes and computers and telephones and banks that move capital freely—all of that is in danger from religious fanatics who wish to destroy this secular edifice that feeds and clothes and houses billions of people. They want to create chaos, prove the primacy of their cause. In the new dark ages that will follow they will build their holy empire. Think of it—billions of ignorant, starving people bowing toward Mecca five times a day."

"They haven't won yet, and they won't win in the future," Jake Grafton shot back. "If they succeed in bringing about a holy war—Islam on one side and civilization on the other—Islam will lose."

"From your vantage point that would appear to be a safe prediction," replied Janos Ilin. "These fanatics wish to shatter the primacy of the rich nations, foremost of which is America. They think that the struggle will radicalize the Islamic masses and destroy the secular Arab governments that attempt to straddle the cultural divide. The goal is to re-create the glorious past, build a united Islamic nation intolerant of dissent, obedient to their vision of God's laws. *They think they will win because God is on their side*."

"Whirling Dervishes," Grafton muttered.

"Many Muslims thought that bin Laden was the Mahdi, the Islamic messiah. He certainly saw himself in that role. In any event, the Muslim world is under severe stress, so we're doing holy war again."

"The terrorists have won some and lost some," Jake said thoughtfully. "People are indeed terrorized."

Ilin turned to face upriver, leaned back against the railing. "In all my years in intelligence, I have never seen a covert operation as large as the September Eleven attack. Quite remarkable." Ilin sighed. "It was only possible because Americans are so trusting, so unsuspicious."

"Not anymore," Jake Grafton said sourly.

"Your countrymen have had an expensive education," Ilin agreed. "One would suspect that future terror attacks will be low-tech, with only one or a few perpetrators. Poison in a municipal water system, adulterated food, something along those lines would maximize their chance of success, minimize the risk, and create terror. Yet, someone paid General Petrov a large sum of money for nuclear weapons."

He flipped away his cig. It took a curving path into the dark water. "This talk of justice I see in the press worries me," he continued. "This war is beyond courts and lawyers, with their sophistry and legalisms. Your enemies will win a victory if you give them a courtroom forum. If you people don't understand that, you are lost."

Ilin held out his hand. Jake shook.

"Good luck, my friend."

"Thanks for coming, Ilin."

Ilin nodded once, glanced again downriver, then walked away. Jake watched him walk the length of the pier and disappear up the sidewalk into the naked trees.

One of the closest fishermen reeled in his bait and disassembled his rod. When he had his gear stowed in carrying cases, he came over to where Jake stood, still looking downriver.

"What did he have to say, Admiral?"

The questioner was Commander Toad Tarkington, Grafton's executive assistant. He had been with Grafton for years. He was several inches shorter than the admiral, with regular, handsome features marked with laugh lines.

"He says that several weeks ago some Russian general sold four missile warheads to an outfit calling themselves the Sword of Islam."

"Do you believe him?"

"Well, the story sounds plausible. He claims that the SVR doesn't know he is giving us this information, which he is donating to the cause of civilization out of the goodness of his heart."

"Where are the weapons now?"

"He says he doesn't know."

Toad pursed his lips and whistled softly. "Four warheads! As usual, we're right on top of events."

"Makes you want to cry, doesn't it?"

CHAPTER TWO

When Jake returned to Washington that afternoon, he went straight to CIA headquarters at Langley. His boss was a man named Coke Twilley. He was heavyset, balding, and, Jake gathered, had joined the CIA when he graduated from college. He had once mentioned that he was a Yale graduate, which was no surprise; in the 1950s and '60s, the CIA had recruited heavily from the Ivy League. He wore what appeared to be his college class ring on his right hand. Twilley had the look and mannerisms of a college professor. On rare occasions his fleshy features registered faint amusement, but usually his features betrayed no emotion except boredom. One was left with the impression that the only part of his professional life he enjoyed was intellectual give-and-take with his social peers, who were few and far between in the down-and-dirty trenches of espionage and office politics. His one human quality was an addiction to Coca-Cola, the sugared variety, which he sipped more or less all day, hence his nickname. What his beverage of choice did to his blood sugar level only his doctor knew.

His assistant department head was a man named Khanh Tran, though everyone called him Sonny. He was a whippet-lean Vietnamese who had come to the States when he was seven years old. He didn't speak a word of English then, and today still had a trace of an accent. A graduate of Cal Poly, he had spent his adult life in the CIA.

This afternoon in Twilley's office, Twilley and Sonny Tran listened to Jake's report without interruption. He carefully covered every point.

When Jake finished, Twilley asked, "Do you have any suggestions for verifying this tale?"

"Get it from another source," Jake replied dryly.

"So where do you think the weapons are now?" Twilley idly played with an expensive fountain pen, a Christmas or birthday gift from days gone by. As usual, today he looked mildly bored, and perhaps he was.

"I haven't the slightest idea. Neither did Ilin."

"Richard Doyle? I've known him for years. A Russian spy? Do you believe that?"

"It strikes me that allegation is certainly worth checking. If it's not true, no harm will be done. If it is . . ." He left the comment hanging.

"I've never liked Russians," Twilley said now, apropos of nothing. He took a sip of Coke from a coffee cup, then leaned back in his padded swivel chair and laced his fingers across his ample middle. He had a habit of staring owlishly at people, which he indulged in now with Jake, blinking so rarely that some people thought he never blinked at all.

"An intelligence gift from the SVR—that KGB crowd . . ." Twilley snorted derisively. "Worst collection of scum on the planet. Stalin's thugs. Murdered thirty million of their own people! I'd bet my pension those bastards have been selling weapons to terrorists for years and pocketing the proceeds. Now they're worried that the terrorists are going to pop a nuke somewhere and the shit is going to splatter on them, so they're covering their ass by whispering to us, blaming it all on some weenie brigadier rotting out in the boondocks. That crowd would sell coal to the devil!"

"You've had past dealings with Ilin, Admiral; you probably know him better than anyone in our government," Sonny Tran said smoothly. "Have you any other thoughts that you wish Mr. Twilley to pass along?"

"Yes, I do," Jake Grafton said. "Ilin gave us a place to start. The Sword of Islam. Regardless of why Ilin passed this information to us, we must investigate. It would be grotesquely irresponsible not to."

"We *will* investigate, Admiral," Tran assured him.

"And it goes without saying that the allegation against Doyle must also be investigated."

"Then why say it?" Twilley shot back.

"I want to be on record as strenuously recommending an investigation. Just in case Ilin's allegations fall through a bureaucratic crack."

Twilley's face was a mask. "I find that comment offensive, Grafton. The implication is that this agency is full of criminal incompetents."

"No one can win every battle," Jake replied, "but we'd damn well better win the war. You can take that remark any way you please."

It had been that kind of day. He was in a foul mood, and this little session with Coke Twilley hadn't improved it. He got up and left Twilley's office, closing the door behind him.

When he got home that evening to the apartment in Roslyn, Jake Grafton found that his wife, Callie, and daughter, Amy, were serving dinner to guests. Toad Tarkington's wife, Rita Moravia, was seated with her three-year-old son on her lap beside Jack Yocke, a reporter and columnist for the *Washington Post* that the Graftons had known for years. Yocke had brought a date, a tall woman in a business suit who appeared to be about thirty years of age. Her name was Greta Fairchild. After the introductions, Jake followed Callie into the kitchen and kissed her.

"How'd it go in New York?" she asked in a voice barely above a whisper.

"So, so."

"How is he?"

"About the same, near as I could tell. Still smokes incessantly."

"Hope you don't mind the crowd. I didn't know when you were coming home, and we invited Yocke and the Tarkingtons weeks ago. Rita says Toad will be along in a few minutes."

"Don't mind at all." He kissed her again. "I missed you, lady."

"Be careful," she cautioned as he pulled off his sweater and tossed it on a chair. "Fairchild is a lawyer, sharp and, I suspect, a wee bit argumentative."

"Afraid I'll get sued?"

"Afraid you'll get in an argument. You look like you could chew nails and spit tacks."

Jake took a deep breath, exhaled, then smiled broadly. Holding the grin, he asked, "How's this?"

"Fine. Go sit down and I'll bring you a glass of wine."

The Tarkington toadlet squirmed off his mother's lap and ran to Jake as he pecked Amy's cheek. "Uncle Hake, Uncle Hake, I pooped today."

"Made his mama proud," Rita proclaimed as the adults laughed. "Keep that up, son, and you'll make your mark in the world."

"You're getting to be a real big boy," Jake said as he lifted the youngster and gave him a smooch on his cheek. He took his usual seat at the head of the table and kept the boy on his lap.

Yocke was tall and lanky. He grinned as Jake listened solemnly to the three-year-old tell of the day's toilet adventures. When that topic had been exhausted, he said to the admiral, "I didn't realize the navy had gotten so casual. Jeans, no less."

"We try to keep up with the times." Away they went, chattering lightly. Greta Fairchild specialized in administrative law, had been with a Washington firm for five years. She was from California and, Jake gathered, had been dating Yocke occasionally for a year or so.

"Do you have any spare time now that you're stationed in Washington?" Callie asked Rita.

"Only on weekends. I've gotten my civilian flight instructor rating. Tommy Carmellini is my first student. Getting time to fly is difficult, but I've given him four lessons."

"Is he still scaring you?"

"Not so badly now. He's learning. I think he likes it. Afterward he drinks beer with Toad and tells him all about it."

Toad arrived fifteen minutes after Jake, carrying a high chair. He shook hands all around, pulled Amy upright from her chair and bent her over in a passionate matinee kiss, then dropped into the empty chair beside his wife. Amy seized the back of her chair to steady herself and gasped, "I love it when the Tarkingtons come to dinner."

"Two days you've been gone," Rita said icily to Toad, "and *I* don't get the romantic treatment. Is this a hint?"

"Stand up, babe."

As everyone cheered, Toad gave Rita a movie kiss like the one he had bestowed on Amy. When they broke, Rita's cheeks were flushed.

"Well," Toad demanded, "are we still a number?"

"You've sold me, Toad-man. Sit down and behave yourself."

Trust the ol' Horny Toad to lighten the mood, Jake thought. He winked at Callie and had a sip of wine.

"Is this what we have to look forward to?" Fairchild asked Jack Yocke, who put his hand on hers.

"Toad may have one more good smooch in him, if you ask him nice," Yocke replied. Fairchild joined in the laughter. Tarkington rescued his son from his boss's lap and installed him in the high chair.

After dinner Rita insisted on helping Callie with the dishes. Toad got into a conversation with Amy about college—she was a student at Georgetown—so Jake led Yocke into the living room. Greta Fairchild stayed with the men.

"How goes the war against terror these days?" Yocke asked. The fact that Jake was currently assigned to the antiterrorism task force was public information, but his duties were not. After knowing Grafton for years, Yocke well knew that he would not get anything classified from him. Nor could he use Jake as a source, even an anonymous one. Grafton was, in the lingo of journalists, deep background.

Grafton's answer to the reporter's question was a shrug. Yocke glanced at Greta, who blandly met his eyes. She had no intention of being shuffled off to the kitchen. Yocke gave up. He leaned back in his chair and crossed one leg over the other.

They talked politics for a while. Greta was not shy about voicing her opinion, which the admiral listened to with interest. Finally he said to Yocke, "So what's wrong with the CIA?"

Yocke snorted. "The organization was put together after World War Two to keep an eye on the Russians. The mission was to prevent World War Three, and everything else was secondary to that."

"Yet they missed the collapse of communism and the breakup of the Soviet Union," Grafton mused, "the most significant political event in Russia since the 1917 Revolution. Not a soul at the CIA even suggested that the collapse of communism was a possibility. Then, bang, it happened, leaving every policy maker in Washington stupefied with surprise. Why was that?"

"All I can tell you is what my sources say—"

"Larded with your own opinions," Greta Fairchild interjected.

"Naturally," Yocke said, not missing a beat. "The KGB was very good at rooting out Soviets who were spying for the U.S. And various American traitors were busy betraying these people to the KGB for money. Add in the natural aversion of liberals for intelligence bureaucracies—gentlemen don't read other people's mail, and after all, it *is* cultural imperialism—and you have an outfit that decided it could find out what it needed to know by signal intelligence and imagery, which is satellite and aircraft reconnaissance. The agency never had enough good sources in high places in Moscow to let them see the big picture of what was really going on."

"They missed nine-eleven, too," Jake murmured.

"From what I hear, analysts at the agency were saying that the 1993 World Trade Center bombing was not an isolated threat. The Clinton administration didn't want to hear it. Then came the USS *Cole*. But still, the agency is structured to warn us if the Russians are preparing for World War Three, not tell us who in the mosques and bazaars of the Islamic world is plotting atrocities and making them happen."

"Can the agency be reformed?" Greta asked.

"Certainly. Reorganized and refocused. Yet I don't think it will ever be as good as the KGB was. I think the American people and the politicians will lose interest in the war on terrorism—hell, you read the newspapers—and those are the consumers the agency serves. Frankly, the politicians don't want to pay people to hunt for bad news and they don't want to hear it when it's found."

"Jack, you're a terrible cynic," Greta remarked, and winked at her host. "But what about the FBI? Nineteen suicidal saboteurs running around the country with no one the wiser—J. Edgar Hoover must be pounding the lid of his coffin."

"I'll bet he is," Jake muttered.

The conversation had moved on to other subjects when Amy came to the door and announced, "Pie and ice cream."

Richard Doyle lived in a middle-sized, middle-class, three-bedroom, two-and-a-half-bath house with a two-car garage in the endless suburbs of Virginia. His house sat tucked between two very similar houses on a quiet, tree-lined curvy street in a subdivision full of curvy streets and speed bumps, a subdivision indistinguishable from a hundred others sprawled across the landscape west of the Potomac.

The Doyles had an above-ground pool in their backyard. They purchased it years ago for the kids when they were small, but now that they were in high school the kids wanted to go to the community pool in the summer to hang with friends, so the Doyles' pool was empty. Indeed, it had not contained water for several years.

Martha Doyle sold real estate from a nearby mall office of a national chain. She drove a late-model white Lexus, which she used to haul clients around to look at houses. The expenses on the car were a nice tax write-off. Many of the people looking for houses were government employees, like her husband, or worked for civil or defense contractors or consulting firms that did business with the government. Some worked in the high-tech industries west of the Beltway.

All in all, Martha Doyle was in a great place to sell real estate. Few people in the area owned a house more than three or four years; the constant turnover kept the market hot, hot, hot. She worked out at a racquet club and belonged to a variety of civic groups, which she had joined when she realized that the contacts she made there would bring her listings.

The Doyles also belonged to a church. They attended services several times a month and participated in church events. Whether the motive was listings for Mrs. Doyle or because the Doyles enjoyed belonging to a religious community, no one could say.

Richard Doyle worked for the CIA, although none of his neighbors knew it, not even his pastor. His wife knew, of course, yet never mentioned it. Both the Doyles told anyone who asked that he worked for the "government" and let it go at that. Anyone who pressed the issue was told he worked for the General Services Administration, a vast, unglamorous bureaucracy that maintained federal office buildings.

There was little to distinguish the Doyles from the tens of thousands of people who lived in similar houses and similar subdivisions in every direction, except for one astounding fact: Richard Doyle was a spy.

None of his friends or neighbors knew his fantastic secret, not even his wife. He had been passing CIA secrets to the KGB, now the SVR, for fifteen years. He was paid for his treason, yet he didn't do it for money—indeed, he had never spent a dollar that the Russians had paid him. He had it hidden away in safety-deposit boxes scattered through the Washington metropolitan area.

Richard Doyle committed treason because it made him different from all these other middle-class schmucks slogging it eight-to-five, five days a week, forty-eight weeks a year, waiting for that magic day when they turned fifty-five years of age and could retire. He was *special*. He had almost two million dollars in cash stuffed in a half-dozen safety-deposit boxes and when he reached fifty-five, he wasn't going to Florida. Oh no! He was going to *live*.

He had seven years to go before that happy birthday, so he didn't really dwell on how it would be. The truth was he hadn't really decided how he was going to spend the rest of his life. There was plenty of time.

This evening Doyle was home alone—his wife was showing a house and the kids were at a high school football game. He was thirty minutes into a Dirty Harry movie on television when the telephone rang.

"Hello."

Richard Doyle listened for a moment, glanced at his watch, then said, "Okay," and hung up the receiver.

He used the remote to kill the television, put on his shoes, then stood and stretched.

His wife wouldn't be home for at least an hour and the kids were planning on catching a ride home with the neighbor down the street. He had plenty of time. He went to the kitchen and helped himself to a soft drink from the fridge. He took the can with him. Martha was driving her Lexus, so he took the vehicle he usually drove, a three-year-old maroon Dodge Caravan.

He made sure he closed the garage door, then headed for the subdivision exit. In minutes he joined the traffic on the highway.

Ten minutes later he rolled into the parking lot of a fast-food restaurant in Tyson's Corner. He knew from past visits that the restaurant's security cameras did not tape activities in the parking lot, yet he remained in his car.

Two minutes later another vehicle, a sedan, drove into the restaurant's lot and stopped with the engine running. Doyle glanced around, then got out of his car and walked over to the sedan. He opened the passenger door and seated himself.

"Good evening."

"Hi." The other man put his car in gear and drove out of the parking lot.

"I've got a document I want you to see, but I didn't want to copy it. Too many pages."

"Hot, huh?"

"Too risky to use the copiers at the office. The ones we have now have a computer memory. I've got to get this thing back into the file tomorrow. You can read the summary and key passages, get the gist of it."

"Okay."

"Once I have it back in the file, we're safe and we've left no tracks."

"You're really worried about giving me a copy, aren't you?"

"Hey, I haven't gotten caught yet. If they bust you, they still got nothing on me."

"They're not going to bust me," Richard Doyle said dismissively. "Shit, I've been doing this forever. Fucking FBI couldn't catch a cold."

The driver pulled into the parking lot of a fast-food joint that had gone out of business. "Did you ever eat here?" Doyle asked, gesturing at the sign. "Terrible food."

The driver stopped the car behind the building, put the transmission in park, and turned off the ignition. He jabbed a button under the dash to release the trunk lid. Then he got out of the car and walked back to the trunk. He took out a folder, then slammed it shut. He came up to the passenger side of the car and opened Doyle's door.

He handed Doyle the folder. "Here it is. Turn on the light over the mirror. It's that button up there."

As Doyle was looking up, trying to find the light switch, the driver used a silenced pistol to shoot him once just behind the right ear. Richard Doyle slumped in his seat.

The driver closed the passenger door, walked around the vehicle, got in, started the engine, and drove away.

An hour later the sedan pulled up to a gate in a chain-link fence at an airport near Leesburg. The killer flashed his lights. Another car drove up and the driver used a pass card to open the gate. The two vehicles drove between rows of sheet-metal hangars until the first car stopped. Two men got out. The killer helped them carry Richard Doyle's body into the hangar. Only when the hangar door was closed did they turn on the light.

"Who is it?" one of the men asked the killer.

"If you really want to know, look in his wallet before you put it in the acid."

"Don't guess it matters."

"You know the drill. Clothes, wallet, everything, in the acid. Concrete shoes for our friend, then put him in the water at least fifty miles off the coast."

"We'll get the concrete on him tonight," one of the men replied, nudging Doyle with his foot, "let it set up, then give him his last flight tomorrow night before he starts getting too ripe."

"Fine," the killer said, and snapped off the hangar light. He opened the door and went out without another glance at Richard Doyle's corpse.

The limo with dark windows cruised slowly through downtown Washington. Traffic that Saturday night was heavy, as usual, even though the hour was near 11 P.M. In Dupont Circle the chess games had their usual players and onlookers. Skateboarders zoomed on the sidewalks and a few hookers strutted hopefully, their pimps watching from a distance.

The driver of the limo looked at his watch from time to time. He was a block from Dupont Circle at two minutes before the hour, waiting for the light. He didn't fidget, didn't drum his fingers—he sat with both hands on the wheel watching traffic and pedestrians. When the light turned green he looked both ways to ensure no one intended to run the light, released the brake and fed gas.

He caught the light at the circle and stayed right. He glanced at the chess game nearest the streetlight—and saw a man rise from the board and shake his opponent's hand. He was late. He should have already been on the corner.

The driver moved left and drove completely around the circle, then pulled to a stop at the light by the drugstore. The man from the chess game was wearing jeans, a pullover shirt, and tennis shoes. He stepped off the curb, grasped the rear door of the limo, and seated himself.

The chauffeur rolled immediately.

In the back the chess player nodded at the passenger on the left side of the car, a tall man with thinning blond hair, wearing a blue suit and dark red tie. "Sorry I'm late," the chess player said. "My opponent used a gambit I haven't seen in years."

"Meeting like this is dangerous," responded the suit.

"The agency and the FBI have learned about the warheads."

"We knew they would."

"A lieutenant general from the SVR told them. He also told them about Richard Doyle. We couldn't wait, so I removed Mr. Doyle from the board."

Mr. Suit sat silently. The news about Doyle was unexpected and created problems, but complaining to the man who had found the problem and solved it was not productive.

"The warheads are at the airport in Karachi," the chess player continued. "They'll leave Friday on a Greek ship, the *Olympic Voyager*."

"Why Friday?"

"We couldn't do it sooner."

"So what is the government's response to the news?"

"It's on the president's desk."

The suit chuckled dryly. "So far so good. This is going to be a very profitable operation. My office got a call just two hours ago. The national security adviser has asked me to have breakfast with him tomorrow."

"As you know, I have never sugarcoated my advice," the chess player said, watching Mr. Suit. "The world is changing very quickly.

I argued against Pakistan. I don't think you appreciate the dangers. The militants are playing their own game."

"We have good people there. And we've paid them well."

"Let's hope it all goes swimmingly. Whatever happens, don't say I didn't warn you."

"Dutch is a good man. He'll get those warheads delivered."

The chess player said nothing.

"Doyle? Will we hear anything from that?"

"I don't think so. He has completely disappeared. I used reliable men. The FBI are already mounting a major manhunt. They will conclude that he defected or was assassinated. Regardless, there are no loose ends."

The limo had been rolling through the downtown and was now approaching Union Station. "You may let me out anywhere along here," the chess player said. The suit used the intercom to speak to the chauffeur, who acknowledged the order by clicking the mike.

"So what drives you?" the suit asked as the limo came to a halt near the curb. "The money or the game?"

"The game, of course," the chess player said with a smile. He opened the door and stepped out.

The chess player stood for a moment watching the limo merge with traffic, then shrugged and walked toward the station. Once inside he took the escalator to the Metro stop, used a token to pass through the gates, and went down onto the platform.

Standing there waiting for the train, he permitted himself a grin. The game at Dupont Circle this evening had been excellent, but this one was going to be sublime. The man in the limo thought that money was the way we keep score in life. People with money always thought that.

The chess player laughed aloud.

CHAPTER THREE

The Walney's Bank building in the heart of Cairo was a small replica of the Bank of England building in London, and in that setting it jarred the eye. Walney's Bank was founded to help finance the export of Egyptian cotton to Britain during the American Civil War. The current building was completed during the siege of Khartoum in the Sudan, and had withstood war and riot and political turmoil ever since.

The dark, spacious interior projected a sense of deep calm, a striking contrast to the cacophony, dirt, intense sunlight, and gridlocked traffic in the streets outside. The floors were marble, the counters, lintels, and doorjambs dark, highly polished wood.

Walney's still maintained a cozy relationship with a large group of British banks—and Swiss, German, Italian, Russian, Saudi, Kuwaiti, Iranian, Pakistani, Indian, and Indonesian banks. Walney's advertised heavily in British magazines, publicizing their slogan far and wide: "Walney's treats you right." British tourists on holiday regularly dropped by to cash traveler's checks and purchase more; English tellers made the tourists feel right at home.

While Walney's looked as British as tea and toast, it wasn't. In the aftermath of World War II British taxes became confiscatory, so the descendants of the original Walney—one Sir Horace, dead now for over a century—sold out to a group of Egyptian investors. The bank today was managed by Abdul Abn Saad, a large-nosed, lean, hawkish man in his fifties who spoke excellent English with a slight Egyptian accent.

He didn't stand when Anna Modin entered the room. She seated herself in front of his massive desk and waited for Saad to address her. He finished reading the sheet of paper in front of him before he looked up.

"How was Russia?" he asked in Arabic.

"Dismal," she said. She kept her knees together and sat perfectly erect, as if the chair were a stool, with her hands folded on the purse in her lap. She was wearing a well-cut dress from a Roman designer, a matching jacket, and high-heel pumps. Her purse was also Italian and very expensive. A single strand of pearls encircled her neck. Her long hair hid her matching pearl earrings.

"Report."

"Zuair arrived on schedule at the Russian arms depot with the money. General Petrov sold him four warheads, which he selected from hundreds that were there. He and his men loaded the weapons on a truck and left. Petrov was quite pleased with the transaction. He didn't rob, cheat, or kill them, hoping that they would soon return with more money for more weapons."

"Very good," Saad muttered as he looked at her through narrowed eyes. "Did you have any trouble getting into or out of the country?"

"No, sir. I stayed at the Metropole Hotel just off Red Square, visited the banks we discussed, then took a holiday. It was during the holiday that I traveled to meet Petrov, who was expecting me. Trusevich recommended me to him, as he said he would."

Trusevich was a Russian mobster who controlled much of the drug traffic in southern Russia. He was one of Walney's better clients.

"Trusevich also recommended Walney's to Petrov, who deposited a million and a half American with the bank. I gave him a receipt and deposited the cash with one of our correspondent banks in Moscow. They should have wired the funds."

For the first time Abdul Abn Saad grinned. He picked up the sheet of paper he had been perusing when she entered. "They did," he said, indicating the paper, then centered the sheet on his desk.

He was grinning, Anna Modin knew, at the irony. Walney's supplied the money to Frouq al-Zuair for his weapons purchase; now a significant chunk of the money was back as a deposit from a Russian general, a deposit that could and would be loaned to the people who were helping finance *jihad* around the globe. Truly, modern finance was a marvel, a weapon that could be turned against its inventors and used to crack the foundations of secular civilization, and ultimately bring it down. And Walney's was making a profit on every transaction!

"Miss Modin," said Abdul Saad, "you have been with the bank almost five years. I confess, I had misgivings about hiring you, but your fluency in various languages, your knowledge of finance, your contacts in Russia, and your discretion have made you invaluable."

"Thank you, sir."

"Especially your discretion," Saad added.

Modin lowered her gaze modestly for a few seconds.

"I am sure you will enjoy a few days to recover from your journey. Still, business is pressing, and I must ask you to travel again on Friday."

She nodded.

"I shall give you your destination and errand on Thursday afternoon. Four o'clock."

"Thank you, sir," she said, and rose.

Abdul Saad watched her walk from the room, then went back to his paperwork.

Anna Modin went to her office, a small cubicle on the top floor of the building. She had one window, from which she could just see the top of the Great Pyramid of Cheops on clear days. She didn't look today.

She stirred through the paper in her in-basket, settled down to scan a report on nonperforming loans, then leaned back in her chair. Abdul Saad's crack about discretion was on her mind; it was a veiled threat, and it bothered her.

She was a Russian woman working in a male-dominated Islamic society . . . naturally she had little or nothing to do with bank business in the Arab world. She had been employed at the bank because of her experience at Swiss banks. She kept her job because she was damned good at what she did, which was to deal almost exclusively with European and American merchants who often felt more comfortable with a European woman than they did with "inscrutable" Arab males who didn't speak their language fluently.

What none of the customers or bankers knew was that Anna Modin was a spy. She was not an agent of any government—she provided information to Janos Ilin, who had approached her ten years before, when she was at the university in Moscow. She turned to the window and stood looking out as she thought about those days.

Janos Ilin, a senior officer in the SVR. Those were heady days, in the early nineties. Communism had just collapsed and a new day was dawning in Russia. A boyfriend introduced her to Ilin, who over the course of four dinners, one a week for a month, felt her out about her political views.

She was not a communist and she told him so. She labeled herself a citizen of the world who happened to be Russian. She believed in democracy, she bravely told Ilin, and the rule of law.

Finally, at the fourth dinner, Ilin asked her to leave Russia, to get a job in European finance and provide him with information, when and if circumstances required it. Of course she refused. She thought he was asking on behalf of the KGB, now the SVR, the senior officers of which had just tried to overthrow Gorbachev in a coup d'état and were now under arrest.

"I am not asking for anything," Ilin said. He laid a passport and exit visa on the table and pushed it across to her. "No strings. I shall provide you with a drop, which is a way to communicate with me. If you ever discover anything you wish to tell me, you may use the drop. If you don't, never use it."

She refused the offer, but two weeks later, when Ilin called again, she decided to talk with him one more time. The thought of leaving Russia intrigued her. She had never been abroad. She had heard so much of the West—seeing it, living there, working there would be a great adventure. She could always return to Russia if she ever wished to. Her parents were elderly, and she talked about the possibility with them, leaving out Janos Ilin and his conversations with her. Seeing her enthusiasm, they gave a reluctant approval.

So she listened carefully to Ilin and decided to take a chance. This time, when he handed her the passport and exit visa, she had put them in her pocket.

Upon graduation six weeks later she went to Switzerland and began hunting a job. Her linguistic skills landed her in a Zurich bank. She heard nothing from Ilin for five years.

One day she ran into him on a street corner as she left her building for lunch.

He picked the bistro and the booth. Over a sandwich and glass of wine, he asked how she was, how she was doing. Finally he got around to it: "I would like for you to apply for a job at Walney's Bank in Cairo. They have an opening for an experienced European banker, and I think they might hire you."

"Are you asking me to spy for the SVR?"

"No. I have a friend inside Walney's. I want you to carry messages from me to him, and him to me. I want you to be a courier."

"That sounds like spying to me," she retorted, thinking of her Swiss friends and a man she thought might be in love with her.

Ilin had taken his time answering. They were in a corner booth where no one could overhear their conversation. "Walney's is involved in financing Islamic terrorist organizations. These groups are composed of fanatics who murder people for political or religious reasons."

"What if I'm caught?"

"You will be tortured for every scrap of information you know, then murdered."

"And you thought of me. I'm flattered."

"Someone has to do it."

After a week's thought, she had applied to Walney's. They asked her to come to Cairo for an interview. Then they hired her. That was five years ago.

Anna soon decided there was no spy at all. The drop, an opening in a brick wall behind a loose toilet paper dispenser in the ladies' room, was never used. One had to reach behind the dispenser with two fingers to extract whatever was there while sitting on one of the commodes. At first she checked it daily, then weekly, finally once a month or so. Nothing. Until five months ago, when she found the first wadded-up candy wrapper in the drop.

The information was on a tiny roll of film inside the wrapper. The candy wrapper seemed innocuous. The film certainly wasn't. Someone was risking their life photographing records, just as she was risking her life carrying the film.

She carried the wrappers in her purse and left them in various drops in cities all over Europe. Ilin didn't offer to pay her, and she didn't ask. She was helping *him,* not the Russian secret police.

She never learned the identity of Ilin's spy on the inside, and in truth didn't want to know. What you didn't know you couldn't tell, inadvertently or intentionally, even to save your life. All she knew was that the spy was probably a woman; the drop where she picked up information was in the third-floor women's room. The janitors were men and cleaned the rest room at night, and one of them was a possibility. Yet it was more probable that the person leaving the information for her to find was one of the women clerks in the wire transfer division. Among the countries in the Arab world, only in

Egypt, and perhaps Iraq, did women work in banks, and then only in back-office clerical jobs. And that is where the hard intelligence is. That is where the information that Janos Ilin wanted could be mined, the who and how much and when.

Two years ago Abdul Abn Saad had begun sending her on missions that were outside the sphere of legitimate banking. Indeed, he and the bank were involved in funding and directing terror.

Four nuclear weapons.

She had written a report of Petrov's sale on the inside of a candy wrapper and left it in a drop on the Moscow subway for Ilin to find. She hadn't telephoned or made any other attempt to contact him. Abdul Abn Saad and his people might be watching.

These people were cutthroats, and hers was the throat they would slit if they learned that she told a solitary soul about the bank's business or theirs.

Saad paid her well for working at the bank, almost twice the salary she had been getting in Switzerland. She fancied that she earned it, but when the secret missions began she understood that she was being paid to keep silent and go along.

They were evil men. And ignorant. They thought all Westerners were motivated by money. Virtue, they thought, was theirs alone. Women were some subspecies of human, useful only for recreation and procreation.

She abandoned the window, sat at her desk, and examined her hands. They were shaking. The trembling was barely perceptible, but it was there.

She was burning out. Saad had never threatened her before. What did it mean? Did he suspect?

What if they had discovered the drop in the women's room, or caught the spy and learned of it?

It would be a simple matter to install a hidden security camera to see who serviced the drop. Interrogation and torture and death would swiftly follow.

Four nuclear weapons . . .

Perhaps she should have stayed in Moscow. Called Ilin, told him what she knew, and told him to get another courier.

She hadn't done that. She hadn't wanted to abandon whoever was risking her life to acquire information here. The fact that it was a woman, probably an Arab woman, made it doubly difficult. No, she could not abandon a woman who was risking her life to fight evil.

Yet now her hands shook all the time.

Anna Modin stood, straightened her skirt, checked her reflection in the glass of the window, then went down the corridor to the women's room. She pushed open the door and went inside. No one was there.

She paused at the sink, studied the room in the mirror, then turned and scrutinized every square inch, looking for any changes to the room since her last visit two weeks ago. There seemed to be none.

She entered the stall and removed her jacket, which she laid across the toilet paper dispenser. Then she rearranged her clothing and sat down.

She glanced at the ceiling, at the walls in front of her. Everything looked as before.

Finally she reached for toilet paper. Keeping the jacket over her hand, she reached into the hole behind the dispenser, felt with two fingers. Nothing there—the drop was empty.

The rest of the day passed doing routine paperwork. She waited and waited for the ax to fall, and it didn't. The waiting—that was the life of a spy. Waiting, always tense, always pretending, always trying to project a calm one didn't feel.

When she finally left the office that evening, she didn't look back.

In the days that followed Jake's interview with Coke Twilley and Sonny Tran he heard no more about Ilin's missing weapons, nor did anyone whisper Richard Doyle's name. Jake's job as military liaison to the antiterrorism task force consisted mostly of coordinating the use of the military in roles that couldn't be performed by civil agencies of the government. He spent long hours on the telephone talking to various commands throughout the country and to the civilians, to whom he had to explain precisely what the military could and couldn't do.

Commander Toad Tarkington was also there, of course, working the phones alongside his boss. Jake was too busy to worry about the bombs, so Toad worried for both of them. "Do you think maybe you should have another talk with Coke?" he asked hopefully. "Maybe find out what's going on?"

Jake shook his head and pushed a button on his phone to answer a waiting call. An hour later, during a momentary lull, Toad suggested, "Wha'daya think about arranging another meet with Ilin, see if he's heard anything else?"

"There's nothing we can do, Toad."

"Goddamn, Admiral, the world is on the brink of the abyss. You and I are the only two sane people on the planet who know about it, and I've got my doubts about you."

Grafton chuckled and started to reply to that bon mot, but the telephone rang, so he answered it. Whatever he was going to say to Toad was never said, because when he finally hung up the phone he was thinking about something else, then finally he forgot it altogether.

On Thursday evening the telephone rang at Jake's apartment. The voice on the other end of the line was that of the deputy chief of naval operations. After a muttered greeting, the admiral said, "An hour from now, at nine, be waiting downstairs in front of your building. You jog, don't you?"

"Yes, sir."

"Wear jogging shorts, tennis shoes. Do you have a distinctive sweatshirt with a college logo or something?"

Jake had to think for a moment. "Slick Willie's."

"What's that?"

"A whorehouse in Nevada, sir."

The admiral chuckled drily. "Wear that. Nine o'clock, down front."

"Want to tell me what this is about, Admiral?"

"Somebody wants to meet you."

So Jake dressed in his jogging duds, stood in front of the building feeling like an idiot as light traffic rolled through the Roslyn neighborhood and a light Thursday evening crowd strolled by, heading to or from the Metro or to get a coffee drink.

A large black sedan with dark windows pulled up to the curb about a minute before nine. A sedan stopped in the street in front of it, and another sedan pulled in behind. A fit man in his early thirties wearing a sports coat got out of the front passenger seat and opened the rear door. Then he motioned to Jake.

Jake walked over and climbed in—the man shut the door firmly and got back into the car.

"Rear Admiral Grafton," the man sitting beside Jake said as the car pulled away from the curb. "It's a pleasure." He held out his hand.

"Pleased to meet you, sir," Jake Grafton said, and shook hands with the president of the United States.

"Cool shirt," the president said, and nodded to the Secret Service agent behind the wheel, who put the car in motion.

"It's a pleasure meeting you, Admiral," the president continued. "I've heard a lot about you."

Jake tried to think of an appropriate response. This was the first and only president he had ever met. He seemed like an okay guy, but after all . . . "Heard a lot about you too, sir," he muttered, and felt like an idiot.

"Tell me about your meeting with Janos Ilin last week. I've read the CIA's summary, but I want to hear it firsthand."

Jake covered it all, who Ilin was, explained how he and his wife had met Ilin about a year ago when the Russian was assigned to the military liaison team for the SuperAegis antiballistic-missile defense system. He mentioned the FBI's surveillance efforts to ensure Ilin wasn't followed to the meet in New York, then carefully related the substance of the conversation, the revelation that a Russian general had sold four missile warheads to the Sword of Islam, and the name of the CIA officer that Ilin said was a Russian spy, Richard Doyle.

"Four nuclear warheads with two-hundred-kiloton yields," the president said softly to himself. He took a deep breath. "Do you think Ilin was lying?"

"When he told me about the missing weapons I thought he was telling the truth. It had the right . . ." Jake rubbed his fingers together as he searched for the proper word. ". . . the right feel, I suppose you could say. Since then I've gone over and over it in my mind, weighing it. For the life of me, I can't see what the Russians would gain by telling us a lie like that. The story isn't one I would want told if I were them. It makes them look like incompetents, criminal incompetents who can't control rogue generals—and if the story is true, that is precisely what they are.

"Was Ilin spilling the beans on his own responsibility or was he playing a role? I don't know the answer to that one. Ilin always struck me as a man with his own agenda. On the other hand, I doubt that he would have made lieutenant general in the KGB or SVR or whatever they call it this week if his superiors had the slightest doubts about his loyalty or judgment. That said, judging abstract qualities like loyalty or honor is always difficult."

"Russians have been defecting from positions of trust since the communists took power way back when," the president observed.

"In any event," Jake continued, "it seems to me we must take a hard, careful look at Richard Doyle. I can't see what Ilin or the Russians would gain by defaming an innocent CIA officer. If it's a gambit, I don't see how it helps them. A lie like that would be a dangerous precedent. On the other hand, if Doyle is indeed spying for the Russians and the weapons story is a lie, giving him to us may be a way to make the lie plausible."

"Yes," the president said. "I see that."

Jake rubbed his head, then said, "The heck of it is that I'm not an intelligence professional. I'm an ex–attack pilot shuffling paper and telephone calls."

"I'm not an intelligence professional either," the president said matter-of-factly. "But the buck stops here."

"Seems to me," Jake remarked, "that the mistake here would be to overthink this. We should proceed—cautiously of course—on the assumption that Ilin was telling the truth and see where that takes us. If we ever discover that he was lying, then we can reevaluate."

"I agree."

"Until we are absolutely convinced that no weapons left Russia, we should pull out all the stops to find those four. I don't think we have any choice here, Mr. President."

"Nor do I," the president said, and looked at his hands. He made a face, then looked out the window at monumental Washington. "The terrorists' attacks laid bare some of the problems that the American political system has been unable to solve for the last thirty or forty years. Since the end of World War Two we've needed a secure place to store all our nuclear waste, and we still don't have one. No one wants the dump near them, so the stuff is sitting in cans in poorly guarded warehouses all over America." He held up a finger.

"We have an estimated six million illegal aliens in the country and no effective way to track or get rid of them. The Immigration and Naturalization Service has just twenty-two hundred people to find, process, and deport illegals. It's unbelievable, yet nothing has been done to fix this mess because many industries want cheap labor and everyone feels sorry for the illegals, many of whom were starving in Third World sewers." Another finger went up.

"Then there is the FBI, which is supposed to build cases for federal prosecutors and catch spies and terrorists. There are exactly eleven thousand one hundred forty-three FBI agents. That's all of them, counting the director." He flipped fingers up as he ticked agencies off. "The CIA is still watching to see if the Russians are going to start World War Three. The Customs Service is so overwhelmed and undermanned that they merely do spot checks of shipments coming into the country. The DEA has been fighting and losing the war on drugs for a generation."

"Democracies are messy," Jake remarked when the president paused for air.

"Aren't they ever!" The president made a chopping gesture. "The hell of it is that the bureaucracies are what governments have to work with to protect human lives. Every bureaucracy has its rules and regulations, rivers of forms and reports and memos and correspondence, in- and out-baskets, federal holidays, people sick or on vacation, plus the usual cast of feudists, fatheads, fools, fanatics, hotshots, incompetents, tattletales, suck-ups, backstabbers . . . and a few dedicated people who do all the real work.

"The challenge is to put all the information from all these bureaucracies together and use it in a timely manner. That is what I want you to do. You must mesh the information from everywhere and prevent future mass murders." The president's eyes flicked over Jake's face. "I've been talking to the folks at the Pentagon; they tell me that you are the man I want. They say you've got good judgment and common sense and you get results."

Jake was surprised. He hadn't heard that the White House had been asking questions. He kept his mouth shut as the president continued:

"I want you to find the weapons. On paper you'll be operating inside the antiterrorism task force, but you are on your own. Put together an independent covert team to find the weapons. Get people and supplies from wherever you need them. Find the weapons before they explode."

"Yes, sir."

"The bad guys have kicked us in the teeth," the president said as he looked out the windows of the limo at the government buildings lining the boulevards. "Should never have happened. Thousands murdered, tens of thousands of lives maimed . . . the shock waves are still ricocheting around America and will be for years to come. The America you and I grew up in is changing. Our freedoms . . ." The president passed a hand in front of his face. "In any event, it's not going to happen again. *Never again!* You understand me?"

"Yes, sir."

The president took a deep breath as he collected himself. "We've got to get better, we're going to get better. We're going to overhaul the CIA, the FBI, the INS, change the priorities. We're going to emphasize HUMINT. We're going to use all the tools we can lay hands on to prevent American citizens from being murdered by criminal fanatics. We must go after our enemies wherever they are, whoever they are, without regard to national borders or political connections or Supreme Court decisions or the rules of criminal procedure or the Code of Federal Regulations or the federal holiday schedule. *We've got to find these people before they hurt us.*"

"All our enemies aren't in Kandahar," Jake said. "Janos Ilin remarked on that fact, and it struck me as critical."

"I think we understand each other," the president said, meeting Jake's eyes and measuring him.

"To do what you want me to do I'm going to have to put together some kind of computer center," Jake said slowly. "Everyone in today's world leaves tracks—electronic tracks on government and nongovernment computer databases. Credit card receipts, bank records, insurance bills, car rental contracts, airline reservations, hotel bills, utility bills, telephone records, e-mails, Web-surfing records—everyone's life is on computers, a tidbit here, a fact there, a shadow in that corner. In Germany in the 1970s the police used computers to pull together all the information in the various databases that existed then to fight the Red Army Faction and the Baader-Meinhof Gang. They got 'em. And because they did it overtly, the German people rebelled. The threat didn't justify the invasion of privacy. Yet today it isn't just murder and kidnapping, it's nuclear weapons, airliners full of passengers used as kamikaze bombers, murder of the innocent on a grand scale."

"It's war," the president said simply. "Move fast and hit hard. I want results, not excuses. You'll be a branch of the antiterrorism task force, but you'll answer to me." The president handed Jake a card. "The top telephone number is for my aide, Sal Molina. Call him when you need help. The other number on there is mine. You can reach me anytime, anywhere with that."

Jake glanced at the card and put it inside his runner's wallet, which was velcroed to a pocket in his shorts.

"If the press gets this, you'll be impeached and I'll go to prison."

"I'll take my chances," the president said. "We're not going to be a nation of victims on my watch. The people who wrote the United States Constitution didn't intend it to prevent us from defending ourselves. The president has the inherent power to defend the nation. I'm using that power here and now."

"I'll buy that. But why me?"

The president cleared his throat but didn't answer immediately. The car was gliding by the Supreme Court. "Our thinking," he said slowly, feeling his way, "is that we want the operation handled by someone outside the intelligence community."

"The folks at Langley and down at the Hoover Building will have to be told. I'll need their cooperation. Hell, I'll need a lot of their people. I'll need the help of experts from the National Security Agency."

"I wanted a tough sonuvabitch with a hatful of brains who wasn't worried about getting another star," the president said. "The chairman of the Joint Chiefs, CNO, the army chief of staff, they tell me you're my man."

Jake didn't reply to that comment. While he had never worked to earn a promotion, getting another one wouldn't hurt. Yet the president of the United States just said that the military chiefs thought another promotion unlikely. Thank you, sir. Thank you, thank you.

"Someone will bring some paperwork to your apartment in the morning," the president continued. "A copy of the appointing document will go to the director of the antiterrorism task force, and the directors of the FBI and CIA. Tell them what you want in the way of people and offices and support. Your budget will come from the CIA."

"Who in the CIA or FBI don't you trust?"

"I didn't say that."

"I feel like I'm on the high wire without a net."

The president's face showed no expression. "We don't have a choice, Admiral. We're in a war we didn't want and didn't start. By God, we're going to *win*."

"If you trust me enough to give me this job, then trust me enough to tell me all of it."

"I've told you what you need to know. Use good judgment and common sense and go where your nose takes you."

Jake Grafton thought it over as the car rolled along, and he looked at the people on the street, men, women, and children from every racial and ethnic group on the planet.

"I'd rather go to Afghanistan," he murmured, "hunt down bin Laden and his thugs."

"You may end up there, Admiral. I don't have a crystal ball."

Jake grinned. "Okay, Mr. President. I'll give it a try. You and I may spend our retirement years in prison, but by God, we'll hit the bastards a hell of a lick between now and then."

The president extended his hand. "They said you were the man."

"If you don't mind, sir, how about letting me out at the next corner? I need to do some thinking. I'll walk for a while and catch a cab later."

"Fine," the president said, and pushed the button on the intercom to talk to the driver.

Jake Grafton got out of the car and didn't look back. He was on the Mall near the National Air and Space Museum.

He broke into a trot. For the first time in months, he felt good.

Yeah, it's a war. And war is my profession.

He jabbed his fist in the air and increased the pace.

Miguel Tejada had never liked the plains. He had grown up in Sonora and for the last ten years had lived in Los Angeles. Western Kansas had no resemblance to either. The plains rolled gently away in all directions as far as the eye could see. Overhead clouds were building, but even at this time of the spring, it was too dry to rain. Tejada knew about clouds in dry air.

He was in the lead vehicle, a sedan, sitting in the passenger seat. The man at the wheel was named Luis, and in the backseat cradling an Uzi was a man named Jose. These weren't their real names, but they were the names Miguel knew them by. There were two more men in the van behind them, Chico and Chuy.

They were two miles along the old road, driving carefully along the cracked, broken asphalt, when they topped a low rise and saw the old airfield. It was an abandoned World War II army air corps base. The runways formed a triangle. Weeds were growing up through the cracks in the asphalt. The only building still standing was the control tower, which stood on the edge of a giant parking mat, one that sprawled over at least five acres beside the north–south runway. Sitting at the foot of the tower was a tractor-trailer rig, an eighteen-wheeler.

Luis slowed the car to a crawl as they approached the hole in the rusting wire fence.

"Parate ahí!" Miguel said. He used the binoculars to inspect the truck. No sign of the driver. He scanned the tower. The glass was gone from the windows, birds were perched on the window ledges, so the man wasn't in there. Hmm . . .

He looked all around the airport, taking his time. No other vehicles, no people in sight. He looked at the fields of green wheat that stretched away in all directions. Also empty.

"Marchate!" he said, and Luis put the car in motion, threading his way through the hole in the fence. Miguel could see the ruts the truck had made going through.

If he didn't know this guy, Miguel would have been more cautious, but he had done business with him twice before. He was a long-haul trucker who occasionally added marijuana or cocaine to his load, buying it here, selling it there. Today he had ten kilos of cocaine.

The man has probably been driving all night, Miguel thought, and is asleep in his tractor.

Miguel had Luis pull up in front of the control tower. Luis killed the engine and all three men got out of the car. The cold wind had a bite to it.

Chuy stopped the van behind them. He and Chico got out, took their time looking around, then walked over to the truck. The wind whipped at Miguel's thin trousers. He zipped his jacket shut.

He heard a thud and a grunt from Jose, who was behind him, and turned in time to see him fall, just as the sound of the shot reached him. Jose's weapon clattered on the asphalt.

"Vámonos!" he roared, and started for the car. Something slammed into his right leg and he went down. The shock and pain were so bad he didn't even hear the shot. He began crawling.

Luis jerked open the car door and threw himself behind the wheel. The engine roared into life just as the driver's window shattered and blood spattered the windshield. The engine roared mightily, but the car didn't move.

Miguel kept crawling, cursing.

He heard another shot, then seconds later another.

The hell of it was that he didn't know where the shooter was. Behind him, he assumed, because of the way the driver's window shattered. But maybe not.

When Miguel reached the dubious safety of the car he crawled under it, dragging his injured leg. He was hit bad and knew it. Blood was soaking his trouser leg, he was leaving a streak of it on the asphalt. He tried not to think about his leg. Somehow he managed to get his jacket unzipped and the Glock out of its holster. It felt good in his hand.

Where the fuck was the shooter?

"Chico!"

No answer. Given the wind and the hum of the car engine, Chico would have had to shout to be heard.

"Chuy! You see the bastard?"

One of them was lying on the asphalt, his weapon beside him. Chico maybe.

There was so little room under the car that Miguel couldn't turn, couldn't go backward or forward. Shit!

Another shot, and a scream. The scream wavered on the wind and finally died as the screamer ran out of air. When it came again, it was more shrill.

Making a superhuman effort, Miguel managed to extricate himself from under the car. He backed out and was looking at the mess that had been his leg when a bullet ricocheted off the asphalt under the car and hit him in the lung. He dropped the Glock.

As his blood pressure dropped he found himself staring at the mud on the car tire. That was the last thing he saw.

The screams had ceased when the shooter approached the car fifteen minutes later. He carried a Remington Model 700 with a scope in the ready position. He took his time, approached each man carefully, ensured that he was dead.

One man, Chuy, was still alive. He had ceased screaming. Only his eyes moved.

The rifleman backed off twenty feet, took careful aim at Chuy's head, and shot him again. The head exploded.

When he was sure that all five of the men from the car and van were dead, the rifleman cradled his rifle in his arms and lit a cigarette.

He collected the weapons from each man, opened the trunk of the car, and pulled out a pillowcase full of money.

Five pistols, three submachine guns, a shotgun, and $200,000. A good day's work.

The rifleman loaded the weapons and money in the back of his tractor, behind the seat, and started the diesel engine. When it had warmed sufficiently, he eased the transmission into gear and got the rig under way.

CHAPTER FOUR

Nooreem Habib was a modern Egyptian woman. She had spent much of her youth in England, where she attended private school. Her father was a progressive—he sent her to an academically challenging school for girls, where, among other things, she learned a great deal about computers.

Just before graduation the headmistress had called her in for a private interview. "Miss Habib, you have a fine mind and have been an outstanding student. What do you plan to do with your life?"

"Return home to Egypt," she explained. "Marry an acceptable man. This is what my father wishes me to do."

"You have crossed a great cultural divide in the last few years," the headmistress observed. "Will the life that you describe be enough?"

"It is what my father wishes."

"There are those in the Arab world who feel that murder in the name of Allah is their holy duty. Do you feel that way?"

"No," Nooreem Habib said curtly and forcefully. "Those people pervert Islam. They are enemies of the human race."

They talked for several hours, not as student and headmistress, but as two adult women. The upshot was that the lady gave her a telephone number. "If you ever feel that you know something that you must share, call that number."

Her father had an account at Walney's and had done business with Abdul Abn Saad from time to time, so when she wanted a real job, she got one at the bank. In the back office. As a bookkeeper, making meticulous entries in huge, bound ledgers. She felt like a clerk in the illustrations of one of the Dickens books, wearing the eyeshade, writing all day. . . . The only thing she lacked was a stool. And she needed one.

Then last year Walney's got around to purchasing computers. Soon Nooreem Habib was heavily involved in making the transition from ledgers to computerized records. She was intellectually challenged for the first time since leaving school, and she enjoyed it immensely.

She remembered that she had the telephone number six months into the computer project. When the bank's cash flows and wire transfers were sorted electronically, patterns emerged. Nooreem Habib was a very bright woman, and she recognized the patterns for what they were. Walney's was transferring money around the globe for terrorist organizations. Knowingly or unknowingly. Instinctively she knew not to discuss her observations at the bank, but she called the number that the headmistress had given her four years earlier.

One day a woman passed her a Minox camera and six rolls of film in a bus on the streets of Cairo. A note inside the camera told her where and how to leave the film after it was exposed. She used the camera to photograph computer printouts, then wrapped the exposed film roll in a candy wrapper and left it behind the toilet paper dispenser in the ladies' room.

Nooreem had never heard the name Janos Ilin, had never seen him, and didn't know her contact, the person who serviced her drop. The fact she knew nothing to tell if she were caught was not lost upon her.

Sometimes she wondered who received the financial information that came from the bank records. The British, she supposed, MI-5. Whoever they were, they were enemies of the terrorists, as she was.

She had only one roll of film left, certainly not enough for the vast mountain of transactions that she thought needed to be sorted through for the patterns that she knew were there. Today in a quiet moment she began downloading critical files onto a compact disk. She filled the CD with file after file until the computer said it was full. Only then did she remove it from the computer.

Later that morning when she went to the rest room, she took the CD along and tucked it into the space behind the toilet paper dispenser.

The morning after his ride with the president, Jake Grafton broke the news of his assignment to Toad Tarkington when he arrived at the office. Jake had already been there for an hour.

"You're kidding!" Toad exclaimed. "Find the bombs?"

"I have got an interview in a half hour with the director of the CIA, and an hour later, the director of the FBI. I suspect that half my time is going to be spent in meetings with people from all over government, so that means you are in charge of getting the work done."

"Whew!" Toad said, still trying to come to grips with Jake's—and his—new assignment. "Where do we start?"

"With office space and a staff. And computers and a budget. I want people working tomorrow morning."

"Who?"

"You and Tommy Carmellini for starters." He looked at his watch. "The first thing, I think, is to find out what everyone knows about the hunt for the bombs. And what the FBI is doing about Mr. Doyle."

"I thought you said the president just asked you to find the weapons?"

"He did. Presumably the FBI will take care of friend Doyle, but I've got this feeling. Ilin linked the bombs and Doyle together, if only by discussing them both in the same conversation. The commander in chief gave me a lot of authority, so I'm going to use it."

"Why not?" Toad muttered. He was beginning to see the dimensions of this mess. "You're going to be out there on the tightrope all by yourself, aren't you?" he demanded. "Without a net."

"Oh, no. You're going to be right there beside me, shipmate, all the way across. If we make it, we'll probably get adjoining cells in some ritzy federal penitentiary."

"There's a happy thought," Toad said without enthusiasm.

The director of the Central Intelligence Agency was a tall, portly man, almost bald, named Avery Edmond DeGarmo. He and Jake had crossed swords before. His round, jowly features wore a frown as Jake entered his office, which Jake knew from past experience to be DeGarmo's usual expression. He looked like a man who rarely heard good news.

This morning the director had the president's letter on his desk. Jake knew because he had been kept waiting in the reception area while DeGarmo called the White House, confirming the authenticity of the letter.

"At it again, I see, Grafton," DeGarmo said testily.

"At what again, Mr. DeGarmo?"

"Charging off to save the republic."

"I didn't ask for this assignment."

DeGarmo made a rude noise.

"I would think that you would welcome all the help you can get to find those missing Russian warheads."

"Amateurs mucking up the water won't help much," DeGarmo snapped. "If I thought they would, I'd have called Arnold Schwarzenegger."

Jake was losing his patience. He and DeGarmo had first butted heads a year ago when USS *America* was hijacked and Jake assisted in the investigation. DeGarmo apparently thought that the less the public knew of the inner workings of the intelligence bureaucracies, the better. Certainly better for the bureaucrats, Jake reflected. "The president appointed me, and we're both stuck with it," he said dryly. "I'd like a look this afternoon at everything this agency knows about the weapons and where they might be. I want to see every file."

"I guessed as much."

"I want a personal commitment from you to actively assist in my investigation."

"Are you implying that I would do less than my duty?"

"I've been ordered to find those weapons. I intend to do just that. You can help in every way possible, or I'll run right over you, Mr. Director, and leave you bleeding in the road. The choice is yours."

Avery Edmond DeGarmo's finger shot out as he leaned across his desk toward Jake. "I was appointed to this post by the president of the United States and confirmed by the United States Senate. You will get all the cooperation this agency can give you, I promise you that. And if you screw up, Admiral, I guarantee that you will never hold another position of trust in the United States government as long as you live."

Jake Grafton stood. "If we don't find those warheads," he said evenly, "there may not be a United States government."

Before DeGarmo could respond, Jake walked out of his office.

In the outer office, Jake retrieved his hat from the coffee table and nervously ran his fingers through his hair. He hadn't handled that interview well. *Off to a fine start,* he thought.

Toad had rounded up a car and driver for Jake, so he rode to the FBI building in style. After credentials checks and a trip through a metal detector, he was led through long halls and into elevators. Eventually he ended up in the director's office.

The director was Myron A. Emerick, who had spent his career in the FBI. He was, as Jake knew, the insider's insider, a man who had ruthlessly worked the system to get to the top.

Emerick was waiting at the door to shake Jake's hand when he came in, then seated his guest in a black leather chair. "Good to meet you, Admiral. I've heard your name many times through the years." He took a seat on a leather couch to Jake's left. It was an intimate setting, yet Jake had to turn his head about forty-five degrees to talk to the director. Jake got out of his chair and turned it so that it faced Emerick, then sat down in it again.

Emerick's executive assistant sat to the director's left with a legal pad on his knee and a pen in his hand. Two other men were there, Emerick's top two deputies. Jake was introduced and shook hands, then promptly forgot their names.

"I got the president's letter this morning," Emerick said earnestly. He was a slim, athletic man of no more than 150 pounds, balding on top, with the rest of his hair cut very short. The top of his head was as tan as his face and hands. Today he was wearing an expensive dark suit and a yellow silk tie. Jake suspected that Emerick worked out—racquetball, probably—every day of his life. A photo of his wife and college-age children was displayed prominently on his desk.

". . . The FBI will do everything in its power to cooperate, Admiral," Emerick was saying, "rest assured of that. Still, as an attorney and official of this government, I think it important to warn you of the minefield you are apparently about to enter."

"At the order of the president," Jake said carefully.

"Ben Franklin was the man who pointed out that those who trade liberty for security end up with neither."

"I appreciate that truth, sir. I am not a fascist."

"I am not implying anything of the kind. As I understand it, reading between the lines, you are going to ride roughshod over the privacy safeguards carefully erected in American society over the centuries for the admirable purpose of catching wild-eyed terrorists. Is that a fair characterization?"

"Something like that," Jake acknowledged.

"Regardless of what the judges say, the right against self-incrimination is designed to protect the guilty, not the innocent. Nor is the right of privacy intended to protect people with nothing to hide—it, too, protects the guilty, all those people who break the law or violate social mores by lying on résumés, loan applications, or financial documents, having secret or homosexual affairs, enjoying pornography, cheating on their income tax, using illegal drugs, doing all manner of little things they don't want their spouses or neighbors or the church or the police to find out about. The world is full of guilty people, Admiral, and they'll burn you and the president at the stake if you misuse what you learn."

"That's terrific, sir. I'll wear my asbestos longhandles, the ones with the flap in back. Obviously I wanted to meet you, let you know who I am, but the one concrete thing I hoped to accomplish this morning is find out what the intelligence committee and the FBI plan to do about Richard Doyle. As you will recall, he was the CIA officer named by Janos Ilin as the Russian spy."

A strange look crossed Emerick's face. "Haven't you heard? We're investigating his disappearance."

Jake was stunned. "Disappearance?"

"Disappeared last Friday night. Drove off in the family minivan while the wife was showing a house—she's in real estate—and the kids were at a high school football game, and he hasn't been heard from since. His wife called us about five the next morning. She was pretty upset. His minivan was found parked behind a bankrupt fast-food joint in Tyson's Corner."

Jake shook his head to clear it. "Any sign of violence?"

"Not so far. The forensic people are going over the van. Right now it looks as if he merely parked his vehicle there, locked it, and left."

"And you don't know where he went?"

"We don't know—that is correct."

"Money?"

"Doyle's wife said he didn't have over forty dollars cash on him. She saw his wallet when he gave her a twenty just before she left. Doyle has written no checks and hasn't visited a cash machine. We've canceled his credit cards, even though no one has tried to use them. His wife is really frantic—either she's an Academy Award–winning actress, or she really doesn't know where he went or why."

"His passport?"

"Canceled. We've done all the routine things. Every policeman in the country is looking for Doyle. So far, false alarms only."

"Does DeGarmo know about Doyle?"

"Oh, yes."

"I had an interview with him an hour ago, and he never mentioned the guy's name."

"Maybe he assumed you already knew."

"Maybes don't cut it anymore," Jake growled, and shifted his weight in this seat. "So what about Doyle's office?"

"We're going through his desk, his files, his computer. His wife gave us permission to search their house. She also let us borrow the family computer so we can look at the hard drive."

"Any way to find out if he's in Russia?"

"If he's there he didn't go on his own passport. I promise you that."

"Friday night?"

"That's right."

"About twenty-eight hours after I met Ilin in New York." Jake took a deep breath. "I want to know the name of every person in the United States government who knew that Friday night that Ilin had mentioned Doyle's name. The list couldn't be that long."

"We're investigating. I asked for that list on Monday. As soon as I get it I'll send you a copy."

Jake nodded. "Okay," he said, "let's talk about terrorists and nuclear weapons."

An hour later, when Jake left, Myron Emerick dismissed his executive assistant and waved his hand at his deputies, Hob Tulik and Robert Pobowski. He seated himself behind his desk; they took the chairs immediately in front of it.

"You didn't tell him about the suspected terrorist cells we're tracking."

"He didn't ask," Emerick answered curtly. "The bureau got caught with its pants down by the September eleventh terror strike. It isn't going to happen again."

Emerick had a limited number of agents. Those agents still had all the usual federal crimes to investigate, plus security investigations and counterespionage duties, all of which had now taken a backseat to the hunt for possible terrorists. God knew there were enough of them. The United States had been scattering student visas around the Arab nations for many years, and the INS had no way to track the students once they were in the country. Tens of thousands of tourists arrived daily at the nation's airports. Illegal aliens walked across the Mexican and Canadian borders daily, and like the tourists and students, disappeared into the American maelstrom. Finding those on terrorist missions was akin to cleaning the Augean stables, a task for Hercules. Then cases had to be built, ones that would justify arrests and prosecutions.

Like every military branch and law enforcement organization in the country, the FBI's responsibilities exceeded its assets. Emerick and his deputies had risen to the top because they had learned through the years to pick the responsibility that was the most important to the bureau's clients—the public, press, and Congress—and work the system to get visible results. Arrests got made and the charges stuck—i.e., those arrested were successfully prosecuted. And the FBI got the credit.

Now Emerick told his colleagues, "J. Edgar Hoover didn't build the bureau by doing the work and letting local police make the collar. We investigate, build the cases, and we bust 'em. The world hasn't changed that much—if Grafton gets the credit, the bureau is going down the ceramic convenience."

Tulik nodded. "We don't catch 'em, the press and Congress are going to start asking, Do we really need an FBI?"

"They're asking it now," Pobowski said sourly. "Did you see this morning's *Wall Street Journal*?"

"We have a job and we're going to do it," Emerick said. "The friggin' politicians can send Grafton to chase anyone they want, but the FBI will still be here when he's whacking little white balls around some golf course."

The two lieutenants nodded. Emerick was preaching to the choir.

"Four nukes are coming in," Emerick continued, all business now. "That's our working thesis. The people who are going to receive the weapons are already here and making plans. What are we getting, Hob, sixty, eighty calls a day about possible terrorists?"

"Yes, sir. At least that. Usually more. They're seeing them in every convenience store and motel."

Emerick nodded. "Police work one-oh-one: we have to sort out the good leads and follow up. I want these sons of bitches found before the bombs arrive. Sit on 'em, wire 'em up, wiretap, infiltrate, whatever we have to do. Then we arrest them with the bombs. *In their possession!* Shoot videotapes to give to the press. I want the bastards red-handed and sewed up tight. No asshole lawyers are going to get 'em off. Understand?"

Pobowski and Tulik did. The bureau was going to get the credit, not Jake Grafton or his collection of amateurs. They believed body and soul that the nation needed the FBI; by God it wasn't going to die on their watch.

Just before lunch that day Tommy Carmellini's department head called him into his office. "Tommy, I hope you aren't too busy just now because the folks at the antiterrorism task force have asked for you by name. They've got the priority, so you're going. They said they'd like to have you tomorrow morning. It'll be temporary duty; they didn't say when you'll be back."

Carmellini was used to temporary assignments. Some days it seemed as if half the people in government wanted bugs planted or someone burgled. He took a deep breath, discussed who might run his branch while he was gone. The department head agreed that Carmellini's assistant could run things for a while.

As he stood up to leave, Carmellini asked, "Who called from the task force, sir? I didn't know that I was on Rolodexes over there."

The boss consulted his notes. "A naval officer, a rear admiral named Grafton."

Uh-oh, Carmellini thought. He knew Jake Grafton. The navy didn't use him to push paper. Oh, he was a nice enough guy, but he was always up to his eyeballs in the smelly stuff.

He found Grafton in the basement of one of the newer buildings on the CIA campus, installed in an SCIF, which was a Sensitive Compartmented Information Facility, a cage designed to prevent electronic emissions from leaving the area. Toad Tarkington and a secretary, just assigned, were cleaning up the space and supervising the arrival of office furniture.

"Hey, Toad," Carmellini said, looking around at the mess.

"How are you?" Toad responded.

"Hanging left today. How about you?"

"Just hanging. These boxes are full of office supplies. Grab one."

They had most of it stowed when Jake Grafton came in. He was in whites and looked tired, Carmellini noted. He waved Tommy and Toad into a vacant cubbyhole and closed the door.

"Okay, guys," he said, and proceeded to tell them everything he knew about the bombs and his new assignment. He also filled them in on the disappearance of Richard Doyle. "I don't know that Doyle and the bombs are related, but there is no way in the world that Doyle's disappearance is not related to Ilin's tip. Twenty-eight hours after Ilin pronounced his name, he's gone."

"Off to Russia?"

"Your guess is as good as mine. Maybe the FBI will come up with something—they're investigating."

"How'd your meeting with the FBI director go?" Toad asked.

"He told me frankly that good intentions don't mean shit in this town."

"Hell, Admiral," scoffed Tommy Carmellini, "I could have told you that."

"Your boss, DeGarmo—"

"Ah, you mean the great Avery Edmond. Known affectionately among the troops—or as they refer to them in the executive suite, the little people—as 'A.E. DeG.' That's the way he signs his initials. He's a truly sick man. A mind that twisted would make a shrink's career if he could get his hands on him."

"Sick or not, Avery Edmond doesn't like amateurs."

"I've never really fit in here at Langley," Carmellini said dejectedly. "I don't have the professional career outlook to be a good spook. Alas, I, too, *am* a loathsome amateur. My heart is pure."

Tarkington made a wretching noise.

"Can a missile warhead be made into a bomb?" Carmellini asked.

Jake thought about what he wanted to say before he spoke. "If the right expert works on it, I assume that he could rig up a wiring harness, timers, batteries, all of it. The person who could rig it to work as advertised would be a weapons professional, an expert."

"What about taking the plutonium out of the warheads, using it as a pollutant with some kind of conventional explosive, like a truckload of fertilizer?" Toad asked. "Is that possible?"

Jake sagged in his chair. "Plutonium is the deadliest substance known to man. Anyone who cracked a warhead would need a clean room, body suits, containment devices for the plutonium, scrubbers, all of that. They'd have to have a well-equipped lab or they would be dead within minutes after they got to the plutonium. If they mishandled the stuff, it could go critical on them right in their hands."

"Probably be dead of radiation poisoning if they didn't do all the work in lead vaults," Carmellini suggested.

Jake took a deep breath, then exhaled slowly. "If I were doing it, I'd be afraid to crack the warheads. Why bother? Packing conventional explosives around a warhead and setting it off would result in a conventional explosion that would spray microscopic bits of plutonium over a huge area, a dirty bomb. The harder the wind was blowing when it went off, the worse the contamination would be. It'd be nearly impossible to clean up. The half-life of plutonium is something on the order of a quarter of a million years. It would be the worst ecological disaster in the history of the world."

Carmellini whistled softly. "A dirty bomb or a nuclear explosion."

"Those are the options."

"Two hundred kilotons apiece," Toad said softly.

"Right."

"Sweet Jesus!"

"This assignment is going to be like charging hell with a bucket of water," Tommy Carmellini remarked. "This would be a great time for me to ask for a transfer to Australia. You know, I hear the beaches there are all topless and the women love Americans."

"Less fallout there," Toad observed. "But if I were you, I'd buy a ticket to Mars."

"Man, if I could put the fare on my American Express card, you could color me gone."

When Tommy Camellini unlocked his apartment door and carried in his small bag of groceries—a six-pack of beer, a loaf of bread and a wedge of cheese—he didn't immediately turn on the lights. He walked to the kitchen and flipped on the light in there. He helped himself to a beer from the six-pack, then stowed his purchases in the refrigerator.

With beer in hand, Carmellini walked out into the living room and turned on the floor lamp by the couch. As he stood sipping the beer, he sensed something was wrong. He froze. Listened.

His eyes roamed the room. Then it hit him. Things were slightly out of position, as if they had been moved. This lamp he had just flipped on was two inches closer to the wall than usual—the circle on the carpet gave away the position change.

Someone had been here. Or was still here.

The apartment was not large. In seconds he verified that the bedroom, bath, and closets were empty.

Things were subtly adrift in the bedroom, too. His books, his clothes, the shoes in the bottom of the closet . . . everything had been stirred slightly.

Carmellini went into every room, inspected everything.

Nothing appeared to be missing. The windows were intact and closed.

He went back to the apartment door, inspected the lock carefully. They had either used a key or picked the lock.

He finished the beer and sat on the couch in the living room, staring at the blank television screen. What was here that anyone would want?

No money, no drugs, no classified documents. . . . He owned a computer, a sound system, and a television, and all three items were still sitting in plain sight. He went into the nook he used as an office and went through all the drawers of the desk. Files, piles of paper, letters, bank statements, bills, all of it was apparently there, although all of it had been pawed through.

Carmellini remembered the pistol in his sock drawer . . . he went into the bedroom and looked. Yep, it was still there, along with a box of ammunition. Shirts, suits, underwear, jeans . . . everything seemed to be there, yet the closets and drawers were not as neat as he left them—he was certain of that. His CIA ID card and building pass were in his pocket, as was his wallet containing his credit cards and driver's license.

Had someone bugged the apartment? If so, why, for Lord's sake?

He didn't look for bugs. Tommy Carmellini spent a significant fraction of his working life planting bugs in other people's homes, cars, and places of business, and he knew how devilishly difficult properly planted bugs were to discover. It was possible that the bugger was an amateur, or incompetent, or both. Or perhaps the bugger wanted him to know the bugs were there.

The second possibility was more likely. The person who planted the bugs wanted him to search and find some. Eventually he would abandon the search, concluding that he had found all the bugs, which would not be the case. Carmellini occasionally used that technique himself on paranoid subjects.

So who would want to know what Tommy Carmellini said in his own apartment? He had friends in occasionally to watch football or play poker, and several times a woman had spent the night . . . but lordy, who would want to listen to that?

It was a mystery, he decided. He turned on the television and flipped the channels, looking for a ball game.

The following evening Tommy Carmellini took a sensitive electronic device home from Langley. He had borrowed it from a man in another division who owed him a favor, so no record had been made of the loan. As he removed it from its case and tested the battery, he again wondered why anyone would want to bug his apartment. What could be said here that would be of interest to anyone?

True, he had been a thief in his younger days. He and a friend had taught themselves the finer points of burglary and safecracking. They had stolen diamonds, then fenced them to a jeweler who recut them and sold them from his store. The jeweler had been a piece of work, advertising that he went to Antwerp and bought diamonds wholesale and sold them cheaper than his competition because he cut out the middleman. And he did go to Antwerp and buy diamonds. And Carmellini and his friend provided more diamonds, cheaper ones than the diamond merchants in Belgium.

Then Carmellini's friend was busted and sold him to the feds. Carmellini had been in his last year of law school then. Fortunately the feds offered a deal—if he would work for the CIA, they wouldn't prosecute. It was, as they say, an offer he couldn't refuse. He was still with the CIA in charge of a branch that specialized in breaking and entering, mostly in foreign countries and, even though it was illegal, occasionally in this country when the FBI requested expert assistance.

The heck of it was he enjoyed his work. He liked the challenges of burglary when he was stealing diamonds and he enjoyed cracking safes around the world to photograph the contents now. He was paid a reasonable salary and enjoyed the travel. Of course, he had thought of resigning from the CIA and getting back into burglary . . . and one of these days he might.

Tonight he used the wand, which was an antenna, to look for the telltale energy that microphones emit. He quickly found two, one in the living room and one in the bedroom. He left them right where he found them.

He turned off the sweep gear and repacked it in its case. He would return it to his friend in a few days.

Carmellini opened a beer from the refrigerator and stood gazing out the window as he sipped it. Four nuclear weapons. Missing.

Jake Grafton, he decided, would not have bugged this apartment. He had worked with the admiral before and felt certain Grafton trusted him. If Grafton didn't, he wouldn't have asked for him by name or included him in brainstorming sessions. On the other hand, Jake Grafton was nobody's fool. Maybe . . .

Augh! He was overthinking this. He had worked with the spooks in the labyrinth too long—he was starting to think like them.

Whoever planted those bugs wants something, he decided. They expect to hear something on the bugs that they want to know.

Carmellini went back to the kitchen and tossed a TV dinner in the microwave. When it was warm, he took it to the living room and turned on the television. He flipped channels until he found a ball game.

I hope they like basketball, he thought, and attacked his dinner. He didn't think about basketball, however; he thought about bombs.

CHAPTER FIVE

Ivan Fedorov pointed the sniper rifle at the small warehouse three hundred meters down the street and stared at it through the night-vision scope. That was the warehouse where Frouq al-Zuair and his friends had parked the truck that they had driven more than fifteen hundred miles from central Asia.

Fedorov had the handguard of the Dragunov sniper rifle resting on a rolled-up blanket on the crumbling brick wall atop the building he was on. He pulled the rifle in against his shoulder, made sure the rubber eyepiece of the scope was against his face, and panned the rifle up and down the street, which was lined with ramshackle warehouses, shacks, light industry, and junkyards. There were no streetlights in this district adjacent to the Karachi airport, so the street was fairly dark at this hour of the night. No one moving that he could see.

"Nothing," he muttered to Zuair, who was sitting on the roof beside him with his back to the wall. A bundle lay beside him, something rolled up in a blanket and secured by strings.

The Egyptian was obviously worried. The warheads were still on the truck, and he couldn't drive the truck to the dock where the *Olympic Voyager* was loading until tomorrow night. "We can't load them aboard the ship until it has loaded its cargo and is ready for sea," the man in Cairo said. "Bribes have been paid for the officials to look the other way at the last minute. If we push too hard, the authorities will be forced to take notice to protect themselves."

Zuair hadn't mentioned this conversation to Fedorov, of course, but he had hired him and two other Russians to guard the warehouse with sniper rifles, which he had supplied. "My men know how to fire assault rifles and throw grenades," he had told Fedorov, "but they are not snipers. I wish to hire you and your friends to guard the warehouse."

Naturally Fedorov had asked what was in the warehouse. "Weapons," he was told, "in a truck." Nothing else.

Fedorov had bargained hard. Zuair had agreed to his price, which was a hundred dollars American for each of them for four nights' work. The Egyptian thought that Fedorov and his friends deserted the Soviet Army in Afghanistan—and Fedorov was not about to tell him he was wrong. Nor did he mention the fact that he had never been a sniper.

This evening he was working, playing the role. He had fired a Dragunov once, years ago. When handed the weapon he managed to open the battery compartment on the night-vision scope and check the battery for corrosion. It still had a charge and the sight seemed to work properly. He inserted the ten-round magazine in the rifle and chambered a round, ensured the safety was engaged. Zuair had watched. Fortunately he didn't fumble too much or drop the rifle. Now he was earning his hundred dollars watching an empty street.

"You don't really think anyone will assault the warehouse, do you?" he asked the Egyptian, who didn't bother to answer.

The monotony was relieved only by the passage of an occasional vehicle. After a few minutes spent looking toward the warehouse they were guarding, Fedorov shifted position and used the scope to glass the buildings and streets right, then left, then behind. He took his time, examined everything, then started all over again.

The Russian was systematic and thorough, which were good qualities in a soldier, Zuair reflected. He also asked too many questions.

No, he did not think it likely that any of the militant Islamic groups would attempt to assault the warehouse. They knew that eight men were inside the building with the warheads. A force sufficient to kill them might also damage the weapons. What Zuair feared was an ambush when he tried to drive the truck away. He was hoping that Fedorov and his friends would spot anyone moving into position on this street and were good enough shots to kill at these distances. Better to pay a mercenary who could shoot than pray with a brother who could not.

This warehouse district was the most likely place, the Egyptian reflected. Not many witnesses, the truck would be moving slowly in the narrow streets, and after it was over, the weapons could be transferred to another truck and driven away.

A hijacking on the crowded streets leading to the docks seemed less likely, he reflected.

Perhaps he had figured it wrong.

He looked again at his watch, the hands of which were luminescent. Two-fifteen in the morning. This was the third night on this roof. Tomorrow night the truck would move.

He would have bet money that an attempt would be made. Too many people in the militant community knew of the weapons. Having four nuclear warheads would catapult any group that had them to instant credibility.

Glory. They all wanted glory.

Frouq al-Zuair hadn't believed this plan would amount to anything when he had first heard it. Plots, conspiracies, plans that came to nothing—he had had a lifetime of those. He was not told what the leaders of the Sword of Islam planned to do with the weapons, only that they had a source and money to buy them. He had become a believer when he saw the money. Two million American dollars—it was a fortune beyond the dreams of avarice. With such a fortune a man could live like a sultan with a compound in a major city, with wives, prestige, and position. On the other hand, if a man used the money to buy warheads to wage *jihad*, he could earn a place in paradise for all eternity. Frouq al-Zuair was a true believer—he knew life was short and eternity was forever. The man from Cairo knew who he was, which was the reason he was selected for this mission.

To lose the weapons now would be ignominy. The brothers would think him a traitor to God. Better death than that.

To be on the safe side, he had hired Fedorov and the other two. While the Russians were infidels, they had lived here for many years and ran errands occasionally when asked. They always demanded small sums for their time and risk, which was reasonable, and they performed as promised.

If Fedorov did betray the brotherhood, Zuair would kill him. He had a knife in his belt and a loaded pistol in his pocket for that very purpose. He had never threatened the Russian, but of course the man knew.

Indeed, Ivan Fedorov *did* know that Zuair would execute him if he got the slightest hint that the Russian had sold him out. He knew it because he knew these fanatics. He had spent ten years getting to know them, working his way into their confidence. They would kill a nonbeliever as quickly as they would a mongrel dog, and with as much remorse. Fedorov moved his head back from the black rubber eyepiece for a moment and glanced at the Egyptian. Even in this dim light he could see that he had one hand in his coat pocket. Fedorov would have bet his life that there was a pistol or grenade in that pocket.

Fedorov was not worried. He had lived with the possibility of murder for seventeen years. He was an officer in the SVR. He had come to this part of the world when the First Chief Directorate of the KGB was the foreign intelligence arm of the Soviet state. He spoke the language, was accepted by these fanatics as an expatriate renegade, a minor dope smuggler, and he reported everything he could learn of their activities to his superiors in Moscow. If these raghead sons of bitches had an inkling of the truth, he would have been dead years ago.

Unfortunately tonight he was on thin ice. He had never served in the military and never killed a man. Zuair's offer of a job was an opportunity to work his way deeper into this dangerous group of fanatics, who he knew had purchased weapons from a rogue general in Russia. A rare opportunity if he could act the part.

Could he kill a man with this rifle? Hold the crosshairs steady while he squeezed the trigger? If he shot and missed, Zuair would not be happy. He had no way of knowing if the rifle was properly sighted. Even with the crosshairs dead on his target, he might miss; with Zuair standing beside him with a pistol. Just thinking about that eventuality made him perspire.

He hefted the long rifle and moved to the other corner of the building, to scan the street in the other direction.

The *Snayperskaya Vintovka Dragunova,* the SVD or Dragunov rifle, was unique in that the wooden stock had a large cutout in it to keep it light, and a pistol grip that allowed him to wrap his right hand completely around it. A soft rubber cheekpiece was glued to the top of the stock. The rifle was a semiautomatic that fired a 7.62×54 cartridge with every squeeze of the trigger. Other than the fact the cartridge was rimmed, it was roughly equivalent to the 7.62 NATO round used by the West. The lengthy action and slender twenty-two-inch barrel with attached muzzle brake made the Dragunov a long, elegant weapon, yet the stock cutout helped keep it light, for a sniper rifle. No doubt Zuair and his friends had obtained these three from Afghanistan.

Ivan Fedorov wiped his palms on his trousers and scanned the street with the night-vision scope yet again. He was desperate for a cigarette, yet was afraid to light one.

Zuair got up once to relieve himself in a corner, then resumed his seat. He let Fedorov do the looking, which was wise. The fewer heads moving about on top of this building, the better.

Another hour passed.

Fedorov was beginning to hope that nothing would happen when he spotted a truck creeping without headlights slowly down the side street opposite the building, heading this way.

He spoke to the Egyptian, motioned to him to come look.

Zuair was beside him when the truck stopped short of the intersection. In the scope Fedorov could see the glow of the engine's heat. The range was only about fifty meters—as he aimed the rifle his head and shoulders must extend well above this wall and be silhouetted against the night sky—easily visible—if the bad guys just bothered to look.

"This may be it," he murmured. God, he hoped it wasn't! At that location, he was the only Russian who would have a shot. If he left any of these men alive, they might hunt him. He remembered in exquisite detail the dark stairway that he had climbed to the roof, the wooden doors leading off the three landings. He had to go down that stairway to get off this roof.

A man got out of the passenger door of the truck cab, walked slowly to the corner, looking around. Fedorov could see him plainly in the scope. "One man, no uniform. No visible weapon." The man flattened against the building, eased his head around the corner to look down the street at the warehouse.

This corner fronted on the only street out of this district. This idiot Zuair had a hideout on a dead-end street! Terrorists were like that, Fedorov well knew—cunning and murderous and sometimes amazingly stupid.

"He's going back to the truck," he whispered, his eye glued to the rubber eyepiece. The soft rubber atop the stock felt hard against his face. Behind him he could hear Zuair doing something. He looked back. The Egyptian was unwrapping the bundle.

Fedorov concentrated on the picture through the scope. His hands shook and his breath came quickly, as if he were running. The entire picture in the scope quivered. He rested the handguard of the rifle on the wall before him to steady it.

"He's reaching into the truck . . . other men getting out. They are armed! Four of them."

"This is it!" Zuair hissed.

"Watch this! This is pretty neat," the technician said. He used a trackball to zoom the camera in on a couple walking out of Union Station. The images were displayed on a giant vertical monitor mounted against the wall. The zoom continued until the faces of the man and woman filled the monitor. They paused and embraced, and she said something to him.

"I don't read lips," the technician said wistfully, "but, boy, if I did!"

Jake Grafton and Toad Tarkington were standing in the command center on the fifth floor of the District of Columbia police headquarters. The technician was showing them the camera system that monitored public places throughout Washington. "We have over two hundred cameras installed and more going up every day. The new ones are digital, merely broadcast a signal, so there are no wires. The cameras are expensive, but the installation is cheap. We just install them on light poles or rooftops or cornices, wherever we can get electrical power to them, and control them from here."

The video feed from the cameras was displayed on dozens of monitors stacked like boxes against the wall. Then there were the large, thin plasma monitors, a wallful of movie screens—Jake stood mesmerized as he watched the intimate moment outside Union Station.

The couple kissed tenderly, then the woman walked toward the cab stand. The man watched her go. The camera followed the woman.

Jake turned and surveyed the command center. He counted—there were forty video stations angled around the wall of floor-to-ceiling screens. The FBI and CIA both had command stations here. The officer in charge sat in a soft armchair on a raised platform beside a teleconferencing screen.

"We are set up to do crowd control from here," the technician said. "Dozens of cameras monitor public places. We are installing two hundred cameras in the school system, over two hundred in the Metro stations, and a hundred more to monitor traffic. The merchants in Georgetown are installing cameras at their own expense. It won't be long before there are cameras in every public place in the city."

"And you can monitor them all from here?" Toad asked.

"Right. Of course, we have a computer setup ordered, a big project that will allow us to process digital images and search for that person in the database, see if he or she is on a wanted list. It'll cost a bundle and take a while to procure and install."

"What about all those cameras in hotels, elevators, and stores?" Jake asked. "Can you access their video from here?"

"Not yet. One of these days. The Supreme Court says that people don't have a right to privacy in public places, and in this day and age, people don't want to be mugged or robbed. Of course, the civil libertarians are squalling, but that's inevitable."

"Can you record the feeds you do get?"

"Oh, sure. We record them all, but no one ever looks at them. We need a computer program that digitizes the data and allows us to search the data for one person, follow them through the city. That's coming, too."

"Check an alibi," Toad suggested.

"The possibilities are staggering," the technician admitted. "*1984* is almost here. And people want it."

He got a telephone call then. As he talked into a lip mike, he manipulated the controls on the screen.

"Are you thinking what I'm thinking?" Toad whispered to Jake.

"The INS already has the software," Jake said. "If someone cobbled it together with the video feeds we could glue all this together right now. Hack into the system in hotels and stores . . . we could track anyone in this town in real time."

"Or see what they did yesterday or last week," Toad murmured. "Here and in New York. Los Angeles. Chicago. This system could put the dopers out of business."

"Dopers, armed robbers, drive-by shooters . . ." Jake mused. "And terrorists."

"And terrorists," Toad said firmly.

Jake slowly walked the length of the room, looking at everything. When he returned to Toad's side, he said, "We're going to need serious help. What do you think of getting Zelda Hudson and Zip Vance out of prison and turning them loose with some computers?" Hudson and Vance had been convicted a few months ago of helping steal USS *America*. They hacked into U.S. government computers, defense contractors' computers, everyone's computers. They were probably the best two hackers alive.

Toad whistled. "Jesus, Admiral. You must be desperate."

"I passed desperate last week."

"If the press ever finds out those two aren't in the can, you're toast, sir," Toad said as he carefully examined his boss's face. He had known Jake a long time and thought he knew him pretty well. Grafton was a high-stakes gambler if ever there were one, but he never took foolish risks.

"Can they help find those bombs?" Jake demanded. "If there is a decent chance, I'll take the risk. If not, give me some better ideas."

"They can get into databases that no one else can get into," Toad mused. "Even terrorists and mad bombers leave computer tracks."

"People use credit cards, they fly on airplanes, they make telephone calls, they rent cars, they stay in motels." Jake made a gesture of frustration. "We don't have time to build a case the old-fashioned way, even if we had the entire manpower of the FBI and CIA to help. We're going to have to take serious shortcuts."

"How much time do we have?" Toad asked, tugging at his lower lip.

"Your guess is as good as mine."

"So how do we go about springing Hudson and Vance?"

"Damned if I know," Jake muttered. He got out his wallet, removed the card bearing the telephone numbers that the president had given him, and reached for the officer-in-charge's secure telephone.

Four men, Ivan Fedorov thought. This was insane! He couldn't shoot all of them before one escaped! Yet if he didn't, he would have to shoot Zuair.

He flicked off the safety of the Dragunov and settled the sight on the chest of the first man, the man who had gotten out of the passenger seat. He was probably the leader. The man was checking his weapon.

Fedorov looked behind him at the Egyptian, trying to decide. If he shot at those men and didn't get all of them, they might trap him in the stairwell. Shoot him in the street below.

He had the weapon off his shoulder, ready to turn, when Zuair rushed to the wall beside him carrying a long tube. He lifted it to his shoulder. "Shoot after me," he hissed. He steadied the tube on his shoulder.

A ball of fire leaped from the weapon, shot across the space toward the truck as the deafening report walloped Fedorov in the face. The truck exploded.

A grenade launcher! Zuair had fired a rocket-propelled grenade!

The men lay on the ground, thrown there by the blast.

"Shoot them," the Egyptian ordered. "Shoot them now!"

The order jolted Fedorov from his paralysis. He put the crosshairs on the man in front of the truck, the leader he had aimed at before. The reticle danced. He forced himself to exhale, gripped the rifle tighter, and squeezed the trigger. The rifle bellowed and jumped slightly.

He brought the crosshairs down on the man again. Fired a second time.

"Shoot them all!" Zuair urged, hissing in his ear. "Ensure they are dead."

Fedorov forced himself to pan the scope. The truck was on fire, creating a heat source that threatened to overwhelm the scope. There, a man crawling . . .

He shot him. Once, twice, then searched for another target.

One man was staggering away, on the other side of the truck, back along the street they had driven down. Fedorov shot him in the back, and he went forward on his face.

The other man . . . he couldn't find the other man! The scope was being overwhelmed with heat.

"He's under the truck," the Egyptian said.

Fedorov looked around the scope at the scene. The truck was burning fiercely, lighting the scene. Now he saw the fourth man. He went back to the scope, searched the brightness . . .

There! Two more shots.

"Let's go," Zuair said hoarsely. "Before the police come."

"The rifle—here, you want it?"

"Leave it," Zuair said over his shoulder. He had already thrown down the RPG launcher and was striding for the stairs.

Fedorov dropped the rifle and followed the Egyptian. They hustled down the dark stairs, making enough noise to wake the dead. The truck was still burning when they exited the building.

He tried to follow Zuair, who turned toward the warehouse. "No," the man said roughly. "Go away. I will meet you this evening at the usual place."

Ivan Fedorov walked quickly away from the truck. He forced himself to walk, not run. He heard a siren moaning blocks away. When he came to a dark alley between the buildings, he turned and went down it. There in the darkness the realization of what he had done hit him like a hammer. He stood in the darkness on shaky legs, retching. It took several minutes to get his stomach completely under control.

No one came into the alley. The siren went in the direction of the burning truck and finally ceased its moan.

He would get off a report to Moscow as soon as possible, he decided. Maybe the men there could figure out whom he had just killed.

Tommy Carmellini was in his office, making telephone calls for Jake Grafton, when a fellow he knew from another department, Archie Foster, stuck his head in the door. "Ah, Carmellini, I wonder if you might have a minute?"

Tommy looked at his watch. "I'm pretty busy."

"Later this morning in my office? This is important."

"Ah, you want to tell me what—?"

"Not here. My office. I've cleared your visit with security."

"Sure. In a half hour."

Archie Foster gave him his room and building number, smiled his thanks, and disappeared. Carmellini checked his watch again, then went back to work.

He had done something for Foster once . . . what was it? Something in Colombia. Several years ago. *He probably wants me to go back there.*

Only five minutes late, Carmellini gave his name and showed his badge to the guard at Foster's building. The badge, of course, was worn on a chain around the neck, where it was visible to anyone who looked, and to electronic devices. He took the elevator, then did the security thing again with the guard on the corridor that led to Foster's office. As he walked down the hallway an electronic device on the ceiling read his badge again. He knocked on the door, which wasn't locked, then entered. Another man was sitting in one of the guest chairs, a man Carmellini had met on several occasions through the years and knew by sight, Norv Lalouette.

"You know Norv, don't you, Tommy?"

"Sure." Carmellini shook hands and dropped into an empty chair.

"Thanks for taking the time to drop by. We have a videotape—actually a copy of a videotape—that we wanted you to look at. See if anything in there is familiar." He used a remote to fire up a small portable television with a built-in VCR in the corner.

"Wow, how did you rate a TV in your office?" Carmellini asked as the VCR clicked and whirred.

"Brought it from home."

"Nice little unit," Carmellini said as the tape began running.

"There's sound, too," Foster said, and put on his glasses so he could see the buttons better.

The tape was obviously shot by an amateur on a bright sunny day. The girl in the picture was college age, not bad-looking; the camera-person—apparently a male—was talking to her. Between them they were giving the viewer a tour of the campus. Yes, it was a college campus, with buildings of red stone and trees without leaves—obvious late autumn or winter—but a nice day.

"It's sorta strange how we got this tape," Archie Foster said, speaking over the narrator. "The FBI is working on an old murder, three years old now, of a college professor at the University of Colorado. Name of Olaf Svenson. Guy was a microbiologist or something like that. Bugs and germs. Anyway, someone popped him in his office with a twenty-two on a weekday, about three years ago. No one saw anything, no one heard anything. Someone pumped two bullets into Svenson's brain, apparently while he sat at his desk, one in the forehead, the other over his left ear. No bleeding, so death was pretty much instantaneous."

The girl in the video was walking along, the cameraman trailing her, as she pointed out various buildings on the campus. Students could be seen in the background coming and going, but they paid her and the camera no notice.

"There were just no clues," Archie Foster continued. "No fingerprints in Svenson's office that couldn't be accounted for, no spent cartridges, no matchbook covers or glasses with lipstick, none of that crap. Oh, the doorknob in and out had been wiped—no prints except for the janitor who found Svenson. The local police were pretty sure he wasn't the shooter. It looked like a professional hit to them, so they called in the FBI."

Now the girl on the screen was standing in front of the main library. Archie Foster pointed the remote at the television and waited. In seconds someone passed behind the girl. When he did Archie froze the picture.

The man on the screen was Tommy Carmellini.

"Anyway," Archie said, facing Carmellini, "Norv occasionally liaises with the FBI . . . and a month or so ago they asked him to look at this tape, which the Boulder PD acquired during their investigation, to see if he could pick out any professional hitters. So ol' Norv is busy watching this thing, stopping the tape on every face and making digital records and doing computer studies and all of that, and bingo!

It's good buddy Tommy Carmellini, all the way from the fourth floor at Langley."

"Looks like me," Tommy Carmellini agreed.

Archie Foster chuckled. "Oh, it's you, all right. Norv and I did some checking. You were down in Cuba with Bill Chance when he got killed. You were both armed with Ruger twenty-twos with silencers and neither weapon came home. The FBI tried to put together a case against Olaf Svenson for helping the Cubans develop a biological warfare agent, but they could never get enough to satisfy the U.S. attorneys. You know how those friggin' lawyers are, proof beyond a reasonable doubt and all that crap. They finally gave up on Svenson, decided not to take him to a grand jury. Then a month later he gets popped in his office while you were on leave, somewhere out there in the big wide world vacationing all to hell. That's the way it stood for years.

"Then voilà! There you are on videotape, big as life, walking across the campus of the University of Colorado within minutes of the time that Svenson went to meet the devil. See those little red numbers in the bottom right-hand corner of the screen? Date and time."

Tommy Carmellini glanced at his watch. "Why are you two wasting my time with this? You're not FBI."

"No, but we could tell them what they have. We haven't yet. We wanted to talk to you first, hear what you have to say."

"Golly, gee, that's sweet of you guys," Tommy said. "I didn't know we were that kind of friends. Be that as it may, let me tell you the sad truth. There's no case here, amigo. What you got is shit. Even if it is me on that tape—and I'm not admitting that it is—the FBI and U.S. attorney will be delighted to tell you that you gotta put me in the building with a gun in my hand before you have a shot at an indictment. We're not talking conviction, we're talking indictment."

Carmellini rose from his chair and headed for the door. "You two tell the FBI anything you want," he said as he reached for the doorknob. "And have a nice life, fellows." He closed the door behind him.

"So what do you think?" Norv Lalouette asked Archie Foster when Carmellini's steps had faded.

"He's good, damn good. No question about that."

"I watched his face. He didn't turn a hair."

Archie Foster studied the image on the television screen. "He's one damn cool customer," Archie muttered finally, and used the remote to kill the television.

"If he really killed Svenson, he might come after us," Lalouette pointed out.

Foster snorted. "He's smarter than that."

Patsy Smoot ran a motel on a road in Broward County, Florida, near Fort Lauderdale. Like hundreds of others, hers was built in the 1950s, before the age of interstates, to serve an increasing tide of motor tourists who were venturing south in the fall and looking for a place to spend a few days, or a few weeks, or the whole winter. The air conditioners were in the windows of the units, each of which had one double bed, a small bath with a shower, and a twenty-something-year-old television wired to an antenna on top of the motel office, which contained the tiny apartment where Patsy and her husband, Fred, lived.

Patsy ran the desk and filled out the forms that it took to stay in business these days. Fred was the handyman and groundskeeper. An illegal Mexican woman named Maria cleaned the units and made beds seven days a week, 365 days a year.

Smoot's Motel stood between a Burger King and a sleazy beer joint, and across the highway from a used car lot. Similar businesses lined the highway—now a four-lane—in both directions as far as the eye could see. The most prosperous of the businesses, like Burger King, had asphalt parking lots, but Smoot's and the used car lot and the beer joint made do with crushed seashells, which a local contractor delivered, spread, and rolled every third or fourth year when the inevitable potholes developed or grass and weeds got too much of a start.

"We need to do the parking lot again," Fred told his wife this morning as she looked out the office window at the cars in front of the units.

"We did it two years ago," she replied curtly.

"I know, but the guy didn't put all that much on, and the weeds are growing through again. And we got a soft place where the RVs go around the building."

Ten years ago the Smoots had installed hookups for ten recreation vehicles behind the motel in a patch that had been weeds and trash. More and more people are out on the road these days in those things, Patsy Smoot thought distractedly. She focused again on the car in front of Unit Six. It was a good-looking new car, apparently a rental. She didn't see many of those at Smoot's. People who rented from the big agencies rarely stayed at $24.99-a-night motels; they stayed at a major chain's facility near the interstate.

"I think we should call the FBI on that bunch in Six," she told Fred now.

"What for? They ain't done nothin' and their money's good. They're paid ahead, ain't they?"

"Yes. Renting by the week. Four single men in that unit with one double bed. Been here almost four weeks now. And driving that rental."

"Hell, we're half-empty. They leave and Six will sit empty most of the summer. You know that."

"They're Arabs," Patsy Smoot said, almost as if she were merely thinking aloud. "Or Palestinians or Iranians or some such. Can't tell 'em apart."

"Lebanese, one of them told me. Working at one of those food warehouses."

"Seems like we ought to call somebody."

Fred snorted. "Think they sneaked a whore in there?"

"No. If that was it, I'd have done called." She was a little peeved at Fred. She ran a decent place, and he damn well knew it.

"Hell," Fred said hotly, "what about that guy from Ohio in One? Claims that girl is his daughter, but for all I know he's some schoolteacher who ran off with one of the students. She oughta be in school. He's probably porkin' her. Maybe we oughta report him for traveling with a minor female. Don't think that's a crime, but what the hell."

His wife didn't reply.

Fred reached his peroration without further ado. "We go calling the law on our quiet customers and we might as well put the Going Out of Business sign up right now," he declared. "We aren't the morals police or the INS. Half our customers are from some Third World cesspool. Came here to make it in America, so they did. Work hard and send money home every month, just like Maria. Goddamn, Patsy, we've had 'em packed in four to a unit many a time."

Patsy shot back, "So you think they're poor working slobs staying in a cheap motel because it's all they can afford and driving a rent car that must cost them two hundred, maybe two-fifty a week?"

Fred had argued enough. He drained the last of his coffee and slapped the cup down on the counter. "You do what you damn well want, woman. You always do. I don't know why you even talk to me about stuff, anyway. But I'll tell you this: Just because these people don't look like us don't mean they're fuckin' terrorists out to blow something up. I don't like siccin' the law on people minding their own damn business. Goes against my grain, so it does." He stomped out to fix the leaky faucet in Unit Two, muttering, "Maybe we need a damn Gestapo to arrest all these little warts we don't like."

The window drapes in Unit Six were drawn, as they were every morning. Job or no job, those four never went out before noon, then they stayed out until midnight. Patsy Smoot waited until she could hear Fred mowing the grass around back, then she looked up the FBI's telephone number in the phone book and dialed it.

The call wound up being taken by a female FBI agent in the South Florida Joint Terrorism Task Force. She wrote down all the information on a form—including the name and driver's license information of the man who rented the unit—thanked Patsy for calling, and promised to follow up. Then she sent the form to one of the bureau teams that was tracking possible terrorist cells.

The form was on a clipboard the next day when Hob Tulik, down from Washington for an inspection, flipped through the forms on the board and saw it. "This cell, Number Eleven, you've had what, seven calls on them?"

"Yessir. Four male suspects in their twenties, from Arabia we think, all here on student visas. Two were at the University of Illinois, one at Stanford, one at the University of Missouri. They're packed in one little room at Smoot's Motel on Route One, north of Fort Lauderdale."

"Studying hard, are they?"

"No, sir," said the agent, ignoring the sarcasm. He pulled a file on Cell Eleven and opened it. "We've been working this cell for three weeks. Two suspects are working at a food warehouse, one is a laborer at a tire store, and another is a part-time convenience store clerk. Strange thing is that they drive a rental car from an airport agency. Displayed a California driver's license for a man named Safraz Hassoun and used a credit card in that name. Los Angeles address on the license. We're having the records pulled on the driver's license and have requested a copy of the credit card app."

Hob Tulik leafed through the file, which contained four photos, all candid snaps with the subjects unaware of the photographer. "Which onc is Hassoun?"

"None of them. There was a Kuwaiti student named Hassoun at UCLA last year, but as far as we know he's left the country."

"Terrific. What are we doing in the way of surveillance?"

"We think one of them has a cell phone, sir. We're trying to find out the number and get court authorization for an intercept and the records. Their motel room contains no telephone. Smoot's Motel does have a pay phone on a car window mount in front of the place, and we have an authorization to tap that. We'll get it done in three or four days, whenever the technicians can process it. We don't have the people to stay on the suspects around the clock, so we have a man in the motel and follow them to and from their jobs. If they leave their jobs before their shifts end, we won't know it."

"That the best we can do?"

"We're working seventeen possible cells."

"I understand."

Jake Grafton was watching the news on television when his daughter Amy came in that evening. She had lived in a dorm for her first year of college, then shared an apartment with two other girls for three semesters—now she was bunking at home. The move home was Amy's idea. Jake resisted the return to the nest at first, until Callie noted that in a year or two Amy would be gone for good. "Better enjoy her company while you can." Now Jake looked forward to Amy's evening arrivals home from the library where she studied and worked part-time.

Amy kissed his cheek, then dropped onto the sofa beside Jake and kicked off her shoes. "I've got to write a paper," she said, "and I don't know what I want to say."

"Been there myself," her father muttered.

"The question is: Can constitutional democracy survive in the age of terror?"

"That's a good one."

"I don't know the answer. I'm really worried, Dad. The news is scary. There seem to be many people in the world who don't have a stake in civilization—they don't *want* civilization."

Jake used the remote to turn off the television.

"Rome fell to the barbarians," Amy continued, "because it could no longer defend itself. Are we like the Romans?"

"There's the format for your paper. Compare America today to ancient Rome."

Amy thought about it. "That's a good approach. Thanks. But it doesn't answer the question: Can we survive?"

"I don't know the answer, Amy. No one does. Civilizations have been rising and falling since the first farmers built huts close together for protection."

Amy wasn't in a philosophical mood. She picked up her books and stood. As she did, she said, "I don't want my grandchildren growing up in a new dark age, ignorant and starving and dictated to by illiterate holy men ranting about evil and preaching holy war against the infidels."

"Nor do I," Jake agreed.

"I'd rather see all those sons of bitches dead," she added grimly. "That isn't politically correct, but I'm getting sick of political correctness, too."

Jake smiled as she went to the kitchen to get a glass of milk and a snack. A chip off the old block, he thought. He didn't know if that was good or bad.

CHAPTER SIX

"Here's the first copy of the magazine, Mr. Corrigan," the secretary said gleefully. She handed him a magazine. "A courier brought it directly from New York."

"Thank you, Miss Hargrove."

Thayer Michael Corrigan was riding a stationary bicycle. He placed the magazine on the stand on top of the *Wall Street Journal* and examined the cover likeness. *Looks good*, he thought. *For an old fart, you aren't half-bad*.

He kept riding as he scanned the cover story. He had already seen most of it, of course, traded back and forth as e-mail. The reporter wanted to ensure he had his facts right, he said, "standard procedure." Corrigan snorted. Preapproval of cover stories was the only way that the magazine could ensure that captains of industry would continue to grant interviews for future cover stories. No one wanted to be sandbagged by some scribbler out to make a name for himself.

Yep, the story was the one he had seen, with only minor editing changes. He used the towel to wipe his face and settled down to serious riding.

The view out the corner office windows was of a duck pond teeming with birds. The groundskeeper fed the ducks and swans every morning to keep them there. The shrubbery around the pond was manicured in the Japanese style, very arty. And labor-intensive. All in all, the scene made a nice statement about Corrigan Engineering, Inc., "Building a Better World" as the slogan under the logo proclaimed.

Thayer Michael Corrigan had started out forty-six years ago with a contract to inspect New England railroad bridges. When people asked about the old days, he liked to talk about those bridges, about wading through the trash and poison ivy, jumping out of the way of passing trains. He had talked about those days for the magazine reporter, who had devoted a long paragraph to that humble beginning.

He didn't tell the reporter that he would probably still be inspecting railroad bridges if he hadn't had a chance meeting two years later with a man in Cambridge. He had never talked about that meeting with anyone.

As he stared at the duck pond, he remembered. The acquaintance began casually enough, and ripened rather quickly into a friendship. Dinners here and there, cigars and whiskey afterward. The man's name was Herbert Schwimmer. He too, he said, was a consulting engineer. Or so Corrigan believed for several years. He was ten or fifteen years older than Corrigan, had a nice accent, and said his parents came to this country from Europe before the war.

One evening Schwimmer made the observation that in the post–World War II era American companies were the technological star cores, the place where research and engineering, competition and the possibility of profits fused old materials into new things that had never before existed. These places, Schwimmer said, were the wealth generators in the age of capitalism.

Somehow, Corrigan couldn't remember exactly how, the subject of industrial espionage came up in their conversation. "You understand," Schwimmer said, "that industrial secrets are impossible to keep. People talk shop to lovers and friends, they leave the company for a competitor, patents are infringed, competitors spy on their rivals and do reverse engineering.... Yet there is a time, a brief window, when knowledge has value, when it can be converted to gold."

Weeks later Herbert Schwimmer confided that he was a broker in intellectual property. "I am not interested in the atomic secret," he said with a grin. "Nor do I deal in political intelligence. I wouldn't pay a nickel for the latest war plan. I need products that I can sell to other companies."

"Where?"

"Here and in Europe. Everyone guards their secrets and buys those of the competition. Of course, the value of intellectual property decreases over time, and one must know the market."

Today Corrigan's reverie was broken by the buzz of the intercom. "Your wife is on the telephone, Mr. Corrigan. Line two."

Corrigan pushed a button to put his wife on the speaker. He kept pedaling.

"Yes, dear."

"Congratulations on the story. *Power*, no less."

"You've seen a copy?"

"A friend in New York faxed me a copy of the cover. A good likeness."

"They got me, I think."

"Oh, Mrs. Everett from the symphony is in the other room. It's the annual fund drive. I was thinking of giving them a hundred. Is that okay with you?"

"Fine," said Thayer Michael Corrigan.

She discussed their dinner plans, then said good-bye.

Corrigan looked at his watch. Ten more minutes. As he wiped his face his thoughts returned to Schwimmer and his business proposition. It hadn't come out all at once, of course, but in dribs and drabs over the course of six or eight weeks. Actually, he had been the one who asked Schwimmer what secrets he wanted.

Two months later Corrigan sold his first secret to Schwimmer. He went looking for it. He was the low bidder for a consulting contract for a division of a company building radars. He couldn't get into the lab, of course; he was hired to help with the structural design of a new building. He spent his spare moments mining the trash. Fortunately he wasn't caught. His excavations yielded blueprints and technical notes that he used to write a coherent summary of a new radar design. Schwimmer paid him $10,000 for the summary. Personally mining the trash was a huge risk, one he never took again. From that day forth he bribed garbage collectors. Thayer Michael Corrigan was on his way.

The intercom buzzed again. "Your wife again, sir."

"Yes, Lauren."

"I'm sorry to bother you, T. M. Everett says Rebecca DuPont gave the symphony two hundred. I knew you thought it important . . ."

"Give them a quarter million."

Corrigan pedaled on, thinking about his wife. She was modeling in New York when he met her at a party five years ago. God, she was gorgeous. She wasn't one of those half-starved, flat-chested fashion horses, but a model for women's fitness magazines. How to get great abs, lose cellulite, sculpt the buns, that kind of thing. She was really built. And she was thirty-five years younger than he was and loved to fuck, so he did a half hour on the damned stationary bike every day. And popped the little blue pills. She didn't know about the pills, and he wasn't about to tell her. Thank God for little blue pills.

Of course, Schwimmer wouldn't have been interested in the formula for blue pills. Back then he had wanted leading-edge high-tech stuff in aviation, radar, computers, sonars, the space program. Corrigan had founded a company and recruited engineers and was making serious money when he finally realized Schwimmer was after the information for the Soviets. He braced him on it. Yes, he was KGB.

But there was little risk, Schwimmer insisted. The FBI was looking for spies in the political arena and in government laboratories. "I told you I am not after the atomic secret, and I don't give a damn what Washington is plotting." Of course not. The Soviets had other sources for that information. The real question, Corrigan realized, was who was going to earn the money providing the industrial secrets that Schwimmer and his colleagues were going to get in any event, from someone. They would buy the information they wanted or some liberal half-wit would pass it to them gratis for ideological reasons. Schwimmer was absolutely right, the stuff was valuable and impossible to keep secret. Corrigan decided that he wanted the money.

Today on the exercise bicycle he grinned to himself. He had made the right decision. He had built a large consulting firm that did business all over the world. The most profitable division was the smallest, industrial secrets, and it had made him filthy rich. The cover of *Power* magazine, no less!

Sure, there had been problems through the years. He hired men who solved those kinds of problems and he paid them very well, more money than they could ever have made doing anything else.

Schwimmer was long gone. Other contacts had come and gone, and the money kept flowing. Business had boomed during the Reagan years, when American industry led the world into space and the computer age had dawned. Stealth airplanes, quiet submarines, guided weapons, networkcentric warfare, space-based sensors, encryption technology, the Soviets had paid top dollar for all of it. Ironically, they couldn't use even a small portion of what he sold them—they lacked the industrial capacity. Thayer Michael Corrigan had enjoyed that delicious irony.

Then the Soviet Union imploded, and money from the new Russia had dried up.

The bicycle beeped at him. One more minute. He increased the pace, worked the pedals as fast as he could. At the end of the minute the machine beeped again and he slowed down, pedaled slowly during the cooling-off period.

The world changed in 1991. Now it was changing again. The age of terrorism was here, and once again there was big money to be made. Security was the top-dollar commodity now and the American government was the customer. *Thank you, Osama bin Laden, you stupid raghead fanatic, plotting mass murder in your mud hut. You are going to make me a billionaire!*

He got off the bicycle, wiped his face and hands, and picked up the magazine. He examined the cover art closely. It was a good likeness. He pushed a button on the intercom for his executive assistant.

"Frank, call *Power* magazine. Tell them I want to buy the portrait they used for the cover. Get it framed for the reception area."

"Yes, Mr. Corrigan. Right away."

Alderson, West Virginia, was a sleepy coal town tucked between two steep, wooded hillsides with a gorgeous river, the Greenbrier, running through it. Tommy Carmellini parked on the main street on the north side of the river, got out of his car, and stretched. He was several inches over six feet tall and wore a baggy light sports coat and trousers that didn't quite fit. In an age when men picked clothes to show off their physiques, Tommy Carmellini's clothes hid his wide shoulders, long, ropy muscles, and washboard stomach. Cut an inch or so too long, his sleeves partially obscured the massive wrists, oversize veins, and superstrong fingers that years of rock climbing had developed.

After working the kinks out, Carmellini went into a small grocery store. He bought a cold can of soda pop and stepped back out on the sidewalk to drink it. The river was wide here, flowing along in the summer heat under the shade of huge oaks and maples. Several boys were fishing along the banks. A couple of them eyed his car curiously—you didn't see many old red Mercedes coupes parked in coal country.

When Tommy finished the soda he went back into the store. He was the only customer. He asked the female clerk, "Where's the women's prison?"

"Cross the river on the bridge, honey, and stay on the highway. It's a ways down the river, but there's signs. You can't miss it."

"Okay."

"You here to visit someone?"

"My mom. She's got a few more years left to do."

He ditched the can in the trash by the door and walked back to the car.

The visitors' room at the prison was divided by a table that ran from wall to wall. The prisoners and visitors were separated by a wall of bulletproof glass that ran the length of the table. Carmellini was the only visitor. He took the middle of five seats. The place smelled of disinfectant. Massive walls, puke green paint, tiny windows, the bars, the vast silence . . . the hopelessness of it washed over Tommy Carmellini.

When the guard brought Zelda Hudson into the room he was stunned at the change in her appearance. She wore no makeup at all, her dark hair was cropped just below her ears, and her beltless prison shift hung on her like a sack. She looked years older than he remembered her.

She took a seat opposite him and stared at him through the glass without a flicker of interest.

"Name's Carmellini," he said into the intercom mike after the guard left the room and they were alone.

"I recognize you."

"Was sort of surprised when you pleaded guilty without making a deal with Justice." Zelda had masterminded the theft of USS *America* last year. After she was indicted by a grand jury she pleaded guilty at the arraignment, which left the media aghast at her effrontery, cheating them out of a show trial.

"I don't know what you want, Carmellini, but I've told you people everything I have to say."

"Well, I was in the neighborhood, just thought I'd drop in and say hi."

"Right."

"So you got what, about thirty years to do before you're eligible for parole?"

"So you read newspapers."

"Not really. You know how death penalty cases are—fame and fortune. You and Hillary Clinton were on the cover of the supermarket tabloids every time I bought beer."

"I hope you kept a scrapbook."

He tugged at an earlobe "You always did have a difficult personality, as I recall."

"Listen, Carmellini. You helped put me here. Oh, I know, I fucked up and all that, but you shoved me into this hellhole. Say what you came to say and hit the road."

"How'd you like to get out of here, Zelda?"

She didn't even look at him.

"I'm here to offer you a job. If you take it, you're outta here."

She snorted in derision. "Who do I have to kill?"

"Nothing messy required," Carmellini said. "I work for an agency of the United States government, and we happen to have an opening for a person of your talents."

Her eyes were on his now. "What agency?"

"Don't get cute. It doesn't become you."

"Last year you were CIA. Still with them?"

"Yes."

"I conspired with murderers and thieves to steal a submarine. I pleaded guilty to *thirty-seven felonies,* Carmellini! They didn't charge me with espionage, but I'm guilty of that, too. The only thing I haven't done is have sex with a farm animal like you. Why in God's name does the CIA want me?"

"You're good with computers."

"That's not exactly a rare skill."

"A lot of people play basketball, but there's only one Michael Jordan."

She was incredulous. "You're offering me a job in the CIA? When I get out in thirty years, or is this something I can do from my cell?"

"Osama bin Laden changed the world. Your skills are in demand. You'll sign the security agreements, get the building pass and green paycheck. Keep your nose clean and you'll have a new life. You can rent an apartment, buy a car on time, get in debt to your eyes—it's the American way, baby. 'Course, if you cheat or screw up, you'll ride the magic carpet right back here to Alderson. We won't do parole or probation or any of that to get you out, so there won't have to be a hearing to put you back in—we'll just call the federal marshals and they'll whisk you back to the joint before you can kiss your ass goodbye. Don't know if we can get you the same cell—you might have to take whatever they have available."

She put her elbows on the counter in front of her and lowered her face into her hands. After a long minute it occurred to Carmellini that she might be crying.

"Hey," he said into the intercom mike. "Hey. Just say yes."

She straightened. Her eyes were as dry as his. "So I give you assholes a good education and you say what the hell and call the marshals. That the way it'll go down?"

Carmellini shrugged. "This Christmas I'll send you a canary. You can become the bird woman of Alderson."

"What guarantee do I have that you'll play fair?"

"None."

"I love it when you sweet-talk me."

"How's the pasta here? I heard they do really good mac and cheese in these federal crypts."

"Of course, the newspapers will never learn that I'm out."

"We'll have to give you a new identity," Carmellini admitted. "I thought you made a good Sarah Houston, so I had them use that name on the birth certificate, driver's license, all of that. We used the computer on your photo, dyed your hair and reshaped it. I'll bet you always wanted to be a blonde."

"One condition," she said. "You have to get Zip Vance out." Zip had helped her steal the submarine. He also pleaded guilty at the arraignment.

Tommy Carmellini scrutinized her face. "You don't have a lot of chips left to throw on the table, lady."

"I don't care how you do it. If you get me out, you must get him out of prison, too. Or no deal."

"I'll bet you don't get a lot of job offers here in the joint. What if I say no?"

She rose from her chair and headed for the door. She was about to knock on it to call the guard when Carmellini said into the intercom. "Funny, Vance also refused the job unless we got you out."

She turned, stared at him.

"I think the fool is in love with you, Sarah Houston."

She rubbed her face with her hands, then muttered, almost inaudibly, "That's his problem." She took a deep breath, then came back to the chair opposite him.

"You can really do this?"

"I've got low friends in high places."

"Zip, too?"

Tommy Carmellini nodded affirmatively. "This is how it'll go down. A few days from now the prison will get standard transfer orders saying you're going to a federal country-club joint for white-collar scumbags. The following day two real, honest-to-God federal marshals will show up to take you there. They'll have all the proper papers, signed and sealed and genuine as hell. The marshals will bring you to Washington instead. Don't tell anyone anything. And this conversation never took place."

She didn't say anything.

"See you in Washington," he said, walked to the door, and knocked.

In the corridor outside the visiting room, Tommy Carmellini told the female guard, "I need to see the warden."

The guard was bored, overweight, and surly. "Hey, I know you're some kind of federal officer, but the warden makes appointments and all."

"Why don't you take me to talk to his secretary?"

The guard decided maybe that was okay. She led the way.

The secretary wanted to know if Carmellini had an appointment. It took five minutes for him to get in to see the warden.

The warden's name was Gruzik, according to the sign on his desk. He didn't get out of his chair or offer to shake hands. Carmellini produced an envelope from his inside pocket and passed it across the desk. Inside the envelope was a letter from the director of the Bureau of Prisons. Carmellini watched Gruzik's face as he read the letter, which directed him to call the director immediately. Gruzik picked up the telephone and punched buttons.

When he hung up the telephone he looked at Carmellini with interest. "Who are you, anyway?"

"Nobody you want to know. Give me the audiotape you made of my visit with Zelda Hudson and forget you ever saw me. And I want the page I signed in the visitors' log."

"We don't tape conversations between—"

"Don't give me that shit. You heard the director. 'Full cooperation.' I want the tape and the log."

In two minutes he had the tape in his hand, a cassette. Three minutes later the visitors' log came into the room. Carmellini ripped out the page he had signed, folded it neatly, and put it in his shirt pocket. "I'm going to listen to this tape on the way to Washington," he told the warden. "It had better be the right one."

"The guard said it was," the warden said sourly.

"I notice you have video cameras in the visitors' waiting area, in the corridors, and outside this office. I want the tapes. All of them."

That took three more minutes. While they were waiting Carmellini reached across the desk and snagged the letter on Bureau of Prisons stationery. "Might as well take this, too."

It turned out there were four videotapes. Carmellini put the audiocassette in his jacket pocket and carried the tapes in his hands.

Before he left he said to the warden, "I want to make sure you're crystal clear on the situation. If you or anyone on your staff mentions my name, my visit, or this conversation with anyone at all and we hear about it, you'll be looking for another job. And there won't be a corrections facility in the country that will hire you, not even to peel potatoes. That's a promise."

He closed the door carefully behind him.

After his shower, Thayer Michael Corrigan dressed in a dark power suit and red tie before he began the rounds of appointments and meetings that filled his days as the head of a large organization. When the schedule permitted, he and his executive assistant tackled the in-basket.

Yet in this mountain of paper that crossed his desk, not a scrap hinted at anything illegal. Naturally Corrigan never saw stolen documents of any kind, nor did he handle money. Other people procured and paid for documents and delivered them to the buyers. Money in payment came through various foreign consulting contracts. The head of the accounting department made sure the money came and went in innocuous ways and was properly accounted for. He didn't know why payments were made or money received—and didn't want to know, because he was paid twice as much as he would have been at any other company in New England. With stock options and bonuses, he was a rich man getting richer, and he liked it like that.

The only man Corrigan routinely dealt with who knew what was really going on was Karl Luck. He had two or three private audiences with Corrigan every day. A former CIA agent, Luck, too, was rich and becoming richer, although money didn't motivate him. He loved the action.

As usual, today he was waiting when Corrigan finished dressing in the private apartment beside the corner office. One of his duties was to sweep Corrigan's offices for bugs. He did a thorough job every morning before anyone came to work, then used a small unit for a spot check before he and Corrigan discussed anything. He was stowing the device in its case when Corrigan came through the door from the apartment.

"Morning, Karl."

"Good morning, sir."

"What do you hear from Dutch?"

"There was a firefight last night near the warehouse where the weapons are parked. Tonight"—he glanced at his watch while he mentally calculated the time difference—"actually about two hours from now, the weapons will be transported to the dock and loaded."

"Tell me about the firefight."

"A rival militant group. The news of the warheads' presence has spread like wildfire. We knew it would. There was no way to keep that secret."

"Why are the weapons still there? They should have been on that ship days ago."

"Problems getting the ship loaded and cleared for sea. Bribes were paid, but we could only push so far."

"The Egyptian?"

"Zuair is primed and ready. He's going to smite the infidels."

"Problems?"

"None right now."

"This has to go right. No screwups."

"There won't be any."

"Fine."

Karl Luck left the office. Corrigan watched the door close, then smiled. Luck's name was misleading. He was effective because he didn't believe in luck; he made his own.

Corrigan didn't believe in luck either. He had made his fortune by ensuring that chance events couldn't ruin him. Get good people, pay them well, and back them to the hilt. That was the formula he gave to the *Power* reporter. Amazingly enough, it really worked . . . most of the time. Random chance and human weakness were always present in human affairs and occasionally created problems. One had to attack the problems ruthlessly and without remorse. Thayer Michael Corrigan and Karl Luck were very good at that. He didn't mention that to the reporter, though.

Mohammed Mohammed was another man who didn't believe in luck. He had been entrusted with the leadership of an attack upon America because he was smart and a meticulous planner who left nothing to chance. Too many holy warriors, in his opinion, believed that since Allah was on their side, they would succeed. *Inshallah,* "God willing," was their creed, the blueprint for their lives. What they forgot was that the forces of evil were everywhere, eternally at war with the forces of Allah. It must be so, he reasoned, or Earth would be a paradise where Allah ruled. It wasn't.

No. Victory goes to those who earn it. Allah had arranged the universe that way. Mohammed Mohammed intended to earn his ticket to paradise.

This afternoon at the Liquid Sunshine Citrus Warehouse in Florida he paused in his task of loading crates of oranges onto pallets to watch the forklifts zipping around the building. He had been unable to operate a forklift yet, and he must learn how.

The foreman was a Mexican, fat and balding. Most of the workers were Mexicans and chattered to each other in Spanish, of which Mohammed spoke not a word. Although he and the Mexicans barely spoke English, that was the language they conversed in. Sometimes he couldn't understand the other workers or the foreman, nor they him. Mohammed had suggested to the foreman that perhaps he could learn to drive a forklift so he would know how if another forklift operator were ever needed. The foreman seemed to understand, yet an invitation to climb onto one and learn the levers hadn't happened yet.

He was going to need a forklift to get the bomb out of its shipping container and into a truck. It would already be on a pallet, but he couldn't risk dropping it. He needed to practice ahead of time.

Timing. Everything depended on timing. After the late shift left work, Mohammed and his men would load the bomb aboard the truck, then fill it with crates of citrus bound for Washington, D.C. The next morning when the truck pulled out, they would follow it, kill the driver at a rest or fuel stop, and steal the truck.

A fine plan it had seemed when they had discussed it in Cairo, God knows. Load the bomb into a truck, drive it to Washington, and detonate it in the heart of the city. They would die instantly of course, and immediately be ushered into Paradise.

Everyone died eventually. That was an immutable fact, the one certainty in our uncertain existence. To earn Paradise as a martyr in Allah's war on the infidels was infinitely better than waiting to die of old age and trusting all to Allah's infinite mercy. *Allah Akbar!* Still, some people went to Paradise and some didn't; everyone knew that! Why take the chance? And why wait? Paradise was there now.

Mohammed picked up another crate and carefully placed it in the stack. Here in Florida, he mused, the plan seemed much more complicated than it had in Cairo. First there was the timetable. Until the bomb arrived, nothing could be done. Once it was here, they could not wait. The container must be emptied, and they must be on their way before anyone became suspicious.

Mohammed knew how to drive an eighteen-wheeler. He even had a commercial driver's license in his pocket. Not in his name of course, but the Americans couldn't tell one Arab from another. Displaying the license would be sufficient.

Waiting was the weak point of the plan. Being put under surveillance by the authorities or arrested would of course cause the mission to fail—and the best place in the United States for the team to live, work, and fit in during those weeks was Broward County in south Florida, among all the other people from all over the planet who flooded this place. Here the local people would be the least suspicious, here the team had its best chance of remaining anonymous, unknown to the American FBI.

Mohammed knew about the FBI. The men and women of that agency were hunting him and others like him. So were other arms of the federal government. That was the danger he and his three team members faced daily.

As usual in terror operations, there was a timetable. The attack would be most effective if it could be coordinated with others. Of other planned attacks Mohammed knew nothing, but he knew there must be others, because the people in Cairo had given him the date.

Yet he could not go until the weapon arrived, and when it did, he must act quickly, regardless of the date. Regrettable, but there was no help for it.

He was wiping the sweat from his brow when he saw the foreman approaching, walking quickly. He paused.

The man pointed at an idling forklift. "You, Mohammed, drive it today. Learn the levers. Today Ramon teach you. Ramon very good forklift operator. Learn good."

Mohammed nodded and flashed his teeth. Americans like to show their teeth. He showed the foreman his several times and went trotting toward the forklift, where Ramon was standing.

"Ah, Ramon, the foreman said—"

"*Sí.* Yes, yes. Into the seat." Mohammed climbed into the seat and began his first lesson in operating a forklift. He was very attentive. This was another rung on the ladder leading to Paradise.

When he reached the interstate that led east, I-64, just north of the town of Lewisburg, Tommy Carmellini didn't make the turn. He continued along the two-lane asphalt that led northeast up the Greenbrier River Valley. Low mountains covered with green forest lay to the right and left.

As he drove his thoughts were on Archie Foster and Norv Lalouette. They had probably planted the bugs in his apartment. Whoever did it had undoubtedly searched it first. If Arch and Norv had found the silenced Ruger .22, they would have had the evidence to send him up for life. Of course, they didn't find it—the silencer was in the mud on the bottom of the Potomac River, the barrel of the pistol was buried in Maryland, the action in Virginia, and the handle in North Carolina.

Arch and Norv or their friends had bugged the apartment, then dropped the bomb. Now, Carmellini thought, they were probably listening to see how he handled it.

His office was probably bugged, too. Hoo boy!

They certainly weren't putting together a case for the FBI, not with illegal searches and listening devices. They wanted something. But what?

No doubt they would let him know in their own sweet time.

Whatever it was, they knew he wouldn't like it, so they were wrapping him up, strand by strand.

Tommy Carmellini saw a country store ahead and pulled into the parking area. There was a woman in her thirties behind the counter. Carmellini bought a soda pop and left. He tossed the unopened can on the passenger's seat.

Every little crossroads and village had its country store that sold essential food items, like bread, beer, and soda pop. Five miles farther up the road was another store, this one with a gas pump in front. Carmellini went inside. A man in his fifties sat on a stool behind the counter.

Carmellini bought a pop and leaned against the counter to drink it. "Pretty country around here."

"Yep. Lived here all my life. Nothing like it. Pretty and peaceful. Quiet-like, not like over in those big cities."

"Friend of mine has a cabin on one of these mountains and has invited me over for deer season. Are there many deer around here?"

"I hope to shoot." The man launched into a story about the hunters that came for the deer, which were plentiful as rabbits, he said. "People hit 'em all the time with their cars. You see 'em dead along every road—cars kill more deer than hunters. Never been as many deer as now."

"I need a rifle if I'm going to hunt," Carmellini remarked at an appropriate time. "I've been thinking about an old thirty-thirty Winchester."

"Them's good guns, so they are. Had one for years. Gave it to my boy. Can't go wrong with one of them. 'Course some folks like scope sights and you can't put one on a Winchester without a special mount and all that. Like scopes myself since my eyes ain't what they used to be."

"Know anyone around here who might have a thirty-thirty for sale?"

"Well, no, I don't. Any gun store would have one though."

"I'll keep my eye out for one," Carmellini said, smiled broadly, and said good-bye.

At the next store Carmellini went through the conversation again. Nope, no rifle like that for sale around here.

At the third one Carmellini struck pay dirt. The proprietor was at least fifty pounds overweight, with a scraggly beard. He said, "Heck yeah, I've got an old Model Ninety-Four thirty-thirty over to the house. Don't use it no more. I might sell it if the price was right. Now this one ain't no collector's item like those pre-sixty-fours. No, sir. I bought it from a neighbor when I got out of the army. Ain't much to look at, but she shoots good."

"I don't want to spend much money for a rifle," Carmellini said, shaking his head. "Going to try hunting, might not like it. And that would be my only use for a rifle. I would have to be able to sell it later for about what I have in it."

"Know how you feel," the proprietor said. He held out his hand. "Name's Fred."

"I'm Bob," said Tommy Carmellini, and shook.

"Got the rifle over to the house." Fred jerked his thumb. "Come on over and I'll show it to you. We'll lock up the store for a while."

Carmellini waited on the porch of the house, which was right beside the store, while Fred went inside. In minutes he was back, rifle in hand.

The Winchester had apparently spent much of its life collecting dings and scratches in a pickup truck and had rarely if ever been oiled. Rust had eaten at the finish in a variety of places, although not too badly. With a twenty-inch barrel, the little lever-action rifle was compact and handy.

"Just needs a little oil," Fred said, "and that rust will come right off. Sharp little gun."

"Can we shoot it?"

"Got some shells." Fred produced four cartridges from his pocket. "Shoots good. Just shoot at the roof of the doghouse over there. Ol' Buck died last winter, ain't gonna get another dog. No, sir! Hard seeing them go."

The doghouse was about forty yards away. Carmellini raised the rifle, lined up the sights, and squeezed one off. Worked the lever, fired again, for four shots. The four holes in the roof could be covered by a pie plate.

"Not bad," Fred said "Offhand like that and all. Little practice and you'll be okay."

"How much?"

"Two hundred."

Carmellini shook his head sadly. "I was afraid of that. Too pricey. With this rust, one-fifty."

They went back to the store while they dickered. Carmellini ended up paying $200 cash for the rifle, a well-used gun case, two boxes of shells, and a can of gun oil. He put his purchases in the trunk of the Mercedes and drove away.

CHAPTER SEVEN

"Good to see you again, Mr. President," said Thayer Michael Corrigan as he shook hands in the Oval Office.

"How's your family, T.M.?"

"Fine, sir. And yours?"

"Busy," the president said, and indicated a chair for Corrigan and the national security adviser, Butch Lanham. "This," the president said, gesturing at a naval officer in whites, "is Rear Admiral Jake Grafton." As Grafton shook hands with Lanham and Corrigan, the president dropped onto the couch. Corrigan didn't pay much attention to the naval officer so intent was he on the president.

"T.M.," the president said, "I know your company has been talking to the government for months about licensing your proprietary sensor technology, and I know we are pretty close to a deal. I asked you here today to try to cut the process short, to twist your arm, make a deal and get on with the program."

Corrigan laughed easily. "You don't have to twist very hard."

"You've always been a big supporter—I know that," the president said earnestly. He meant financial supporter, which in the world of big-time politics was the only kind that mattered. "But this matter is urgent. We have credible intelligence that a terrorist organization has purchased several nuclear warheads from a rogue general in Russia. That is top secret, by the way."

Corrigan didn't even nod. He was not a gossip, and the executives who populated the world in which he moved knew it—although they didn't know that he would not ignore an opportunity to make a profit on someone else's secret if it could be done in such a way that no one knew that he had done it. That kind of maneuvering never troubled his conscience—he honestly believed that he saw opportunities that others didn't because he was smarter than they were.

"We need that technology now," the president continued. "The Customs Service has been carrying ordinary Geiger counters for years. They're worn on belt clips—about the size of a pager. Simple and unsophisticated, with limited capability. We're now deploying gamma ray and neutron flux detectors, putting them wherever we think the threat is greatest, but it's not enough. We must do more."

"I hear you're also doing basic research on detecting radioactive material."

The president nodded. "I've ordered a crash program at the government labs to build the next generation of detectors. We're working on it. But our scientists tell me your technology is better than what we are using, and it's ready to go into production now."

"Well . . ."

"T.M., we need it *now*! Heck, we need it yesterday."

"Mr. President, the Customs Service and I have discussed price. They made an offer that I thought low, but I'll take it. Today. Now."

Lanham, the national security adviser, broke in smoothly. "We need four times more sensors than the Customs Service and Coast Guard were discussing, and we need your company to drop everything and help us get these sensors produced and operational."

They discussed the government's projected needs. Corrigan was willing. "I have the best engineering brains in the country working for me," he said at one point. "Nothing is impossible for them."

"When can we start?" the president asked Corrigan.

"Now. This afternoon," T.M. replied. "As soon as I can get back to Boston. We'll get to the paperwork later."

The president stood and stuck out his hand. Corrigan shook it. As they walked to the door, the president said, "Saw the article in *Power*. Good write-up."

"Thank you," said T.M. matter-of-factly, without a trace of humility. Well, it *was* a good article.

"You know," the president continued, almost thinking aloud, "in five or six months the ambassadorship to the Court of St. James may come open. I can't offer you the post at this point. Still, if things work out the way I think they might and I can offer you London, would you be willing to consider it? It would mean leaving the management of your company, which would, of course, be difficult."

"I'd be honored to be considered for such a post," Corrigan said, his sincerity evident. "And if it were offered, I'd do everything in my power to arrange my affairs so that I could accept it."

The president smiled. "I'll be talking to you," he said, and shook Corrigan's hand again.

He came back to the couch. "You're sure these sensors will help?" he asked Jake Grafton.

"No, sir, I'm not. But I heard Customs and the Coast Guard have been negotiating on and off with Corrigan—they haven't had the money to buy the sensors—and I thought they sounded good. Hell, it's only money."

"So what's your plan to find these bombs?"

"Mr. President, we're working on that. Obviously more and better sensors are part of the mix. I've had a talk with the chairman of the Joint Chiefs, General Alt, and the army chief of staff, General Cahn. We're putting together a plan to use army and national guard forces to search trains and trucks going through choke points and entering major cities. Take about a week to deploy the forces and get operational, and we'll need your authority to make it happen. We'll search with conventional Geiger counters until we can get better equipment. The Delta Force is on standby to take out anyone found with a nuclear weapon, but finding them . . ."

"Are bombs the threat?"

"They are one of the possibilities, certainly. Another is that a warhead will be seeded in with a truckload of conventional explosives—like the Oklahoma City bomb. The explosion will spread deadly radioactive plutonium, creating a major ecological disaster. Every time I see a tractor-trailer I think about that."

"So you want to use the army to search trucks and railroad cars?"

"Precisely. The load would be pretty hot and easy to detect with conventional Geiger counters."

"I'll approve that."

"We're also talking to the Coast Guard, FAA, and Customs about harbor searches, ship searches, airplane searches. The agencies are doing everything in their power. If we can find something they aren't doing, help them do more, I'll make recommendations and offer assistance. I'm getting people and offices and computers and money. We're up and running."

"I've given the orders," the president said, "but you'll have to get the cooperation." He rose from the couch and went to the window. As he stood looking out he said, "We've hundreds of years of statutes, federal regulations out the wazoo, and armies of career bureaucrats all trying to protect their rice bowls. Getting the government to do anything is a major triumph. Harry Truman said he spent a large part of his time kissing ass, trying to make things happen."

"Amen," Jake said.

The president turned to Lanham. "What do you think, Butch?"

"I don't think we have many choices, sir. The challenge will be to keep from panicking the public." He opened both hands wide. "We don't need another stock market meltdown or everyone deciding to stay home, bankrupting the airlines and gutting the economy. The press will learn we are using troops with Geiger counters and ask questions. You need to decide what you want us to say. It will be impossible to keep the activity of thousands of soldiers and guardsmen secret, and we'd be fools to try."

"Do we want to keep it secret? Wouldn't we be better off letting the world see what we're doing to counter the threat?"

"It's telling people about the threat that I'm worried about," Lanham remarked.

"What do you think?" the president asked Jake Grafton.

The admiral took a deep breath before he answered. "If we can search a high enough percentage of the nation's cargo, we can dissuade the enemy from doing something conventional. That means they'll get creative. The challenge is to prevent a really creative attack from succeeding."

"Thanks for sugarcoating it, Admiral." The president slapped his leg. "The public is entitled to know what their government is doing to ensure their safety. Obviously intelligence and intelligence sources are secrets and must stay that way. We'll tell the public that we're taking security measures that we deem appropriate and stop right there."

"I'll brief the press secretary," Lanham said, and excused himself.

"The age we live in . . ." the president muttered sourly. "I can tell you for a fact that stopping 'right there' will prove impossible. Too many people will know too much. Sooner or later the secret will get out, and God help us then."

Jake Grafton was philosophical. "When you wake up in the morning, turn on your television. If the crowd on CNBC is talking about stocks, America is still in one piece. I listen to about half a minute of that, then say, Thank You, Jesus, and get out of bed."

Jake Grafton wasn't sleeping nights. He had a plan, although he didn't like it very much. He hoped to use Zelda Hudson—soon to be Sarah Houston—and Zip Vance as key members of a team to bring information together from disparate places to see if they could find patterns. And terrorists. The main thrust, he thought, should be to find out what anyone knew about the Sword of Islam. He wasn't sanguine—he needed a crack to pry at. And he didn't have one.

The government was deploying an army to search for radiation with conventional equipment. That was strictly a short-term solution. He needed high-tech sensors so he could turn the job over to a small cadre of searchers. Of course, the United States was a huge place, with thousands of ports of entry, and it would take years to procure and deploy enough sensors to cover every intake hole. Still, some ports of entry were more probable than others . . . it shouldn't take long to have a significant chance of finding radioactive material being smuggled in.

Significant chances . . . terrorist hunts.

It was enough to make a grown man cry. After his meeting with the president he went back to Langley and huddled with his new staff. He had asked for and got an officer he knew from several years ago to be his chief of staff, Captain Gil Pascal. He had three people from Customs, three from the National Security Agency, and two from the Coast Guard.

"We have four problems to solve," Jake said, "before we can deploy and use these new sensors. First, we have to figure out where and how we will employ them. What is an acceptable level of probability of detection? Is it fifty percent? Sixty? Eighty? What is achievable with the technology and sensors we have? And what can we do to counter attempts to thwart or evade the search?"

Everyone nodded.

"Second, we must decide how we will respond if we detect radioactive material. It could be anything from hospital waste to a ticking bomb. If it is a bomb, we must gain control of it before the bad guys detonate it."

"That'll be a snap," the senior Coast Guard officer, a captain, commented.

"To accomplish this, we must decide on and appoint someone with real-time tactical decision-making authority. We are talking a major responsibility. It almost goes without saying that the consequences of those decisions could be catastrophic if they turn out badly."

Silence followed that comment.

"Finally," Jake continued, "we need to devise a plan to control public and insider information about our search efforts. The news will get out, and if we don't manage it right, we could have mass panic, which might lead to a public safety or political meltdown. Or both."

After an afternoon of intense conversation, Captain Pascal drafted a memo to the president outlining Jake's four issues and proposing answers. Toad Tarkington delivered it to the White House.

When Toad left on his errand, Jake called his FBI liaison officer, Harry Estep. "What are you doing on the Doyle investigation?"

"Interviewing everyone in the government, Admiral, who knew that Ilin named Doyle."

"Then what?"

"We'll follow leads, if any. The thinking here is that we should follow up the interviews with polygraph exams."

"How accurate are they?"

"Well . . ."

"Oh, hell, let's do it. Tarkington and I will be first."

"Stop by this evening, around seven, at this address." Estep gave it to him.

At six that evening Toad brought the memo he had hand-delivered to the White House back to Jake in a sealed envelope.

Jake opened the envelope at his desk. The president had written in longhand at the bottom of the memo, below Jake's signature: "Approved. You, Admiral Grafton, are the tactical decision maker." Then the president's signature, written boldly.

Jake tossed the document to Toad, who read it, then commented, "You knew he was going to do that."

"Yes."

"Boy, he didn't initial it—he wrote his full name in big letters."

"That's for me," Jake muttered, rubbing his head. "If it goes badly, he wants the congressmen to be able to read his name without their glasses."

"Goes badly? You mean if it blows up in our faces?"

"No more puns, Toad. I'm not in the mood. Don't get comfortable. You and I are going to take polygraph exams. Let's lock everything up and set the alarms and go do it."

"Darn," Toad said with obvious disgust. "They better not ask me about my old girlfriends. Or that time I got in trouble in the fifth grade. Or the night of the senior prom—I did a lot of lying about that evening afterward. How come I have to do this anyway?"

"Rita gave me a list of questions she wants answers to."

"Uh-oh. Another life-threatening experience."

The polygraph operator asked if either of them had ever taken a polygraph exam before, and they both had, several years ago, when they were being processed for Special Intelligence (SI) security clearances. Jake went first. A cuff was placed around his arm, a sensor put over a finger, and a multitude of contacts placed on his head.

The questions were straightforward—his name, social security number, military rank, address, then a series of yes or no questions. Did he know Janos Ilin? Had he ever met him? Then he was asked about Richard Doyle. Using his statement that he had given earlier, the operator went into possible unauthorized disclosures while he watched his printouts and used a pencil to mark them after every question. Finally he handed Jake a stack of photos facedown. "Please read the number on the back of each photo and turn it over and look at it. Then place it facedown and do the same for the next, and so on. If you recognize any of the photos, please tell me who that person is."

Jake didn't recognize the first or second picture, but the third was of Janos Ilin, and he said so. The shot had apparently been taken by a surveillance camera while Ilin walked along a New York sidewalk—at least the city looked like New York. Ilin seemed oblivious to the camera.

There were nine more pictures, a total of a dozen, and he recognized none of them.

As Toad went into the room for his session, Jake headed for the Metro and home.

How was he going to find those damned bombs and make sure they didn't explode?

Jake Grafton thought about that question every spare minute, riding the Metro, in the head, even when he was out walking with Callie in the evenings. She knew he had a new assignment, knew he was worried, yet she didn't know what the job was or what he was worried about.

He wanted to go walking when he got home, regardless of the hour. "Aren't you too tired?" she asked that evening after dinner, which was leftovers from the fridge.

"I want to make sure America is still there."

As usual, they strolled the sidewalks, looked in windows, smiled and said hello to people they recognized as they made their usual pilgrimage to the Potomac. "It's a grand river," Jake had once said as he stood watching the brown water and listening to the people and traffic and airliners. Callie thought of that this evening as she stood beside him, watched him take everything in.

He was thinking of people as he walked along. The lady who sold coffee from a pushcart near the Metro stop was a Filipino . . . she married an American sailor who brought her to America, then deserted her. She had raised a son and owned her pushcart and worked every day, rain or shine, selling coffee and pastries. For years she sold sticky buns, then bagels when that fad hit, now she was selling doughnuts. Jake habitually bought a cup of coffee and a doughnut on his way to work. He always drank the coffee, sometimes he threw away the doughnut—but he bought one whether he wanted it or not.

The art gallery—well, it sold prints and framed whatever you carried in—was owned by a black woman whose father was murdered in Mississippi during the civil rights marches of the 1960s. She wrote up the orders and gave good advice on colors and frame styles. Five years ago her son had been convicted of shooting someone in a dope deal gone sour; he was still in prison somewhere. The guy who did the framing was a Brit who lost a foot in the Gulf War. He came to America to live with a woman. The romance didn't last but he stayed.

The neighborhood Italian restaurant was owned by a guy from Hoboken who got angry at his brother ten years ago and left the family business, moved here, and started over. One of the daughters wanted to be an opera singer. Occasionally she sang the old Italian songs on Sundays at the restaurant. Alas, the music didn't help the food, which was only so-so.

Most of the business at the Chinese restaurant was take-out, so they had just three tables. It, too, was a family place—only the son spoke English; he took orders and the parents cooked. Jake and Callie liked to eat there. When Jake walked in the son always asked if he wanted Tsingtao beer. He never did. When he ordered a glass of chardonnay, the son filled it to the brim. "Three dollars, seventy-five cents, you get full glass," he told Jake.

So it was a neighborhood, like tens of thousands of neighborhoods all over America, filled with people living their lives well, poorly, or screwing them up beyond redemption.

"We'll put Corrigan's damned sensors in vans," he muttered.

"What did you say, dear?" Callie asked. She was holding on to his arm as they climbed the hill away from the river.

"I was just thinking about people," he told her. "I like these people." He gestured with his free hand.

She gripped his arm tightly as they climbed the hill toward home.

The following afternoon an FBI agent and two CIA internal investigators interviewed Coke Twilley and Sonny Tran individually, apart from each other, about the Richard Doyle matter. They wanted to know the names of everyone who knew that Janos Ilin had named the missing Richard Doyle as a Russian spy. They asked all the usual questions and reviewed office security procedures. They went over the report that Tran had prepared for Twilley's signature, questioned both men closely about drafts, counted the copies, and exchanged the hard drive of Tran's computer for a new one. They took the old hard drive with them. The entire process took six hours.

The hard fact was that the Russians might have whisked Doyle off to Russia or eliminated him. If he fled to Russia, the CIA would eventually learn that fact. If he were never heard from again, one would be forced at some point to conclude he was dead. He might have been betrayed and killed by the SVR because his usefulness was about over or they wanted to score points with the Americans but didn't want Doyle listing his thefts through the years. Or the SVR might have killed him after they learned that Ilin had betrayed him. Sorting through tangled conumdrums like this would take years, untold man-hours, and would probably never provide a conclusive answer.

Coke and Sonny also knew that regardless of the outcome of the investigation, their careers also on the line, so they cooperated fully and cheerfully with their colleagues, answering every question. Only when the ordeal was over did their resentment flare.

When the door closed behind the interrogators, Twilley muttered, "The prez promotes Grafton and the snoops start harassing us. Anyone who thinks that isn't cause and effect is a dope. The snoops can't find Doyle but they can afford to harass us at their leisure."

"At least they didn't ask us to take polygraph exams," Tran said philosophically.

"Oh, they will," Twilley grumped. "When their little investigation leads nowhere, Grafton will probably order polygraphs for everyone. He's that kind of guy."

"Some FBI type is leading the hunt for Doyle."

"Sure," Twilley replied acidly. "With Grafton breathing down his neck. Remember his little cover-my-ass speech in this office? A mess like this is made to order for an amateur climber. It's a goddamn snipe hunt, that's what it is. He can stir the shit for years, getting money and staff and attention from the very top, all the while looking for a leak that may not be there."

Tran puttered desultorily in his office until quitting time. Coke Twilley grabbed the latest copy of *Chess Monthly* from his in-basket and went home early. Tran locked the safe and filing cabinets, then armed the office zone alarm on his way out.

Olympic Voyager was an old, tired, single-screw freighter of ten thousand tons. She made her living hauling bulk cargo—usually grain, steel, or fertilizer—between the Indian subcontinent and Europe. Profit margins were razor thin, so her owners had not spent a penny more than absolutely necessary on maintenance—her sides were so rusty that from a distance she appeared to be orange.

Her captain—Pappadopoulus—was Greek, her first mate—Erik "Dutch" Vandervelt—South African, and her second mate—Lee—from Singapore. Her crew were lascars. Vandervelt was new, having just joined the ship four weeks before in Marseilles after the previous first mate was hospitalized following a bar brawl.

This evening, with *Olympic Voyager* moored to a pier in Karachi, Vandervelt stood on the wing of the bridge smoking as a crane loaded the last of the cargo. Lee was in the engine room with the black gang; Captain Pappadopoulus was drunk in his cabin. The old man had been in a state of continuous inebriation for the entire three weeks Vandervelt had known him. He varied between tipsy, walking drunk, puking drunk, and dead drunk, depending on the time of day and the state of the moon.

The pungency of the cigar Vandervelt smoked helped make the air palatable tonight. Karachi was a large, filthy Third World city often obscured by a noxious pall of smoke, engine exhaust, and the smells of rotten garbage. The sewage floating in the black waste of the harbor didn't help, not on an evening like this, with the breeze off the land.

Dutch Vandervelt checked his watch. Three and a half hours. Where was Zuair?

Vandervelt had spent most of his adult life around rough men ruled by their passions and addictions. He understood what motivated them. But not the Egyptian, Dutch thought, who was a maniacal, homicidal zealot, and perhaps the most dangerous man he had ever met. On the other hand, there was that American. . . . What a pair they were, one driven by a warped vision of God, the other driven by greed. Truly, he was a fool to allow them to learn his name or see his face. Or to take money from men like that.

Dutch had accepted money. One million American dollars. Would he live to spend it?

Despite the heat and humidity, Dutch Vandervelt shivered.

As Frouq al-Zuair wheeled the truck into the warehouse at the head of the pier, one of his men stood by the door. The door was closing before Zuair turned off the engine. He slapped the side of the truck's cargo bay three times, then opened the door. Eight of his men climbed down.

"Everything all right?"

"I have men on buildings in every direction. No strangers or strange vehicles in sight."

Zuair inspected the four empty shipping containers sitting inside the dark, dirty building. He used a flashlight. Meanwhile, his men rigged chain hoists and wheeled dollies.

It took two hours to get the four warheads into the containers—one to a container—and secure them. Properly securing the warheads was critical.

The Egyptian inspected each weapon when his men were finished. Satisfied, he then watched them fill the container with stuffed animals, each wrapped in cellophane to keep it clean, then loaded into a clear plastic bag containing fifty of them. The bags were thrown in until the container was as full as possible. Anyone opening the container to inspect its contents would only see the bags.

An hour later, Zuair watched from the bow of the ship as the four containers were loaded aboard *Olympic Voyager*. At his feet lay an RPG launcher wrapped in carpet. The pier was dark—the area was lit only by floods mounted on the ship. One by one, the ship's forward gantry picked up the containers and swung them to the ship's main deck, where they were stacked two deep and chained down.

Finally the lights were extinguished, leaving only the ship's running lights. A man the Egyptian knew to be a port official went down the gangway, then motioned the dockworkers to remove it.

Obeying orders shouted from the deck of the ship, the dockworkers removed the giant hawsers that held the ship to the pier. They had removed the rat guards earlier. When the last rope end was tossed onto the pier, the ship began to move. She backed away from the pier under her own power, drifted to a stop, then began to move forward. Her head began to swing as she answered her helm. Slowly increasing her speed, she made her way between anchored ships into the harbor, heading for the sea beyond.

Using his binoculars, Zuair searched the harbor for boats. If someone wanted the cargo badly enough, the harbor, he thought, or perhaps just outside it, was the most likely place to board and hijack the ship. That was how he would have done it if another group had weapons he wanted. He had learned through the years that there were other men just as clever as he, although few as ruthless. His willingness to do whatever needed to be done regardless of the consequences made him a leader, a man who could accomplish the impossible.

And he had done it! He felt the rush of victory as the breeze began blowing from ahead of him as the ship gained way. He scanned with the binoculars. A few fishing boats, a harbor fuel boat, a Pakistani customs boat . . . none of them attempted to approach the ship or turned to an interception course.

Zuair turned his binoculars to the bridge. He saw Dutch Vandervelt there with the pilot beside the wheel. One other man on the bridge, one of the crewmen apparently.

Beyond the breakwater were several ships on their way into or out of the harbor. They made no attempt to approach *Olympic Voyager*. The ship was an hour outside the harbor, with the lights of Karachi making a smudge upon the horizon, when the pilot boat loomed alongside.

Zuair looked it over as it came against the rope ladder. He knew the man at the wheel of the boat, and he was alone. Not another boat in sight.

The Egyptian retrieved his rocket launcher and walked back to the rope ladder amidships, almost under the bridge. He motioned to the men who had come aboard with him. There were three of them, all armed. They joined him at the rail, then followed the pilot down the ladder. The little boat pitched and rolled and bobbed in the swells, its single-cylinder diesel engine thudding lazily and spewing noxious fumes. Bracing themselves against the gyrations of the boat, the men with weapons went forward and hunkered down to stay out of the bow spray. Frouq al-Zuair was the last man down the ladder. When he was aboard the boatman paused, timing the swell, then spun the helm and gunned the engine. The pilot boat veered smartly away from the freighter's rusty hull.

Up on the bridge, Dutch Vandervelt breathed a sigh of relief and rang up ahead two-thirds on the engine telegraph. He glanced at the four containers on the deck, then turned his back and lit a cigar. Later tonight, after he was relieved by Lee, he would stop by the radio room and tell the man in America that the weapons were aboard and the ship was under way. Months ago they had agreed on a simple, unbreakable code—ten nonsense words, one for every possible contingency, launched into the ether on a preagreed frequency. He ran through the list in his head again, reciting the words silently.

Well, they were pulling it off. A man would come aboard when the ship docked in Marseilles and pay the rest of the money owed to Vandervelt, the captain, and the crew. The man from Cairo who recruited him for this job had originally proposed half in advance, half when the job was done, but Vandervelt balked. The risk of getting stiffed was too great, and who was he going to complain to?

He demanded eighty percent in advance. The man from Cairo was smooth, a true fanatic. He reminded Vandervelt of a snake he once saw in a zoo staring at a mouse. When the haggling began Vandervelt settled for seventy-five. Two days later a man brought the money, $750,000 American, in a cheap, hard suitcase, the kind one rarely sees anymore.

Vandervelt had paid the captain a hundred grand and shared a hundred with the crew, promising more. He didn't intend to pay it, of course. He intended to collect the additional quarter million and vanish as quickly as he could. Although Lee and the captain didn't know it, Vandervelt's maritime career was ending in Marseilles.

He already had a false passport, Dutch no less. It belonged to a sailor who had been lost at sea one stormy night a year ago. Vandervelt took it to a man he knew in Amsterdam, who had substituted his picture for the one of the dead man, for a price, of course.

Smuggling bombs. The truth of it was that if he hadn't agreed to do the job, someone else would have. It was that kind of world.

Standing on the deck of the pilot boat, Frouq al-Zuair watched *Olympic Voyager* gain way. She grew smaller and smaller, shrinking in the darkness as the pilot boat hammered through the swells back toward the lights of Karachi. Soon the freighter's lights disappeared into the sea haze and she was lost in the vastness of the night.

CHAPTER EIGHT

At midnight Lee, the second mate of *Olympic Voyager,* came to the bridge and relieved Dutch Vandervelt.

"Where's the old man?" Vandevelt asked.

"He was drunk when I saw him an hour before we sailed. He went to his stateroom, I think, and hasn't been out since. Passed out in there, probably."

Vandervelt discussed the ship's location, speed, and course, pointed out other ships on the radar and plot, then lingered for a moment as Lee surveyed the horizon with his binoculars.

"This is my last voyage on this ship," Lee said matter-of-factly. "You and I have stood port and starboard every minute when we're at sea since the day you arrived. With Pappadopoulus drunk all the time, it's not going to get any better. No one has suggested a pay raise. And I guarantee you, if there is a problem, we'll lose our licenses."

Vandervelt grunted. The statement was true. The owners should put Pappadopoulus on the beach and hire a new captain. "Maybe after this trip the captain will ask to go. We're all going to make some serious money."

"Yeah," Lee said, unenthusiastically. He brushed the money away.

Vandervelt left the bridge in a thoughtful mood.

He stopped in front of the one-guest stateroom, the so-called owner's cabin, and knocked once. The man who opened the door and admitted him was of medium height and dark, in his early forties, apparently. Vandervelt didn't know his name. Didn't want to know it. He was of Middle Eastern origin, Syrian or Palestinian or, perhaps, Iraqi—somewhere in there. Vandervelt didn't want to know his nationality either.

When Vandervelt was inside the cabin with the door closed, the man said in English, "Are they aboard?" He spoke those words with very little accent—Vandervelt thought the man had spent a good many years in some English-speaking university, probably British, but it could have been American.

"Yes. No hitches."

"Shall we examine the patients?"

The wind was over the port rail, a good stiff sea breeze that was putting up four- or five-foot swells. The brisk wind and motion of *Olympic Voyager* in the seaway meant that both men needed to hold on to something on the weather deck. No one was topside that the mate could see. Of course Lee was on the bridge watching, but he had been paid.

Vandervelt wondered if Lee had told anyone about this adventure.

Dutch Vandervelt opened the padlock on the first container and helped the passenger open the doors.

The bomb was strapped to a pallet. Under it was a sheet of lead. Bolts went through the pallet into the lead.

The passenger inspected it carefully and fully with a flashlight. As he bent over looking, the container door banged as the ship rolled.

"So what do you think?" Dutch asked. "Can you do it?"

The passenger flicked off the flashlight. From the darkness his voice came, "This weapon was not designed to withstand this salty environment. The contacts are already beginning to corrode. I'd say after five or six weeks it will become unreliable."

"What's that mean?"

"It may be a dud."

"Not my problem," Vandervelt said. "You need any help working on these things?"

"No."

Dutch handed him the keys to all four containers. "Work during the night. You have four nights."

"I can be done in two."

"The crew has been told to leave you alone. Let me know if anyone keeps track of your activities or asks questions."

After Vandervelt left, the man went to another container and opened it. He used a flashlight to select a toolbox and carried it back to the bomb. After two more trips carrying items he wanted, he put a temporary latch on the container door. The latch was cunningly made of pot metal. Satisfied it would hold the door closed against curious eyes, he turned on a battery-powered lantern and began unpacking his tools.

Dutch Vandervelt had been correct about the man's education—he held a Ph.D. in engineering from MIT—but wrong about his nationality. Dr. Hamid Salami Mabruk was Egyptian, a colleague of Dr. Ayman al-Zawahiri, a medical doctor, the longtime leader of Egyptian Islamic Jihad. They had spent years trying to topple the secular regime that ruled Egypt by murdering government ministers and tourists with bombs and gunfire. They left the country only when the government fought back ruthlessly, making it impossible to operate there. Interrogated and tortured until they told everything they knew, the militants of Egyptian Jihad were then imprisoned or secretly hanged, every one that the authorities could lay hands on.

When Dr. Zawahiri fled to Afghanistan and joined Osama bin Laden, Mabruk returned to America and secured a teaching position. Just now he was on sick leave. He escaped Egypt just in time, for now the authorities there knew his name—not his real name, his name in the movement—and would hang him if they ever caught him. He had no intention of returning to Egypt until the movement was triumphant. As Zawahiri and bin Laden had argued so eloquently, Egypt's ally America would have to fall before that day would come.

Hamid Salami Mabruk was going to help make it happen. He arranged the lantern just so and began cleaning corrosion from the warhead's detonator contacts.

Jake Grafton had big plans for Tommy Carmellini. Although he hadn't yet laid them out, Carmellini thought he knew what was coming when he sat in a staff meeting with the brain trust, Jake, Toad, Gil Pascal, and senior people from each of the federal agencies.

First the admiral wanted to know the status of each agency's hunt for the missing bombs. The National Security Agency, NSA, was monitoring—eavesdropping upon—radio and telephone communications throughout the Middle East, trying to intercept conversations that might be referring to the bombs. So far they had come up dry.

The FBI was investigating the disappearance of Richard Doyle. The list of negatives that FBI special agent Harry Estep recited from his notes was impressive. Doyle had not returned home, called his wife or his supervisor. He had not made an airline reservation or purchased a ticket, written a check, used a credit card, made a cash withdrawal from a bank machine, or used his passport since the evening of his disappearance. Every police agency in the Western world was looking for him; so far there had been four false sightings, but no credible ones.

"Could he have been kidnapped?" This possibility was not as bizarre as one might think. The KGB/SVR had a long history of kidnapping people, usually Russians, whom they didn't want talking to Western governments.

"We've checked every airport up and down the East Coast, with negative results. Of course he could have been stuffed into a van or the trunk of a car and driven to Canada or Mexico. On the other hand, it is difficult to see how he could have been removed from the country by air." Estep discussed what the bureau was doing to check out charter and corporate flights the evening of Doyle's disappearance. "He's dropped off the face of the earth," Estep concluded.

"Or been buried under it," Grafton shot back.

"It looks that way," Estep admitted.

"A professional hit."

"At this point, that appears to be a strong possibility."

The CIA had also been busy. Coke Twilley was the officer who presented Jake with a dossier on General Petrov and the base he commanded. Jake flipped through it while Twilley talked. The file looked, he thought, as if it had been put together with newspaper clippings and photocopies of pages in reference books.

The dossier did contain, however, the intelligence summaries from the former Soviet republics and the countries on the Indian Ocean rim. "What about this shootout in Karachi the other day?" Jake asked as he perused the summaries. "What was that all about?"

"Rival gangs, we think," Coke said. "Our contacts there are talking to Pakistani intelligence, but so far we know only that a shootout took place in which all the parties were armed with Soviet-bloc weapons. Four dead, as I recall, and no arrests."

The national imagery system had seen nothing of consequence.

Finally, the admiral got around to it. "Zelda Hudson and Zipper Vance will arrive tomorrow," Jake said. "Gil, are the arrangements made?"

"Coming together, sir. The new identity documents are coming over this afternoon from the Federal Witness Protection Program. Sarah Houston and Matt Cooper. Carmellini has rented them an apartment under those names. If they don't want to live together, I figured they could sort out their own arrangements. I have informed security, and we'll get them badges and stuff when they arrive."

"Fine. Tommy, they will work directly for you. I will brief them tomorrow afternoon when they arrive. I want you to sit through the brief."

He paused and automatically Carmellini said, "Yes, sir," which surprised him after it slipped out. He tried to avoid sirring the brass on the theory that few of them deserved it. On the other hand, Jake Grafton was kind of guy who rated a "sir."

"Okay," Jake said, "that's it. Coke, stay for a moment, will you?"

Twilley remained in his seat as the other people filed out of the room. When the door closed, leaving him alone with Grafton, he said, "I think you're running some damn dangerous risks, Grafton."

"That's true," Jake Grafton acknowledged, eyeing Twilley without warmth.

"Are you sure you want me on your team?"

Grafton let that question hang for a moment before he answered. "I didn't ask for this job."

"I know that."

"A few days ago I was working for you. Now the roles are reversed. Are you uncomfortable with that?"

Twilley shrugged. "A little, I guess."

Grafton's lips formed a straight line across his face, and his gray eyes showed no warmth as he examined Twilley's face. "You're a professional. I expect you to do a professional job. This is our country. If you can't do that, say so now, and I'll ask DeGarmo to replace you."

This course of action would not look good on Twilley's record, and both men knew that. Twilley backpedaled. "No need for that, unless you want someone else."

Grafton began gathering his notes.

"But I want to say I find the request that Sonny Tran and I take polygraphs demeaning."

Grafton glanced up again. "Everyone who knew about Doyle, including me, is taking polygraphs. Hell, I already had one."

Twilley threw up his hands. "A waste of time."

"Perhaps." Grafton stood. "I want you to send Tran to Corrigan Engineering in Boston to look at these new radiation sensors. I want a report on what they will do, when we get them, how big they are, how much power they take, our deployment options, all of it. Get him on the road as soon as he gets through with the polygraph people. Toad Tarkington and one of the Coasties will go with him."

"Why Tran?"

"Man, I only have so many people."

"What about deploying some of these new Corrigan sensors overseas?" Twilley asked. "A terrorist might conclude that an attack against one of those cities would rock a major American ally and leave the U.S. isolated diplomatically."

"The big kahunas will make those decisions."

"London and Paris would be good places to start."

"Indeed, they would," Jake agreed. "But we'll need sensors. Send Tran to Boston."

"Sonny Tran, Boston," Coke Twilley said, and rose from his chair.

After Twilley left, Jake found Tommy Carmellini waiting in the corridor. "I'd appreciate a few minutes of your time, Admiral."

Jake glanced at his watch, then led the way back into the conference room. Carmellini sat one seat away from Jake.

"What's on your mind?"

Carmellini scratched his face. "This is a little embarrassing. Truthfully, I'm going to put you in a bad position, but I think I owe you the truth."

"Okay," Jake said, scrutinizing Carmellini's face. He had piercing gray eyes, Carmellini suddenly noticed.

"Last week someone bugged my apartment. The bugs are still there. I think it was two guys from the CIA, Archie Foster and Norv Lalouette. I couldn't figure out why in the world anyone would bug my apartment, then Arch asked me to come down to his office. Norv was there. They showed me a videotape taken several years ago by a tourist at the University of Colorado in Boulder on the day that someone assassinated Professor Olaf Svenson."

Jake's brows knitted. "Svenson? The microbiologist that Justice thought developed a polio virus weapon for Castro?"

"That's the guy. The FBI couldn't get enough evidence to prosecute."

"I remember."

Carmellini shrugged. "I was on that videotape, walking across the campus."

"I see."

Suddenly Tommy Carmellini's mouth was very dry. He swallowed several times, reached for the pitcher of water in the middle of the table, and poured himself a cup. He drank it.

"I told Arch and Norv they didn't have a case. They knew that, of course. They want something from me."

"Is there any more evidence for them to find?"

"I don't think so. Of course, the existence of that tape was a big surprise too, so"—he shrugged again—"maybe the best answer is, I don't know."

"If they want something from you badly enough they might manufacture some evidence."

"There is that possibility. That's why I thought we should have this conversation."

"What do you think they want?"

"Anything I said would be pure guesswork."

"What do you want me to do?"

Carmellini poured another cup of water and sipped it. "I just want you to know where it stands, what's happening. I don't know what in hell these clowns are up to, but whatever it is, it's bad. When the deal goes down, I want you on my side."

A shadow of a smile crossed Grafton's face. "I appreciate that."

"That's it," Carmellini said, and stood. "That's my little tale. If you don't want me working for you, I understand."

The admiral nodded slowly, looked at his hands. Then he raised his eyes again to Carmellini's. "A bunch of people died in Cuba."

"Yes."

"One of them was a colleague of yours, as I recall. A fellow named Chance."

"William Henry Chance," Carmellini said. "A genuinely good man."

"This day and age they're hard to find," Jake said. He stood and picked up his papers. As he and Tommy walked toward the door, he said, "Keep me informed."

"Yes, sir," Carmellini replied. The "sir" just slipped out.

Zelda Hudson and Zip Vance arrived on Thursday afternoon. The federal marshals had a paper they wanted signed, a receipt for two prisoners. Toad Tarkington scanned it and was about to put his John Hancock on the dotted line when Jake Grafton loomed beside him. "Uh-uh," he said. "I'll sign. They jackrabbit, it'll be my ass, not yours."

The marshal looked at Jake's signature and his uniform—he was in whites today—then said, "They're all yours." His female colleague took the handcuffs off Hudson while he removed the cuffs from Zip Vance.

"Be seeing you," the marshal told Vance, then disappeared through the door after the female officer.

Jake surveyed his prizes. They were wearing clothes that looked as if they had been slept in. "My office," he said, and led the way. "Carmellini," he called, and gestured for him to follow.

When the door was closed and his three guests were seated, Jake said, "It took an order from the president of the United States to spring you two, but with one telephone call I can pop you back in."

"I can't wait to thank him," Zelda said. Her hair was a mess, but in civilian clothes she looked more like her old self, Carmellini thought. Zipper Vance looked slightly overwhelmed. He chewed pensively on his lip and gazed fixedly at the corner of Jake's desk.

"Ms. Hudson," Jake Grafton said, "over six hundred people died as a result of your crimes, which were apparently committed for money. About two hundred of those people were American servicemen and women. I know you two didn't personally murder anyone, but they would still be alive if you had obeyed the law."

Carmellini noticed that the scar on Jake's temple was an ugly red splotch.

The admiral's voice developed a hard edge. "Out of necessity, I have pulled every string and jerked every lever to get you out of prison. The American people desperately need your skills. Don't think for a minute that I have forgotten what you did or the debt you owe. I'll never forget. The families of those who died will never forget. As it happens, the fortunes of war have given you a chance to redeem yourselves. You may not believe in redemption, but I do. If you wish to stay out of prison you will obey Mr. Carmellini and throw yourselves into our work, giving it your best efforts. This can be the first day of the rest of your lives—it's up to you. I will not threaten you, but I will make you this promise: If you give less than your best, violate the security regulations, or cut and run, I will be delighted to hold the cell doors open while the federal marshals throw you through them."

Grafton's finger made a tiny circle on the desk as he continued in a voice Carmellini had never heard him use before. "If you betray the trust that I am placing in you and people die because of it, you won't go back to prison—I'll personally send you to hell. Do you understand?"

Zip Vance couldn't meet Jake's eyes. Zelda wet her lips, swallowed once, then nodded affirmatively.

The edge went out of Jake's voice as he continued: "As of today you are on the federal payroll as probationary GS 5s. Your supervisor is Mr. Carmellini. Whatever he says goes. He'll give you a detailed brief, give you the documents that prove your new identities, and show you your workstations in the SCIF. That's all."

Out in the hall Carmellini loosened his tie and unfastened the top button of his shirt. He pursed his lips in a silent whistle.

"Do you think he really would?" Zip muttered. "Do what he said?"

Tommy Carmellini glanced at him, decided he didn't deserve the courtesy of an answer, and led the way toward security. The paperwork, photographs, and fingerprints took an hour. When they were accoutered in their new security badges, he led the way to the ad hoc computer center in the SCIF.

Once there he watched as Hudson and Vance inspected the equipment. They didn't have much to say to each other, he noticed. He had no idea of how long the marshals had had them together. Perhaps they were waiting until they were really alone.

"Here's the deal," Carmellini said after they sat down. He planted his bottom on the table and sat facing them. "The admiral wants you two to put together the world's finest surveillance network. He wants into every computer database in the Western world and access to every video camera in every hotel, business, airport, and intersection in the country. We want to be able to research airline reservations, driver's licenses, passports, credit card balances, hotel reservations, rental car receipts, video game rentals—in short, every database in the nation, *every*thing. Can you do it?"

"Jesus Christ!" Zip muttered. "We get out of prison on a pass and you got fifty new felonies lined up for us to commit. This is fucking unbelievable!"

"The reason I ask, the D.C. police are trying to put together a setup like this—well, maybe not quite so ambitious—but they are going to spend beaucoup bucks and wait years to get the right software."

"Thanks, Carmellini, you asshole," Zelda hissed. "We needed this. Another fifty felonies and they'll crucify us on the steps of the Capitol Building."

"By the time the prosecutors get to you," Carmellini replied, "the newspapers will have run out of ink. The president and Jake Grafton are going to be first."

"What's the rush?" Zip Vance asked.

"I know you've been in prison, but didn't you hear about nine-eleven?"

"So?"

"There are a lot of bad guys out there in those mud huts."

Vance looked pensive. Even Zelda seemed subdued. She caressed one of the keyboards with her fingers. After a bit, she said, "We're going to need to be hardwired into some of the databases that you want us to access, with or without permission. Others we can get into on-line. Can you or Grafton do anything about that?"

"Little problems like that are my specialty," Carmellini admitted. "Breaking and entering is my life."

"Another straight arrow."

"Hey, lady, let's forgo the personal remarks. I'm just a civil servant doing my job."

"Serving the civils by breaking and entering—that's a new twist on an old gig."

"Well, yeah. I do what I'm told. I'm no knight in shining armor, but I guarantee you, Jake Grafton is one of the real good guys."

She took a deep breath, scratched her head, then said, "We're going to need bandwidth, and a lot of it. I'm talking fiber, not copper."

"Got you covered. You are in the second-most-wired place on the planet. The first being NSA, the National Security Agency." Tommy tossed Zelda a pad. "Write down what you want, hardware and software."

"You're not really going to do this, are you?" Vance asked her.

"You want to go back to the joint?" she asked him.

"No, goddamn it, I don't. That's precisely the point. I want to do something legal and respectable. I want to earn a commuted sentence. Grafton doesn't want to give us an honest-to-God legal job, for all I care he can stick it up his ass. You and I got troubles enough to last a lifetime!"

Tommy Carmellini hopped off the table and hotfooted it toward the door.

He stood in the hallway listening for a moment. "You're a computer junkie," Vance shouted at Zelda. "You're hooked on this cyber-crap. What about *us*? You and me? Have you forgotten those letters you wrote me?"

"It's this or prison," she replied coldly. "You think Grafton is going to make you his press spokesperson?"

Carmellini decided it was time to go to the men's room. When he returned he heard only silence. He opened the door, saw Hudson and Vance sitting silently glowering at each other. He went in and closed the door behind him.

"So what's the verdict?" he said brightly.

"We'll do it," Zelda said.

"What about software? We can't wait years for this. We need this up and running like yesterday."

"Multiple Oracle databases with some heavily modified off-the-shelf software for data mining should do the trick."

Carmellini sat again on the desk. "I'm a techno-turkey, but I have to explain stuff to Admiral Grafton from time to time. How are you going to do it?"

Zelda eyed him. "What do you know about networks?"

"Very little."

"Networks are ubiquitous in modern nations, private networks, the Internet, wireless—even Starbucks is using WiFi, which is wireless fidelity, to create a continuous on-line wireless network for store managers in an urban area. Universities have WiFi networks, businesses, law firms, banks, the Senate and House of Representatives. Most are not encrypted, easy to gain access to, and you get to look at anything on the network."

"Okay," Carmellini said, nodding.

"The commercial networks that you mentioned, like credit card databases, bank, telephone, medical records, what have you, can be exploited—in fact they're exploited all the time; the companies just never tell the public because they don't want the bad publicity. They lose business and their stock price sinks when people find out how stupid they are. They have enough security to keep out the 'script kiddies'—the teenagers who use attack scripts they get off hacker Web sites—but every commercial network has holes. What we want to do is quietly gain access while coming in under their radar."

"How do we do that?"

"All networks have security patches they forgot to install, or former users with dumb passwords that haven't been deleted from the system, or have gear attached to the network that came with factory-set passwords they forgot to reset. We go after these because it's so easy. Once we get into their networks, we're an authorized user and we get whatever we want because we have library cards."

Carmellini grinned warmly. "I knew you two were the right folks for this job."

"Can it, creep," Zelda said bitterly. "I'm not in the mood."

"Let's make that list," Tommy said, and handed her a pen.

"Zip and I are hackers," Zelda explained. "We are going to need a small team of specialists that can build a data center with huge amounts of horsepower to process data. And we're going to need a team to write the software to mine the data as it comes in. Without a data mining team, we'll be looking for needles in a three-thousand-acre hayfield."

Carmellini was taking notes.

"And we're going to need some serious hardware. NSA uses hundreds of RISC-based Sun and IBM machines to process data."

"We'll get you the people and equipment," Carmellini promised, "but you are in charge. Grafton wants you to make it happen."

Before Hudson and Vance left the building, Carmellini visited with Jake Grafton, who perused Zelda's list. "I'll bet various government agencies own darn near everything on this list. Tomorrow you jump on it. Get the White House involved. I want that equipment in here Monday. You have all weekend."

"Yes, sir. Zelda also wants maps from the network companies so she can figure out where we will need to hardwire permanent access."

"How are you going to get those?"

"Steal them."

Jake merely nodded. "So what do you think? Will Zelda and Zip work out?"

"As the saying goes, they have issues."

"Keep me advised. I want them on the job. They're the sharpest computer geeks I ever met, and they know how to cut corners. We need them badly, but don't let them know that."

"If they haven't figured that out, they soon will."

"So are you going to take them to their new apartment?"

"Yes, sir."

"Pick them up in the morning and bring them to work. This weekend they need to get a set of wheels."

So Tommy Carmellini took Zelda Hudson, now Sarah Houston, and Zip Vance, now Matt Cooper, home to a one-bedroom, one-bath walk-up in a massive complex. They rode silently, looking at everything, and said not a word.

He drove into the parking lot, stopped, and pointed to the entrance. "You're in twelve forty-one. Elevator's in there. A suitcase with new clothes in your sizes is upstairs, along with the usual toilet items. I'll pick you up tomorrow morning at seven right here." He handed each of them a key to the apartment. As he handed Zelda hers, he added, "You have a hair appointment in thirty minutes at the salon on the ground floor. Get a cut and dye. Blonde, to match your driver's license photo." The photo on the license had been altered on a computer before it was affixed to the license form.

Carmellini took out his wallet, extracted two twenties and a ten, and handed them to Zip. "Get something to eat."

"This agency money or yours?"

"Mine."

"Then thanks."

Carmellini snorted and put the car in gear.

They were standing side by side looking up at the building as he drove away.

The apartment was small, a Pullman-sized kitchen, a living room, one small bedroom, and a bath. The furniture looked as if it had been purchased at a motel liquidation sale; the sheets, blankets, pillows, and kitchen utensils were from Wal-Mart. As Zelda walked through the place inspecting, Zip Vance dropped onto the sofa and kicked off his shoes.

"I wish we were back in Newark," Zelda said as she stood at the living room window looking at the view, which was of a freeway.

Vance took a deep breath, stretched, then studied his toes. Finally he looked at her back. "This is our chance, Zelda. We can make it work."

She crossed her arms and hugged her elbows.

"I don't want to spend the rest of my life in prison," Vance said.

"This isn't much better."

"You measure human lives by the amount of money people have. Aren't you ever going to learn?"

She turned to face him. "I grew up in a dump like this. My brains were my ticket out." She waved a dismissive hand at the room. "It's like I never left."

"If you can't see the light, kid, you'll never get out."

"You're one to talk," she shot back. "You're right here with me."

Vance reached for his shoes. "Yep. I fell in love with a woman without good sense, and I wasn't smart enough to walk away. I bought the ticket and I took the ride. The actual number of people who died because we set up that submarine hijacking was six hundred thirty-two by my count." He looked at his hands, then made a face.

He tied his shoes and stood. "Redemption, Grafton said! Six-hundred thirty-two people is gonna take a shit-pot full of the stuff. Maybe I'll always feel like a total slime. But I'm not going back to the can, not for you, not for anybody alive. Frankly, I'd rather be dead." He headed for the door. "I saw a pizza joint next door when we drove up. I'll bring you half. Don't forget your hair appointment."

With that he walked out and closed the door behind him.

Zelda turned back to the window and stood watching the traffic on the freeway. All those cars, all those people, every one of them going somewhere . . . and she was stuck here.

Jake Grafton got home that evening at 9:30 P.M. Amy was at the library studying and Callie was reading a book. "Let's take a walk," he suggested after he kissed her.

She looked at her watch.

"I've been looking forward to it all day," he added. She put down the book and put on her shoes.

When they were out on the street walking along, he said, "I'm going to retire when this is over."

"Because the president said that the brass felt you wouldn't be promoted? Certainly it isn't *that*?"

"A few weeks ago terrorists belonging to a organization called the Sword of Islam bought four nuclear weapons—missile warheads—from a Russian general. I'm supposed to find the damn things."

Callie gripped his hand fiercely. "Can you?"

"There's a chance. But I'm going to break most of the privacy laws in the country. Regardless of whether or not I find the weapons before they detonate, when this gets out—and it will—I'm toast. If I've got weapons in hand, I probably won't go to jail. But any way you cut it I'm done as a naval officer."

"How do you feel about that?"

"It's time. Nuclear weapons, terrorists, spies, traitors—Jesus, Callie, I'm just a farm kid from southwestern Virginia who wanted to fly airplanes for Uncle Sam. And I've done that. I'm way over my head in scalding-hot water, and I don't like anything about it."

They walked along in silence hand in hand. After a while she said, "This started with Ilin, didn't it?"

"He's the one who told me about the bombs. The report went all the way up. The president put me in charge of finding the damned things."

"Why you?"

"That was my question. Apparently he has a sense that something's rotten at the FBI and CIA. I keep getting those vibes, too. It's hard to put a finger on . . . and yet, I get this feeling that the people in these outfits don't trust each other. Then again, maybe I'm wrong, and it's something else. But the prez is getting bad vibes, too, from somewhere."

They found a neighborhood bar and went in. When they were each drinking Irish coffees at a corner table, Callie said, "Terrorisms, mass murder—how'd we get to this, Jake?"

"Populations have been exploding since World War Two in rigid societies that can't change," he said gloomily. "They must change to feed all these new people, and they can't. Or won't. So the pressures build until something pops. Roughly a billion people live in the Islamic societies on less than a dollar a day. Africa is a continent full of those folks. Modern medicine has caused the birth rate to explode, but the people are still ignorant and illiterate, without the trust in each other that holds developed nations together. All those European kings, all those fights with parliament and wars and battles for king and country—they were building nations. Never happened in the Third World. We call them nations, but they aren't."

"The world has experienced exploding populations before," Callie said, frowning.

"Yes, and war and pestilence have always ravaged mankind until populations were reduced to a sustainable level. Hordes of locusts, epidemics like the Black Plague and AIDS, the Napoleonic Wars, the centuries of strife that occurred in China when dynasties fell—all those reduced the populations to levels that could be sustained with the technology available."

"Terrorism and mass murder? Are they the modern plagues?"

Jake Grafton rubbed his fingers through his hair, then looked his wife in the eye. "During the Middle Ages in Europe ignorant, illiterate people were manipulated by appeals to the strains of intolerance and fanaticism that are part and parcel of every religion. The Crusades, the popes' wars on heresy, the Spanish Inquisition, the war between Catholicism and Protestantism . . . all these horrors were committed in God's name. The result was the rise of the secular states, which grew into nations.

"The Muslim world didn't move on—it's still trapped in the Middle Ages. Islam teaches that man should live a life that earns him God's mercy—it's no better or worse than any other religion. Yet the Islamic fanatics are exporting the horrors of the Middle Ages to a developed world that moved on centuries ago. Perhaps this war between religion and secular society is a stage that every civilization has to go through. Maybe it's the only way for a people to gradually learn tolerance, which is the foundation for complex societies that can entertain new possibilities, new visions."

"The future isn't inevitable, Jake. It hasn't been written yet."

"I know. I tell myself that once an hour."

He was sitting on the little balcony of the apartment having a drink when Amy got home a few minutes after eleven that evening. She got a Coke from the fridge and joined him on the balcony. "What are you doing?" she asked.

"Looking at the North Star," he said, and pointed. "Most nights you can't see it because of the light pollution, but the air is very clear tonight."

"How do you know it's the North Star?"

"Find the Big Dipper. See it? The two stars at the end of the dipper point to Polaris—the North Star. If you were standing on the earth's North Pole, it would be directly overhead. The stars seem to wheel around it during the night as the earth rotates."

"I didn't know that."

"It's an old friend," Grafton said. "I got to know it years ago when I was flying A-6s in Vietnam."

Jake rarely talked about his combat experiences, so Amy led him on. "What was it like, flying up the Gulf of Tonkin looking at the North Star, knowing that in a few minutes the enemy was going to be trying to kill you?"

Jake thought about his answer. "Winston Churchill once said that one of life's most sublime experiences was to be shot at and missed. He was right. We always went in low, trying to get under the radar coverage, so up north they shot like wild men when they heard the sound of our engines. Streaks of flak, muzzle flashes, volcanoes of shells . . ." He fell silent, remembering.

"One night we were supposed to hit a target southwest of Hanoi, pretty deep in-country. There was a low stratus deck, and our usual tactic was to get down under that stuff and go roaring in at five hundred knots, four or five hundred feet above the ground. That night I had a feeling . . ." He shrugged, thinking about how it was.

Amy was watching his face, which she could just make out in the glow from the city.

"Anyway, I decided to vary the routine. We went in at about ten thousand feet, about a mile above the stratus clouds. Lord, I never saw so much flak. The flashes from the guns and tracers and exploding shells pulsated the clouds under us, illuminated them like continuous sheet lightning. Then there would be a pause, they would listen for our engines, and everyone would shoot again. The only thing . . . all that stuff was under us. They thought we were down there, and we weren't."

"Did you attack your target?"

"Oh, yeah. The BN found it, locked it up, and I dived during the attack. The bombs came off just above the clouds, and I pulled the nose up and did a long climbing turn to go back to the coast, trying to keep my speed up. You didn't want to get slow over the north; they had a bad habit of shooting SAMs at us. They didn't shoot any missiles that night, though."

"Did you hit the target?"

"No way of knowing. It was modern war, I guess . . . we dropped the bombs and often didn't know what we hit, if anything. If anyone died. The photo recon guys probably took pictures a day or two later—I don't remember. I do recall that when we got back to the ship that night several other pilots who had seen the show told me that that was the worst flak they had ever seen. They didn't know that we weren't down there in it, so they thought we were real studs. I didn't have the moral courage to tell them different."

"Who was your BN that evening?"

"Morgan McPherson."

"Did you like combat?" Amy asked.

"Yeah," Jake said. "Getting shot at and missed—I loved it. But the thing was, you knew you weren't invulnerable. You knew if you kept playing the game long enough, they would eventually hit you."

"Which made the game exciting."

"I suppose. They killed Morgan a few weeks later." He sighed. "Strange, he hated it and I loved it and he was the one who died."

He finished his drink, rattled the ice. "When I see the North Star on clear evenings I think of those nights, flying up the Gulf, see the flak again. And wonder if I would still be alive if we had gone in low that night they shot everything they had."

"Playing the game . . ." Amy mused. "It sounds like an addiction."

"Yep. People who play those kinds of games always play too long. I certainly did." He stood. "Let's call it a night."

She hugged him.

CHAPTER NINE

Corrigan Engineering's facilities sat on an industrial campus in the western suburbs of Boston. The senior engineer, Harley Bennett, was a stringy sack of bones with a fringe of hair framing a bald brown pate. He looked to be in his fifties. "You must be a serious runner," Toad remarked when he shook his hand.

Bennett beamed. "Do the marathon every year, finish in the top hundred."

"Wow." Actually Toad thought he was crazy, but he was too polite to say so.

Sonny Tran was also skinny—he didn't weigh 120 pounds, but he had a small bone structure and ate like a bird. He'd had a third of a muffin at Reagan National Airport for breakfast, and said he wasn't hungry when asked about lunch. Nor was he gregarious. On the plane that morning he sat beside Toad and didn't say ten words. He read the morning paper cover to cover—except for the classifieds—looked out the window a while, then worked a crossword puzzle.

In contrast, the Coast Guard officer, Captain Joe Zogby, was a veritable chatterbox. As they waited that morning to board the plane, before he settled in with his copy of the newspaper, he remarked on the weather, the fortunes of two baseball teams, and even noted that the stock market had gone up the previous day.

"So the government's buying these things?" Harley Bennett remarked. "Getting cutting-edge stuff, I can tell you. C'mon, let's look, then we'll talk."

When the little party entered the lab, he swept his arm and asked, "What d'ya think of that?" The Washington delegation stood staring at a complex electronic instrument chained down to a wooden pallet. Toad bent down for a look. The thing looked a little like the inside of a computer, everything solid state.

"What does it do and how does it do it?"

Harley jumped right in. After he had spent five minutes discussing the sensors and detection technology in general terms, Toad asked, "Does it really work?"

"Of course." Here Harley got technical, talking about various types of radiation and detection ranges. "The detection range will vary widely," Harley explained, "depending on the type and strength of the radiation. And that will depend on the amount of shielding around the emitter. A well-shielded reactor, such as one in a late-model nuclear-powered submarine, would probably be undetectable unless you were within a few dozen yards. Perhaps not even then if it were an American sub. A Russian sub—I'm guessing—maybe a mile."

"A Russian warhead—how far?"

"Missile?"

"Yes."

"They don't have much shielding because the shielding is too heavy. Of course, the plutonium inside is not critical, but it's decaying, radiating. Given the amount of shielding in a missile warhead, and a leaky Russian one to boot, I should say we can detect it at five miles. Maybe six."

Toad whistled. "You're the man," Joe Zogby said with a grin. Even Sonny Tran smiled.

"Give us a demo," Toad suggested.

First Harley screwed a sensor cable into one of the wire sockets. He laid the cable in a straight line along the floor. On a nearby table sat an instrument containing a rotary drum and stylus. He turned it on.

"You'll notice that the detector is physically connected to the operator's instrumentation and recorder. In later versions of this gear the sensors, detector, and instrumentation can be at three different sites and communicate through data-link. For short-range versions we will put the sensors on belt clips and everyone can carry them around. We aren't there yet, though."

From a lead vault, Bennett produced a small lead box. "Inside here we have a radioactive isotope for use in certain medical diagnostic procedures." He carried it into the lab and set it on the table near the machine. As he lifted the test tube containing the isotope from its lead box, the recorder on the nearby table emitted a high-pitched noise. On the recorder the stylus began squiggling. Harley carried the test tube from the room. The instrument continued to scream. The noise stopped, finally, when Bennett was in the parking lot outside. He called in on the lab's telephone to report his location.

An hour later Toad Tarkington called Jake Grafton in Washington. "You better sit down, boss. You aren't going to like this."

"Shoot."

"Corrigan has hand-built prototypes of his detectors that he has been using for testing purposes. He has no manufacturing facility. The outfit he was dealing with to build the things is in China."

"Which China?"

"The big red one."

"Has he given them the engineering drawings or specs?"

"These people say no. Apparently he was negotiating with the government for a technology export license. That's how the administration learned what he had."

"What has friend Corrigan been doing to get these things built since he shook the president's hand?"

"He's got a couple of custom shops lined up to hand-build the things, so they'll be pricey. Another screwing for the taxpayers."

"They're used to it. Do these detectors work?"

"Seem to. The head engineer gave me a demonstration and a classified capability sheet. These things would be very nice to have."

"Get a delivery schedule and call me back."

"Yes, sir."

Jake went back to his paperwork. He was inundated. He needed someone to handle it for him, but he had to do the paperwork to get that someone.

And four warheads were missing. *Where are they?*

Tommy Carmellini knocked on his door. He was wearing an electrician's outfit. A&B Plumbing and Electric. His shirt proclaimed that his name was Junior. Jake waved him in.

"Just wanted you to know, sir, that Zelda and the Zipper are hard at it. I wouldn't have believed it if I hadn't watched it—they went right into the credit card databases of three large banks bang, bang, bang. Nothing to it. They know how security systems are set up, they know how to go around them, and they know how to get what they want."

"Where did they learn all that?"

"I didn't ask, sir. I don't want to know. I don't think Zelda or Zip wants the FBI to ask either."

"We need permanent access."

"They're working on it. They actually designed one of the systems, left themselves a hole to go in and out of."

Jake made a face.

"You know, Admiral, I hate to be the one to tell you this, but I don't think they're honest."

"I like your duds."

"Yessir. I'm going to visit the D.C. police department about their cameras. We'll be wired in by tomorrow."

"New York. We need every video feed in that city."

"New York is going to be tougher because there is no central place to tap in. We need to let a subcontract."

"For an illegal wiretapping?"

"It's a couple of independents the agency uses from time to time. I can get them in here for an interview if you like."

"You trust them?"

"Yes."

"Sign 'em up."

A half hour later Tarkington called again. "One every two weeks, Admiral. Each has to be tested for a week before it can be put in service."

"Terrific," Jake muttered, wondering what the president would say when he heard. "Leave Tran and the Coastie up there to learn all they can. You jump a plane back. I want to see that capability sheet."

"See you this evening."

The little bell on the door rang when Tommy Carmellini pushed it open on Tuesday morning. He went inside, stood by the counter looking at the televisions and VCRs stacked on the back wall. There was even a computer. A black man came through the door at the far end of the counter and walked along behind it. "Hey, Carmellini, my man. What's happenin'?"

"Hey, Scout. How come you guys got all these televisions and VCRs and stuff? These for sale?"

"We got 'em 'cause the owners couldn't pay their bill, man, and we needed some security. You see anything there you like?"

"Ah . . . no. Came to discuss a business proposition."

"Hey, Earlene, come out here," he called. "Carmellini is here and wants to make us rich."

Earlene was a striking, statuesque woman. She was fit and looked it—she had spent two years in the WNBA. Now she was half of S&A Electric. Carmellini didn't know if Scout and Earlene were married; he had never thought to ask.

"Hey, Tommy."

"Hey, Earlene." He jerked his head toward the partition. "Anyone else back there?"

"Nope."

"Mind if I look?"

Scout and Earlene glanced at each other. "It's like that, huh?"

"Yeah."

Carmellini walked around the counter, stepped to the door, and looked. There was no one. He came back to the counter and leaned on it again. "I need some serious help. The agency wants access to some computers around the country, like the video control computer at D.C. police headquarters, the mainframe at various credit card processors, airline reservation computers, all of it. A lot of this work will be in New York."

"The agency? That mean CIA?"

"Yeah."

"Man, I thought they already had wormholes and trapdoors and all that shit."

"If they did, I wouldn't be standing here."

Scout laughed. "Oh, man, this is heavy. The CIA?" He slapped his leg. "They know I'm a convicted felon?"

"Hell, no, they don't know. My boss told me to get some people I trust. I trust you. I'll give him an invoice from S&A Electric and he'll sign it and you'll get paid."

"We're electricians, not telephone or computer experts."

"Oh, don't give me that. I'd bet a paycheck that you do interior telephone wiring from time to time."

"Well, yeah, sure. Got the stuff and know which wire is which, but we don't have the passwords and phone company numbers and all that."

"I do."

"How much?" Earlene asked sharply.

"Your usual rate."

Disgust registered on Scout's face. "You a fuckin' comedian, man.

I'm going to take a chance on gettin' arrested and losin' my fuckin' electrician's license for my fuckin' usual rate? Enough already. I ain't got time for your shit today, Carmellini."

"If we get popped, the charges will get squashed. We're working for the CIA, not some cracker hacker."

"We?"

"I'll be there, too, for some of it. I have a lot of projects and I can't do them all. I need help. I told my boss I trust you. He trusts me, so that's good enough for him."

"I don't want to bust your bubble, Tommy, but what if I get a little tempted?"

"Like I said, I trust you, Scout. You and Earlene. We know each other. You decide to cross me, better kill me first."

"So that's how it is?"

"Yeah."

"I hear you, man."

Earlene snorted. "Hell, we're so far down the food chain that when we finally get a government contract, the work is illegal."

"I brought you this deal because you're a minority-owned business."

"Female-owned, too," Earlene said. "I got fifty-one percent."

"The rising tide of social progress has lifted your boat. Money only lightly soiled? How can you say no to an offer like this?"

They arrived at police headquarters an hour later. Tommy Carmellini presented a work order bearing the signature of a senior civil servant in the district public works department—Carmellini had signed the work order himself—and fifteen minutes later he was standing with Scout and Earlene in the main trunk room of police headquarters.

Carmellini had briefed them on the way downtown. Now they identified the incoming video lines, the camera control lines, and the feed to the main computer. As Carmellini suspected, there were bundles of unused telephone and fiber-optic lines coming into the police station, a legacy of the massive bandwidth build-out during the final days of the great tech bubble that caused every street in the center of the city to be dug up and poorly repaved, sometimes numerous times as company after company laid their own lines willy-nilly under the streets, one atop the other. The bandwidth gold rush was aided and abetted by the city fathers, who pocketed campaign contributions and refused to force the network companies to pay for the damage they did to the pavement and underlying roadbase. As usual in America, when the bubble popped and the dust settled it was the taxpayers driving on ruined streets who got the bill for the incompetence, greed, and stupidity of their elected leaders.

When they finished in the police station, Carmellini and company went outside, set up four barricades around the nearest manhole, and pried off the lid. As Scout and Earlene worked underground, Carmellini consulted the maps he had stolen during the weekend from the network companies. When Scout called for it, he passed down equipment.

By six that night the ad hoc computer center in the basement of CIA headquarters was receiving the feed from police headquarters. Carmellini stood behind Hudson and Vance and watched as they manipulated the video cameras in public sites all across the city, zooming in, focusing, tracking specific people.

"How is your recognition program coming?" Carmellini asked.

"We should be ready for a trial by tomorrow night. Get it up and running, start hunting glitches."

"Okay."

"We managed to hack into three of the larger banks' credit card operations today," Zelda Hudson reported. "We can do data searches, construct time lines and credit histories, get addresses and references, basically see whatever they have."

Carmellini clapped.

Zelda bowed her head in acknowledgment as her cheeks flushed with pleasure. The security measures had been unexpectedly challenging, and she had enjoyed every minute of it. With Zip watching, tossing in suggestions, they had gotten it done. "We're a good team," she told him now, and he grinned at her.

Tommy Carmellini slapped them both on their shoulders, then headed for the cafeteria to get a sandwich as the campus emptied out. Zelda and Zip didn't yet have a car, but they had arranged to ride with a car pool, so he was relieved of chauffeur duties.

He was getting more than a little peeved at Arch Foster and Norv Lalouette. He had been waiting for them to drop the other shoe, and they hadn't. The waiting was hard.

Arch and Norv were slimy and had an odor about them. In contrast, Scout had done a stretch in the joint for stealing money and drugs from people's houses while he was working on their wiring systems, yet he didn't stink like Arch and Norv. Those two . . .

When he finished his sandwich, Tommy walked back across the Langley campus to his building. The guard inspected his badge, then admitted him. On the third floor another guard also inspected his badge. As he walked down the hall the sensors in the ceiling read his badge electronically. He opened the cypherlock to his office, turned on the lights, and punched his secret code into the keypad, disabling the zone alarms. He sat in his chair, stirred through the stuff in his in-basket, looked at the evening through his window, and thought about things.

It would be interesting to see what was in Arch Foster's house or apartment. And Norv's, for that matter. What in the devil were those two jerks up to?

He picked up the telephone book for the Metro area and looked up Foster. Let's see . . . Foster, A., Alice, Allen, Archibald . . . Archibald C. A house in Silver Spring, looks like.

Lalouette . . . He wasn't in the book. Probably an unlisted number.

The days passed one by one, and Jake Grafton felt the pressure intensely. He could almost hear the doomsday clock ticking. Each day, each hour, each minute that passed was gone forever. He couldn't sleep, couldn't eat, and he couldn't get the problems he faced out of his mind.

The computer teams made up of NSA and CIA experts worked hard on software programs, integrating information from dozens of sources, all unauthorized, to which Tommy Carmellini and his friends provided access. Jake put Zelda to work researching Frouq al-Zuair and the Sword of Islam.

He talked to the president's aide twice a day, talked to federal agencies and individual members of his staff at all hours of the day or night. The president, state department, and federal law enforcement agencies were working their foreign resources, covertly and overtly. Everyone was putting in brutal hours. Tempers were short, the pressure intense—and *that* worried him. If he got too focused on the here and now he would lose track of the big picture. His job, he well knew, was to drive the ship, not stoke the boilers. Fortunately Gil Pascal was shouldering a huge share of the load, which helped enormously.

He forced himself to take time to read the papers, to keep up with world events. He even took his wife to a movie, but it didn't help.

He ignored the actors on the screen and thought about nuclear weapons.

Toad briefed him every morning on progress with the new radiation detectors before Jake sat down with Pascal to review progress. "The problem," Toad said one morning, "is that they detect everything. Tons of radioactive materials move through our cities and ports every day, radioactive waste, hospital isotopes, research materials.... Food processors even use isotopes to radiate produce."

"We're running in place," Jake muttered. "We don't have anything to grab on to."

"Hey, CAG," Toad said, "something good will happen. We'll get a break. You gotta have faith."

Jake stared at Tarkington, who hadn't called him CAG in years. The old naval aviation acronym stood for Commander Air Group and was pronounced to rhyme with "rag"; it had been Jake's title when he and Toad met years ago on a cruise to the Mediterranean.

"You gotta have faith," Toad stated dogmatically. "The good guys always win in the long run."

If only that were true!

"That clock—" Jake pointed at the government-issue electric clock that hung on the wall opposite his desk. "Take it down and get rid of it. I'm tired of looking at it."

Toad bit his lip. "Yes, sir," he said.

On the evening of the seventh day after leaving Karachi, *Olympic Voyager* passed Sharm el Sheikh and entered the Gulf of Suez. The next morning at dawn she picked up a pilot at the port of Suez and entered the canal. Nine days after leaving Karachi, she eased against a quay in Port Said, at the northern end of the canal,

From his perch on the wing of the bridge, Dutch Vandervelt watched as the passenger went down the permanent ladder on the starboard side of the ship to the gangway the dockworkers had pushed against the lower steps. Once on the quay they crossed it and disappeared from view. The first mate had only spoken to him on two occasions after their conversation on that first night. Once the man asked for a ladder to get to the containers stacked above deck level, and the next time, as the ship entered the Red Sea, he reported that the job was done.

"I am finished. I shall leave the ship at Port Said."

"What about your tools, your gear?"

"Everything is in the other two containers. Off-load all six at Port Said."

"Are the weapons armed?"

"Don't ask foolish questions," the man snapped. "I have installed new shipping documents on the containers. Off-load them at Port Said and forget you ever talked to me."

That, Dutch Vandervelt knew, was sound advice. He lit a cigarette and watched a dock crane lift the first container from the top of its stack. Lee, the second mate, supervised the hookup. Once he looked up at the bridge at Dutch, who pretended not to notice.

The stevedores were hooking up the second container when Dutch realized Captain Pappadopoulus was standing beside him. Fortunately the breeze carried away his stench. An unshaven, heavyset man, the captain wore filthy trousers, carpet slippers, and a shirt that had once been white. He hadn't bothered to tuck his shirttail into his trousers. He put a hand on the railing to steady himself and peered myopically at the containers on the deck.

"Get them off my ship," he shouted hoarsely at Lee, and waved his other hand, making a brushing gesture. "Get that shit off my ship."

"Captain," Vandervelt said, "this isn't the time or place to make a scene. Why don't you go below?"

Pappadopoulus glared sullenly at his first mate. "Don't give me orders, you son of a bitch. I'm the master of this vessel."

"I'm not giving you orders, sir. I merely made a suggestion. Your officers and crew will get the containers unloaded expeditiously and have the ship under way in about an hour."

"Never should have agreed to this fucking deal," Pappadopoulus muttered, and turned to look again at the offending containers. "I've spent my life sailing from Third World shithole to shithole, hauling trash, dealing with trash." He glanced again at Vandervelt. "Trash like you. All my wasted life. But I was honest, did honest work, earned honest money. Not much of it, you understand. Still, the money was clean. Didn't stink. Wasn't bloody."

"Yes, sir."

"Clean money, by God. Not like this Arab shit."

For the first time he looked at the quays and piers and warehouses and the pollution cloud tailing out to sea from the city. "The asshole of the world, by God." He snorted. "Appropriate, I suppose."

Now he half turned and stared owlishly at Vandervelt. "I haven't got that many years left. You're young. Sold your fucking soul young. I pity you, you miserable bastard."

Pappadopoulus headed for the ladder. He kept his hands on the railings or hatch or bridge fixtures as he went, whatever he could reach, steadying himself against the nonexistent roll of the ship.

Dutch Vandervelt caught a glimpse of his own reflection in a bridge window. He looked pasty-faced and drawn.

The old man was a sot, a worthless friggin' drunk, but he called it right. Vandervelt had sold his soul for money, and he knew it. "I pity me, too," he muttered.

Oh, shit, what *had* he done? Why oh why had he ever agreed to do this?

For money!

He did it for the money. And if those bombs ever exploded, he was going to have to live with it the rest of his life.

He paced the bridge thinking about that.

On her fourth day in Zurich, Anna Modin returned to the hotel in the afternoon after another round of meetings with Swiss bankers. A consortium of companies wanted to sell computers and software in the Middle East; their European banks wanted Walney's to finance the buyers and bear the risk if the buyers defaulted. Of course, the credit ratings of some of the buyers were less than sterling. Negotiations had been tense.

She had three messages on her voice mail. The first two were from bank officers in Cairo—she had already called them before she left the host bank. The third message was from a man who merely said the name of a local restaurant and a time—nothing else. She played the message three times before she erased it.

It was Ilin's voice. Modin was sure of it. She hadn't talked to him in three years, but she was certain.

Anna Modin glanced at her watch. She had thirty minutes.

Frouq al-Zuair sculled the rowboat along the waterline of *Olympic Voyager* on the side of the ship away from the quay. The filthy water of the harbor had the clarity of motor oil and in a pinch could be used as a substitute for it. With zero visibility, there was no way for a diver to work except by feel. Consequently the diver was under the boat, being towed along with a rope around his waist. Fortunately the swell from the sea was almost nonexistent here in the harbor. Bubbles from the diver's scuba gear merged with the ripples of the boat.

Zuair glanced upward at the wing of the bridge. Anyone standing there could see this boat near the ship's hull, but that was a chance he would have to take. He glanced at the other ships in sight. No one seemed to be paying any attention to this rowboat.

Sinking a seagoing ship before she could get off a distress signal or a passing Samaritan could rescue the crew was not a job for an amateur, a fact of which Zuair was keenly aware. He had given the problem much thought. Starting a fire in the engine room would do it, of course, but the ship might drift for days. He could carry plastique aboard, yet knowing where and how to place the charges so that she would sink quickly would require a demolition expert with a thorough knowledge of the ship's systems.

The best bet, he decided, was to place charges below the waterline, then detonate them. No doubt there were acoustic transmitters that could be reliably used for underwater charges, but he didn't have access to those. He was using what was available.

He had made up four bombs containing twenty-five pounds of plastique in each. He had rigged up motorcycle batteries to fire the fuses, three for each charge, and a twenty-four-hour timer to trigger them. Each bomb was wrapped in thick polystyrene and sealed to keep the water out. This package was placed inside another polystyrene bag, one containing six powerful electromagnets and two batteries, and after all the air was carefully squeezed out, sealed again. The switch to turn on the power to the electromagnets was inside the bag; the diver would have to manipulate it by feel.

The four bombs lay in the bottom of the boat. He had sealed them up just an hour ago, immediately after he started the timers. The timers were ticking.

He stopped the boat about seventy-five feet aft of the bow and tugged on the diver's rope. The hull of the ship was encrusted with weeds and crud that the diver had to scrape away with a tool he had attached to his wrist, or the electromagnets would not stick. Zuair checked his watch. The minutes passed slowly. Three minutes . . . four . . . five. At six minutes the diver's head reappeared in the narrow gap between the boat and the ship's hull. The man's head broke the surface, then a hand. The diver was in a black wet suit, wearing a mask, scuba tanks, and a mouthpiece.

After another glance at the empty bridge wing, Zouair braced himself and carefully picked up one of the bombs—which weighed about sixty pounds each. The boat rocked dangerously. Trying not to capsize, he passed the bomb over the stern to the diver, who let the weight push him under.

Less than a minute later a hand rose above the water. A thumb in the air signaled success.

Zouair sculled the boat another hundred feet aft, then tugged on the line again.

When Anna Modin entered the restaurant she saw Janos Ilin sitting at a table at the back of the room. He looked exactly as she remembered him. He stood as she approached and helped her with her chair.

They chatted for several minutes as if they were old acquaintances. Ilin led the conversation along innocuous lines. After dinner they left the restaurant together.

Walking the streets of Zurich, he strolled briskly and kept a wary eye peeled to ensure they weren't being followed. As he walked he talked. "That CD you brought from Cairo is full of Walney's Bank records. They show how the money flowed to Frouq al-Zuair for the purchase of those four warheads. It's a long, convoluted trail."

She nodded.

"I want you to take it to a man in America. His name is Jake Grafton." He gave her Jake's address in Washington.

"When?"

"Now. In the morning on the first flight. The weapons were put aboard a freighter, *Olympic Voyager,* in Karachi nine days ago. He needs to know that, too."

"Don't you have any other way of getting him this information?"

"No." He said the word abruptly. "I'm operating on my own. There are factions in the SVR and Russian government that would call what I'm doing treason. I faked up a reason to go to America several weeks ago, but I cannot go again now. I do not have a plausible reason in position. Perhaps I should have, but I don't. If I go to America, the people in Moscow will suspect treason and everything I have worked for all my life will collapse."

"I guess I always knew you were on your own," she admitted. "That's the only reason I did as you suggested, went where you wanted me to go."

Ilin nodded, his lips a thin line. "Perhaps we're both fools." He gestured irritably. "I'm asking you to risk your life. Abdul Abn Saad and his friends will suspect you betrayed them. They'll come after you. The fact that you've already told what you knew won't matter—they'll want revenge. Tell Jake Grafton that and he will try to protect you."

"I saw the bombs."

"I know you did. Grafton will believe you. That is why I'm asking you to do this. Abdul Abn Saad is one of the most dangerous men alive—he's up to his eyeballs in this mess. The Americans must be told."

He stopped and faced her. "You understand, if those weapons explode, the world that we know will cease to exist. The world will enter a new dark age. Billions of people will starve. I don't know what your politics are, and I don't care, but that outcome must be prevented."

"When I don't return to Cairo Saad will look in the bank for an accomplice. He'll find your agent."

Ilin made a gesture of helplessness. "Perhaps he won't find her. If he does, she knows nothing that will help him. She, too, is a soldier—she must take her chances."

"No," said Anna Modin, shaking her head. "I must return to Cairo and get her. I shall take her with me."

"Too dangerous. *I forbid it.* They may capture you both, which is an unacceptable risk. You know too much. *You know me!* They'll torture you until you tell them everything. If the woman in Cairo dies, we've lost a soldier. If I die, we've lost the army and the war. There will be no one between us and them."

Janos Ilin cocked his head and examined her eyes.

"Do you understand?"

"I *do* understand. Years ago you bet your life on your ability to find people with integrity to help you. If you made a single error you would forfeit your life. As a person who grew up in communist Russia I appreciate the magnitude of the risk you chose to run and your courage. You are either the greatest man who ever lived or the biggest fool. That question remains to be decided."

Anna Modin paused and touched Ilin's arm. "I do not question your assessment of the risk. On the other hand, if we abandon this woman we will be no better than Abdul Abn Saad or Frouq al-Zuair or General Petrov. They are the evil I am fighting against."

His eyes looked as hard as the steel in a rifle barrel. "No."

"Yes," she said simply. "I will not abandon that woman. There is no other way, unless you go to America yourself. Give me the CD and tell me her name. She and I shall go to America together."

Ilin had no choice. He didn't like it, but he gave her the name and the disk.

Dutch Vandervelt made a decision as the containers were being off-loaded to the quay. He decided he would send a message telling about the bombs in the clear on the international distress frequency as soon as the ship was out of Egyptian waters. Every ship in the eastern Med would copy the message, and they would relay it to governments around the world. . . .

He had grabbed for the gold ring and knew now that it had been a horrible mistake. Oh, Christ, what had he done? Even that sot Pappadopoulus had seen the evil of it.

He stared at his hands. They would put him in prison, probably. Being human, he thought about that.

When the last container from *Olympic Voyager*'s deck was on the quay, the pilot came up the ladder with a port official. They climbed to the bridge. Dutch Vandervelt had never met the pilot, who had little to say. The port official was overly friendly, unctuous.

"Your friends suggested that you wanted no written record of your port call, for private reasons, all legitimate of course, and we wish to help you in any way we can. . . ."

After negotiation, five hundred dollars American was agreed upon. Vandervelt removed a wad of bills from his pocket and peeled off ten fifties.

Dutch Vandervelt surveyed the horizon. The brisk wind off the desert carried a load of dust, restricting visibility. Five or six miles, Dutch thought idly, trying to get his mind off bombs and fanatics and his own stupidity. He was looking with unseeing eyes at the gulls wheeling and soaring about the bridge when the radio operator ran onto the bridge.

"The com gear is ruin! Someone smash the radios!"

"What?"

"Someone hammer on the radios—probably before we dock. Smash the radios all to hell."

One of the crew? Naw! It couldn't have been the pilot—he never left the bridge. The port official went ashore immediately after he got his bribe.

That fucking nuclear engineer! He must have done it just before he went ashore! But why?

Then he knew: They didn't want anyone on *Olympic Voyager* sending messages.

He looked about desperately. There were people on the quay, men of course—Arabs—everywhere. The port official was walking across the deck, heading for the top of the ladder that would take him down to the quay.

My God, they must intend to sink the ship, to kill everyone aboard! Suddenly his legs would no longer support his weight. He grabbed for the rail to keep from falling.

Of course, they can't leave a shipload of sailors to tell who, what, where, and how after . . . afterward.

What in the name of Christ have I done?

"What I do, sir?"

He shook his head, trying to clear his thoughts.

"What to do, sir?" It was the radio operator, speaking to him.

Maybe they wouldn't kill him.

"Here," Dutch said, and reached into his pocket. He pulled out the wad of bills and thrust them at the man. "Take this, get off the ship. They're going to kill us all, I think. Go down the ladder—right now—and walk away. Don't look back."

The man stared at him.

"For God's sake, you fool, take the money and go!" He wrapped the man's hand around the money and pushed him away.

A moment later Dutch saw the radio operator crossing the deck. He paused at the top of the starboard ladder, looked back at him, then disappeared down it behind the port official.

Vandervelt waved feebly to Lee, the second mate, on the deck. Ten minutes later the ship was moving away from the dock under its own power.

The pilot boat was waiting outside the harbor, as usual.

Vandevelt signaled all stop on the engine telegraph. He had no money for the pilot, and told him so. The pilot was horrified.

"You must pay me!"

"Write a letter to the company, you wop bastard. Now get the fuck off this ship."

"That no way to talk. Talk respectly. I a pilot. Highly skilled."

"Get off this ship. Now! Get down there."

After a last look at Dutch's face, the pilot stepped back several paces, then turned and made for the ladder to the main deck.

As the ship slowed, the little pilot boat moved in toward the starboard ladder. The pilot waited at the top with the mate, talking volubly and gesturing grandly at the bridge.

Lee looked at Vandervelt, who stood impassively.

The truth was there was nothing he could do—he had realized that standing on the bridge when the ship was at the dock. If he left the ship, they would kill him. If they intended to sink the ship, they probably would. He and the crew had no weapons aboard—they were completely defenseless.

He was mulling all this, trying to see a way out, when he realized with a start that Lee was signaling to him, waving his arms . . . and four men carrying weapons topped the ladder. Backpacks hung from their shoulders.

In less than a minute they were on the bridge, pushing Lee in front of them with a gun in his back.

"Get under way," Frouq al-Zuair snapped, and pointed a submachine gun at Vandervelt's midriff.

Lee stared at him, his eyes big as saucers, as if to say, See, this is where our greed has taken us.

"We had a deal," Vandervelt managed.

The burst hit him in the stomach and hammered him against the engine telegraph pedestal. Dutch Vandervelt felt everything inside coming loose. With his hands on his stomach, he slid toward the floor, unable to stay erect.

As his blood pressure fell, Dutch heard the jingle of the telegraph, heard Zuair say something to Lee. The last thing he saw was the dirty green tile on the deck, then he lost consciousness. Sixty seconds later his heart stopped.

Zuair and his holy warriors were merciless. As the ship worked up to fifteen knots, they went methodically through the ship killing the crewmen, shooting them where they stood. Lee they left alive, on the bridge conning the ship, with a man standing behind him with a submachine gun against his back.

As the afternoon wore on Zuair set charges of plastique explosive that he and his men had carried aboard in their backpacks. It was possible, he knew, that the charges on the port side of the ship, below the waterline, might be torn off by the sea. He had to allow for that possibility.

He planted charges around the pipes that fed oil to the boilers and the water intakes from the sea. Just to make sure, he set incendiary charges with delay fuses on the ladders leading up from the engine room.

At sunset, with the charges set, he climbed the ladder to the bridge. From the wings of the bridge he used binoculars to survey the surface of the ocean. One ship in sight, on an opposite course, apparently heading for Port Said. Several miles behind *Olympic Voyager* and offset from her wake was a cabin cruiser on a parallel course.

Satisfied, he walked back across the bridge. As he walked he pulled a pistol from his waistband. When he passed behind Lee, he shot the second mate in the back of the head.

"Put them in there," he said to his man, and nodded toward the hatchway to the radar shack. "Lock the door. We don't want bodies floating."

The sun sank into the sea and black night enveloped them. An hour later a large container ship appeared from the haze behind them, overtaking. It was a bit to port. He watched the lights of the ship through his binoculars, then turned the helm and let the ship's head come starboard twenty degrees. Then he recentered the rudder.

It took almost two hours before the other ship's lights were fading into the haze again.

He consulted the radar display. He didn't know how to operate it or the scale of the presentation, but he saw no blips close by. That would have to do.

With his man tending the helm, trying to hold a steady course, Frouq al-Zuair climbed down the ladder and went along the deck to the ladder leading below. Once in the lower deck passageway, he made his way to the ladder well that led down to the engine room.

Two bodies lay sprawled on the deck. Zuair ignored them as he studied the engine controls. Tentatively he closed the lever he thought must be the throttle. The beating of the engine slowed, and the revolutions dropped on the RPM gauge.

He didn't know how to secure the flow of fuel to the fireboxes, so he didn't try. He scurried up the ladder well and left the hatches open behind him.

On the weather deck he could feel the absence of vibration as the ship began to respond to the swells.

The man from the bridge was already standing by the starboard ladder. The other two arrived as the cabin cruiser made its approach.

When he and his men were aboard the boat, Zuair removed a radio controller from his backpack and turned it on. The green light glowed in the darkness. He pushed the button . . . and heard the thump of the charges within the ship going off.

Olympic Voyager's running lights were still on, so the ship was easy to see at a hundred yards from the cockpit of the boat.

He didn't know how long it would take for the ship to sink. A half hour passed as the ship lay motionless on the sea, then another.

He could detect no noticeable settling. Frustrated, Zuair pushed the second detonator to explode the incendiary charges.

Five minutes later a dull glow could be seen amidships. Fire must be coming up the passageways and ladder wells from the engine room. Soon the watchers smelled smoke, noxious, oily, greasy fumes.

The glow finally became open flame. Still Zuair waited. One of the men wanted to go before a ship came into view, but Zuair cut him off with a curt word.

He looked at his watch repeatedly. Finally he heard the explosions from the charges he had set while the ship was moored in Port Said, one boom, then two quick ones ten seconds later, and a fourth fifteen seconds after that. At last!

They pulled off and waited as the flame from the burning ship lit up the sea for a half mile in every direction. The ship soon began listing.

Frouq al-Zuair took the helm himself and steered the boat back toward the burning, sinking ship. He used a powerful spotlight to inspect her. She was visibly settling, listing at least twenty degrees. Satisfied, he turned the boat away from the ship and told the helmsman to take over.

As the boat sped away from the derelict, Zuair watched the burning ship in his binoculars. He hoped it would sink before dawn. *"Inshallah,"* he whispered, God willing.

CHAPTER TEN

Anna Modin didn't leave Zurich on the next plane. Her business required that she stay another day and she was afraid to leave before it was concluded. Her meetings ended too late the next day for her to catch the last flight out, so she was forced to wait for the first flight the following morning.

Before she checked out of her hotel room she made her morning call to Abn Saad, as she did every day, reporting the results of her meetings with the Swiss bankers and European businessmen. She tried to keep her voice calm and businesslike, the way she normally spoke. If he became suspicious now . . .

When she rang off, her mouth was too dry to swallow. She sipped bottled water from the hotel room minibar, felt the pulse throbbing in her forehead.

Oh, she sounded brave when she talked to Ilin, full of courage and noble purpose, ready to charge off to save an Islamic woman she had never met who might not even be in danger. In fact, she was risking her life to attempt to rescue a woman who might refuse to leave Egypt. Nooreem Habib might be married, engaged, happy . . . Ilin didn't know. All he could tell her was that Nooreem attended an English school for six years and was a brilliant pupil, a woman with a fine mind and much promise. The headmistress had believed in her, which was enough for Ilin. Enough to trust her the tiniest little bit. The risk was small: She had never heard his name, knew nothing about his operation.

And yet, Nooreem Habib was a woman of courage. That Anna Modin knew for a fact. She had risked her life to supply evidence of terrorism, and that fact outweighed all the unknowns.

They would need American visas, Ilin told her. On such short notice, he could do nothing. She knew a man in Cairo, she said. . . .

Anna Modin felt her stomach churn. She ran to the bathroom and vomited up her breakfast.

Courage? Ha! You are a fool, Anna Modin. A complete, utter fool.

Freddy Bailey! When she got to Cairo she would call Freddy Bailey!

Fool or not, she completed her packing and called the bellboy. Soon she was on the way to the airport in a taxi.

When he found the note on his desk that Jack Yocke, the *Washington Post* reporter, had called, Jake Grafton felt a twinge of anxiety. This was a professional call, obviously, or Yocke would have called the house and left a message with Callie. He did that a time or two a year, dropped an invitation to dinner, occasionally an evening at a Kennedy Center concert.

Jake waited until the noon hour, then called the reporter on his cell phone while he was on his way across the CIA campus to the cafeteria.

"Hey, Jack. Jake Grafton."

"Admiral, thanks for returning my call."

"Sure."

"I wanted to ask you some questions, deep background."

"Uh-huh," Jake said, and stopped in his tracks. He looked around for a seat. There was a wrought-iron bench nearby, so he parked his fanny on it and gave Yocke his full attention.

"I'm sorta digging into this army story. All these troops around New York, Washington, Los Angeles, San Diego, Miami . . . all over, using Geiger counters to search railroad cars and trucks. Have you heard anything about that?"

"I read your paper, Jack."

"So you know what the Pentagon and White House are saying about 'routine precautions'?"

"I read that."

"Is there anything you could tell me, off the record, for deep background?"

"No," Jake said, the word rolling right off his lips. "Can't think of a thing. Isn't that army and national guard?"

"Well, yeah, and of course you're navy, but I kinda thought you might know something about it."

"Want to tell me why?"

"I heard a rumor."

"Uh-huh."

"That you're involved in a search for a nuclear weapon."

"Where did you hear this vicious slander?"

"You know I can't tell you that."

"Shipmate, I can't confirm or deny anything. This conversation never happened. But I want to know where that rumor came from. This is very important, Jack."

"Maybe you can track it down."

"You could help me on this. Your name will never come up."

"All I can say is that I thought the rumor credible. The person who told me was talking out of school about a matter that I thought was probably highly classified."

"I appreciate that. Think this person will ever call you again?"

"It's probable."

"Have a nice day, Jack."

"Thanks, Admiral."

When Grafton got back to his office after lunch, he wrote a note to Tommy Carmellini. "Jack Yocke, a reporter for the *Washington Post,* said he has a source who told him I was hunting for a nuclear weapon. Have Zelda put someone to work finding out who his source is. He or she will probably call him again."

Cairo is one of the world's great cities, a sprawling urban mass split by a great, legendary river. People have lived and farmed beside it since the first farmers learned to grow grain, yet the city of Cairo was not founded until 969. Its Western name, Cairo, comes from the Arabic al-Qahira, the victorious. In Arabic, both the city and the nation are known as Misr.

Modern Cairo is a curious amalgam of East and West, old and new, the past and the future sweltering amid the dirty, foul, gridlocked present. The influence of Europe and America is plain in modern buildings and boulevards, yet not far from the urban splendor is old, Islamic Cairo, a city of narrow streets and vibrant humanity.

If, when arriving on an airliner, the flight path brings one over the city, dazzling white stone can be glimpsed on some of the larger buildings, mosques mostly. The citadel and some of the older mosques are constructed of white limestone, the facing stones of the pyramids, removed from the pharaohs' monuments centuries ago when the Islamic civilization of Egypt's Arab invaders approached its zenith of glory and power.

And there is the river, that ever-present moving brown highway that flows northward from the desert, carrying water and mud from the tropical heart of Africa. Somehow it seems fitting that for millennia the descendants of the ancient Egyptians who inhabited this desert city never knew the source of the river that formed the center of their civilization.

At the airport Anna Modin passed through customs and immigration and walked upstairs. In a quiet nook with some empty chairs, she dialed her cell phone.

"Freddy, this is Anna," she said in English.

"This is a surprise," he said bitterly. "I didn't think I was ever going to hear from you again. What's it been, three months?"

"Freddy, I need a favor."

"I must have called you a dozen times. At least you could have returned my calls."

"Freddy, you are a sweet man, but we aren't right for each other."

"Isn't it amazing? I didn't have a clue until you dumped me."

"I didn't mean to hurt you, Freddy, and I apologize. An emergency has come up at the bank; a colleague and I need to go to America immediately. We need American visas."

"Stop by the embassy during working hours, and we'll run you through the computer and put you on the list."

"Freddy! I have never asked you for a favor, and I wouldn't be asking now if I had a choice. Please."

There was a long silence, so long that Anna thought the connection had been lost. Then he said, "You broke my heart, woman."

"I'm sorry, Freddy."

"I'll get in trouble, you know that."

"Freddy, I speak to you from the heart. My colleague's life is in danger—"

"Yeah. Right."

"We must go to America. That is all I can tell you. The bureaucrats at the embassy may be unhappy at you, but the people in Washington will not. That I promise you."

He sighed. "Tourist visas, two weeks."

"That will be sufficient, thank you."

"Meet me at the bar in the Marriott at ten tonight. Have you forgotten it?"

"You know I haven't."

"Sorry about the hour, but I have a date."

He broke the connection without saying good-bye.

Anna Modin joined the queue at the Lufthansa ticket counter, pulling her valise on wheels. She purchased two tickets to Switzerland on the first flight in the morning for herself and Nooreem Habib, paid cash for them, then went out to join the mob seeking to engage a taxi. As usual, the driver of the vehicle she commandeered was not happy to hear her speaking Arabic with an Egyptian accent—he had taken her for a European tourist. He argued the fare halfheartedly, then muttered *"Inshallah."* Away they went for the hour ride into the heart of the Cairo.

As the taxi driver charged through traffic, Anna Modin took stock. She had money in her purse and her bra and underwear, American dollars she had withdrawn from a small bank account she had opened years ago when she worked in Switzerland. She didn't dare touch her Cairo account at Walney's.

She hoped Nooreem Habib had a valid passport and could get to it. If she didn't . . .

The risk was that Abdul Abn Saad would send someone after them. If they managed to get out of Egypt. Nominally Egypt was a limited democracy, but in reality it was ruled by a small number of very powerful men. Saad was not one of the elite, but he was definitely in the second tier. He had money and he knew people with more money, and they knew people with even more money . . . and he was in bed with the religious fanatics. Underestimating his power would be fatal.

Her stomach was calm as she watched the familiar sights pass the car windows, the hordes of people, the animals, small groups of police with automatic weapons carried every which way. It was very familiar. She had not thrown up again, perhaps because she had not eaten all day. She certainly wasn't hungry.

As was her habit on returning from a business trip during business hours, she went straight to the bank and took the elevator to her office. Then she went to Abdul Abn Saad's office and greeted the male secretary. In minutes she was seated across the desk from Saad, reporting on the business that she had conducted in Zurich.

He seemed as he always was, engaged and sharp.

She concentrated fiercely on reporting the results of her trip, the discussions and decisions she had made and the commitment she had given on the bank's behalf. Saad knew most of this from her daily telephone calls, but he liked to go over all of it again after every trip while he watched her face and listened carefully to the reasons she had made the decisions she had.

"I, too, believe the business will be profitable for us," he said finally, his eyes still on her face. "You have done well."

"Thank you."

"Please attend the morning meeting with the staff. I want them fully informed."

Tomorrow morning. He wouldn't know she was gone until then. A great sense of relief flooded her, one she was afraid he could see. "Yes, sir," she managed, then she was on her feet and walking out of the room, past the secretary at his desk, along the corridor to her small office.

She checked her watch. The back-office staff would be leaving soon. She must intercept Nooreem.

There was no alternative. The clerks didn't have telephones at their desks, so the office manager, a man, would answer. He would want to know the reason for the call, then might or might not call her to the telephone, might or might not pass on the message. She had no plausible reason to ask the office manager to send the woman to her office. She never had in the past.

If Nooreem was there.

Please God, let her be there.

She walked down the stairs and went along the corridor to the new computer center.

Through the door, looking. . . . A half dozen Egyptian women were in sight, wearing Western business clothes.

The office manager was standing there. "Nooreem Habib, please."

If he was suspicious, it didn't show on his face. He pointed her out to Anna Modin.

She walked that way. Nooreem was sitting at a computer terminal. She looked up as Anna approached, then stood when she saw Anna was heading straight for her. She appeared in her mid-twenties, had an intelligent face.

"Miss Habib, I am Anna Modin. May I have a moment of your time?"

Nooreem looked up at the Russian woman with large, intelligent brown eyes.

Modin spoke softly, almost inaudibly. "I am your courier. Follow me to the hallway, please."

She turned and walked from the room, nodding respectfully to the manager, who was now seated at his desk near the door.

Habib was quick. As Anna walked from the room she heard her speaking to the man, then she followed her into the hallway.

Anna faced her. "I am your courier," she said again, so low that she could barely be heard. "You must leave Cairo and come with me."

Nooreem Habib's eyes widened. "Because of the CD?"

"Yes. Have you put another in the drop?"

"No."

"Do you have a passport?"

"Yes. At home. I live with my parents, of course."

"When do you get off work?"

Habib looked at her watch. "In twenty minutes."

The man from the computer center opened the door and looked out. "At the coffee shop around the corner," Anna said, then said in a normal tone of voice, "Thank you for your help," and walked away.

She would have liked to have said more, but there was no time.

No time!

When Nooreem Habib entered the coffee shop, she walked over to Anna Modin's table and sat. The small room was rapidly filling with vociferous office workers seeking coffee and a snack before tackling the trek home.

Modin was surprised at the determined look on Habib's face. She didn't look like a woman facing the abandonment of home and family.

"You must come with me to America," Modin said, watching Habib's face intently. "You may never be able to return to Egypt."

"I understand. Yesterday I finished loading a computer file with the names and amounts of secret contributors to the fundamentalists' *jihad*. It was all there, names, dates, amounts, everything. I downloaded it onto a CD a few minutes ago."

Modin stared at the other woman. "After I talked to you?"

"Yes." She opened her purse, showed Anna a glimpse of a compact disk, then closed the purse again. "I didn't realize that Ahmad was watching when I did it. Still, I don't think he knew what I was doing."

Modin tossed money on the table. "Come," she said. "There is no time to waste."

First they had to go to Habib's home so that she could get her passport. They took a taxi, which crawled through traffic, bearing generally east. Modin and Habib sat in the back without saying anything. Anna thought about Freddy Bailey, wondered if indeed he would meet her with American tourist visas, wondered if Ahmad the records clerk was busy talking to Abdul Abn Saad.

The ride, Anna thought, was the longest of her life.

The Habib residence was an imposing single-family dwelling in a fashionable neighborhood. It stood directly across the street from the City of the Dead, a huge, sprawling cemetery that had been used to bury people since at least the ninth century. The cemetery was huge beyond belief, a sea of stones and monuments and crypts that stretched away as far as the eye could see in the haze and smog. Around the cemetery were walls, with guard towers every few hundred yards. Atop the towers were troops with machine guns, yet the guns were pointed at the cemetery. The walls and troops were designed to keep the living residents of the cemetery inside. Some of the poorest people in Cairo lived there, tomb squatters, criminals, army deserters, the homeless, and so on. They had even built their own mosques in the cemetery, where the imams preached Islamic fundamentalism and *jihad*.

Anna got out of the taxi to caution Nooreem. "You mustn't tell them you are leaving," she said. "Gossip has wings. If Saad hears from any source that we are leaving, he will send men to the airport to find us."

"I understand," Nooreem Habib said noncommittally, glancing at the house.

"I suggest you say you are going out to dinner with friends, get the passport, and leave everything else. I have enough money for both of us on my person."

The taxi driver wanted to be paid. Habib entered the house while he and Anna haggled. She gave him some money, promised more, then sat in the back of the vehicle so he couldn't leave.

She glanced past the cemetery wall at the nearby sepulchers, crypts, and waist-high walls around family burial plots. Because of the masonry mazes, the place was nearly impossible to police. At night the authorities didn't even try, apparently on the theory that anyone there after dark deserved whatever he got.

The cab radio blared popular Egyptian music. Traffic and people walking filled the crowded street in front of the Habib house as the shadows disappeared and dusk settled over the city.

Time passed glacially. Finally, the cab driver turned to Anna, asked for more money. She looked again at her watch. They had been here for twenty minutes. She passed the driver more bills. The realization congealed in Anna's mind that Nooreem hadn't done as she asked. She must have told her family that she was leaving, perhaps permanently, and now the family was having a scene.

A car pulled to the curb and stopped fifty feet beyond the cab. Two men were in the car. They looked back this way, then adjusted the mirrors of their car, a newer sedan.

Ten minutes and another payment to the taxi driver later the Habib door finally opened . . . a man in his fifties stood in the door looking across the street at her, then closed it again. Uh-oh.

The waiting car with the two men didn't move. The men were still there, sitting calmly.

Forty minutes passed, then forty-five. The last of the light faded from the sky.

Headlights and lights from windows and open doors illuminated the street. Puny streetlights were mounted on street corners, but they didn't seem to help much.

Finally, an hour and a half after Nooreem went into the house, the front door opened again and a horde of people came out. She was apparently surrounded by her family, the father, mother, a sister or two, and several younger brothers. A woman that might be an aunt. The whole procession crossed the street toward the taxi. One of the boys carried a valise.

The two men in the car ahead opened their car doors and got out. Each had a pistol in his hand.

Anna stifled a scream. The taxi driver took one look, started the car's engine, and engaged the clutch. The taxi lurched, then shot forward.

One of the gunmen was on Anna's side. She grabbed the door latch and pushed it open with all her strength.

The door hit the man with a sickening thunk.

"Stop the car," Anna Modin shrieked in Arabic at the taxi driver, who had braked when he felt the impact. Anna reached across the back of the seat and twisted the ignition key, then jerked it out. The car coasted to a stop as the taxi driver swore lustily in Arabic. With a firm grip on her purse, Anna bailed out.

She sprinted back toward the gunman lying in the street. Beyond him the Habib family was scattering, all except Nooreem, who stood rooted, staring at the lone standing gunman. He, too, stood transfixed, mesmerized at the sight of his partner crumpled in the street.

Anna Modin slowed to a walk, bent over, picked up the wounded man's pistol. She pointed it at the standing gunman, who took a step backward, then glanced at the car he had arrived in.

She knew nothing of firearms, had never handled one in her life. She pointed the pistol at the standing man and squeezed the trigger . . . and nothing happened.

The specter of the pistol pointing at him caused the lone assassin to duck, then hurriedly retreat toward the car. When Modin didn't shoot, his steps slowed. He glanced about to see who was watching, then lifted his own weapon.

Oh, my God!

Anna Modin turned and fled toward Nooreem. "Run," she shouted.

Nooreem took off like a rabbit through a gate by the nearest guard tower, with Anna Modin right behind. Atop the tower the soldiers watched . . . and did nothing.

The two women ran into the darkness along a path that led directly away from the lit street. Once Modin glanced over her shoulder and glimpsed the running gunman following.

Something smashed into the dark wall on her right, then Anna Modin heard the shot. And another, although she didn't know where the second slug went.

The path turned hard to the right, Anna hit the wall and bounced, then ran after Nooreem, who was just a darker figure in the darkness ahead. The stones were uneven under her feet; several times she almost fell. She realized with a start that she still held the pistol. It was useless to her—she didn't know how to use it—so she threw it into the darkness.

Seconds later they passed a shadowy someone who tore at Anna's purse, which was slapping against her shoulder.

Seizing it with a death grip, Anna ran on, panting fiercely, her heart threatening to leap out of her chest. She caught up to Nooreem, who was slowing down.

Behind her she could hear running feet. Coming closer and closer.

"Run faster," she urged, "don't quit."

"I can't," the younger woman panted. She pushed her purse at Anna. "Take it—the disk is in it."

Anna grabbed Nooreem's arm. "Over this wall," she urged. "Let's hide."

They scrambled over the wall beside them as the running footsteps approached. They were crouched there as the footsteps passed.

They crossed the small plot and tackled the wall on the other side.

The next plot contained a monument of some type that Anna hit unexpectedly. She fell, then rose and scrambled after Nooreem.

The exertion required to climb wall after wall was tremendous. Skinning knees, ripping hose, they were crawling over wall after wall when a flashlight beam illuminated them. Shots followed.

They fell on the far side of the wall, listened for several seconds to the gunman coming after them, cursing all the while, then as one they rose and started on.

The grave they were crossing collapsed. They tumbled into the hole. Despite herself, Anna Modin screamed.

Dirt, cobwebs, something slimy . . . Nooreem was first out of the hole, and she reached back for Anna, who clawed at the earth and fought her way out. As Anna rose, Nooreem again thrust the purse at her and shoved her down at the base of a wall, then she threw herself on top and scrambled across.

A spear of light shot out, caught the fleeing girl two walls over, struggling to get a leg up. A shot . . . two . . . three, and Nooreem Habib collapsed.

The shooter crossed the walls to Anna's right. She heard him, saw the flash from his flashlight as he crossed a wall.

He would be looking for the purse, and Nooreem didn't have it on her. Anna knew he would search the area quickly with his flashlight, then come after her.

Keeping low, she felt her way in the darkness along the wall around the open grave. Once on the other side she crossed the wall as silently as she could, determined to try for the path that they had used to enter the cemetery.

From behind her she heard a scream, then a single shot.

The odyssey took twenty minutes, all the while the gunman was flashing his light into family plots, crawling over fences, cursing mightily. Breathing heavily, sobbing, fiercely biting her lip, Anna Modin refused to give up.

When she once again stood on the path, she staggered toward the distant streetlights. Clutching both purses, she wiped her face on the hem of her dress. She stopped for a few seconds, collected herself, and squared her shoulders. Grimly determined, she walked on as briskly as she could. When she reached the wall she walked toward the nearest guard tower and the gate. The troops saw her but pretended not to notice.

She called Freddy Bailey on his cell phone. Her voice was shaking, even though she tried to speak calmly. "You must come get me in your car." She described where she was, in a small restaurant near the City of the Dead.

The tone of her voice convinced Freddy, who didn't argue. "What's wrong?" he demanded.

"I'll tell you whatever you wish to know when you get here. I need your help, Freddy."

"I'm coming. Wait for me."

"Yes," she said, and pushed the button to end the call.

In the rest room she looked at her face in the mirror. She was scraped and cut—her legs bleeding in several places.

At least she was still alive. Her face was filthy, streaked with sweat and dirt. She used the hem of her skirt to swab off the worst of it.

Killers of women and children—no wonder Nooreem had hated them.

She had courage, Anna thought. You had to say that for her. In a world where many people are afraid to board an airliner, Nooreem Habib was ready to wrestle with the devil himself.

Anna well knew who the devil was—Abdul Abn Saad.

"You haven't seen the last of me," she whispered fiercely.

"Got a minute, Admiral?"

The head sticking through Jake Grafton's door belonged to Harry Estep, the FBI liaison officer. "Come in, Harry, please."

"What I've got, sir, is the results of the polygraph examinations you requested on everyone who knew about the Ilin/Doyle connection."

"Okay."

"First, though, an explanation. Do you recall when you took the polygraph, all the leads that were connected, including EEG leads on your head?"

"I remember the leads. I didn't know they were EEG leads."

"The EEG leads were the important ones. The other stuff we use to make the session look like a conventional polygraph examination, but it wasn't. Polygraphs look at blood pressure, respiration rate, pulse rate and so on, trying to detect involuntary emotional responses to lying. Skillful or chronic liars can and do defeat the system. The new technology ignores emotional responses to lying—we now look for something called the P300 bump in the EEG trace. This is a characteristic bump in the trace which happens about a third of a second after you notice something significant. It's like a mental click of recognition, automatic and utterly predictable. In effect, we are looking for 'guilty knowledge,' which is specific knowledge that only a guilty person would have. The difficulty with the technique is constructing the questions."

"Never heard of it," Jake muttered.

"The theory is that the perpetrators of crimes have details stored in their brains that innocent people won't have, even people trying to confess falsely. People with secret knowledge show a P300 response to otherwise innocent-looking pictures or phrases. Our success rate is about ninety percent with no false positives."

"So you are saying that the guilty devil may not show up as a hit, but if you get a hit, he's the guy?"

"Precisely. The beauty of this technology is that the person being examined doesn't have to say a word. We're looking straight into the cognitive processes of the brain. The right to remain silent is now irrelevant."

Jake Grafton smiled. "I'm sure the ACLU will love to hear that."

The FBI agent continued, "When you and Commander Tarkington took the test, both of you recognized Janos Ilin's picture. Neither of you recognized Richard Doyle."

"Never met him."

"One of the people we questioned also recognized Ilin—the national security adviser, Butch Lanham. He didn't name him, but the P300 bump said he recognized the photo."

"Okay."

"Two persons recognized Doyle. Twilley recognized him and pronounced his name. Tran didn't say his name, just laid the photo down and picked up the next one."

"Did you ask if he ever met Doyle?"

"He denied knowing him."

Jake looked thoughtful. "He could have seen him in the cafeteria, parked beside him a time or two, something like that."

"That's true," Estep acknowledged. "All we know is that there was that flash of recognition."

"Okay."

"Butch Lanham was really pissed that he had to take this test—so were Coke Twilley and Sonny Tran."

Jake Grafton said nothing.

"There's more, Admiral," Harry Estep said. "Under questioning, while they were hooked up, both Twilley and Tran admitted telling unauthorized persons about Doyle."

"You're kidding me!"

"Nope." Estep scratched his face. "Could be quite innocent, of course, but admitting a small crime to hide a big one is a common technique for foiling polygraph exams."

Jake Grafton played with his pencil for a moment, then said distractedly, "Thanks, Harry."

Arch Foster's house was in a quiet subdivision in Silver Spring, Maryland, just south of New Hampshire Avenue and about a mile from the old Naval Surface Weapons Center. The neighborhood consisted of endless rows of little brick houses, with mature maples shading quiet yards. Foster's home had a sharp drop-off behind it, so from the street it looked as if it might have a walk-out basement. No garage. The lights were off, no car in the drive.

Tommy Carmellini parked the Mercedes a block away. He snagged the backpack containing his burglary tools from the floor in front of the passenger's seat, then locked the Mercedes. He consciously placed the car keys in his right trouser pocket. He strolled back through the neighborhood, taking everything in. At 11 P.M. there were still lights on, and through the windows one could catch an occasional glimpse of a television screen. A dog barked one street over, but otherwise the neighborhood was quiet, lit only by streetlights.

He had no idea where Arch was tonight or when he might return. If Arch came home while he was in there, things were going to get interesting.

From his left trouser pocket Carmellini removed a set of latex surgical gloves and pulled them on. He had already dusted the inside of them with talcum powder, so they slid right on. He pulled them tight.

Still strolling, glancing around yet not obviously turning his head, he walked up the block to Foster's house, then angled across the lawn and down the hill to the back of the house. Now he looked carefully around. There was a creek back here full of weeds and brush, not a place for joggers or walkers. No one in the adjoining yards.

It was dark back here. No, there wasn't a walk-out basement. The house must be fifty years old, built long before anyone ever thought of walk-out basements. The basement door was under a deck off the kitchen. Using a small, shielded penlight, he checked the door and looked through the single pane of glass. No visible alarms. There was a little sign from a security company, faded from the sun. It had obviously been on the glass pane of the basement door for many a year.

The smart thing to do would be to cut the telephone wire, just in case ol' Arch did have an alarm on the door, or motion detectors or infrared sensors inside the house. The power service came in from a pole near the creek. Carmellini walked over, found the telephone wire running down the brick to a hole in the foundation.

Well, if Arch had spent some bucks on a good burglar alarm, the technician that installed it would have insisted he do something about this telephone wire, which any thief could cut.

The lock on the back door was a Yale. It took Carmellini about a minute to open it with his picks. The door opened inward into an unfinished basement. He stepped in, closed the door behind him, then examined the frame with his penlight. No alarms. He scanned the room. A hot water heater, a furnace, shovels and tools on a bench, and stacks of cardboard boxes, but no sensors.

There was a light switch on the bottom of the basement stairs. He flipped it on. Better to have lights in the house than for the neighbors to see someone using a flashlight inside. The stairs creaked under his weight. He tried the door at the top. Unlocked. It opened in his hand.

He walked through the house taking inventory. Arch obviously was a bachelor. The house was neat enough, but there were no women's things, no feminine decorations or women's clothes in the closets.

It would be impossible to search a house and rearrange everything so no one knew it had been searched, so Tommy Carmellini didn't try. He quickly went through the collection of mail and brochures in the kitchen, then went straight to the spare bedroom that Arch Foster apparently used as a home office. A computer sat on the desk. Tommy flipped on the desk lamp, checked the room for sensors, then began quickly searching the desk. A bank statement . . . Arch was single and made a good salary. He had $27,000 in savings and about two grand in checking. He also had a brokerage account worth $137,000 at the end of the previous month. Files of bills paid and unpaid. . . . It all looked pretty normal. He made a conscious effort to put everything back the way he found it, as near as possible, yet he could feel time pressing on him. Breaking in without knowing when Arch was coming back was dumb, he told himself.

From the study Carmellini went to Arch's bedroom. He checked the nightstands first. Arch was obviously a connoisseur on fine fuck books. He abandoned that collection and quickly pawed through the stuff in his closets and dresser, trying to disturb things as little as possible. And found a 9-mm Walther automatic. Loaded. He left it there.

Under the bed, under the furniture . . . he was looking for something out of the ordinary.

He glanced at his watch. Almost 11:30. He had been here long enough. Well, he could always come back some fine day when Arch was at work and take this house apart.

Carmellini turned off the bedroom light and went back through the house, snapping lights on as required, looking at everything. Nothing attracted his curiosity.

He was in the basement, reaching for the light switch, when the cardboard boxes caught his eye. Old paperbacks? Stuff from Arch's mother's estate? He looked at the stack. No dust on it.

A layer of dust all over this basement, and none on the boxes?

Working swiftly, he opened the top box, which turned out to be full of old pots and pans. He restacked the boxes to get to the bottom one. Opened it. Wadded-up newspaper on top. He dug down.

Currency. In bundles.

Well, what do you know! He counted bundles. Over a hundred grand.

Time to go. Carmellini restacked the boxes, turned off the lights, and headed for the basement door. He looked through the pane, then eased the door open and checked left and right. The yard was empty, no one about. He checked the door lock to ensure it would latch behind him, then stepped outside and pulled the door shut. It locked.

A minute later he was walking down the street with his latex gloves in his pocket, the backpack dangling from one shoulder.

Mohammed Mohammed was having his troubles keeping his troops in line. After two years in America, Ali, Yousef, and Naguib liked certain aspects of American culture, such as pizza, video games, and television. Products of a closed, male-dominated society in which the traditional way of life was believed to be required by God, their first impression of America had been horror, then wonder.

The brazen display by women of their faces and figures—and bare arms, legs, and stomachs—had led to the immediate assumption that they were all sluts or prostitutes. A few regrettable incidents had clarified that error, but still, the singing, dancing, and role that women played in all aspects of public life shocked them profoundly. Magazines such as *Playboy* and *Penthouse* were horrifying . . . and titillating, something to be perused in secret.

Ali had acquired a taste for pornography that was catholic and insatiable. He liked all of it, and he liked it a lot. These days he made little secret of it. His job as a convenience store clerk allowed him to steal adult magazines, which he perused in the bathroom of the Smoot's Motel unit he shared with the others, with the door locked.

Mohammed braced him on it—no fool, he knew what was going on—and was told that since Ali was going to Paradise as a *jihad* martyr, why not sample a few forbidden pleasures before the day of glory?

Yousef's sin was more benign. He found music videos fascinating and watched them by the hour on MTV when he had the chance. Unfortunately they weren't available on the Smoot's television, which received only the local broadcast stations from an antenna atop the motel office, so he watched at work or in bars, video parlors, and bowling alleys, which he liked to patronize when he wasn't actually working. The sight of women crooning suggestive words and moving in sexy ways mesmerized him.

Naguib liked beer and women. He thought beer a heavenly drink. He had also managed to pick up a half dozen women in bars during the last two years; these adventures had been the high points of his life. He was fascinated by the fact that certain American women found him attractive. He attributed that extraordinary fact to his looks and his ability to say witty things in a delightful accent, even though Mohammed told him that having plenty of money in his pockets and buying drinks for any woman in sight might have something to do with it. He practiced oozing charm whenever there was a female within fifty yards. His bedroom triumphs, such as they were, had given him a fierce self-confidence that made him a poor military order-taker.

All of them, even Mohammed, liked video games. Driving games and shooting enemy space fighters for a quarter a pop kept all four amused for hours.

Still, Mohammed worried that the resolve of his troops was being subverted by the temptations of the devil's culture. He questioned them occasionally, tried to limit their participation in sinful pastimes, and fretted. "The authorities may be watching our every move," he told them. "We are engaged in a holy mission. It would be a sin to fail."

"We will succeed," Ali assured him, *"Inshallah."* If God wills it.

"He will not will it if we are incompetent and wicked," Mohammed snapped.

Obviously they didn't believe there was any danger. They *knew* no one was watching. They had lived in America for two years. No one watched, no one cared what they did. America was not Arabia.

Mohammed had a sinking feeling that this was an argument he could not win. The sooner the better, he thought. Before they ruin everything.

This evening he awoke to answer a call of nature and found that Naguib was missing. He wasn't in the bathroom either. It wasn't the first time. Mohammed dressed in the dark and closed the door to the unit behind him. He walked to the nearby beer joint and went in. Naguib was seated at the bar nursing a draft, talking animatedly to the woman beside him, a trashy sort in tight jeans and a short shirt that displayed her belly button. Frowning in disapproval, Mohammed saw as he approached that she had painted lips and short blond hair and an upthrust bosom that Naguib was openly admiring.

"Come," Mohammed said when he reached him.

Naguib gave him a guilty look and shoved the beer away with one hand.

"Come," Mohammed repeated in Arabic. "You aren't supposed to be here. You know that. Allah is watching."

"There is no harm," Naguib argued halfheartedly as he climbed down from the barstool. He pulled money from his pocket and left it on the bar for the drinks.

Mohammed laid a hand on Naguib's arm and led him away. He missed the wink the blond woman gave Naguib and the smile she got in return.

When the two Arabs had left the room, the blonde reached for her purse. She removed a notebook, glanced at her watch, and wrote something in it.

CHAPTER ELEVEN

When he awoke on Saturday morning, Tommy Carmellini padded into his kitchenette and fired off his coffeemaker. As he waited for the dark brown liquid to drip through, he rubbed his eyes and examined the new day out his kitchen window. Sunbeams were peeping through gaps in the clouds.

You gotta admit, having a box full of money in the basement must be a warm fuzzy for Arch Foster. So how did good ol' Arch come by a hundred grand in cash? A hundred and fifteen grand, to be precise. Maybe he saved his lunch money for the last 152 years.

Carmellini eyed the amount of coffee in the pot, then slipped the pot from the maker and held a cup in its place. Only spilled a few drops. When the cup was full, he reversed the process. He blew on the steaming brew, then sipped experimentally.

The real question was, What was he, Tommy Carmellini, going to do with the information he had acquired? If he reported the money in Foster's basement to the honchos at the agency, they would want to know how he knew it was there. Confessing to a felony didn't appeal to Carmellini, this morning or any other. What about an anonymous letter? In all likelihood someone would whisper about the letter to Foster or even question him about its allegations, so the money would be long gone when the cops or FBI arrived with a search warrant.

A pretty problem.

As he showered and got dressed this morning he thought about it. About going back and getting the cash. After all, sending postcards to the police wasn't going to accomplish anything. Arch had probably gotten the money doing something slimy. Why shouldn't Carmellini do something a wee bit nasty to keep that miserable peckerhead felon from enjoying the fruits of his ill-gotten gains? It wasn't like Foster inherited a box full of cold cash from his kindly, white-haired uncle who adored him. Or did he? Well, it would be easy enough to find out.

He paused at his dresser as he considered what he knew of Archie Foster and his buddy, Norv. He thoughtfully removed his pistol from the drawer and loaded it. Put it in his pocket. Just in case.

Those two bastards were listening on the bugs. He wondered what they were listening for?

Oh, well. Time to go get a bagel and a cup of real coffee. He cycled through the kitchen to turn off the coffeemaker, then left the apartment, locking the door behind him.

"He's coming down," Norv Lalouette told Arch. "The front door just closed." They were sitting in a van parked near the service entrance to Carmellini's apartment building.

Arch was in the driver's seat. He started the van, drove it over to where Carmellini's red Mercedes was parked. He turned off the engine. Watching in the rearview mirror, he spotted Carmellini coming out the main entrance of the apartment building. Arch had parked in such a way that Carmellini would probably walk right between the van and another vehicle to get to his car. Yes. He was walking their way.

"Here he comes. Get ready."

As Carmellini walked by the rear of the van Arch opened the door and pointed a pistol at him. "Freeze!"

Carmellini stopped in midstride, about four feet from Foster, who had dropped out of the driver's seat and now had the pistol leveled belt-high, with both hands on the butt.

"Hey, Foster, what's this—"

That was as far as Carmellini got, because Norv Lalouette had gone out the rear doors of the van, and now he whacked Carmellini in the head with a sap, a hose weighted with lead. The lights went out for Tommy Carmellini, and he collapsed.

"Quickly, now," Arch said, pocketing his pistol and scanning the parking lot to see if anyone was watching. Apparently not. "Get his legs. Let's get him in the van and get going."

Sixty seconds later, Foster jumped back into the driver's seat and started the engine. He pulled the shift lever into gear and fed gas.

In the back Lalouette used a plastic tie on Carmellini's wrists and ankles, then put a strip of duct tape over his mouth. Working quickly, he produced a syringe and bottle of liquid. The next time the van stopped at a traffic light, he drew some liquid into the syringe, then turned Carmellini's right arm so he could see the veins. Carmellini worked out, obviously. Lalouette picked a vein and jabbed in the syringe. Only after he had given the big man the injection did he take the time to search him. He passed Carmellini's pistol, wallet, and keys up to Arch.

When Tommy Carmellini awoke, the process was gradual, a gentle dawning of consciousness. He tried to move . . . and couldn't! He was lying on his back.

He could feel his legs and hands and arms, feel himself lying on something, but he couldn't make his arms and legs move. He couldn't focus his eyes. He was looking up, but he couldn't decide what he was seeing.

He tried to make a noise. Something on his mouth. He filled his lungs with air and tried to talk. He couldn't make a sound, not even a moan. He couldn't turn his head, couldn't move. He was totally helpless.

"Hey, he's awake."

Someone came into his field of view. He recognized the blurry face. Foster!

"How you doing, Tommy?"

He didn't try to speak.

"Sorry it had to be you, Carmellini. You shouldn't have broken into my house. My stuff was a little out of place—not much, but a little. I could tell someone had been in there pawing around, and you are the only burglar I know. And you weren't in your apartment when this little crime was being committed. Then this morning, you're packing heat—a rod in your pocket. Tsk, tsk, tsk. It's all circumstantial, I know, but Norv and I are the judge and jury and we've convicted you. Not going to take a chance on you, Tommy. Wish it could have been different, but you are too much of a nosy asshole.

"You *are* an asshole—do you realize that, Tommy? Probably don't give a shit, do you? Yeah, I know. Just lie there and don't say a word like the asshole you are.

" 'Course you couldn't say a word if you tried. We've given you an injection, Tommy, to make you easier to handle. We're going to kill you. Going to put you in an airplane with concrete around each foot and haul you fifty miles out over the Atlantic. Then we're going to shove you out. Maybe you'll get lucky. Maybe you'll get killed on impact with the water. Needless to say, you'll go down feetfirst. If the impact doesn't kill you, I doubt that you'll swim far with thirty pounds of concrete on each foot."

Arch Foster leaned over, placing his eyes inches from Carmellini's. "We'll have to wait for the concrete to set up. Takes at least twenty-four hours. Tomorrow night, Carmellini, we put you in the plane for your last ride." Foster chuckled. "Could kill you now, of course. You'd be sorta stiff tomorrow night, but not too bad. Yet killing you now would spoil the fun. You see that, don't you, Tommy? For thirty-six hours we get to savor the thought of that asshole Carmellini lying here paralyzed, unable to move, thinking about the fall. Oh, yeah, you'll be thinking about it, all right. You'll lie here thinking about how it will feel when you hit. Kersplat! It'll be like falling off a twenty-story building. Oh, yeah, you're going to think about *dying*."

Arch Foster chuckled. He walked away still chuckling.

Tommy Carmellini tried by sheer force of will to move one finger. Just one.

And failed.

Arch chattered with Norv Lalouette while they stirred water into premixed concrete. Tommy Carmellini could hear the water running from the hose into the buckets, the sounds of bags being ripped, the shovel clanging against the metal pails. He was completely unable to move. He couldn't even focus his eyes on the ceiling. He could hear okay, though.

"Too bad, Carmellini, that you couldn't see the advantages of working with us. You weren't man enough to just up and ask what the deal was. Naw, you had to break into my place and snoop. I always said you were the kind of guy who couldn't be trusted, didn't I, Norv?"

Norv grunted.

Arch returned, looked at Carmellini's face. He reached and ripped the tape from Carmellini's mouth. "You might drown in your own spit if I leave this on," he said, and laughed. "Hey, Norv, he can't even close his mouth." He addressed his next comment at the paralyzed man. "Drool all you want, big guy."

"I told you that was good stuff," Arch told Norv. "It's some sort of ketamine derivative. Never seen it work before, but I got it from a guy who used it in China a couple of years ago. Said the effect was awesome."

"Okay, I'm a believer. Go easy on the water in the concrete, man, or it'll never set up. Don't let it get soupy."

They worked with the shovel for a few seconds, then Arch said, "Yeah, that's enough water. Stir it up good. When it's ready we'll jam his feet in."

"Shoes on or off?"

"Off."

Tommy Carmellini could feel someone peeling off his shoes, but he had no control over his legs. Or his bladder. He could feel a spreading cold wetness.

"Hey, he just pissed himself."

"What did you expect?"

"Maybe we ought to shoot him. Won't stink up the place so much." That was Norv. He was a hell of a guy.

"Naw," Arch told him. "More fun this way." He chuckled.

They pulled Carmellini down the table and jammed a foot into each bucket. He felt the slimy cool wetness. The buckets were sitting on something below the table level, so Carmellini's knees were bent ninety degrees. He knew that, too, although for the life of him he couldn't move those legs.

"Whad'ya think? Should we give him another injection?" Norv asked that.

"The juice is good for forty-eight hours. Another shot would stop his heart and breathing."

Arch put his head over Carmellini's face, and grinned. "See you tomorrow night, asshole. I'm going to think about you all evening, lying here paralyzed, waiting to make the big splash tomorrow night. That's as old as you're going to get."

"That's enough, Arch. Let's lock up and get going."

"Okay."

"I still think we should shoot him now."

"Waste of a bullet," Arch replied. "And we'd be doing the bastard a favor. I don't like him that much. The fall will probably kill him, and if it doesn't, he'll drown. That's more his speed."

He stepped over to Carmellini and whispered in his ear, "Think about the fall."

The lights went off. A little daylight leaked through the joints in the tin siding, so the building didn't become truly dark. Carmellini heard a door close and the sound of a padlock clicking. A moment later he heard a vehicle start, then it drove away.

He listened for minutes. He was alone.

He tried to move his arms. No. Then his head. Close his mouth. Move a finger. Speak. All to no avail. He couldn't move a single muscle. He was totally and completely paralyzed.

He lay there on the table motionless for the longest time. He heard airplanes start and taxi, occasionally a plane went overhead. The motors sounded like piston engines. Once he thought he heard a jet, but it wasn't loud. Every now and then he heard car doors slamming far away, twice he heard voices. He concluded that he was at a general aviation airport, probably in a private hangar.

When his vision got extremely blurry he realized he was crying.

"Where's Tommy this morning, Zelda?" Jake Grafton asked, then winced. He kept forgetting that her new name was Sarah. Sarah Houston.

"I don't know, Admiral. We haven't seen him."

"Probably breaking into a bank or something," Zip Vance said grumpily. They were in front of the computer terminals in the SCIF, or technocenter, as Tarkington had labeled it, in the basement of a CIA building on the Langley campus.

"I suppose," Jake agreed. He produced a list from an inside pocket. "Here are three names. I want you to construct dossiers on these people, find out everything you can about them."

"Everything?"

"Everything. Money, telephone records, e-mail correspondents, Internet sites visited—whatever you can get. I'm looking for something—anything—that shouldn't be there. It's time to try out the system you've been constructing. These people knew that the Russians had given us an American traitor named Richard Doyle, who was spying for them. When they learned that he had been fingered, one of the three probably told someone they shouldn't have told, someone without access. It's probable that Doyle was killed by someone who had the time and money to dispose of the body so it couldn't be found."

"He's missing?"

"Vanished into thin air."

"Perhaps Doyle was spirited out of the country," Zelda mused.

"It's possible," Jake said, "but I doubt it. If he was in Russia we would have heard something, a hint over a telephone, a sighting, something. He's dropped completely out of sight. I'm betting he's dead."

"Lanham, Twilley, and Tran," Zip said, glancing at the list.

"We'll do our best, Admiral," Zelda said.

Jake left thinking about Janos Ilin, the tightrope walker. If the Russians killed Doyle or kidnapped him to keep him from talking, one had to assume they knew that Ilin sold him out. If that was the way it went down, Ilin was dead or in prison or soon would be. And Jake had no way to contact him. He felt helpless, as if he were living a nightmare in some dark, smoky room filled with mirrors that distorted every image and made it impossible to separate the real from the unreal.

An hour later Toad Tarkington bounced into Jake's office upstairs with Sonny Tran bobbing along in his wake. "Got 'er down front, boss. Let's take a ride, see what she'll do."

Jake grabbed his hat and followed the two men from the office.

"There she is," Toad said when they reached the parking lot. He gestured to an unmarked white van, a fairly new one by the look of it. Except for two small windows in the back doors, it had no windows behind the driver's and passenger's seats. "Sonny, you drive and the admiral and I will sit in back and play with stuff. Sir, the technician's name is Harley Bennett." He opened the door. Bennett was sitting at the control consol. Toad introduced the two men.

As Bennett explained the Corrigan detection unit, Sonny Tran got the van under way. He threaded it through the parking lot, which was only about half full on Saturday afternoon, stopped for the guard at the gate, then dropped down the ramp onto the southbound lane of the George Washington Parkway. Traffic into Washington was flowing well. Tran accelerated to sixty miles per hour and held the van there.

Harley Bennett chattered on as the van swung onto the George Washington, headed toward the heart of the city. "We hunt alpha particles, X rays, gamma rays, and free neutrons. Each has its own characteristics. These types of radiation generally do not propagate far, especially in the atmosphere, and therefore detection ranges are limited. We think our arrays of sensors, which are mainly banks of crystals, push the technology as far as practical."

"Crystals?"

"Yep. Remember all those crystals that NASA was trying to grow in space to advance pure scientific research? Crystals are used to detect radiation. In any event, Corrigan Engineering couldn't get really big crystals in sufficient quantity. We have ganged little ones together to achieve the same effect and invented some new ones. Other sensor improvements and digital signal processing enable us to determine the amount and specific type of nuclear material being detected, which we think pretty much solves the false alarm problem."

"False alarms?" Jake hadn't really considered that problem.

"The problem is that our society is full of radiation. Darn near every electromagnetic device is radiating on some frequency. We want a device that won't ring fire alarms when we drive by a dentist's office and he's X-raying teeth." Bennett was an enthusiastic talker and Jake Grafton was a good listener, so Bennett charged on, discussing the truckloads of radioactive waste that crisscrossed the nation's highways daily. Hospital waste, medical and industrial isotopes, even some types of concrete give off radionucleides.

"The innovation that makes the Corrigan detection system unique," Bennett confided, "is the patented active measures we devised—mainly e-ray sources and neutron generators—for interrogating the emitter and inducing it to increase its emissions rate."

"All that is in this thing?" Jake asked as he inspected the aluminum cabinet in the center of the van.

"It's in there," Harley Bennett said warmly, and patted the box.

Sonny drove to a hospital, which excited the Corrigan device. "Medical radiation," Bennett said after he actively queried the emitters. He showed Jake and Toad the instrument readings. "Occasional X rays, and some low-order medical isotopes."

"Naturally you've tested this thing on a real warhead?"

"Oh, yes, sir," Harley said, slightly offended. "The air force made one available to us last week."

"We also went by Three Mile Island on the way down here, Admiral," Toad said. "This thing lit up like a drunk on Saturday night."

They talked about the readings, what each meant.

"Let's drive south to the Beltway," Toad suggested. "Sit beside the road and see what goes by."

Jake nodded. Toad spoke to Sonny, who started the engine and got the vehicle under way. They ended up on the I-95/I-495 interchange. Sonny pulled over and turned on the emergency flashers.

He came back to join Bennett and the naval officers. The men sipped coffee and watched the gauges. "We got some hits with radioactive waste being transmitted while we were driving down from Boston," Toad said.

"We've got one detector and a whole city to protect," Jake said to Bennett. "How should we proceed?"

"I recommend that we make a map of the city, a grid, and take a sample in every sector, establishing a baseline. Then we keep going back over the sectors sampling radiation levels. I imagine we could do the whole city a couple times a week. When we get more detectors, we will get more proactive, visit the airports daily, for example."

"Do you think the goal of finding the weapons as they come in is unrealistic?"

"It is until we get more detectors. When we have enough, put one at every airport, establish corrals on all the major highways coming in to force the trucks to pass by. But since we can't build a wall around the city and limit traffic to a few gates, I don't see how you'll ever get away from sector searches."

"How about an airplane? Put one in a plane and have it fly over the city?"

"That would work, if we could fly low enough."

It wasn't long before a truck hauling medical isotopes went by. The device squealed an audible warning.

When the excitement died down, Jake said, "Sonny, let's get this thing rolling. I want to drive around the Capitol, then the White House and Lincoln Memorial and the Pentagon."

"You don't really think the bombs are already here, do you?" Toad asked.

"If our source was telling the truth? No, let's get busy establishing a baseline right now."

Sonny moved back into the driver's seat.

The van was proceeding north on I-295, past the old Naval Station Anacostia, when the detector began squealing again.

"That's strange," Bennett muttered. As the van rolled north, the emissions faded. "Must be some kind of radioactive waste around here."

"Here?" Jake said, and went forward so he could look out the windows. He could hear the audible tones sounding behind him. As the van rolled, the sounds faded.

Bennett scratched his head. "That was something, anyway."

"What?"

"I don't know, Admiral."

False positives! Jake cursed under his breath, then told Sonny to turn around. He got off at the next exit, crossed the overpass, and headed south.

The Corrigan detection unit came alive again. An hour later the van was sitting on the waterfront. Reagan National Airport was across the river.

"Something's triggering this damned thing!" an obviously frustrated Harley Bennett exclaimed. He had put out sensor cables, gotten the direction of the strongest reaction.

Jake and Toad got out of the van and consulted the map. "Could be something at Fort McNair," Toad said, pointing across the Anacostia River. "Or at Reagan National, or maybe over on that golf course at East Potomac Park."

"Let's do Fort McNair first," Jake said. Traffic was building, so it took a while to get there. At Greenleaf Point the machine was indicating the presence of a weapon.

"I don't believe it," Toad said. "There is no way in hell that terrorists have got a bomb here from Russia in five weeks."

"We haven't found the locus of the signals yet," Jake said. He pointed toward the golf course on Hains Point, across the Washington Channel that led to the Tidal Basin. "Roll it, Sonny."

The golf course security guard didn't want to let an unmarked van onto the grounds. While he called the course groundskeeper, Jake used his cell phone. Ten minutes later two squad cars and a car full of FBI agents arrived within a minute of each other. Opposition from the groundskeeper vanished. He unlocked the access gate and let the van and police cars through.

They ended up at the southern end of the island behind a seawall made of pilings. Harley Bennett unwound sensor cables and plugged them into sockets in the van, then flaked them out on the ground. After consulting his machine, he announced, "We're right on top of it, almost. Within a few feet." He and Jake joined the police officers, who were searching the grounds, looking under bushes and hedges.

There was a small building nearby. The goundskeeper unlocked it. The building was full of shovels, rakes, mattocks, tools, and spare parts to repair the course's watering system.

"This is all fill dirt, isn't it?" Jake asked the groundskeeper as he gestured at the area around them.

"Yessir, it sure is. About five, maybe six years ago, the city hauled in dirt and piled it on this mudflat. They built the wall around here to hold it all in and made that fairway over there longer. Moved that putting green. Moved some trees, too."

"Any digging around here lately?"

"Oh, no. Nothing like that."

"I seem to remember the construction five years ago. I was living at Fort McNair around then."

"The environmentals didn't make much noise about this mudflat, not like they would today."

"Five years," Toad muttered to Jake. "Something's wrong with that gadget."

"Let's go."

Bennett was embarrassed. "I can't explain it, Admiral. Unless maybe someone dumped a drum of Three-Mile Island waste into that fill."

"I want you to go over this gizmo with a fine-tooth comb, Harley, check every lead and sensor. Call Toad in the morning, check in with him."

Bennett nodded sadly and checked his watch.

"Sonny, take me back to the office." He thanked the law enforcement officers and groundskeeper for their time, and led the little procession back toward the clubhouse.

When he returned to the office, Jake Grafton found a telephone message waiting. He had received a call from Sal Molina, the president's aide. He was requested to attend a meeting at nine o'clock that night at the Executive Office Building adjacent to the White House.

Jake removed the card with Molina's telephone number from his wallet and dialed the telephone. "What's this meeting tonight about?" he asked.

"The heads of the FBI and CIA are hearing about your plans from their liaison officers. They want to argue about your decisions."

"I see."

Molina sighed. "The president asked the national security adviser, Butch Lanham, to referee. DeGarmo wants you canned. You're a lightweight, Emerick told the president, in over your head."

"And Emerick's such a nice fellow."

"Right."

"How about inviting the chairman of the Joint Chiefs to this soiree,

General Alt? Maybe even the guy I work for, Stuffy Stalnaker?" Stalnaker was the chief of naval operations.

"I'll talk to Butch, see what he thinks," Molina said. "Nine o'clock."

Lying on the table totally paralyzed, Tommy Carmellini's mind wandered freely. He thought of his parents, friends, places he had been, things he had done, stupid things he was ashamed of, things he regretted.

The night had come, and the building was totally dark. He heard some airplanes for the first few hours after the sunset, then silence.

Complete silence, broken only by the gentlest whisper of the breeze around the gaps in the metal siding of the hangar.

His mind resumed its aimless wanderings. Norv and Arch were going to kill him—of that he had no doubt. If they didn't kill him, he would kill them, and they knew that.

He certainly never thought it would end this way. Or this soon. He was still a young man, with a lot of great years left.

He was thinking about dying when he heard a plane coming. The noise grew louder and louder. It seemed to be taxiing up right outside the building. Then the pilot cut the fuel to the engines and they died. Engines—Carmellini was sure there were two.

He filled his lungs, tried to shout. And couldn't.

Tommy Carmellini tried to moan, to speak, to say a single word. He couldn't make his lips or tongue move. He couldn't swallow, couldn't move his head. . . .

The door of the hangar opposite the one he was in creaked as it was opened. Voices reached him, although he couldn't distinguish the words. A small gasoline engine started . . . probably a nose tug of some kind being used to move the plane.

After a while he heard the hangar door being closed.

This was his only chance! He had to make a noise now!

He filled his lungs, tried by sheer strength of will to move his cheeks and tongue to form a word.

And failed.

When he heard a car start and drive away, he stopped trying. He lay staring up into the darkness, concentrating. If he could move a finger . . .

CHAPTER TWELVE

The conference room in the bowels of the Executive Office Building was stuffy that Saturday night. Only half the lights were on and the air-conditioning was apparently off, no doubt as a result of some bureaucratic decree.

Jake Grafton arrived a few minutes early and discovered that he was the first arrival. Admiral Stuffy Stalnaker, the CNO, and General Alt, the chairman of the Joint Chiefs, arrived within seconds of each other, followed by Sal Molina and Emerick of the FBI. Molina was half-Hispanic, a lawyer from Texas who had been with the president for many years. He was short, balding, with a spare tire, and freely admitted that he wanted to run for the Senate someday. Jake remembered seeing op-ed pieces in the newspapers that opined that Molina was a real power in the White House owing to the high regard in which the president held him.

The CIA's Avery Edmond DeGarmo and General Newton Cahn, the army chief of staff, came in next. As people came in they engaged others in private conversations. Emerick and DeGarmo were huddled in a corner whispering inaudibly when the national security adviser, Butch Lanham, bustled in and surveyed the crowd as he dropped into a chair at the head of the table. Two of his aides, both women, sat in the corner to take notes.

Lanham was one of the new breed of managers in business and government who worked very hard at trendy athleticism. He didn't just play tennis and racquetball, lift weights and jog—he competed in triathlons and participated in strong-man competitions. How he managed to sandwich the sweat in around his work and family responsibilities was a minor mystery. Jake had seen Lanham on television a few times, but had never before met the man in the flesh. He didn't now. Lanham didn't speak or look at him. Without a word to anyone, he glanced at the women to ensure they were seated with pens poised over notebooks, and began.

"We're here to discuss Rear Admiral Grafton's decision to deploy the Corrigan radiation detectors only in Washington and New York City. Is our information accurate, Admiral?"

"Corrigan can only deliver one detector every two weeks," Jake said, and found that his voice sounded unnaturally harsh. He made a conscious effort to sound calm, unflustered, and normal. "We're hoping each has a five-mile detection range under average urban conditions, but we won't know until we play some more with the first one, which we just received. In my judgment, we are better off covering those two cities, which I would call the primary targets of terrorists, until we have enough of them to ensure complete coverage. Then we can start covering lower-priority targets."

"Who sets the priority?" DeGarmo muttered.

"Is that a question of Admiral Grafton, or an incisive comment?" Lanham retorted sharply.

"Question."

"Sir, I put New York and D.C. at the top of my list," Jake replied calmly. "Economically and politically, they're the most important cities in the world. I think we should keep adding detectors as they become available in those two cities until we reach some reasonable level of protection. Then we can focus on other cities, which I suggest be picked based on strategic criteria. The idea is prevent attacks. Preventing all attacks is an impossible goal—a realistic strategy is to prevent the ones that will hurt us the most."

"Mr. DeGarmo, your thoughts, please," Lanham said.

"I don't think New York and Washington are in much danger. After the terror strikes of September eleventh, I think it most likely that the terrorists will strike somewhere else, if they strike at all. The newspapers and television have aired the hell out of the troops with Geiger counters manning roadblocks and searching railroad yards. Any terrorist with a television has to know that we're looking for nukes."

"Keeping the fact that we're using Geiger counters a secret was impossible," Jake said mildly, without a trace of rancor. "Indeed, one of the things we're looking into is the possibility of building Trojan detectors and publicizing them. We could always substitute real detectors for the fakes as they become available."

"Hmm," said Lanham, and glanced at Emerick, the FBI man.

Emerick took his time before he spoke. "If there is an attack anywhere in the U.S., the decision to protect only those two cities with Corrigan detectors will undoubtedly be revealed by the press. If the attack hits one of those two cities despite our precautions, Grafton will look like an incompetent. If an attack hits elsewhere, the president looks incompetent."

"Jesus, you make it sound like we're damned if we do, damned if we don't," General Alt rumbled. "If it's heads they win, tails we lose, why'd we even bother coming over here tonight?"

Emerick eyed Alt without warmth. "I'm merely pointing out how the cookie will crumble. The public's perception of the government's competence is damned important, and you know it."

"I don't give a flying fuck what the public thinks," Alt shot back. "Our job is preventing terror attacks. That's Grafton's mandate, and by God, he's working hard at it."

Butch Lanham stirred around, making some noise and moving until he had everyone's attention. "Mr. Emerick's point is well taken. If the government allows itself to be perceived as protecting some citizens and abandoning others, it jeopardizes its mandate to rule."

"Deciding how and where to employ radiation detectors strikes me as a military decision," General Alt said. "Admiral Stalnaker?"

"Yes."

"General Cahn?"

"Of course it's a military decision. No commander has the luxury of protecting every inch of the home terrain. Risks must be weighed, assets counted, decisions made."

"And the thrust of that remark is . . ." Lanham asked, pretending to be obtuse.

Alt looked Lanham square in the eye. "The president has appointed Admiral Grafton to a military post. In the natural order of things he's going to have to make military decisions—all military commanders do. The discretion and authority to make those decisions go with the job. If it doesn't, the president needs to can him and make the decisions himself. Or appoint someone else and give him the authority. Hell, he could have appointed you, Butch, but he didn't."

Lanham didn't rise to the bait. "The characterization of Grafton's decision is not in question, Mr. Chairman. The question is simply this—was the decision Grafton made in the best interests of the United States? In other words, was his decision correct?"

"He made a judgment call," Alt shot back. "Whether we agree or disagree with his call—whether we would have made the same decision in his place—isn't the issue. The president appointed a military commander. That's a fact. There he sits." Alt jerked a thumb at Grafton, but he didn't take his eyes off Lanham. "You and DeGarmo and Emerick seem to want to second-guess him. Ask the president to fire Grafton and give you the job."

Butch Lanham tapped his forefinger on the table a time or two. "The president has never suggested in my presence that Grafton has complete and total discretion. If you gentlemen think the president lacks the authority to overrule a military decision—any military decision—you need to reassess."

"Oh, he's got the authority, all right," Alt said. "I just don't think he should use it here. I recommended Grafton for this job. Stuffy did, too. I stand by my recommendation. Grafton made a military decision for reasonable, justifiable reasons, and we need to back him up."

"We didn't delegate our responsibilities to Grafton, and neither did the president," DeGarmo said heatedly.

"The president gave the man the job. Are we going to let him do it or aren't we?"

"I'm not questioning his integrity or fucking military honor, just his decisions," DeGarmo shot back.

The three of them butted heads for several minutes, and finally fell silent.

Lanham sighed deeply, then scratched his head. Authority flowed from the president—the question, Jake thought, was how much authority the president had given Lanham? Then he found out.

Sal Molina spoke for the first time. "The president has confidence in Jake Grafton. He's appointed the best officer he could find, and he'll back him to the hilt." Molina stood up, picked up a notebook he had been doodling in, and tucked it in an inside coat pocket as he headed for the door.

The meeting broke up quickly. Jake spent a few minutes visiting with Alt, Stalnaker, and Cahn while the civilians left.

"You haven't won," Alt told him. "That isn't the way things work inside the Beltway. DeGarmo and Emerick fanged you for a reason—they are now on record as saying you screwed up. If indeed things don't work out, sooner or later the president will have to pay attention to them."

Jake knew Alt spoke the truth. "I'll continue to do the very best I know how, General. That's all I can promise."

"We know that," Stalnaker replied curtly. "Why do you think we backed you up? Don't mushroom us—keep us informed. No surprises, huh?"

"Yes, sir."

"I don't know who has the backbone at the White House. We know it isn't Lanham. Maybe it's the big banana, maybe it's Molina. Regardless, they may chicken out in the dawn's early light—guts aren't required in politics."

On the way out of the building, Jake informed Alt that the new Corrigan detector was malfunctioning. He explained the problem: "The thing is indicating there's a bomb under a golf course, a false positive. I wonder if the air force could fly a nuclear warhead into Andrews and let us calibrate the thing again."

"I'll take care of it."

The black stretch limo drove slowly around Dupont Circle. Precisely at midnight, one of the spectators at the chessboards walked away from his group and crossed the circle at a crosswalk. The next time the limo stopped at the light, the spectator climbed into the backseat.

"Good evening," Karl Luck said.

The new passenger glanced at the window between the passengers and chauffeur to be sure it was closed. "I thought Corrigan was coming tonight."

"He's at a reception."

"Must be nice."

"I wouldn't know," Luck said testily. He rode silently with his hands in his lap while the chauffeur worked the car around the Lincoln Memorial and then southward beside the river. The limo finally stopped in the parking lot for the Jefferson Memorial; the chauffeur came around to open the door for Luck. The man from Dupont Circle opened his own door and stepped out.

When they were standing by the reflecting pool, Luck asked, "How'd the thing work?"

"As advertised, except for one false positive. They didn't expect perfection. Grafton reported a successful test to the White House this afternoon. Even as we speak the president is presumably shaking Corrigan's hand and thanking him for saving Western civilization from the forces of evil."

Luck was a trim man in his fifties, with close-cropped iron gray hair and a square, chiseled jawline. He glanced speculatively at the other man, then asked, "Do they know where the weapons are?"

"Not yet. They are pinning their hopes on the detection gear."

"They had better start investigating the terrorists. Those clowns probably left a trail a blind man could follow."

"One wonders. Sophisticated systems detect sophisticated networks. Criminals who don't know what a telephone is are not going to incriminate themselves on one."

"Are they looking?"

"The elephant is stirring itself."

"Anything I should pass on?"

"Yes. Our approach to Tommy Carmellini didn't work out. Perhaps I should have undertaken it myself, but I didn't. The two men who tried it have struck out."

"Carmellini? I've forgotten—why did you want him?"

"He's in Grafton's inner circle, and I'm not."

"Are you neutralizing Carmellini?"

"Yes."

"What is your next move? How are you going to get inside?"

"I'm not going to try. Too dangerous, in my judgment. We'll have to make do with the information I can learn and not worry about what's going on behind the door."

"Anything else for Corrigan?"

"Not tonight."

They walked back to the limo and got in.

Thayer Michael Corrigan was having a wonderful evening. He and his wife had received an invitation from the first lady to attend a reception in the Hay-Adams Hotel ballroom to raise funds to refurnish the White House after the rebuild was completed with taxpayers dollars. The core of the executive mansion had been destroyed a year ago by a missile attack from USS *America* after it was hijacked. The Congress would have funded both the rebuilding and the refurnishing, but the president wanted private industry to contribute in a major way. Naturally he and the first lady were heading the fund-raising effort. Of course the nation's top industrialists were lining up at receptions such as this to make six- and seven-figure tax-deductible donations. And to talk to the politicians.

Tonight the president and first lady were flanked by senior congressional leadership as they shook hands and schmoozed about the issues of the day with the leaders of America's major corporations. Money was not mentioned. There were pledge cards on the little table by the door, but that was about it. Anyone curious about how the donated funds were going to be spent could note on the card that he or she would like a call from the foundation staff during business hours.

The folks who were "in," though, got a personal briefing from the first lady, who liked to discuss color schemes and furniture. While Lauren Corrigan hovered with three other women near the first lady, T.M. mixed and mingled with the movers and shakers.

The important thing at these functions, he thought, was to be seen as belonging. Say little, listen, be pleasant, and be accepted as "one of us." He circulated, he spoke to the right people, he greeted people he hadn't seen in a while, he introduced himself to people he didn't know, *all in a way subtly designed to welcome them to the group to which he belonged*. That was the art of it, which he had worked for years to acquire.

The commodity being bought and sold was not antique furniture, carpets, or wall treatments. Oh no. The commodity was access to power. Everyone in the room knew it, and everyone got a little tingle from the thought that he or she was standing dead center on the hub of the universe.

Thayer Michael Corrigan got more than a tingle—he ate it with a spoon. His whole life had been spent on a journey to this place. Standing here now sipping a very dry chardonnay, chatting with two senators and the chairman of one of the largest corporations on earth, he was pleasantly surprised when the president appeared at his elbow, squeezed it as he spoke to the group, and pulled him gently away for a private conversation.

"I've been hearing good things," the president said softly, so softly that Corrigan had to bend down slightly to hear. "But we need more of the latest radiation detectors, and we need them as soon as you can get them built."

"I'll do what I can, Mr. President."

"I wouldn't even mention it on a social occasion, but the matter is urgent. The need is great. This is our country we're talking about, T.M."

"I understand, sir."

"Knew you would." The president patted his arm twice, then moved on.

A waiter walked by with whiskey, so Thayer Michael helped himself. He sampled the amber liquid. Oh, my, yes! Tasted great, and warmed you all the way down. When T.M. finished the first glass, he stepped six feet to the nearest waiter with a tray and helped himself to another.

Yeaaaah, this is the place, the summit of Mount Olympus. From here you can see the little people digging and scratching for a living, see the stupidities and follies, see yesterday and tomorrow, watch the galaxies spin. Zeus on his mountaintop and God in his heaven never had it any better, and that's a goddamn fact!

How happy can one man be?

Tommy Carmellini could smell the shit. His bowels had moved, and he hadn't even known it. The sun was up and light was again leaking into the hangar where he lay. Not a sunbeam, just light.

His feet felt hot, painfully hot, but there was nothing he could do about it. The lime in the concrete must be burning his skin.

He worked hard at focusing his eyes. Could he see better?

He told himself he could, that his vision was coming back. If his visual acuity returned, the drug was wearing off. Soon he would be able to move. He would kill those two greasy sons of bitches, strangle them with his own hands. He would be waiting when they returned, snap their necks like twigs.

The anger ran through him like hot lava. Oh, what he would do to Arch Foster and Norv Lalouette. Just plain murder would be too easy for them. Oh, yes. He would strangle the life from them as he looked into their eyes.

Thinking of strangling, he tried to flex his fingers, make them move. That was the project, and he worked on it. Worked, worked, worked.

Of course, his fingers didn't move, the ceiling of the hangar was still slightly blurred, he couldn't even move his lips or close his mouth. But he had to. He had until tonight.

If he failed he would simply disappear, vanish like Richard Doyle . . . and God only knows how many others.

Jesus, his mom couldn't even collect his government life insurance for seven years. Wasn't that the time a missing person had to be gone before the government declared him dead? Funny he should think of that now. Pathetic, really. *Foster and Lalouette are even fucking over my mother, for Christ's sake!*

As he tried to bend his fingers, he listened to the airplane noises, the noises of cars and people going about the business of life. While he lay here dying.

Without food and water he was gradually getting weaker. If Foster and Lalouette gave him another injection when this one began to wear off, he would lie here paralyzed until he died of thirst. His heart would eventually stop when his blood got too thick.

But he didn't have that kind of time. They were coming back tonight to load him on a plane and take him somewhere—probably over the ocean—and dump him out. Concrete shoes. Foster was right—the impact with the water would probably kill him. The concrete would take his corpse to the bottom, where it would never be found.

He kept trying to flex his fingers and move his tongue. Futilely. The drug held him firmly in its death grip.

On Sunday morning Toad asked Jake, "How'd it go last night, Admiral?" Jake hadn't mentioned last night's summons, but naturally Toad knew.

"I still have a job."

"So what was the flap all about?"

Jake sketched it for Tarkington.

"People in your meetings are going back to the office and spilling their guts to DeGarmo and Emerick?"

"Of course. They work for them."

"They work for you now. Can the bastards and let's get other people."

"Who will do the same thing," Jake muttered. "Let me tell you about life, Toad. You can function just as long as your superiors have faith and confidence in you. When they lose it—your fault, other people's fault, whatever—then you have to leave and make room for the next guy. Your time at the plate is over."

"You're right," Toad admitted. "Marriage is the same way, I guess."

"I suppose."

"These guys who carried tales—you still have confidence in them?"

"They did what I thought they would do. Nothing more."

"You realize, I suppose," Toad said thoughtfully, "that if there is a nuclear explosion in America, low-order, high-order, whatever, you are going to get crucified."

"I figured that out while the president was explaining the job, Toad."

"Admiral, excuse me for asking, but why in hell did you take it?"

"Somebody has to do it."

"You really think Lanham or DeGarmo or Emerick wants to sit on the hot seat?"

"They want me to do it their way so if things work out they get the credit. Yet if things go to hell, they don't want to get splattered. They're bureaucrats, still playing the goddamn game."

After a moment, Jake asked, "What did Bennett find out last night?"

"He spent the night in the van, Admiral. Said he can't find a thing wrong with that gadget."

Jake explained his request to Alt last night for a nuclear weapon with which to calibrate the Corrigan unit. "Follow up, will you, Toad? Call his E.A. If there's anything wrong with the Corrigan unit, we've got to get it fixed. And if the design is bad, I want to know ASAP."

That would be a hell of a disaster, Toad thought. He kept his thought to himself, however. "Aye aye, sir," he told his boss, and went to his office to use his encrypted telephone.

The telephone rang on Sunday as Callie was cleaning away the lunch dishes.

"Hello."

"Mrs. Grafton, this is the security guard in the lobby. You have a visitor. She said her name is Anna Modin."

Callie searched her memory. Modin?

"She said a mutual friend sent her, a Mr. Janos Ilin."

It took Callie several seconds to process it. Then she made her decision. "Send her up."

Callie replaced the instrument in its cradle. She was home alone. Jake was at Langley, naturally, and Amy was having lunch somewhere with friends.

When the doorbell rang, Callie opened it. The woman standing there was perhaps thirty, with long black hair. She was wearing a dress that hung well below her knees and sturdy shoes with modest heels. A large purse hung from her shoulder. She had no luggage. Her stockings were torn in several places, her hands were scraped, and she had a large bruise on one arm.

"Mrs. Grafton, my name is Anna Modin. Your friend Janos Ilin sent me to see your husband." Callie Grafton, linguist, recognized the Russian accent instantly, although it was subdued.

"Please come in," Callie replied in Russian.

Modin smiled. "He said you speak Russian."

"A very little," Callie said as she closed the door behind Modin. "Tell me, please, if Mr. Ilin is Russian, why is his first name Hungarian?"

Modin turned to face her. "His mother was Hungarian," she said simply, meeting Callie's eyes.

Callie nodded. That was what Ilin had told her last year when she met him. "Do you live in the Washington area?"

"No. I just arrived at Dulles Airport and gave the taxi driver this address."

"Oh, my! Are you hungry, thirsty?"

"I slept a little on the plane, but I'm tired and filthy. Something to drink would be nice."

"Come into the kitchen." As she led the way she said, "My husband is not here right now."

"Ilin asked me to talk to him as soon as possible."

Callie poured Anna Modin a soft drink over ice and offered it to her. Then she went to the bedroom to call her husband.

When he answered, she said, "Jake, there is a woman here who says that Janos Ilin sent her. She just flew into Dulles and wants to talk to you as soon as possible."

"Hmm," Grafton said.

"Did you know she was coming?"

"No."

"So what should I tell her?"

"Make her comfortable and I'll be home in about an hour."

Although Anna Modin spoke with a detectable accent, her command of English seemed to be excellent.

"Is this your first visit to America?" Callie asked.

"No. I made trips for business to New York several times when I was working for a bank in Switzerland."

"Do you work for Ilin?"

"He is a friend," she said, which Callie thought evasive.

Callie pressed: "Are you in Russian intelligence?"

"No," the Russian woman said positively, and added, "Janos Ilin is a friend."

Callie pursed her lips thoughtfully. The truth of that statement was an issue for Jake and the intelligence professionals to decide. "Tell me about yourself," Callie said, changing the subject. "Where were you born, where did you go to school?"

When Jake came home he joined the women in the living room. They were nursing soft drinks.

"Janos Ilin asked me to give you this," she said, and handed the admiral the CD that Ilin had given her.

"What is on it?"

"Accounting records from Walney's Bank in Cairo." She removed a second CD from her purse and flicked it with a fingernail. "Perhaps it would be better if I started at the beginning."

"Please do," Jake prompted, and laid the CD she had handed him on the coffee table.

Anna Modin talked for almost an hour. She told how Ilin recruited her years ago, working in Swiss banks, the move to Cairo, Ilin's message about the bombs, Abdul Abn Saad, Nooreem Habib, the killer in the park—she told all of it, including Ilin's message about the bombs. "They were aboard a Greek freighter, *Olympic Voyager,* which departed Karachi sixteen days ago."

Jake's horror showed in his face. "Sixteen days? You tell me now?"

"When Ilin learned of it, he told me to deliver the message to you. I came as quickly as I could."

Jake Grafton couldn't sit still. He rose and went to the window and looked out. Sixteen days! Well, there was no more time to waste. He turned from the window and went back to the coffee table. He picked up the CD she had given him. Anna handed him the second CD.

"This is the one Nooreem Habib lost her life to get?"

"Yes. She said it contained the names of people who gave money to the terrorists, including dates and amounts."

Jake put both compact disks in his pocket. "I would like to talk with you later this afternoon. Will you stay for dinner?"

"If you wish. But first, I have a question."

"Okay."

"Who *are* you? Ilin gave me your name and address, but he never said what you did, who you serve."

"I'm just a guy working for his country, just like every soldier, sailor, policeman, fireman, and civil servant you ever met."

"Just a guy," Anna Modin echoed.

"I'll see that she gets some rest," Callie told her husband, who kissed her on his way out the door.

Sixteen days, Jake thought. A ship that sailed at ten knots—most of them went faster—would cover 240 nautical miles every day. Sixteen days, 3,840 miles. At fifteen knots, 5,760. Twenty, 7,680 miles.

"Tell me about your friend who was killed, Nooreem Habib," Callie prompted.

"She was not a friend. Like me, she was a friend of Janos Ilin, and she made the CDs. Abdul Abn Saad would have found her eventually." Anna was losing her composure. She rubbed her eyes. "Do you have vodka or whiskey?"

Callie inventoried the liquor shelf in the kitchen, then poured Modin a bourbon on the rocks. She accepted it gratefully, sipped it in silence.

She was calmer when she asked for another. As she sipped the second, Callie said, "It sounds as if being a friend of Janos Ilin is dangerous."

Modin thought about that comment, then said, "He said Jake Grafton was his friend."

Callie didn't know what to say to that. She decided that she needed a drink, too. When she returned from the kitchen, she tried to change the subject. "So this is your first trip to Washington?"

"Yes." Modin nodded and blinked, almost as if she were clearing her thoughts.

"You must be exhausted. How about a nap and a bath?"

"I have no other clothes. My bag was in the taxi by the cemetery, and the taxi driver sped away, I think." She rubbed her eyes, then put the empty liquor glass on the table before her. "I thank you for your hospitality. I do not wish to be a burden. I have money. I have delivered my message. After your husband and I talk, I will go to a hotel."

"While we wait I would suggest a hot bath and a nap while I wash your clothes," Callie said. She showed the other woman the towels and soap, then closed the bedroom door to give her some privacy.

The weapons, Callie knew, were the warheads Jake was worried about.

Sixteen days. . . . After she put Modin's clothes in the washer, she went out on the balcony of the apartment and automatically checked the potted violets. She stood in the sun with her arms crossed, facing the city, but her mind was on other things.

Jake Grafton spent four hours Sunday afternoon in the Pentagon talking to people in federal agencies who, like him, were too busy to take the day off. It was the Coast Guard officer, Captain Joe Zogby, who produced the first hard information. "*Olympic Voyager* is a Greek ship. The company that owns it is headquartered in Athens. They tell us that the ship left Karachi sixteen days ago, should have completed her transit of the Suez Canal last week, and is now en route to Marseilles. Estimated time of arrival is Wednesday evening local time."

"Find out if we have a battle group in the Med," Jake said to Toad. "Send an op immediate message, have them find that ship. Ask for a photo overflight, then have them stay on that ship day and night until it's searched."

Toad shot out of the office.

"It's night in Athens," Captain Zogby continued. "State says they will have someone from the embassy visit the owners' office and get a complete crew list and manifest."

"Let's have State request that the French authorities intercept the ship and search it," Jake said. "Maybe we can get them to hold her in quarantine until we can get someone over there with sensitive Geiger counters."

"I've already talked to State, sir," said Captain Zogby. "They're working on it."

"Very good."

"There's more. As she was crossing the Indian Ocean *Olympic Voyager* reported that she lost four containers over the side."

"Reported to the owners?"

"Yes, sir. And the owners reported the loss to their insurance company, Lloyds, which reported it to the Global Marine Distress Safety System. Coast Guard headquarters printed out a portion of the daily listing for me." From his attaché case he produced a dozen pages of computer printout, which he passed to the admiral. The entry of interest was circled in red ink.

Jake looked up from the list. "Do losses like this happen often?"

"It's been estimated that as many as ten thousand containers a year are lost in transit. On the other hand, over a hundred million containers are delivered annually across oceans. Container ships often stack those things six high. A stack that large can weigh eighty tons. Normally only the outboard stacks on both sides of the weather deck are secured with fasteners, which are steel turnbuckles. In a heavy sea the bottom containers can be crushed as the ship rolls, creating slack in the system that causes the fasteners to fail. Sometimes the fasteners weren't properly secured when the ship was loaded. Sometimes the fasteners just fail catastrophically. If the outboard stack goes over the side, occasionally the inboard stacks go, too."

"Why does the Coast Guard get a report?"

"We meet and inspect any ship that arrives in an American port that reported a cargo loss while in transit. We inspect the remaining containers, condemn those that are damaged. Most other countries don't do that, though. The worst of it is, lost containers don't always sink. Occasionally they float around on or just below the surface like little steel icebergs, going wherever the wind and current take them. NIMA"—the National Imagery and Mapping Agency—"tries to track floating containers with satellite data. It's hit-or-miss."

"Does Egypt search ships that report losses?"

"I don't know, sir. I doubt it. The insurance and shipping companies regard the losses as the normal cost of doing business."

An hour later Jake had NIMA searching the databases to see if the analysts could spot the *Voyager*'s lost containers. Since the loss report contained the date, time, and position of the loss, his task was not as hopeless as one might imagine.

He also got on the telephone to Coast Guard headquarters. That evening Coast Guard officers equipped with Geiger counters were on commercial flights to Athens, Marseilles, and Cairo to search the docks for radiation.

He felt hopeful. Finally, they had hard information to work with. The leads might turn up nothing, but the inaction was killing him.

T. M. Corrigan's man in Cairo was an Egyptian who called himself Omar Caliph. He was as loyal and trustworthy a man as money could buy. Honest he was not, but then Corrigan didn't care about that—he wasn't honest either. Omar had worked for Corrigan on numerous projects in the past and had done highly satisfactory work, so he had been picked for this job and promised a mint, so much money that Omar knew he could—and probably of necessity should—retire when this gig ended. He fully intended to do so and had already made a deposit on a house in Argentina.

Omar Caliph lived in a new high-rise apartment building in a wealthy district in Cairo. From his windows on the tenth floor one could look across the sprawling slums of Cairo and the Nile and see, on a good day, the pyramids. He paid the equivalent of $2,000 American in rent and thought he had a bargain. The problem in Egypt—

and most of the Third World—was that there were a great number of very poor people, a few enormously wealthy ones, and very few people in the middle. This absence of a middle class was nearly universal throughout the Arab world except for those few small countries that had spread the oil money around in the hope of buying social peace for the rich. Omar had been born and raised in the slums of Cairo; the journey to the tenth floor had taken him a lifetime.

This evening he was standing at the window thinking about Argentina when he heard the doorbell ring. He glanced at his watch. He was expecting no one, and the security guards in the lobby had not called. It was probably his wife—she was shopping and may have forgotten her key. He went to the door and opened it. Two men stood there with drawn pistols. Omar stared at the guns. It was several seconds before he realized that Abdul Abn Saad was standing behind the gunmen looking at him.

Before Omar could react, the gunmen pushed the door completely open and forced their way in, pushing him back toward the center of the room. Abdul Abn Saad entered behind them and closed the door. He also shot the bolt.

One of the gunmen pushed Omar into a chair while the other man went off through the apartment. Nothing was said for almost a minute, until the man returned. He spoke to Saad. "No one else is here."

Saad took a seat opposite Omar Caliph.

"Did the thought ever occur to you," Saad said, "that you might know too much?"

The color drained from Omar's face. "What?"

"You are a man of the world who has had experience in extralegal matters," Abdul Abn Saad continued smoothly, "so I wondered if it occurred to you that if we didn't kill you, Corrigan probably would? After all, you are the only link between us."

Omar Caliph realized that he was in deep and serious trouble, the worst of his life. "Mr. Saad, I have never whispered a word of our relationship to any living soul. Why in the name of Allah would I? Doing so would be equivalent to signing my own death warrant. We both know that."

Saad stood and walked slowly around the room, fingering the objets d'art, letting the tension build. It was then that Omar realized that Saad was wearing gloves. So was the other gunman whom he could see.

"Someone betrayed us," Saad said slowly. "Bank records were copied and the copies stolen. Why now? I asked myself. Why not six months ago, or last year? Why now? And the answer I came up with is that someone is probably investigating the money trail between America and the Sword of Islam. Someone knows too much. You are not the only possible source for this knowledge, but you are the most probable one."

Omar Caliph tried to speak but couldn't. His eyes were fixed on Saad, who finally turned to face him. "You were the go-between. Now you are the only man alive who can personally testify about the people at both ends of the transaction."

"Abdul Abn Saad, I swear on the beard of the prophet—"

"Someone betrayed us. Was it you?"

Omar tried to sort it out. "I swear on the beard—"

"The attack on our computer records is a serious matter. Lives are endangered—the very movement is endangered. I must identify the traitor. Was it you? Corrigan? Or someone who works for him?"

"It wasn't me," Omar blurted. "I swear on the grave of my father. It must be Corrigan! I never trusted the man."

"It was not Corrigan," Abdul Abn Saad said flatly. "He would have no conceivable use for copies of records. He might wish to destroy the records themselves, but no such attempt was made. This was an operation by an intelligence agency. The question is which one. And where was the leak?"

"In the name of Allah, have mercy on me. If I had betrayed you or knew anything about it, do you really believe I would still be here? In my own apartment? Awaiting your revenge? You know it isn't so! I am not a fool! I have done only what I was hired to do—negotiate with you, transfer the money, and arrange for a ship. Nothing less and nothing more."

Abdul Abn Saad stood in front of Omar Caliph and stared into his eyes. Finally, he sighed. "I believe you," he said flatly. "You have appealed to Allah for mercy, so you shall have it." He glanced at the man standing behind Omar's chair and nodded a quarter of an inch.

The gunman struck Omar on the head with the butt of his pistol. He collapsed in his chair.

"Put him out the window," said Abdul Abn Saad, then turned and walked from the room. Standing in the hallway outside the apartment he tried the door, ensured that it had locked behind him. As he walked down the hall he removed his gloves and pocketed them.

He was out of the building crossing the sidewalk when he saw people on the street pointing upward and heard them saying, "It was a man, apparently a suicide. . . . He fell from up there. . . . Landed on the roof of the foyer." The foyer protruded from the building.

Abdul Abn Saad didn't bother to look. His chauffeur was holding the door to the limousine open, so Saad took his seat and waited for the chauffeur to resume his. Then the limo rolled away into the crowded streets.

CHAPTER THIRTEEN

The hangar had been dark for several hours when Tommy Carmellini heard the car drive up. Heard the engine stop, heard the doors slam.

Heard the key in the padlock on the door.

Heard the door open.

A light came on.

"He's still here."

"Did you think he wouldn't be?"

Arch's face loomed above him. "Still paralyzed, all right. Slack facial muscles, drooling up a storm, can't focus his eyes. Hey, asshole, look at me. Look at me!"

Carmellini couldn't, of course.

Arch slapped him three or four times, stinging slaps that made his ears ring. Then he laughed.

"Tough shit, Carmellini. Hope you've had a hell of a bad day lying here getting ready to die. I went to a ball game. You'll be delighted to hear the Wizards won. Drank beer, ate good food, even got laid last night. How about that? And tomorrow I'm going to keep on living. Go to work, eat, drink, get laid, enjoy life. And you'll be dead!"

Arch tired of taunting him, finally, and checked the hardness of the concrete. Tommy could feel Arch lift his leg. He felt the weight of the concrete in the bucket, too, pulling on his muscles and tendons.

Arch dropped his leg roughly and the bucket banged.

"You're ready to die, Carmellini. And we're going to do it to you. Hope you enjoy the ride."

Foster left him then.

Carmellini heard them opening the doors of an airplane, snapping latches, preflighting it, probably. Time passed—it was difficult to judge how much. They talked about the fuel and oil, even checked the air in the tires. Meanwhile he strained every muscle, trying to move something, anything. He tried so hard he felt his eyes leaking tears.

They came for him finally. Arch took his head and Norv took his feet, each of which had several gallons of concrete attached. With the concrete and his weight, it was all they could do to wrestle him off the table. They dragged him across the hangar floor toward the open cargo door in the right side of the airplane. The concrete was like sandpaper on his skin, ripping off hide. He could feel the pain, but he couldn't even groan.

The two of them somehow wrestled him up and through the opening in the side of the plane. The plane seemed to be a single-engine. He got a glimpse of the fixed gear. It was probably a Cessna 206, he thought, like those he had seen hauling skydivers. He was thrown on a bare aluminum floor. Norv got in and arranged the buckets that held his feet near the aft bulkhead. Then he used bungee cords to secure Carmellini in place, so he wouldn't inadvertently fall out the gaping hole in the fuselage, which had no door.

They left him there while they opened the hangar bay and pulled the plane out onto the taxiway with some kind of nose-tow tug.

He heard them climb into the front seats and the engine start. After a minute or so garbled voices came over the loudspeaker as the plane began taxiing.

Carmellini found himself focusing on a rivet in the floor. It was eight inches or so from his face, but he could see it clearly. He forced his eyes to move.

As the engine roared and the plane began its takeoff roll, he found that he could clearly see the cargo door in the subdued light from the instrument panel. It wasn't much light, but it was enough. He could see! He could move and focus his eyes!

His hands were still tied in front of him. The tie wasn't tight; the blood was still flowing to his fingers. He forced his eyes down so that he could see his hands. He could barely make them out in the gloom. He flexed his fingers. And they moved. Perceptibly. *He could see and feel them move.*

Jake looked exhausted when he got home at eleven on Sunday evening. Callie met him at the door.

"Any luck?"

"We're working the problem, as they say. The next guy who tells me that, I'm going to reach through the phone and punch him out. Have you eaten?"

"We ate when Amy got home. I saved you some."

"What do you think of Anna Modin?"

"I thought she was telling the truth this afternoon. I don't think she's an intelligence professional. She says she's a friend of Ilin's. Says you are, too. I guess I buy that. On the other hand, she may be lying. The world seems to be full of good liars these days."

Jake ran his fingers through his hair. "Okay," he said.

"According to her, Ilin said to tell you that the Egyptians might make an attempt on her life."

That stopped Jake. He sat heavily on the nearest chair. "Has she made any telephone calls while she was here?"

"No."

He shook his head. "I certainly can't protect her from murderous fanatics. The FBI wants to talk to her anyway. Maybe she can file for some kind of asylum—I don't know. She's going to have to talk to the FBI—anything she can tell us that explains those CDs would be a help."

"When will the FBI have the disks analyzed?"

"Not for a couple days anyway. They'll want to see what's on them before they talk to her." He didn't mention that he had Zelda make copies before he passed them to the FBI.

"Perhaps Anna could stay with us until then. I want to get to know her better, and she would really like to see Washington."

Jake glanced at his watch. "You mean here in the apartment, or at a hotel?"

"I thought we could do the tourist thing and then she could sleep in Amy's room. Amy can sleep on the couch. Tomorrow we're going shopping together, get her some clothes. She needs clothes from the skin out."

Jake took a deep breath, then exhaled. "Let me eat something, then let's go for a ride. I need to see it again, too."

Modin wasn't sleepy. She was still changing time zones, and the nap earlier had refreshed her. Tonight she was wearing an exercise outfit of Callie's that seemed to fit fairly well. She and Amy sat at the table while Jake ate. They talked of Washington.

"The city isn't old, like European cities," Amy explained. "In 1791 our first president, George Washington, commissioned a Frenchman, Pierre L'Enfant, to design a capital city for this site." Callie broke out a map, and she and Amy showed Anna the design of the city.

After Jake got the dishwasher going, he drove the three women through the city. They crossed the Potomac and, after a few false turns, parked in the parking lot for the Jefferson Memorial, which was undergoing a major renovation. They walked around the construction barriers and were soon inside, looking at the statue of Jefferson and reading the inscriptions on the lintels.

Back in the car they drove the major avenues. They passed the National Air and Space Museum, slowly circled the Capitol, drove along Constitution Avenue past more museums, then parked and walked to the front of the White House. From there they drove back to Constitution Avenue and went west, toward the river. Jake parked again by a large statue of Albert Einstein; from there they walked to the Vietnam Memorial, the wall.

Amy led the way up the steps of the Lincoln Memorial. "This is my favorite place in Washington," she confided to Anna Modin as they stood before the seated figure of President Lincoln.

When the women came back outside, they found Jake sitting on the steps, looking up the Mall at the spotlighted white obelisk of the Washington Monument against the black sky. Callie sat down beside him and reached for his hand while Amy pointed out various buildings and monuments to their Russian visitor.

"I know you're tired. Thanks for giving us the tour tonight."

"I needed to see it all again myself," he said.

"These nuclear threats, to murder millions or destroy civilization—" Callie mused. "In his column in today's paper Jack Yocke said that even if the terrorists never set off a bomb, they are destroying our innocence."

"They are pouring acid on the trust that holds civilization together," Jake agreed. "The people doing it know what they are doing. They don't want civilization, not as it currently exists. They want the traditional village life. They ignore the fact that the traditional Arab/Muslim lifestyle cannot support all these people living here on earth. Ignore it or don't care."

After a while they stood, dusted off their fannies, and went down the steps to join Amy and Anna Modin.

As they went back to the car Jake walked beside Anna Modin.

He slowed his pace and Amy and Callie walked on ahead. "Tell me again about Nooreem Habib and the men who killed her."

Anna went through it again as they walked. Jake had parked the car across Constitution Avenue on a side of the street near the statue of Albert Einstein. Traffic was light, so Amy and Callie dashed across the avenue. Jake paused on the curb as Anna talked. She covered it all, including Freddy Bailey and the American tourist visa.

As Jake listened he watched her face, listened to the tone of her voice, noted the pauses and hesitations as she searched for the right English words. She told it slightly differently than she had the first time, and that seemed right. He decided she was telling the truth.

"They may try to find you here," he said.

"Yes," she said simply. "Ilin said they probably would."

"Does that worry you?"

"Of course. I do not want to die."

The traffic light changed, and they crossed the avenue. Callie and Amy were already in the car. Jake led the way to the Einstein statue and sat down on a wrought-iron bench. Anna took a seat beside him.

"I want you to talk to the FBI," he said. "They will have many questions, about the CDs, about Saad and his bank, about how he finances terrorism. . . ."

"I will answer those questions," Anna said simply.

"They will also have questions about Ilin, about the SVR, what you do for them."

"I work for Ilin, not the SVR."

Jake's skepticism showed on his face.

"I will not answer those questions."

"You have discussed them with me."

"Ilin trusts you. He does not trust the FBI or the American government. The SVR has penetrated your government. They have spies everywhere. Ilin must be protected."

"But you talked to me," he pointed out. "I am not Superman. I must tell my superiors what I know so that we can protect ourselves and utilize the information you have given us."

"I trust Ilin, and he trusts you," she replied, refusing to yield. "What you do and say is your business, but I will not say words to anyone who might betray Janos Ilin. He has many enemies. I know the identities of some of them, but not all."

"How do you know he's on the side of the angels?"

"He is a good man, trying to do right. That I know to be true."

"How do you know?"

She made a gesture of frustration. "I know!"

Jake pressed. "The risk is that you are wrong. The KGB and SVR have cruelly used people for almost a century. Don't tell me that you haven't thought about it."

"I have," she acknowledged. "Some people believe in God. They cannot prove He exists, yet they have faith and believe. I believe in Ilin. I can prove nothing. Yet I believe." She thought about it a moment longer. "Perhaps some people need something in this world that makes life worth living. Perhaps I am one of them. I believe on this planet there is at least one good man. Janos Ilin is his name."

In the car Amy and Callie sat watching Jake and Anna. They couldn't hear the conversation, but they could see Anna shaking her head obstinately.

"Who is she, really?" Amy asked.

"I only know what she told me," Callie murmured.

"What's this all about?"

"We're in a war, Amy, and your father is fighting it."

Jake had just gotten home when an officer from NIMA called him. "Admiral, we came up dry. We just didn't have a satellite in that area at the time of the container losses. A day later a satellite made a pass, but when we review the data, we don't find anything that might be a container."

"It was a long shot, I know," Jake replied. "I figured the storm would obscure the ocean."

"Oh, there was no storm. We just didn't have a satellite in that area."

"No storm."

"No, sir. Considering the season, the last two weeks were pretty quiet in the Indian Ocean."

The engine noise of the Cessna drowned out all other sounds for Tommy Carmellini. The plane seemed to bounce occasionally, move gently in the night air.

As the plane burrowed through the night he worked his fingers, tried to flex his legs, forced a shoulder to move. The wind coming through the open doorway was cool and welcome. It swirled around his face and dried the perspiration.

He was afraid to do much more. He was still alive only because Arch Foster was a sadist. If one of those guys glanced back and saw him moving, they would shoot him without a qualm.

He swallowed. For the first time in thirty-some odd hours, he swallowed. Worked the muscles in his face. Forced his tongue across his teeth.

The plane flew on and on. Tommy Carmellini lay still as death. His moment would come—he could feel the strength flowing back into his muscles. He forced himself to relax, to not tense up.

The waiting was the most difficult thing he had ever done. Every minute passed glacially.

He was so focused on killing these men that he never thought of afterward. Not for a second.

Waiting . . . listening . . . trying to stay relaxed.

He was lying in a heap, still waiting, when an overhead interior light came on.

Norv put a leg over the back of the copilot's seat. He kicked at Carmellini, then found room for his foot. Now he stepped completely over the front seat. Squatting, he grabbed Carmellini by the jaw, turned his head so he could see his face.

Using iron self-control, Carmellini kept his eyes unfocused, his face slack.

Norv unfastened the bungee cords that held Carmellini and his concrete buckets secured in place, took them off one by one. He slid one of the buckets toward the door, then reached for the other. When the buckets went out, Carmellini would follow.

As Norv pulled and shoved, Tommy Carmellini flexed his right leg, lifted the concrete bucket off the floor, and kicked Norv with it.

Lalouette grabbed for the doorpost, tried to save himself. Carmellini got a glimpse of his face, saw the shocked expression, then the slipstream took him and he was gone.

Tommy Carmellini pulled his legs under him, used his arms and hands to lever himself upward.

The airplane danced. Carmellini could see the whites of Arch's eyes as he looked wildly at the apparition coming to life. Arch tried to fly and pull a pistol from a holster behind his belt. His shoulder and lap harness kept him pinned to the seat. Carmellini saw the fear in Arch's face—and it made him glad!

Carmellini ripped off Foster's headset, pulled it over the seat back. Then he reached for Arch's neck so he could strangle him. Foster's writhing prevented Carmellini from getting his hands around his neck, so he grabbed his head.

Foster banked the plane to the right, toward the open door. Whether it was a conscious move on his part or just a happy accident, the effect was the same—the concrete buckets on Carmellini's feet—and Carmellini—slid toward the yawning blackness.

Unwilling to release his grip on Arch's head, Carmellini used all the strength in his upper body to resist the pull of gravity and get his feet under him. Arch was moaning, a primal howl that mixed with the fierce growl that came up Carmellini's throat.

Arch released the controls and used both hands to fight the vise that was squeezing his head. When he did the plane righted itself, and Tommy Carmellini adjusted his grip. Even with his wrists tied together, his fingers were like steel bands digging into Arch's head.

His left hand was behind Foster's head, his right over his eyes.

Carmellini dug two fingers into Arch Foster's right eye.

Arch filled his lungs and screamed, a demonic scream of pure terror. Using both hands, he fought to pull Carmellini's hands away. His writhing banged his knees against the yoke; the plane bucked viciously.

After all those years of rock climbing, Carmellini's fingers were like steel rods. He forced his fingers deeper into Foster's eye. The eyeball popped out, dangled on his cheek, held there by the optic nerve.

Arch Foster screamed insanely as the airplane stalled and fell off on one wing.

The human eye socket is constructed of bone. With a grip like a steel vise, Tommy Carmellini jammed his fingers into the back of Arch's right eye socket and squeezed with all his strength.

He felt the bone give. His fingers sank into Arch Foster's brain. He jammed his fingers in as far as they would go.

Foster's screams ceased abruptly, and he went limp.

Tommy Carmellini shook the now-limp corpse like a dog shakes a rat. The airplane rolled left.

The antics of the plane brought him out of his killing rage. He threw Arch's body to the right and grabbed for the yoke. For the first time, he looked outside. There was nothing to see in the stygian universe, not sky or sea or land . . . nothing at all.

The gyro was right there in front of him, telling him the nose and left wing were well down.

Concentrating on the gyro, he lifted the wing slowly so as not to tear it off and began pulling back on the yoke.

How high was he?

He looked for the altimeter, felt a moment of panic when he couldn't find it, then realized which instrument it was. He was descending through two thousand feet, still going down.

Somchow he got the nose up, then he let go of the yoke and jammed the throttle forward to the stop.

Back on the yoke, pulling, climbing, watching the airspeed so the plane didn't get slow again, trying to read the gyro and not panic.

Finally he realized he had the plane under control. He looked outside again, searched the darkness. Saw the lights of a beach town far to his left. He gently turned the airplane in that direction.

Carmellini had had a half dozen flying lessons from Rita Moravia in a high-wing Cessna smaller than this one. Those flights had all been during the day, and Rita had demanded he look outside.

As he stared at the gyro he found the sensations of flying disorienting. He kept the aircraft level by sheer strength of will. He also forced himself to glance at the altimeter, checked every now and then out the front windshield to see if the smear of light from the town was still dead ahead, then again stared fiercely at the gyro.

With his hands tied together he could only do one thing at a time, and that thing was handle the yoke. There was no way he could reach the rudder, no way to reach the trim wheel.

But he was alive! *Alive!* Oh, God, yes, *alive*!

The lights were still a smear on the horizon. How far out over the ocean was he? He was down below a thousand feet. He should climb, get away from the ocean, get higher so he could see. He pulled back on the yoke, made sure the altimeter was moving upward, desperately scanned the panel for the airspeed indicator. Oh, there it was, right above the altimeter.

At three thousand feet he decided he was high enough.

Slowly, slowly, the plane approached the city on the shore. Now he could see individual streets, buildings, the lights of a boardwalk. What city was it?

He didn't know or care.

A flashing light off to his right caught his eye. He turned gently in that direction. Yes, it was an airport! In about a minute he picked out the runway lights.

A wave of relief flooded him.

The wind, where was the wind? He couldn't find the wind indicator, so he gave up. He let go of the yoke momentarily and pulled the throttle out several inches. The drone of the engine changed dramatically.

He flew a wide, sloppy, descending circle, trying to line up on the runway that looked the longest. He had to release the yoke and adjust the power several times. Every time he took his hands off the yoke, it jerked forward, and the nose of the plane dropped precipitously. When he grabbed it again he had to pull back quickly. The problem was that the plane was trimmed for cruise, and he couldn't reach the trim wheel and fly, too.

If there were other airplanes about, he didn't see them.

He was still very high when he crossed the end of the runway. Releasing the yoke momentarily, he pulled the throttle all the way out, to idle. He grabbed the yoke as quick as thought, got the nose back up, let the plane settle.

Holy damn, he was going to run out of runway!

He eased the nose forward, dived at the runway, pulled back at the last moment, just before the plane hit the earth. It floated along just above the dark runway in ground effect, slowing slowly, refusing to touch down. The lights at the end of the runway raced toward him.

Now the wheels touched.

He couldn't reach the brakes. He couldn't steer.

How do I turn off the engine?

The red knob! The mixture! He released the yoke and grabbed for the red knob on the throttle quadrant, jerked it out as far as it would go.

The engine died as the plane careened past the lights marking the end of the runway.

Carmellini grabbed the back of the seats and braced himself for the inevitable, which wasn't long in coming. One of the wheels hit something and the nose slewed right. The plane tilted left, then the left main gear collapsed; the wing hit the earth and sparks flew.

The airplane was slewing to the right amid the howl of tearing metal and slowly decelerating when the left wing tip hit something solid. The impact almost tore the wing off, spinning the plane madly to the left. Tommy Carmellini lost his grip on the seat back. His head smashed against the right side of the cockpit and the lights went out.

From the door of the helicopter Jake Grafton saw the wreckage of the Cessna in the headlights and floodlights of the fire trucks. The carcass sat off one end of the runway amid the stanchions that held up the approach lights. The left wing was nearly severed, the gear was torn off the plane, the tail was severely damaged.

The chopper settled onto the grass a hundred feet from the wreck. As the rotors spun down, Jake and FBI agent Harry Estep climbed from the chopper and walked briskly to the ambulance. Tommy Carmellini sat on a gurney with a blanket around him drinking water from a bottle. Nearby lay a body covered with a shroud.

"Zip Vance said you were robbing a bank this weekend," Jake said. "What in hell are you doing here?"

"Fun and games with agency colleagues." Carmellini jerked his head at the corpse. "That's Arch Foster. Norv Lalouette is somewhere out there"—he pointed a thumb eastward—"sleeping with the fishes." He lifted a leg. The skin was raw and bleeding in places. The lime in the concrete had taken off the top layer of skin on his feet and ankles, leaving them red, raw, and inflamed. "The bastards had me in concrete booties. The firemen pounded me loose. See those buckets over there?"

Jake glanced at the buckets and piles of concrete shards.

"Who are those guys over there with the police and firemen?"

"Off-duty cops, I think, and plainclothes. Every cop in eastern Maryland must be here tonight. Crash at the airport, corpse in the cockpit, the only live guy wearing concrete galoshes. . . . The chief himself was by to see if I'd talk without a lawyer. He and some brass from the state police. I told them I wasn't even telling anyone my name until after I talked to you. I told them how to get hold of you."

"They found me, all right." Jake turned to Harry. "Maybe you'd better talk to them."

Harry nodded and walked over to where the police officers stood.

"These two bastards were going to put me in the ocean while I was still alive," Tommy explained to Jake, wanting desperately to make him understand. "I kicked Norv out the door and killed Arch, then flew that thing back here. Screwed up the landing."

"I guess you did."

"They had a plastic tie on my wrists. Thought I was history."

Jake Grafton bent over for a close look at Carmellini's feet, then straightened.

"How'd you kill Foster?"

"Jammed a couple fingers into his right eye socket. Punched them through to his brain."

Tommy Carmellini began to shake. He wrapped the blanket tightly around himself, but the tremors continued. His teeth began chattering.

He told Jake about searching Arch's house on Friday night, finding the money, and being kidnapped on Saturday morning. "They injected me with something that paralyzed me. It's been a long weekend, I want to tell you."

"Sounds like the weekend from hell, shipmate," Jake said, and laid a hand on Carmellini's arm.

"I was fucking scared shitless, man," Carmellini admitted, biting his lip until blood flowed. "When the paralysis wore off, I just . . . like, you know . . . lost it, I guess. Wanted to kill those two bastards with my bare hands. Never thought about how I was going to land the plane—not once. Didn't care, really. Just as long as I could kill them."

He put a hand over his face and took several deep breaths. By the flashing lights from the emergency beacons Jake could see the struggle going on behind Carmellini's hand. The tremors gradually ceased, which surprised Jake—he had never seen anyone demonstrate such iron self-control.

When Carmellini lowered his hand his face was composed.

"Where'd Arch get a hundred fifteen thousand in cash? Did he say?"

"No. You want my opinion, these two dumped people before. They had the routine down. Bet you ten bucks they dumped Richard Doyle out of this airplane into the Atlantic."

"We'll have the FBI forensic guys go over that plane. Maybe they can find some trace of Doyle."

"And the hangar. Don't know where it was—somewhere around Washington, I guess. Took about an hour or so of flying to get out over the ocean."

"You injured?"

"Scraped and scratched, covered with shit and piss. The concrete burned the hell out of my feet—those fucking pricks! God, I'm glad I killed 'em!"

"Sit tight and let us talk to the law. Then maybe we can take the chopper back to Washington."

"We don't have any time to lose, sir. There was a television crew out here, but I told those cops I was CIA, so they ran them off. Don't know what's been on the air. We'd better get the FBI to get agents over to Lalouette's and Foster's houses to sit on them before the news leaks out. Then they can get warrants whenever. Same for their offices, cars, all of that."

"We'll take care of it," Jake assured him. "How do you feel now, Tommy? Are you okay?"

"I'm all right."

"Hey, man, you're alive. It's going to be okay."

"Remember that time in Hong Kong, when you and I went into that ship after Callie?"

"Yeah."

"How you just wanted to do the bastards, regardless? It was sorta like that."

"I hear you."

"I needed to talk to somebody I trust."

Jake Grafton didn't reply, and Tommy left it there. After a bit Jake said, "I'll walk you over to the helicopter," and helped Carmellini to his feet. His feet were so sore he tottered and staggered like a very old man, so the journey took a while. When Carmellini was seated inside the helicopter, Jake walked over to where Harry Estep stood talking to the chief of police.

CHAPTER FOURTEEN

Captain Joe Zogby was waiting for Jake Monday morning when he arrived at Langley after three hours' sleep. According to Zogby, no one knew the exact location of *Olympic Voyager*. Her owners couldn't raise her on the radio. "They think there's probably been some sort of com casualty. When the owners last talked to her, she was in the Red Sea."

"She should be in the Med but the owners don't know?"

"That's correct, sir."

"Uh-oh."

"Yes, sir."

"Call NIMA. I want that ship found and put under twenty-four-hour aerial surveillance. Now! Make it happen. And get someone from the embassy in Athens over to the owners' offices *now*! We need a list of the crew, have them fax it. We need to know everything the owners know about that ship—everything—from photos to maintenance records to how much fuel and beans were aboard this morning."

Zogby glanced at his watch. "It's evening in Athens, Admiral."

"Drag someone away from the dinner table. Get the Greek government involved. Have the U.S. ambassador call a minister or two—I don't give a damn what the people at our embassy have to do."

Jake Grafton dropped into his chair and smashed his fist down on the desk. "No more business as usual!" Bam! "It's time for them to get off their asses." Bam!

The light was flashing on his telephone. "Harry Estep on line one, Admiral," Gil Pascal said.

Jake snagged the instrument. "Whaddaya got?"

"We found the hangar where they kept Carmellini—found Foster's vehicle parked nearby. The judge is signing search warrants for both men's cars and homes, we'll go in within an hour. We've got people guarding them. We'll search their offices as soon as agency security provides access numbers and safe combinations."

"Keep me advised."

Pascal told him the air force was flying a nuclear weapon into Andrews AFB outside of Washington that afternoon to allow Harley Bennett to test and calibrate the Corrigan detection unit.

"How's Carmellini?" The helicopter had dropped Carmellini at Bethesda Naval Hospital early that morning.

"I don't know, sir."

Jake pulled his cell phone from his pocket and dialed. Three rings later he heard Tommy Carmellini's voice. "Hello."

"How are the feet?"

"Sore as hell."

"What do the docs say?"

"Stay off them for a week, which is bullshit. I'm outta here day after tomorrow. See you then."

"So how are you doing, shipmate?"

"Doing okay, Admiral. Feeling better than I did last night. The sun is shining in my window and the nurse is pretty cute and those two crackers are dead. It feels kinda nice."

"Wait until you can walk before you sneak out of the hospital. I don't want you crawling around here."

"The nurse is smiling at me now. She's very empathetic. She obviously understands post-traumatic stress. If she'll bring me another bagel from the cafeteria and hold my hand a little, my recuperation will rocket along. I'll let you know."

Zip Vance and Zelda Hudson were hard at it in the SCIF. Surrounded by computer monitors, they were both so submerged in what they were doing they were oblivious to Jake's and Toad's presence when they walked in. Jake watched for a moment. Zelda was apparently writing a software program; one of the CIA technicians was instructing Zip in the proper way to search a bank's credit card transactions records.

The data scrolled up the screen too fast to read, then paused. Zip looked, made a note, hit a key, and the scrolling continued at a sickening speed. After a couple minutes of this, Zip got out of the file with a few keystrokes, all the while chattering away to the technician.

"Ah," Zelda said. "I was going to call you. We're putting info together on those three men you asked about . . . nothing leaps out yet."

"Here are two more names," Jake said, passing her a sheet of paper containing everything Gil could garner quickly in the CIA personnel office on Foster and Lalouette.

"Zipper has been monitoring the telephone calls of that *Post* reporter—Jack Yocke. He said he wanted to talk to you about one of them."

Vance glanced up when he saw Jake, then handed him a piece of scratch paper. "This guy called Yocke and used your name twice. I have a tape."

Jake nodded.

Getting the tape ready to play and finding the right spot took several minutes. Jake donned a headset and waited, trying to exude more patience than he felt.

Finally Zip pushed the right buttons and Jake heard a voice in his ears. "Yocke."

"Jack, how are you?" A male voice, cultured, a hint of New England, perhaps.

"Fine, sir, and you?"

"Busy. Got a tidbit you might want as deep background."

"Okay."

"There was a meeting Sunday in the old Executive Office Building about Jake Grafton and his task force. A lot of people don't feel comfortable with him or the way he's going. He was there on the carpet."

"I see," Yocke replied, drawing out the words. Jake could almost see the reporter making notes as he listened. "Could you elaborate on that?"

"He's a lightweight, in way over his head. Doesn't have a clue what in hell is going on. Baldly, we're worried that he's incompetent."

"Uh-huh."

"You remember those items I mentioned to you—I don't think he's any closer to finding them than he was before he was appointed. People feel that time is running out."

"Thanks for sharing that with me," Jack Yocke said warmly. "I hope you feel better."

"What do you mean?"

"Amigo, I need something I can put in the goddamn paper," Yocke replied. "I got inches to do every day. This father confessor thing goes with the job, of course. I hope you successfully get in touch with your inner self, but at some point you gotta stop jerking me off and give me something I can use, like from an anonymous source or a highly placed government official. A tidbit, a crumb, *something*!"

"Now is not the time."

"Okey dokey. It's your call. But when the time comes—and I hope it gets here soon—I need something hard, you know? Not gossip column fluff. I need solid nouns and verbs and predicates that I can spin into that who, what, where, when, why jazz."

"I just wanted to bring you up to date."

"Appreciate it."

"Maybe I do need to share. This thing is troubling me, if you know what I mean. Grafton's a featherweight with big friends—I'm damn worried."

"Right."

"Talk to you soon."

"Yeah," and the connection broke.

Jake handed the headset to Zip.

"I have the number of the cell phone that call originated from, Admiral, if you don't recognize the voice. I can get into the telephone company records and get you a name and address."

"I recognized the voice."

"Those items I mentioned to you"—Jake thought he knew what those were.

Oh, well. So Butch Lanham played hardball. He knew that already.

He paused to talk to Zelda before he left the SCIF. "How is it going?"

"The computer experts from NSA and CIA are very, very good. I'm just coordinating and trying to stay out of their way."

"What's the software you're working on?"

"Making the police surveillance cameras useful. I want to show you something I've put together." Jake's schedule was full to overflowing, yet Zelda's enthusiasm made it difficult to refuse her a few minutes. And he knew that sooner or later some senior someone—probably Lanham, who was casting about for ways to torpedo Jake's boat—would get wind that Zelda and Zip were working on Jake's team; when it happened—and it would—he was going to have to use valuable political capital to defend their presence or send them back to prison. So he stood rooted, listening to the life in Zelda's voice, watching her fingers fly across the keyboard and images dance across the monitors.

"It's a movie," she told Jake. "Here goes." The scene was a street in Washington, one of the poorer neighborhoods, from the look of it. The camera zoomed in on several young men standing on a street corner. A car pulled up, one of the men went over, accepted money, passed something into the car. There was a close-up of a license plate as the car accelerated away. A minute later another car arrived and a smiliar transaction occurred.

When the video stopped playing, Zelda stood and faced Jake Grafton. "These are drug dealers doing business. The people in the cars are their customers. With only a little work someone could put names and addresses to license numbers and compile a list of people using this stuff."

"Uh-huh."

"With a little more work, we can identify the car that delivers the product." Her eyes and intensity held him pinned. For the very first time Jake felt the force, the fire, the charisma of the brilliant mind that was Zelda. Inadvertently he glanced at Zip, then found himself recaptured by her. "I wrote software that tells the computer to search the video feeds for whatever license plate we identify. With this tool we can uncover entire networks—wholesalers, dealers, customers—and put together overwhelming evidence to put these networks out of business. We could make a digital movie of the entire network in operation."

Jake glanced again at Zip, who was now watching him.

"Our job is security," he objected, "not law enforcement."

"I understand that. I am not suggesting that we waste a minute on this project that could be used to further the primary mission. I want to put a movie together on my own time, a few minutes here and there, when I'm not busy with something else. Even if the lawyers refuse to use it, the movie would show the system's capabilities."

And Zelda's, Jake thought. "Do it," he said, and headed for the door.

Midnight at the Oasis. Naguib had never heard the song by that name—didn't even know there was one—so the irony of the name of the beer joint escaped him. This establishment was two hundred yards and five parking lots south of Smoot's Motel, which he had sneaked away from ten minutes ago.

He looked around the smoky bar and saw her sitting alone in the booth against the wall. She was facing him. As he walked toward her, her face broke into a smile. He slid into the booth beside her.

"I can't stay long," he said. "Mohammed will awaken before long and come looking."

"He will look in the place next door to Smoot's, honey. He won't come all the way down here." She rubbed her hand up and down on his thigh, pressed a large, firm breast into his arm. "Aren't you glad to see me?"

"Oh, yes."

"I been waiting for you, hoping you'd come in."

He put his arm around her shoulder and kissed her. She opened her lips.

When he finally broke for air, she said, "Oh, honey. You got me so hot! I wish there was something we could do about it."

While he was digesting that comment, she continued, "My husband is such a pig. I sneaked out just to see you. I think he might be getting suspicious, though. And to think, all we've done is kiss."

For the life of him, Naguib couldn't remember her name. Something that began with an S. Sophie? Susan? Sue-something. With a husband.

She rested her head on his shoulder while he took a sip of her beer. "I don't have much time either," she said. "You know what I mean, honey? A man like you, with a job and friends and everything, you must know how it is?"

"Of course," said Naguib, intensely conscious of the location of her hand on his thigh and what she was doing with it.

"You and I could get something going, honey, if we had a little time. You know? A few Saturdays and some nights, you and me'd be friends for life. You ever thought about a woman like that, honey?"

No, he hadn't, not for life, but he didn't want to tell her that. "Sure," he said, lying through his teeth.

"Just lovin' and leavin' ain't enough, honey. One-night stands don't do it for me. I'm looking for something more. Larry is such a pig."

Larry must be the husband, Naguib thought, as that hand moved up, up, up his thigh.

" 'Course you aren't American, so that complicates things. You aren't going back to Pakistan anytime soon, are you?"

"Arabia," Naguib said, too much into the presence of her to bother lying. "Never going back."

"That's good, honey. You aren't already married or living with someone, are you?"

"No," he said.

"But that man who came in last time—who is he?"

"Just a friend I share a room with. To save money. That's all."

"You speak terrific English, honey. Easy to understand. You musta been here in the States a long, long time?"

Five minutes later she said, "Some of the girls are worried about me with you. I like dark, foreign men, they're so cute. I know there's nothing to it, but with the terrorism and all, a girl's gotta be careful."

Naguib's eyes darted around, his jaws worked soundlessly, and he swallowed several times.

Bingo, Suzanne thought.

A half hour later Naguib looked at his watch with a start. He had been here twice as long as he figured. "Suzanne, I gotta go. Gotta get a little sleep and go to work tomorrow."

"Oh, baby," the blonde said, and gave him a kiss that almost caused his heart to stop. "I wish you and I . . ." She left it hanging, her face inches from his.

He walked out into the night. Crossing the second parking lot, Naguib stopped and stared at his surroundings. This was what he was giving up, this place, these women—life so sweet and precious. He was throwing it all away for the great hereafter. Murdering millions for the glory of God. On the word of holy men ranting in Arabia and Cairo, Tehran, Kabul, and Baghdad, preaching the glories of Paradise although they weren't anxious to hurry there themselves.

In a few weeks he would be dead along with millions of others, Suzanne would have to find another fellow to give her what she wanted, the holy men would be ecstatic . . . and *this* was what he was leaving. *This!* The rush when a woman was close, the shock of her hand brushing his groin, the feel of her breast, the warm sensuousness of her kiss, the sliding perfection of her tongue on his. *Life*. When he had a woman pressed against him and his hands on her body, he could feel the beat of life, feel it coursing through him and her.

What a fool he had been, planning to waste life. He could see it plainly.

Mohammed was waiting for him outside the motel unit. In the dim light Naguib could see the fury on his face. He didn't care.

"I don't want to be a martyr," he said to Mohammed.

"Where have you been?"

"I don't want to be a martyr. I want to find a woman who loves me that I can love." Naguib was realistic enough to realize that Suzanne might not be the one. Still, he believed that the right woman would make everything in his life better. "I want to get a job and a woman and have children. Two at least, I think."

Mohammed backhanded Naguib casually across the mouth. The blow was unexpected; Naguib lost his balance and fell. "I hope for your sake you have not betrayed your brothers. If you have I will personally cut your throat. The hour approaches and you speak of treason. What kind of man are you?"

"One who wants to live," Naguib managed as his head cleared. He stood, swaying gently to and fro. When his head had almost cleared, he jabbed Mohammed sharply on the chin, staggering him. He followed and hit him with the left. Then again with a well-timed right with everything behind it.

The cool hardness of the crushed shells brought Mohammed around. He got to his knees, looking around for Naguib, trying to see the attack he knew would come. On his feet he swayed as he waited, then he was aware that someone was standing near him looking at his face.

"Who are you?"

"Fred Smoot. I'm the landlord, laddie-buck. Now hold still and let me see how bad you're hurt."

Naguib was nowhere in sight. "Did you see who hit me?" Mohammed tentatively asked Fred. He was trying to think up a way to avoid the notice of the police.

"Yeah," Fred said as he examined the blood flowing from Mohammed's eyebrow. Cuts there usually gushed. "One of the guys you room with. The big one. He's got a hell of a right on him, fella, so I'd try to keep my head out of the way of it, if I were you."

"This is no large deal," Mohammed said, ignoring the blood, wanting to ensure that Fred would not call the police.

"His left ain't bad either." Fred finished his examination. "You need to get that cut washed out. The old woman can do it and put a couple Band-Aids on it to hold it together so you won't need stitches." Fred sighed. "Like a good fight myself. When I was young I was always ready if somebody wanted some action. Little tussle gets the juices flowing and clears the air, but I want no more of that horseplay around here, understand? You'll get the tourists all lathered."

Brushing the shards of crushed shells from his hair, Mohammed followed Fred toward the office, thinking about how he had lost Naguib and what he would have to do.

At eleven o'clock Tuesday Harry Estep called Jake Grafton. "Those CDs that Anna Modin gave you are gold."

"What's on them?"

"Bank transaction records. Walney's Bank in Cairo is in the business of financing terrorists. One of the groups they finance is the Sword of Islam."

"Where are the bombs?"

"That isn't on the CDs."

"Did any of that money come to America?"

"Don't know yet. But the big news is that a big chunk came from here."

"What?"

"Yeah. Looks like it came to Walney's sorta all at once through eight or ten accounts. The money was shuffled all over hell to try to prevent it from being traced. What we see is the stuff coming into Walney's and what Walney's did with it. We then have to compare that info with the records of other banks. We think we've found a trail."

"Provable in court?"

"No. Maybe one of these days, but not now. The problem is that banks are the ultimate washing machine; they make money a commodity—bucks come in one window and go out another and all the dollars look alike. A transfer could be a loan, a payment to settle a check or a set-off—whatever. If the people at the bank are writing fiction, creating bogus backup . . . you can envision the possibilities. Anyway, what it boils down to is this—a sizable chunk of change, maybe two million, went through Walney's and on to guys we think are dirty. We think it came from the U.S., but it will take a lot of work to nail that down."

"Uh-huh."

"The CDs are a big piece of the puzzle. We still don't have all the pieces and never will, yet with these pieces we can begin to see what the puzzle looks like."

"Tell me about the searches of Foster's and Lalouette's stuff."

"Foster had a hundred and fifteen thousand bucks cash in his basement, right where Carmellini said it would be. Nothing else of interest yet."

"Modin thinks that the guy who runs the bank in Cairo may send assassins to kill her. I agree. What can we do to protect her?"

"You want me to put that on my to-do list?"

"I guess," Jake said dryly.

"I interviewed her this morning. She named names in Cairo. Wouldn't answer a single question about Ilin or the SVR."

"Claims she doesn't work for the SVR. And she's trying to protect Ilin."

"Terrific."

Jake hesitated before he asked the next question. He thought he knew the answer, but he wanted a professional's opinion. "Do you think Anna Modin is telling the truth?"

Harry Estep sensed the gravity of Jake's query, and considered his answer before he spoke. "She thinks she is, I believe. She's letting us see that portion of the picture that Ilin let her see. That's about as good as it gets in this game, I guess."

"We need to get her into a witness protection program or something. She flew here with a Russian passport and took a cab from the airport to my house. If assassins are after her, she won't be hard to find."

"I'll see what I can do. Maybe you should put some pressure on the top echelon."

"That I can do."

"She's given us the disk and named names. Why would they risk an assassination?"

"How would I know? I've heard those guys spell revenge with a capital R. Why are you asking me?"

"You know everything else, Admiral. If you figure out why the sky is blue and male dogs like fire hydrants, let me in on it, huh? I've always wondered about those things."

Callie Grafton and Anna Modin had a late lunch Tuesday at one of Callie's favorite haunts in Georgetown, not far from the university. Callie insisted on practicing her Russian and Anna worked on her English, so they smiled often as they told each other about themselves and corrected grammar and syntax errors. Callie noticed that Anna relaxed as the luncheon went on.

She had not been relaxed this morning when they went to the parking garage for the car for the trip to the Hoover Building on

Pennsylvania Avenue. Before she left the elevator she stopped Callie with a hand and eased her head out. She reminded Callie of a hunted animal, hesitant, listening, looking at everything.

In the car Anna refused to wear a seat belt, preferring to be free to bail whenever and wherever.

"This is America," Callie said gently. "One doesn't normally meet assassins on the way to lunch."

"These people are very dangerous," Modin said matter-of-factly. "They have much money, much hate, and they kill easily, as if it is of no importance."

Callie didn't ask about the interview with the FBI, and Modin volunteered nothing. At lunch the conversation swung to Callie's work, teaching languages at the university, so after lunch she took Anna to her office. The spring semester was in full swing; the place was jumping. Callie had called in that morning and been given a day off, so a chat with the department head was in order. As she visited with him, Anna chatted with two of the instructors in Russian. Callie introduced her as Anna and gave no last name.

As they left the building, Modin paused again in the doorway and surveyed the scene carefully.

"How long do you think they will hunt you?" Callie asked as they walked toward the car. Perhaps Modin's paranoia was catching; Callie no longer questioned Modin's assessment of the situation.

"Until they kill me or die themselves. Even if they die others may try."

"Won't they give up after a while?"

"Never." Modin made a fist and squeezed it. "God is like this with them. They are afraid to be afraid."

"And you agreed to steal from them for Janos Ilin?"

"Someone has to fight them," she said simply. "I do not have his courage—no one I ever met does—but I go where he leads. He is a great man."

"Do you love him?"

Modin looked surprised. "No," she said. "Not lovers." After a moment of thought she added, "Soldiers, I think." She glanced at Callie, apparently wondering if she understood. "A man must have something to fight for, something bigger than he is."

"Some women, too, apparently," Callie shot back.

She drove the car toward the U.S. Naval Hospital in Bethesda. "We will stop and see a friend, if you don't mind."

"Fine, fine. A lover?"

It was Callie's turn to look embarrassed. "No. Friend. Sometimes he works for my husband."

"Sick?"

"Sore feet. Very sore. Some men were going to kill him and stuck his feet in concrete."

"In America, even, where there are no assassins. Shocking!"

"Isn't it?" Callie agreed.

They found Tommy Carmellini occupying one of the two beds in a double room on the third floor. The second bed was empty. When Callie first saw him he was flipping through television channels and looking glum. His face lit up when they walked into the room. "Mrs. Grafton! Wow! Am I glad to see you! Find a chair. Sit on that empty bed. Please sit."

"This is Anna. She's our houseguest."

"Pleasedtameetcha." Carmellini stuck out his hand. "Forgive me not getting up. They stole my pants so I won't boogie."

"Ah, the usual indignities," Callie said.

"Boogie?" Anna asked.

"Run away," Callie explained.

"There oughta be a law," Carmellini stated firmly. "Sit, please!"

"How are your feet?"

"Sore." He peeled back the sheet to display one of the bandaged units. "Did your husband fill you in?"

"Oh, yes."

"It was a long damned weekend, I am here to tell you. Thought it was my last."

Anna Modin scanned the bright, cheerful, sunlit room and marveled at the contrast with the Russian hospitals she remembered. Then she took a careful look at Tommy Carmellini, the broad shoulders, craggy good looks, and ready smile. Even in a hospital gown, the muscled arms and thick wrists and weight lifter's veins told her that he did more than push paper for a living.

"Mrs. Grafton said someone tried to murder you," she said to the patient.

His smile got even broader. "Hard to believe, isn't it? A personal thing, I think. No problem now. What is that accent you have?"

"Russian."

"Ahh, a spy in the house of love. How about dinner tomorrow night?"

"You'll be walking by then?"

"I'm going to steal crutches and blow this pop stand. I'll call you at the Graftons'."

When the women left ten minutes later, Anna Modin was smiling for the first time since she'd arrived in America. "He's very nice," she told Callie as they walked out of the hospital.

"You have a date already," Callie said. "Things are looking up."

"A date," Anna said, savoring the idea.

When the two women were in the car and rolling, Anna commented, "My life is so empty. Men have been interested in me, but I always push them away. One, in Cairo, put his life in jeopardy for me. Then there was the girl in Cairo, Nooreem Habib—I demanded that she drop everything and flee for her life, and instead she took the time to say good-byes to her family. Then they killed her."

Anna Modin shook her head. "They have so much money that they can afford spies everywhere—even here. America is full of Islamic immigrants and illegals."

Callie concentrated on driving and held her tongue.

"Nooreem Habib had a life and lost it," Anna mused aloud. "I have no life, and I remain alive." After a while she added, "Until they find me."

Jake and Gil Pascal spent Tuesday afternoon in a meeting with senior officers of Delta Force, listening to deployment options and scenarios in the event a live nuclear weapon was discovered on American soil. The options were all risky, with horrific consequences if anything went wrong. The whole thing was a nightmare.

Along toward five o'clock a staffer rescued Jake to take a call from Toad.

"There's nothing wrong with the Corrigan unit, boss. I'm sitting out here at Andrews Air Force Base with Harley Bennett and Sonny Tran beside a B-52 with a nuke in the bomb bay. This gizmo is singing and chirping just like it did the first time."

"How does Bennett explain the alarm at the golf course?"

"He can't. Says there must be something there."

"Buried under a golf course?"

"Right."

"Go back to the golf course and do it again. Call me from there."

"Aye aye, sir."

"You're keeping a log of every buzz and beep, right?"

"Yes, sir."

"Terrific." Jake cradled the instrument and stood in his office staring at the wall. Through the years he had watched engineers wrestle with bugs in new systems large and small—but what if something were buried beside that river?

Not in the last three weeks. He inspected that terrain himself. Sure, every day people filled holes and put sod or plants over the fill, but if they had done it within the last three weeks, the disturbance would still be evident. He would swear that area was undisturbed. The soil was compacted, the plants secure in the ground. . . .

So what the hell was going on?

Unable to solve the problem, he dismissed it and went back to Colonel Kiechel of Delta Force.

He was back at his desk at six-thirty that evening tackling the paperwork that had accumulated when the telephone rang again. It was Toad.

"Harley has the sensors flaked out, boss. We're at Hains Point in East Potomac Park, precisely where we were the last time, and the Corrigan giz-mach is singing up a storm."

"Put Bennett on."

After a moment of silence, Jake heard, "This is Harley Bennett."

"What do you think, Bennett?"

"Damn, Admiral. I don't know. I have two recommendations. First, let's get some of the factory engineers down here to check that I'm doing everything right and not missing something. It's possible there could be some internal interference or something that is screwing up the sensors and giving false positives. The wizards are going to have to figure it out."

"I thought you were a wizard."

Harley Bennett's voice sounded tired. "Admiral, I'm just a working engineer. I'm not in the league with the guys who designed this thing; anybody who thinks I am is fooling himself."

"Give them a call. Now. Tell them to get on a plane. What's your second recommendation?"

"Dig a hole."

"Are you satisfied that thing is functioning properly?"

"I am, but like I said . . ."

"Let me talk to Toad again."

When Tarkington was back on, Jake said, "I told Bennett to get the boffins from Boston down here to look at your gizmo. Make that happen this evening."

"You can hear the clock ticking, can't you?"

"Yeah. If they can't find anything wrong tonight, tomorrow morning I want you guys to drive that van up and down both sides of the Potomac from Beltway to Beltway. Drive it through downtown Washington, by the Capitol and White House and Pentagon, all of that. Do Andrews, Fort Meade, NSA—all the high-value targets. Annotate a map. Put down every buzz and cheep and chirp. If a needle twitches, I want to know about it."

"Yes, sir. How long do we have for this project?"

"As long as it takes. But I want the map on my desk tomorrow evening whether you are done or not."

"We'll put this thing in the garage at Langley, and I'll meet the plane from Boston."

"Thanks, Toad. By the way, is Sonny within earshot?"

"No."

"Keep an eye on him. He may be dirty."

By ten that night three of Harley Bennett's colleagues from Corrigan Engineering were working on the van in a garage at Langley. Jake stopped to talk after he left the office. One of them was a pipe smoker. "Dr. LaFontain," Bennett said, "Admiral Grafton." The two men shook hands.

LaFontain played with his pipe as he watched the other two peer and probe under the control panel. He said nothing.

When Jake tired of the silence, he asked, "How long is this going to take?"

LaFontain looked startled. Obviously he hadn't even considered the time element. He shrugged and puffed smoke.

"I'll see you in the office first thing in the morning," Jake said to Bennett.

"Ah, Admiral, I will need to get some sleep at some point."

"We screw this up, a whole lot of people will be sleeping forever. Eight in the morning. Be there."

When a uniformed naval officer wearing stars walks into Bethesda Naval Hospital, even at eleven at night, he is not anonymous. Jake managed to shed his escort—two nurses and a doctor—outside the door to Carmellini's room. He went in and eased the door shut behind him. Tommy Carmellini was asleep. He had an IV catheter in his left wrist, but he was not hooked up to an IV.

Jake touched his arm. "Hey, shipmate."

Carmellini drew back as if stung. His eyes flew open. He relaxed when he saw who was standing beside the bed.

"Hey, Admiral," he said. He looked at his watch.

"How are you doing?"

"Fine, fine, sir. Jeez, I didn't expect to see you. Sit down. Drag up a chair there. Your wife was here this afternoon, and I appreciate that. Brought your houseguest with her."

"Yeah." Jake pulled the chair over by the bed and sat. "Sorry it's so late, but I couldn't get away sooner."

"Sure."

"I want to hear all of it, every word and gesture, everything."

When the limo cruised into Dupont Circle at midnight, the chess player was waiting on the corner. He opened the passenger door and seated himself beside Karl Luck.

"Mr. Corrigan wants to know how the device is working," Luck said by way of greeting.

The chess player looked at him oddly, then removed a small electronic device from his pocket. He ran it over Luck's clothes while he watched the meter, then moved it carefully around the interior of the car. Only when he had passed the instrument over every nook and cranny did he flip off the power and return it to his pocket.

"It worked as advertised this afternoon. The air force provided a live nuclear weapon to recalibrate the instrument."

"Why? I thought it was already calibrated."

"It is indicating the presence of a weapon buried on Hains Point, across from Reagan National Airport."

"The weapons aren't here yet," Luck objected.

"Apparently the device doesn't know that. From all indications, there's a weapon buried under a golf course on Hains Point. Either that, or the thing is giving false positives for some reason Harley Bennett can't figure out."

"What in the hell is going on?"

"I was hoping that you could tell me."

"You are sure the detection unit is functioning properly?"

"I am not. Bennett swears it is, and I don't know enough to doubt him."

"Has Bennett talked to the factory?"

"Several times today."

Luck was clearly puzzled. "Underground, you say?"

"Where are the Russian warheads?"

"We believe they were transshipped at Port Said, as planned. Unfortunately we haven't heard from Dutch Vandervelt to confirm that. Nothing on the radio. And we haven't heard from our man in Cairo, either."

The chess player watched the city slide by the windows while he thought about that. "When is the ship due to reach Marseilles?"

"Tomorrow, I think."

"Is she still afloat?"

Luck stared. "Why wouldn't she be?"

"I was thinking of Frouq al-Zuair and his cutthroat friends. One suspects they adhere to that hoary old axiom that dead men tell no tales."

"The whole ship and crew? I don't believe it! Not a chance. There has been a radio casualty of some kind."

"So what's with your man in Cairo? He ever run off on you before?"

"No."

"He may have been arrested. He may be singing his heart out for the FBI this very second, naming names and places and dates. Personally I think loyalty is an overrated virtue. In this day and age you get about as much of it as you are willing to pay for, and by God it comes high."

Luck said nothing.

The passenger glanced at Luck's face, then said conversationally, "We'll know tomorrow when the ship drops anchor, won't we?"

Luck changed the subject. "What else is happening with Grafton?"

"I don't know. I am not a member of the inner circle, I told you that. That is why we needed Carmellini. By the way, I heard Tarkington talking to him on the telephone today."

Luck's jaw dropped. "What the hell is this? He's supposed to be dead."

"I gathered from what I heard of Tarkington's end of the conversation that he's very much alive and in the hospital."

"So where are Foster and Lalouette?"

"Why don't you find out?"

"Perhaps Carmellini's dead, and they are playing you."

"Perhaps."

"If so, Corrigan will—"

"If they're playing me, you and Corrigan are going to prison for the rest of your natural lives. Think about that."

Luck half turned in his seat and looked through the rear window of the limo.

"If they follow you or me, we won't see them," the chess player said. "If Carmellini is alive, Foster and Lalouette have been arrested or bitten the big one. He probably killed them. And he's undoubtedly talked to the authorities and told them all about those two incompetents. If they have been arrested, they may have talked. Even if they are dead, an attempted contact will lead the authorities to you."

Luck sat back in the seat and pursed his lips.

"The noose tightens, eh? We're playing a damned dangerous game . . . for money." He shrugged. "A lot of money, it's true, a small fortune for each of us. All so that asshole Corrigan can look good and go out in style. Well, Luck, I've got news for you—you and I are going to earn every goddamn dime. And Corrigan's radiation detector doesn't work for shit. Tell the son of a bitch I said that."

Luck keyed the intercom and told the driver to return to Dupont Circle.

When they got there, the chess player said in parting, "See you tomorrow night. You can tell me then about that ship and its broken radios. Let's pray that the ragheads don't change their plans. We've got to find those weapons when they arrive . . . *before* they explode. If one of those things pops anywhere on this planet, there won't be a gallows high enough for you and Corrigan."

Luck's features were set in stone.

"And you fools thought this was going to be easy. Ha!"

Luck made a gesture of irritation.

"The best-laid plans of mice and men . . ." Sonny Tran continued, rubbing it in. The truth was that he hated Luck and Corrigan and all those comfortable bastards with their money and their cute plans to play the system for their own benefit. How he hated them! He wanted to strangle them all, watch them die with his hands around their lily white throats.

Sonny swallowed hard, put the mask back on. "If I'm not at the Circle, Grafton has sent me to chase wild geese. Or the FBI has arrested me."

He got out of the car and walked halfway around the circle, then set off north on Nineteenth Street. Two blocks later he paused in front of a coffee shop—closed of course—and stood looking in the window with mild curiosity. A man walked up behind him, then they fell in step.

"No one paid any attention to you, Sonny," the second man said.

"How would you know? You won't see 'em."

"You overestimate the enemy."

"Underestimating them can be a fatal mistake. You'll only do it once."

As they approached a black sedan in the center of the next block, the chess player unlocked it with a button on his key. He seated himself behind the wheel, started the car, and piloted it away from the curb.

"Luck hasn't heard from Vandervelt," Sonny Tran told the passenger.

"What are the possibilities?"

"He's been arrested. That's the first one. The second is that he didn't do his job so the ragheads killed him. The third is that the ragheads killed him after he had done his job so they wouldn't have to give him any more money and he couldn't tattle on them."

"We don't need him."

"True. But we are going nowhere if he didn't do his job, which was to ensure the weapons were properly armed and deposited in Port Said for transshipment. If he didn't do his job, the weapons won't arrive where they are supposed to, and you and I will be well and truly fucked."

"Not if you kill Luck and Corrigan before they talk."

"That's true," Sonny Tran acknowledged.

"So which of your three possibilities is the one?"

"How would I know? We'll have to play it by ear and see how the bones fall."

"Okay."

"Want a laugh? They've got me running around with the Corrigan detector looking for bombs."

"The government knows about them?"

"Oh, yes. A Russian intelligence officer tipped them off. They found out sooner than I figured, but we are still okay."

"The people you're working for—maybe they know about Vandervelt and how that went down."

"I can't get close enough. The guy running the show is named Grafton. He has me working with his right-hand man, guy named Toad Tarkington. He sent me out of the office and keeps me running around with Tarkington and the Corrigan detector looking for the bombs."

"Why aren't you over at the CIA? And who is this Grafton?"

"He's a naval officer, some kick-butt guy the Pentagon calls when the going gets tough. I can't figure out if he's suspicious of me or doesn't like my body odor."

"Bastard probably doesn't like Vietnamese."

"Maybe. The FBI gave me a lie detector test. Then this assignment arrived."

"You've taken those tests before and always passed."

"Yeah. I just hope I'm not on Grafton's shit list—not at this stage of the game."

"He's a paper pusher," the passenger said dismissively. "From basket to basket. We're going to *win*!"

Sonny Tran was thinking about Dutch Vandervelt. The whole ship! As for the man in Cairo, he was dead or wished he was. The missing ship almost certainly meant Vandervelt was dead. If the terrorists had killed Vandervelt to ensure he never talked, Corrigan's man in Cairo was living on borrowed time.

Those guys were venomous and downright homicidal. *So long, Dutch!*

The thought occurred to him, not for the first time, that Luck and Corrigan were also going to be unhappy if they suspected they had been double-crossed. The terrorists might be poisonous snakes; Corrigan and Luck were cornered rats.

"Don't be so damn gloomy," the man beside Tran said. "Nothing ever goes perfect. Still, for a change, life is breaking our way. For the first time in my life I feel free."

"Right," Sonny said.

Seated beside him, his brother, Nguyen Duc Tran, laughed. "The fall of the American empire," he chortled, "is gonna be one hell of a lot of fun."

"If we live to see it."

"We'll see the big pop, believe me. That'll be enough."

When Nguyen settled down Sonny steered the subject in another direction. "Tell me about Kansas," he said.

"It went well. Two hundred grand in cash to fund the adventure and a sackful of weapons."

"Any chance of the law figuring out you did it?"

"I don't think so. Killed them all. Had a wonderful time. The law will think someone did the world a favor by killing some rats." He laughed. "You and I are going to kill a lot of them."

CHAPTER FIFTEEN

On Tuesday morning Jake Grafton wore casual civilian clothes and rode the Metro to the L'Enfant Plaza station. He exited the train and took the escalator up to the large indoor shopping mall. After one wrong turn, he found the bakery shop he wanted and went in. At a tiny table against the rear wall with his back to the entrance sat Sal Molina. Dressed in jeans and a sweatshirt, he was buried in a newspaper while he munched a bagel and drank coffee. After Jake stood in line and got something to eat, he joined Molina. No one in the place paid any attention to either of them.

"Good morning," Molina said.

" 'Morning, sir," Jake Grafton replied, and checked the interior of his bagel to be sure the cook had left the cheese off the egg.

"I'll say this for you, Admiral—you have more enemies in this town than any other sailor I know."

"The navy teaches you how to make a splash."

"So tell me about this woman who showed up on your doorstep."

After a glance around to ensure no one was eavesdropping, Jake did so. "Harry Estep and I think she's telling the truth, for whatever that's worth," he concluded. "Harry says the CDs are gold."

Molina had asked no questions during Jake's recitation. Now he said, "I got a call last night from Emerick." Emerick was the director of the FBI. "The little weasel was complaining that you want to put that Russian woman in the Federal Witness Protection Program."

"Someone will probably kill her if we don't," Jake said.

"He was bitching that she was in the country illegally, that the tourist visa she got in Cairo was fraudulently issued by an ex-boyfriend."

"Bet he also said that she was probably a Russian spy."

"As a matter of fact, he did. So did DeGarmo when I talked to him."

Jakc bit off a mouthful of bagel and chewed thoughtfully.

"One of these guys is going to leak this to the press," Molina said thoughtfully. "Or to one of their friends on the Hill."

Grafton captured Molina's gaze. "Your problem," he said distinctly, just loudly enough for Molina to hear. "If you want some free advice, cut their nuts off before they do it. Don't wait."

"Uh-huh."

"While you are at it, you might cast a cold eye on your good buddy Butch Lanham. He's trying to screw up the courage to do some leaking to a reporter."

"How do you know that?"

"You don't want to know. Believe me. What is it with that guy, anyway?"

Sal Molina grimaced. "He wants direct access to the president. Access is power in Washington. He wants my head on a plate."

"Hell of a guy."

Molina went on to another subject. "DeGarmo also complained about a CIA officer attached to your staff who had some kind of aerial adventure Sunday evening."

"Guy named Carmellini. Two agency colleagues tried to kill him," Jake said, then sipped his coffee. "They put him in concrete boots and were going to dump him into the ocean still alive. Sort of what Lanham is trying to do to you and me. Carmellini killed them first."

"And the reason?"

"They tried to blackmail him into telling them what's going on in my office. Access. That's what he and I think it was all about, anyway."

"DeGarmo was bitching that you and this guy—Carmellini?—won't tell him or the FBI anything about the blackmail end of it."

"Yep."

"Will you tell me?"

"Sure you want to know?"

"Try me."

"They thought they had Carmellini on the hook for an old killing."

Molina pursed his lips. He had a hell of a poker face, but his surprise showed. Whatever he thought he was going to hear, that wasn't it.

"Did he do it?" Molina asked after a bit.

"I didn't ask him," Jake replied curtly.

"What do you think?"

The admiral shrugged. "Probably did."

"And you want this guy on your team?"

"You surround yourself with people who can do the job you need to accomplish," Jake explained. "So do I. But we play on different fields. I don't care about gilt-edge résumés or family connections or Ivy League degrees. Carmellini's a good thief and a hell of a burglar and he knows how to get stuff done." He turned over a hand. "Trustworthy people with brains and balls are hard to find these days."

Molina couldn't let it alone. "Who'd he kill? Girlfriend or mom or the kid next door?"

"A guy he ran across in Cuba a few years ago."

"You don't seem very upset about it."

"I'm sure he had a good reason. You could find out more if you want to, but I advise you not to try. And I suggest you stop asking questions that you won't like the answers to."

Sal Molina nudged the remainder of his breakfast with a finger and made a face.

Jake pressed. "Don't get cold feet now. You let me spring Zelda from prison."

"You trust her?"

"Not really. Bureaucrats wringing their hands, worrying about the regs and their careers aren't going to get it done. I think she can help. I need to tell her about the items we're looking for. She can't help me search the haystack unless I tell her what the needle looks like."

"She doing you any good now?"

"Yeah. She hacked into the FBI's investigative files. I'm seeing everything Emerick is."

Molina sat frozen, staring at him openmouthed, speechless for probably the first time in his life.

"Just because the president told Emerick and DeGarmo to cooperate didn't mean they were going to do it," Jake explained. "Bureaucrats protect their rice bowls. It's the survival instinct, I suppose."

Molina snorted.

Jake continued: "Now for the bad news—Emerick isn't seeing

much. The FBI's computer systems are hopeless. They have thirty-four different databases over there, most of which can't talk to each other. The systems are difficult to search, and in some cases searches are futile because the field offices are as much as six months behind on data entry. I hear a lot of agents keep private case files on paper."

"Zelda hacked into the CIA computer yet?"

"Not to the best of my knowledge. I told her to stay out of it."

"Will she do what you tell her?"

"That's the question."

Molina tried his coffee and found that it was cold. He made a face. "How many spots are on Emerick's hole cards?"

"The most promising leads are in Florida. The joint task force down there is tracking seventeen groups that might be terrorists. Emerick has his right-hand man, Hob Tulik, down there personally running the show and reporting back daily. They're hoping one or two or three or four of those cells will lead them to the bombs."

"What do you think?"

"I hope to God they're right."

Sal Molina looked slowly around the room, taking in everything. His gaze returned to Jake Grafton's face. The gray eyes looking into his were the color of the North Atlantic in winter. "Find the fucking things," Molina said. "I don't care what you have to do."

"Okay."

"So tell me about this thing you found buried in a golf course."

"We don't know what it is. A bomb is a possibility, obviously."

"You gonna dig it up?"

"Not right quick. Whoever put it there probably has an eye or two on it."

"What do you want me to tell the president?"

"Whatever you think appropriate. He trusts your discretion and good judgment. Use them."

"Brains and balls, huh?" Molina extracted a packet of Rolaids from a pocket and popped a couple in his mouth. As he chewed he said to Grafton, "I can see how you earned your reputation."

"Which is?"

"The toughest nut-cutter in uniform."

Jake snorted derisively. "Don't say that to my wife. She still thinks I'm a nice guy."

"You got her fooled. Congrats. I wish you every happiness."

Sal Molina arose, tucked his newspaper under his arm, and headed for the door. Jake went to the coffeepot for a refill.

Two hours later when Molina briefed the president, he said, "Jake Grafton's the guy for this job, all right. He may be the most dangerous man alive. Emerick and DeGarmo haven't a clue who they're dealing with."

"Can he find those bombs?" the president asked.

"I don't know," replied a pensive Sal Molina. "Maybe we're all walking the plank together, living out the last few days of Western civilization."

Thayer Michael Corrigan and Karl Luck were concerned. Where *Olympic Voyager* had gone they had no idea. Not a word from Dutch Vandervelt or Omar Caliph in Cairo. Obviously things weren't going as planned. The problem was figuring out whether the random friction of life or an unknown factor was hindering the grand plan.

Luck normally communicated with Caliph by the use of encrypted e-mail, yet now Omar wasn't answering. Luck finally sent a man from the law firm Corrigan Engineering used in Cairo. The news, when he received it, was grim. Omar Caliph had leaped to his death from his eleventh-floor apartment this past Sunday, an apparent suicide. Rumor had it he left no note.

Corrigan stared at Luck after he relayed the news. "First Vandervelt, now Caliph. It's almost as if the terrorists knew we were going to help the feds find the bombs."

"They couldn't know that," Luck said. "Vandervelt didn't know and neither did Caliph."

"Perhaps they don't suspect us," Corrigan mused. "It seems more probable that, as a precaution, they are killing everyone who might betray them."

True, he had provided the money for the bombs, but that bought him nothing in the eyes of the terrorists. As far as they were concerned, if a bomb ultimately exploded he would get his money's worth. Even if he and all his friends were dead. After all, if the destruction of your enemies wasn't worth your life, you didn't hate enough. And they did.

They couldn't know that Corrigan didn't want the bombs to explode, any of them.

Precautionary murder. The next move on the board, he concluded, was for the terrorists to murder him and Luck, sever the last of the ties.

Corrigan had never used that tactic himself, preferring to solve his problems with money and occasionally blackmail. Money works wonders, he knew, because he lived in a place and time and among a people where money was very important. Although money meant little to the Islamic terrorists, he had thought he could induce them to play the role he devised for them. And yet, he realized early on that he had never before played such a dangerous game. He had won all his life by preparing for every contingency. He intended to win this game, too.

He got on the exercise bike and began riding while he thought about it. Frouq al-Zuair and Abdul Abn Saad were damned dangerous men, not greedy engineers in Georgia. He knew a killer who could eliminate them. Corrigan hadn't planned on doing it so soon, but every day that passed increased the risk. Why wait? The bombs were on their way, the terrorists had done their job.

"It's time for the Russians," he told Luck.

"I thought so, too."

"After they do the ragheads, they need to eliminate Sonny Tran. His usefulness will be at an end."

"Yes, sir."

"On your way out turn on the television to CNBC so I can watch the ticker. And send my secretary in. Have her bring her notepad and the *Wall Street Journal*."

Luck went to do as he was told.

When he reached his office in the tombs of Langley, Jake Grafton called General Alt on the secure telephone. The executive assistant put him straight through to the chairman. Jake explained the problem. "Either something is buried on Hains Point or the Corrigan detection unit is defective. We must establish which is the case as soon as possible."

"Which is more likely?"

"We calibrated the Corrigan unit again today on a live weapon. Everything seems to be working the way it's supposed to."

"So what's under that golf course?"

"General, I don't know. It's what might be down there that has me worried."

"The heart of Washington," the chairman mused. "Heck, I live right across the boat channel in Fort McNair."

"The seat of American government is within a mile and a half of that site," Jake remarked. "We're talking the Capitol, the Pentagon, the White House, the Treasury, Federal Reserve, Supreme Court, FBI—"

"Well, go dig a hole."

"That was my first thought, sir. Then I had another. If it is a nuke, whoever put it there may be watching it—by satellite if nothing else."

"We can put a tent up," Alt shot back, "a big one, biggest we can find. The following evening we'll bring in a couple of big backhoes and some trucks to haul out the dirt. Work at night and keep the site completely shielded with the tent. Use armed guards to keep spectators as far away as possible."

"All the golf course personnel will know that something is up," Jake objected. "If this thing is what we think it is, someone is watching. We go digging around, the wrong people are going to hear about it before long. I'd rather go to a little trouble and do it in such a way that a direct observer can't tell what we are doing."

"You know, Grafton, I never really appreciated what a sneaky bastard you are."

"That's my second compliment this morning, sir. Clean living and prayer are paying off."

Alt sighed audibly. "Okay. Do it any way you want."

"I'm going to need your aides to help me grease this through the system."

"Of course," Alt said.

Toad Tarkington and Gil Pascal came into the room after Jake cradled the secure telephone. Captain Pascal said, "We've put together a patrol program here in Washington for our one Corrigan unit, Admiral," and handed Jake the document.

The admiral flipped through it—ten pages, he noted—and pushed it back across the desk.

"Not yet," he said. He eyed Toad. "You and Sonny and Harley Bennett take the van to New York. Drive up and down beside the rivers, drive the major boulevards of Manhattan and Brooklyn and annotate a map, establish a baseline."

"Why the rivers, sir?"

"If I were going to attack America with a nuclear weapon, I'd bring in it in a ship or boat. Wouldn't even have to dock it. Detonate the bomb in the harbor."

"Do you think one is already here?"

"I don't know what to think," Jake Grafton confessed, and toyed with Pascal's plan. "That golf course hot spot has me worried. That was unexpected."

"When do you want us to leave, sir?" Toad asked.

"As fast as you can get to the parking lot. Buy a toothbrush and clean underwear in New York. Keep me informed."

"I'm on my way," Toad said, and walked out of the room.

"NIMA can't find *Olympic Voyager,*" Pascal said as he handed Jake a memo to that effect. "They don't think she's in the Med."

"Oh, she's probably there, all right," Jake said carelessly. "On the bottom."

Later that morning he spent a half hour with FBI agent Harry Estep and two of his colleagues. There was no official record of *Olympic Voyager* docking or anchoring in the harbor at Port Said, but several informants were sure that she had been there. If cargo was off-loaded or transshipped, there was no written evidence of it.

"Thousands of containers . . . make that tens of thousands of containers," Estep said, "go across those docks every week. We're chasing down the ships that have gone through that port this past week, but I don't know that we have them all. The port authorities *seem* cooperative, going through the motions, checking records . . ." He ran out of steam.

"Any possibility of bribery?" Jake asked softly.

"That's the third world. Every civil servant has his hand out—all of them!"

"So what if the weapons were transshipped?"

"You know the answer as well as I. They could be sent anywhere, be redirected from port to port, from ship to ship, until finally they arrive wherever the people juggling the shipping documents want them to go."

"Assume they are destined to come here. How do we intercept them?"

"Search every ship, every container. That's the only way."

"Is that possible?"

"No. Too many ships, too many containers."

"What about intercepting every ship at sea, boarding and searching it with Geiger counters?"

"That might work," Harry Estep admitted. "If we use every boat and ship the Coast Guard and navy can get to sea and every airplane that will fly—assuming we're willing to pay the costs and tolerate the delays—what the hell, it might be possible."

Jake shooed them out. He stood in front of the map that covered the wall opposite his desk and used his fingers to roughly measure distances.

"Here are the daily FBI reports on those Florida cells," Zelda said. She didn't do the "sir" thing. Jake Grafton didn't care. She placed the file on the desk.

"Please. Close the door and sit." Jake's regular telephone had a long cord so he could walk around the office while he talked, and as often happened, the cord was twisted into a knot. He had the receiver off the hook and was busy untwisting the thing as Zelda seated herself. She had more files in her arms and rested them on her lap. He glanced up at her, finished the cord, then placed the receiver back on the hook.

He took his time perusing the reports. "What do you think?" he asked her when he finished.

"If these are terrorist cells, they are waiting for something to happen. I don't know what. They aren't really doing anything."

"I think you're right."

He handed the file to her and nodded at the folders on her lap. "What else have you come up with?"

"A lot of nothing," she said, and placed five files in front of him. The top one was Arch Foster. Inside were telephone records, bank statements, credit card records for a year, even copies of the power company's records on his house. His car payments—he was never late. Subscribed to three magazines, belonged to a service club . . . made a complaint to the police six months ago about a loud party down the street.

Norv Lalouette's file was even thicker. He was a heavy user of the Internet—liked to visit porn sites, apparently. Ordered books from Amazon.com, dabbled in on-line investments—nothing huge, just occasional hundred-share lots. The investment account was worth $27,745.

The other three were Butch Lanham, Coke Twilley, and Sonny Tran, the three people who knew that Janos Ilin said the missing Richard Doyle was a spy and flunked the recognition portion of their lie detector tests. He flipped through the files . . . nothing leaped out.

"I'll need to study these," he said. "Is there any way you can put names and addresses to the telephone calls these people made and received?"

"Yes. I have a staffer on that now."

"So tell me what you think. Using the tools we have, how can we find out more about these people?"

"It would help if I knew why I was looking and what I was looking for."

Her hair was shampooed and brushed, she was dressed in a nice outfit, her color looked good. She seemed more relaxed than Jake remembered seeing her. Yet still sour.

"How are you and Zip getting along?"

She shrugged.

"Carmellini says Zip's in love with you."

"I don't think that's any of your business. Or Carmellini's."

"I suppose not," Jake acknowledged.

"You act like a man trying to work himself up to something. Why don't you just spit it out and we'll deal with it."

Jake nodded. "Here's how it is. I don't trust you to do the right thing, yet I need your help."

"Your problem."

He arranged the files on his desk in a stack and checked that the backs were straight. "We're looking for four nuclear weapons." He went into detail, explained what he knew. She asked no questions, just listened. "We need a fresh approach. I want you to think outside the box. If those weapons are coming to America, there will be people here to meet them, perhaps these cells the joint task force is tracking. Perhaps cells they don't know about. In any event, the people importing these weapons have plans. They are making telephone calls, spending money, talking to confederates, traveling. Your job is to find them. Not all of them—one will do. Some one person. Give me a hint, a trail, some little bit of the string. I don't care about arrests or prosecutions—that is for the FBI and Justice. I want the bombs."

"Arch and Norv? Were they part of this?"

"They might have been. It's possible." She had been told of Carmellini's weekend adventure but knew nothing of the blackmail angle, a detail Jake had no intention of sharing. "I think they wanted Carmellini to tell them what is going on in this office. There are other possibilities, by the way. One of them is that they were involved in a Russian spy ring. It's probable someone killed Richard Doyle; they are the likely candidates. The FBI has a forensic team going over their airplane."

"Lanham, Twilley, and Tran?"

"They knew Ilin fingered Doyle."

"I need to think about this," she murmured.

"Think hard. If a nuke pops in Washington, you're dead. If it pops anywhere in the U.S., this nation will be irrevocably changed. Before it's over we may all wish we were dead."

"No one will be able to put Humpty Dumpty back together again," she said flippantly. "I got it, Admiral." She stood. "Anything else?"

"Well . . ." Jake hesitated, played again with the files. Then he made up his mind and looked up at her, meeting her eyes. "Corrigan Engineering invented a nifty new radiation detector just in time for us to start chasing terrorists with nukes."

She snorted. "Ain't it grand the way American industry comes through in the nick of time, just when we need 'em? We needed telephones and there was Bell. Cars, and Henry Ford showed up. Airplanes, and the Wright brothers delivered in time for World War One. We could talk all day about Bill Gates, or Saint Bill, as he likes to be called. Are we lucky or what?"

"Check out Corrigan."

"You're a suspicious bastard, aren't you?"

Jake brightened. "Wow, three compliments this week. Go get 'em, Zelda."

"My name is Sarah Houston," she growled, and marched from the office.

So the feds knew about the bombs. Nguyen Duc Tran thought about that fact as he piloted his big eighteen-wheel rig south on the interstate. He didn't turn on the radio—most of the stations played country music and Nguyen Duc Tran hated it. Country was too schmaltzy, too sweet, too stupid . . . too American. Nor did he want to listen to the smart people on NPR talk to the people who thought they were smart. He had some classical and jazz CDs in the box, but today he wasn't in the mood. He kept the tractor at sixty-five and let the hum of the engine and the unwinding endless highway smooth him over and chill him down.

And the feds had Sonny looking for the damned things! If that wasn't a hoot!

Nguyen Duc Tran hated America. He had lived here since he was five years old and spoke only English, but he hated the place and the people and their decadent, rotten values.

He and his brother grew up in Texas. His parents were professional people with standing in Vietnam—his father a career army officer—but after they escaped from Saigon before the fall in 1975, they wound up in Texas. The only work his father could find was as a janitor. His mother cleaned houses. Sonny and Nguyen grew up as Vietnamese niggers, loathed and endlessly teased about being Viet Cong. Communists. Cong Tran they called him in school.

"You South Viets lost the fucking war, Cong, let those fucking Ho Chi Minh-ers kick your asses. Even the U.S. Army couldn't save your sorry butts. So you came over here and took jobs away from good Americans when you couldn't hold on to your own shitty little country. Why don't you go back there, huh, raise the IQ of Texas *and* Vietnam?" He had gotten a lot of that growing up, back when he was too small to fight back.

Sonny was smart, a great student, and he won scholarships to California colleges. Nguyen was only mediocre in school. He dropped out of junior college after a year and became a commercial truck driver. When he could find work. "Think you're big enough to drive this fucking truck, boy? Hell, you don't weigh 140 pounds. All that fucking rice and fish heads."

He had learned enough karate, finally, to take care of the worst of the big-bellied bastards. It didn't take much. A punch in the throat, an elbow in the pot gut, or a well-aimed kick in the groin would usually put them down. Then they flopped around like whales on the beach.

Sonny hated them, too. Oh, he had played the game all his life, but he hated them as much as Nguyen did. Maybe more. Hated these people and their money and their cultural superiority and the mindless way they interfered with the lives of people all over the globe, because Americans knew best. Knew what was right for everyone.

They poured money and weapons and endless reams of worthless free advice on the lesser folk . . . then they left when the going got rough and let their friends take the fall. Lose everything. Do the dying.

And they didn't care. Didn't care a good goddamn.

Today the spell of the road eased Nguyen past the black mood. And the thought of the weapons.

He and Sonny were going to make the bastards pay. Oh, were they going to pay!

The ragheads had shown them how. You had to hate them enough to be willing to die to make them pay. If you did, it was easy. Oh so easy.

His thoughts turned to Dutch Vandervelt. Did the raghead motherfuckers figure out they were being double-crossed? If they did, his bomb wasn't going to arrive where it should.

He thought about that. About what he would do.

You just have to play hardball. Anyone who thought he could play it tougher than Nguyen Duc Tran was kidding himself.

After the doctor smeared his feet with an antiseptic, desensitizing cream and wrapped them in bandages, Tommy Carmellini carefully donned a set of oversized tennis shoes and rode a wheelchair to the front door of the Naval Hospital in Bethesda. Rain was falling from a slate sky. A taxi was waiting. As a nurse stood watching, he gingerly tried out his new feet. Yep, if he walked slow and easy. . . . He eased himself into the backseat of the taxi and waved good-bye to the nurse.

Thirty minutes later he was back at his apartment building. His car was still in the parking lot. Fortunately the FBI had recovered his keys and wallet and returned them to him, although they never mentioned his pistol and he didn't ask. The pistol would have been no big deal in most of the United States, but owning and possessing one in the District of Columbia was illegal. Like every other law on the books, this one was also ignored by crooks, dope dealers, and gangbangers who continued to use guns as they preyed on the unarmed and each other. Presumably the knowledge that most of their constituents were unarmed made the local politicians feel more secure.

As the rain dampened him down, Carmellini opened the trunk of his car and looked in. Yep, the Winchester was still there. Maybe the FBI didn't search the car.

The agents had carefully searched the apartment. Estep and his colleagues had found twelve bugs, he said, and removed them. He had been reasonably confident that they had gotten all of them, but one never knew.

The place felt stuffy; Carmellini opened several windows. Then he lowered himself into his favorite chair and reached for his remote. He flipped through the channels looking for a ball game. Nope. He clicked the television off.

His feet were still tender. He put them up on his coffee table to keep them from swelling and sat listening to the city noises coming through the window and savoring the cool damp air. Like most people, he rarely stopped to appreciate the moment, celebrate the sublime sensual pleasure of being alive. Just now he was acutely aware of how close he had come to losing it.

He looked up the Graftons' telephone number in a notebook he had lying beside the telephone and dialed it. "Mrs. Grafton, this is Tommy Carmellini. . . . Doing just fine, thanks. Is your houseguest, Anna, available?"

The Russian woman's voice had a delicate, delicious quality—it was almost as if all the languages she spoke gave her a unique personal accent. Carmellini thought he could detect a note of warmth in her voice when she asked about him. Would she still like to go to dinner? He knew a place, he said. She agreed and he set the time, then said good-bye.

He made the effort to put the telephone on the floor beside his chair and stretched out. Actually the chair was quite comfortable and his feet on the table were at just the right height. With a breeze stirring the curtains and caressing his cheek, his mind wandered to his parents and his childhood days. Carmellini drifted off to sleep with the sound of gentle rain pattering on the window pane.

A noise in the hallway outside his apartment woke him. Or perhaps it had been outside. Some noise that shouldn't be there. He lay with his eyes closed, listening intently.

Rain hitting the window glass. Nothing else.

Now he opened his eyes, moved them around without moving his head, looking at everything in his field of view—the objects in the familiar room, the dancing curtains, rain smearing the window glass and dampening the sill.

Arch Foster and Norv Lalouette wanted him dead because they had tried to recruit him for something, and he turned them down. Something they didn't want other people knowing about. He had nothing even lukewarm going in his office right now. They probably wanted him to spy on Jake Grafton. What else could it have been? Did he have that figured right?

He didn't know anything compromising about anyone. Or to be more precise, any live person. Even if someone thought he did, he had had two days to blab to the FBI and the Maryland State Police and anyone else on God's green earth he could telephone or write to.

Damage control for Arch and Norv's friends would certainly not involve silencing him. Would it?

"You're all assholes," he said aloud to anyone who might be listening. "Arch and Norv were assholes, and so are you."

Angry with himself for being in this mood, he levered himself erect and padded carefully into the bathroom to give himself a sponge bath and shave. The dressings on his feet were good until tomorrow, and in any event he didn't want to fool with them tonight.

An hour later he stood in front of the door to his apartment, listening carefully. He put his eye to the peephole. Then he unlocked the door and pulled it open.

In the lobby he stopped at the door to the building and surveyed the parking lot. Still an hour or so before dark. The rain had stopped but the clouds were low and the wind had picked up. No one in sight. Yet even as Carmellini stood there a car rolled into the lot and slid into a parking place. A fit man in his late twenties or early thirties got out and headed for the lobby.

Carmellini stared, trying to recognize him.

Suddenly anger flooded him. "Shit!" he muttered, pushed the door open, and stalked out as confidently as he could on sore feet. He ignored the man going into the building—didn't even glance at him.

CHAPTER SIXTEEN

Tommy Carmellini took Anna Modin to a seafood restaurant on the northern shore of Inner Harbor in Baltimore. He wanted crowds, music, and a fine meal in the company of a beautiful woman. Anna Modin certainly qualified, he thought. She wasn't cover-girl perfect, but she had a presence.

The restaurant was a stand-alone building with a lawn between it and the water, one tastefully landscaped with trees and benches and sidewalks. Along the seawall were moored several magnificent small ships from the age of sail. On the western edge of the little point was a basin for powerboats. Despite the fact that it was a raw, windy evening with low clouds scudding swiftly across the sky, before they went inside Tommy Carmellini and Anna Modin strolled the walkway along the seawall, inspected the sailboats rocking in the swells and straining at their moorings, watched a water taxi swing into a small dock and deposit a load of chilly people from the complex at Inner Harbor. Another group boarded the boat and away it went with the wind behind it, headed eastward for the bars and restaurants at Sewell's Point.

In the growing darkness the lights of the city were illuminating. Carmellini pointed across the harbor at Federal Hill and the barely visible swell of headland where Fort McHenry stood, all the while talking about the War of 1812 while Anna stood with her coat wrapped tightly around her and the tails whipping in the wind.

His world felt normal again. He didn't even notice his tender feet.

After dragging in several deep lungfuls of tangy sea air, he led Anna to the foyer of the restaurant to warm up. He asked for a table. They were lucky; the maître d' seated them at a small table by the window overlooking the harbor and the moored ships. There weren't many empty tables remaining. The hum of conversation, laughter, well-dressed people, subdued classical music—Tommy Carmellini felt good!

Over a glass of wine he decided that Anna Modin was the most interesting person he had met in many a year. She was calm, self-assured, quite at home in a new country, surrounded by people speaking a foreign language. She looked around curiously, then paid attention to him. After they ordered he noticed that she carefully scanned the crowd from time to time and the shadowy strollers on the seawall, barely visible through the trees and shrubs a hundred feet or so away from the restaurant windows.

She had worked in international banking for years, she said, so they discussed that. And places they had both been, movies, music, the arts. Carmellini's recent adventure never came up, nor did the reason Anna was in America. Carmellini would find out about it at the office, he knew, if and when Jake Grafton chose to tell him.

Eventually they discussed the Graftons, Jake, Callie, and Amy. Anna liked them and Carmellini did, too, so Tommy ended up telling her all he knew of the family history, including the recent adventure in Hong Kong.

Dinner was delicious, Alaskan king salmon and Atlantic halibut. They lingered over their meal, had more wine, scrutinized the desserts the waiter brought by on a cart, and ordered carefully. When the desserts came they shared, each sampling the other's, then ended the meal with coffee.

The spell was broken when he noticed she was looking around again, scrutinizing the other diners, staring at the lights beyond the huge dark windows.

She was obviously worried.

"Is someone looking for you?" he asked.

"Yes."

"Husband or boyfriend?"

"No."

"Want to tell me about it?"

She glanced at him. "Who are you?" she asked.

"Just a civil servant."

"Whom people try to kill."

"Sometimes life gets complicated."

"What branch of the government do you work for?"

"I'm working for Jake Grafton just now," Carmellini answered, wondering if she would pick up on the subtlety of that answer. People who worked for the CIA were not supposed to advertise the fact since everything involving their employment was classified.

"Did he ask you to take me out tonight?"

"Nope," he said, slightly relieved that she had moved off the subject of his employer. "Thought it up my very own self."

"Would Jake Grafton have us followed?"

"Were we followed?"

"I'm not sure. There was a car behind us as we drove to Baltimore."

"Why didn't you mention it before now?"

"I thought it might be your police."

"Uh-huh."

"Protecting me."

"I see." He didn't see, but if Grafton thought she needed protection, he was certainly capable of providing some. But not, Carmellini thought, without telling me beforehand. Not in light of my recent adventure. Grafton would not have overlooked that courtesy.

Unless there was some reason that Carmellini didn't know about. Come to think of it, there was little he did know. He considered the situation while the waiter refilled their coffee cups. Frankly, everything he knew wouldn't fill a coffee cup.

When the waiter moved out of earshot, he asked Anna, "Is there anyone here now that you think might be keeping tabs on us?"

"Tabs?"

"Watching us."

"Several couples are possibilities."

"Any single men? Or pairs of men?"

"No."

For the first time the vulnerability of their position in front of the windows struck him forcefully. If someone wanted to kill her, they were outside watching through the glass, not inside.

Cursing silently to himself, he laid a credit card on the table, then fished in his jacket pocket for his cell phone. His stomach felt queasy, his skin clammy.

"The waiter will bring our bill in a moment or two," he said with more confidence than he felt. God, what a fool he was! A normal evening! "It will take several minutes to process the credit card, I'll sign the invoice, then we will leave. Tell me if they are also preparing to leave."

Staring through the window beside their table at the shadows and dark areas of the lawn and the just-visible spidery masts of the sailing vessels, he toyed with the cell phone. He could call Jake Grafton, of course. But what would he say? *I'm scared—send someone to save us?*

Get a grip, Carmellini!

For the love of Christ—why didn't I ask Grafton for a weapon?

The waiter drifted over, presented the bill. Carmellini didn't even glance at it. He nodded, still fingering the cell phone.

"Please, sir," the waiter murmured. "We ask our patrons not to use telephones in the restaurant. They disturb the other diners."

"Do the credit card," Carmellini said sharply, and pushed the plastic at the man.

When the waiter departed he asked Anna, "Who is after you?"

"I was in Egypt. They tried to kill me there." She wanted to tell him more, but she refrained.

He felt a surge of anger. Why didn't she tell him that earlier? He had accepted a table by the window and she didn't even peep!

The manager came over, smiled, laid a hand on the back of his chair. "How was everything tonight?"

"Terrific."

"Please come visit us again."

"You bet."

The waiter brought the bill and credit card invoice, all tastefully hidden in a leather folder. Carmellini bent over to figure the tip. Anna Modin reached for her purse, which was on the empty chair to her right. The strap had slipped over the back of the chair.

"Let me help you with that," the waiter said and walked behind them. As he bent over the chair with the purse Carmellini heard a whap. And the tinkling of glass.

He looked up. The waiter was staring uncomprehendingly at his shirt . . . at a spreading bloodstain. Carmellini's eyes went to the window, to a small hole in the glass.

As the waiter fell Tommy grabbed Modin's wrist and dragged her from her chair.

"Let's go!" he hissed, and ran for the door, pulling her behind him as people in the restaurant screamed and several people jumped up and tried to flee. Carmellini bowled over one woman and pushed another man aside, all the while dragging Modin behind him with a death grip on her wrist.

They could be waiting for them outside!

That thought ran through his head and competed with an overwhelming urge to flee this palace of windows; the urge to flee won. He charged down the hallway toward the foyer, still holding Modin firmly by the wrist.

"My purse," she pleaded.

"Fuck it!" Tommy Carmellini roared, and charged through the crowd waiting for a table and blasted out the door into the night.

"Can you run?"

"Yes," she said, so he released her wrist. Dodging and weaving, he led the way toward the parking lot as fast as he could go, oblivious of his sore feet. He never felt a thing.

Approaching the car he scanned the area . . . and saw no one. The rifle in the trunk—he wanted it in his hand, wanted it desperately.

There couldn't be more than one or two of them, he thought as he savagely ripped his car keys from his trouser pocket. He pushed the button to unlock the thing as he approached and the fucking lights flashed! A 1987 model, the car hadn't come with that feature—he had paid extra to have it installed when he purchased the car two years ago!

Oh, shit!

He jabbed the key into the trunk. It opened.

At least he was still ahead of them.

"Get down, get down," he hissed, and Anna dropped to a crouch.

He grabbed the rifle, felt for the box of shells.

He hadn't fired the Winchester since that day in West Virginia. Hadn't even loaded the friggin' thing. Now he ripped open the box of shells, poured four into his hand, and jammed more into his right jacket pocket. He rammed the brass cylinders into the loading gate on the side of the action. One, two, three, four, all the while scanning for people.

"Get in the car!"

She obeyed instantly.

He worked the lever, jacked a shell into the chamber.

The interior light popped on.

He sidled around the car, opened the driver's door, and slid into the seat. The interior lights went out when he pulled the door closed.

He fumbled to get the key into the ignition. The rifle was awkward, too long. Belatedly he realized that the hammer was cocked and the rifle had no safety. He took time from the key struggle to ease the hammer down, then jammed the key in and twisted hard. The engine caught.

He looked aft as he pulled the transmission into reverse. As he did he saw a car roaring down the lane behind them. He heard its brakes lock up and the tires squall.

"Get down," he shouted, slammed the transmission into park, and bailed out.

The rifle barrel hit something, then he had it and swung it as the sedan behind screeched to a halt and the man in the driver's seat leveled a weapon through his open window.

Tommy Carmellini already had the rifle up. He aimed just in front of the driver's door handle and pulled the trigger. From fifteen feet he couldn't miss.

The rifle boomed and bucked.

Carmellini worked the lever and aimed and fired again, as fast as he could.

After the third shot, the car began moving, crawling away at idle. Carmellini stood, aimed carefully at the shadowy figure of the passenger and fired his last shot through the rear side window, shattering it. The car crept along at an angle and lightly impacted a parked car.

He fed another shell into the loading gate of the Winchester, worked the lever to eject the spent shell and chamber the new round. Walking toward the car he shot the passenger again. Shoved another shell into the rifle, worked the lever.

The driver was lying over on the passenger's lap. Tommy fired another shot into the passenger, rammed another shell into the gun, worked the action, and stuck the rifle barrel through the driver's window. That bullet exploded the driver's head.

Standing there slightly deafened by the gunshots, Tommy Carmellini carefully loaded the rifle as he scanned the parked cars. Suddenly he realized that he could hear screaming, an ongoing scream that started some seconds ago.

He swung toward the sound with the rifle up. A woman stood frozen, staring with wide eyes, her hand over her mouth as her companion tugged at her arm.

He looked again into the sedan. The carnage created by the soft-nosed .30-30 slugs at close range was awesome. The interior was spattered with blood and brains.

Tommy Carmellini reached in and twisted the ignition key, killing the engine.

In the silence he walked back to Anna. She was lying on the seat. She looked up at him with fear in her eyes.

He opened the passenger door of the Mercedes.

"It's okay," he said. "We're okay. Let's wait for the police."

His hands were shaking and his heart racing. He remembered the cell phone, felt for it in his pocket.

He had left it on the table in the restaurant, along with his credit card and her purse.

It was close to midnight when the first-class petty officer pulled the throttles of the cabin cruiser back to idle. The boat was about a hundred yards off Hains Point with its bow pointed upstream. Jake Grafton used his binoculars to scan the seawall. No one visible—which was what he expected. He could hear the faint sound of two army helicopters overhead, just under the clouds. They had been patrolling the golf course with infrared sensors since dark, and they had detected nothing.

Behind him he could hear Gil Pascal talking to the pilots on a handheld radio, and their tinny reply: "Nothing, Dog Leader. It's clean."

Jake touched the petty officer at the helm on the shoulder and pointed. The helmsman nodded and stroked the throttle. Despite the raw breeze, he brought the boat in expertly against the seawall. One of the sailors leaped from the fantail to the top of the wall, and another sailor threw him a line. While they were mooring the boat, two marines wearing night-vision goggles went ashore to act as perimeter guards.

With the help of the sailors, four army engineering officers offloaded several boxes of equipment. They set up their gear in a location that Jake pointed out. Yes, right here. He could see the tracks from the van.

He, too, had night-vision goggles, but he carried them in his hand. Streetlights on tall aluminum poles were sited every hundred or so feet along the top of the seawall, so there was too much light for the goggles. Even without the streetlights, the glow of the city lights reflecting off the clouds raised the light level to perpetual twilight.

The rain late in the afternoon had soaked the turf. Jake watched the engineers work. Their equipment consisted of an ultrawide band radar normally used to look for cracks in concrete bridge structures. It had a fantastic ability to see through solids.

Soon the engineers had a picture on the scope. Jake bent down, examined the image with his reading glasses. Gil Pascal bent over, too.

"What do you make of it," Jake asked the senior officer, a major with a Southern accent.

"Something down there all right, sir, but don't know what. Can't see too well from this angle."

"Looks like rocks to me," Jake said.

"Bound to be a lot of rocks in this fill, sir. Big ones, small ones, and everything in between. We're gonna have to look for something that doesn't look like a rock."

They moved the transceiver several times, trying to find the best angle. All that could be seen on the screen were bright spots of high relativity and dark places of low. The major hooked the video feed to a computer and began playing with the image, seeing if he could improve it.

A shadowy line appeared across the screen, came and went as he increased some values and lowered others.

"What's that line?" Jake asked.

"A wire of some kind," the major suggested.

He and Jake walked away from the unit, inspected the earth. The major pointed out where the wire would be.

"Seems to run toward that streetlight pole," Gil Pascal suggested.

"Seems to be, yes."

"Follow the wire. I want to know precisely where it goes."

"Yes, sir."

Using the UWB radar, the engineers confirmed that the streetlights were wired together by underground cable. In addition, there was this other wire that ran in under one of the poles.

"There ought to be one more wire of some kind, an antenna," Jake muttered to the major. "See if you can find it."

It was Gil Pascal who called his attention to it. "Some of these trees seem to have wires running through the branches." Jake walked to where Gil was standing. "See this wire running up beside the tree? When I saw it I assumed it was a lightning rod."

"Isn't it?" Jake donned his night-vision goggles and inspected the wire running up one of the trunks.

"It could be an antenna. See how the wire loops through the trees. Looks to me like it's been there for years."

Jake Grafton turned to Gil and slapped his shoulder. "The Corrigan unit works. We're getting someplace now."

Pascal was incredulous. "That's a nuclear weapon buried under there?"

"You can bet your last dollar on it," Jake said, and walked away to tell the army engineers to pack up.

His cell phone rang and he answered it.

"Grafton."

"Tommy Carmellini, Admiral. I'm in Baltimore police headquarters with Anna Modin. A couple of guys tried to kill her tonight."

"Baltimore? What the hell are you doing with her in Baltimore?"

"I asked her to go to dinner, and she said yes. Why didn't you tell me the ragheads are after her?"

"I didn't know you were taking her out." He hadn't been home since he left this morning for the L'Enfant Plaza bakery shop and his appointment with Sal Molina, and he had been too busy to call his wife. "She okay?"

"Yeah, but I killed two guys in the parking lot outside the restaurant. This went down about four hours ago. Police been trying to pump me. Every cop in Baltimore is milling around in here tonight. From what I gather, they think it's a drug gang thing. They finally let me make a telephone call, and you're it."

"Don't say anything."

"I'm getting real good at that."

"I'll be there as soon as I can."

Jake broke the connection and walked over to Gil Pascal. "Have one of the helos land and pick me up. Two men tried to kill Anna Modin tonight in Baltimore."

"She okay?"

"Carmellini says she is. He took her to dinner, then killed these guys in the restaurant parking lot. You get this stuff cleaned up and out of here." He used the cell phone to call Harry Estep.

Carmellini was right about the Baltimore police brass—they were all at headquarters when Jake Grafton arrived. They kept popping into the waiting room where a uniformed officer had parked him, introducing themselves, feeding him tidbits of information while they looked him over, then leaving him to cool his heels. He used the dead time to call Callie on his cell phone.

He broke the news of the attempted assassination as gently as he could.

"Tommy said they are both all right. I'm in Baltimore at police headquarters waiting to talk to them."

"My God!"

"They're okay," he said. "According to one of the cops, someone fired a rifle into the restaurant, killed a waiter standing beside Anna."

She took the news pretty well, he thought. After telling her all he knew, he promised to come home when he could.

At three in the morning he was led into a conference room full of brass. Harry Estep was there and introduced him to a senior FBI officer from Washington.

The police chief was a black man named Carroll. "You'll be delighted to hear that Carmellini and Modin were uncooperative. They identified themselves and refused to talk without a lawyer."

Silence followed that remark.

The chief sighed. "We're releasing them. It looks like self-defense. We'll investigate, talk to all the witnesses we can find, give the file to the prosecutors. If self-defense holds up, I assume they'll let it go at that."

"Okay."

"We'll hold on to Carmellini's rifle until our investigation is complete. He killed the living shit out of these two guys. We don't know who they are. They fired a bolt-action Winchester into the restaurant, trying for Modin or Carmellini apparently, killing the waiter instead. New rifle, no visible wear, got both their fingerprints on it. We found it lying outside by a tree."

"Sounds like these guys were real craftsmen."

"Couple of rank amateurs. Fingerprints on the rifle, blew the shot, then drove up to Carmellini and he splattered them all to hell. You oughta see the car."

"No thanks. Who were they?"

"Middle Eastern males in their twenties, looks like. They had wallets and ID, maybe fake. We're working on that. We'll get fingerprints and talk to the INS and FBI, and maybe we'll know more tomorrow."

"I'd like to keep Carmellini's and Modin's names out of the newspapers."

"That we can do," Chief Carroll said. "The reporters will get the rest of it, though. The television crews are outside now. I suggest you get your people out of here through the basement. We'll give them something to put over their heads."

"Okay."

Carroll toyed with his pen. Looking at the senior FBI officer, he said, "I'm going to be frank with you people. The dead waiter was a kid working his way through Johns Hopkins. Name of Newhouse. John Wilson Newhouse. Had a wife and kid. We're lucky only one innocent person was killed."

"And your point is?"

"Keep your goddamn problems in Washington. Don't want 'em in Baltimore."

"There's a war on," Jake Grafton retorted sharply, "or haven't you noticed?"

"I'm just telling you, we've got enough problems with druggies and gang-bangers and all the usual crooks and creeps. We don't need assassins—competent or incompetent—running around killing innocent people."

"Tell it to the terrorists," Jake Grafton snapped, and started for the door.

Carroll wasn't finished. "Your man Carmellini is a real piece of work. The Maryland State Police tell me he killed a man with his bare hands Sunday night. This guy is a walking bomb. Seventy-two hours later he blew these two away before they had time to fire a shot. Oh, they both had pistols in their hands when he did it, but what if they'd been cops responding to a call from the restaurant?"

"What do you want me to say? He should have let them shoot first?"

"He could have stayed inside the restaurant until the police arrived. Any *normal* person would have done that."

No one said anything.

The chief continued: "You people are going to ride off to Washington clucking over this mess, and I'm going to go see Newhouse's wife and tell her she's a widow." Carroll put his face inches from Jake's. "We don't want your goddamn war. That ain't fair, I know. Life rarely is. Oh, I know, everyone waves the fucking flag and wants the terrorists smacked—but they want them smacked somewhere else. And from now on it better happen somewhere else. Keep Carmellini and your other goddamn holy warrior killers the fuck out of *my* city! Got it?" He spun and pointed his finger at the FBI agents. "That goes for you assholes, too."

Jake walked out of the room.

On the way to the basement Harry Estep said, "Boy, the chief was really pissed."

"I know just how he feels," Jake muttered. And he did. The greed and stupidity of everyday criminals he understood—those qualities were inherent in the human condition. The irrational, illogical hatred that drove the terrorists was a ray of evil leaking from a crack in hell. It was frightening—and horrifying.

Anna Modin rode silently in the center of the backseat of the crowded car. Traffic on the wide superhighway was light in this hour before dawn. Tommy Carmellini told Grafton and the two FBI officers about the evening in detail, answered their questions. Harry Estep chattered away on his cell phone, call after call after call.

Carmellini was seated beside her, against the door. She could feel the warmth of his body, the solidity of his upper arm against her shoulder.

The car was dark, so she found his hand and squeezed it. They sat with their hands together, holding them between their thighs so no one would notice.

"Are you certain they weren't after you, Tommy?" Jake Grafton asked, half-turning in the front seat so he could look at Carmellini.

"Not certain, no. Pretty sure though."

Estep stuck his oar in. His superiors wanted Carmellini and Modin to spend the next few days at the FBI barracks in Quantico. Grafton said it was okay and Carmellini agreed, after a glance and nod from Anna Modin.

"I want a pistol," Carmellini announced.

"Harry?" That was Jake Grafton.

"We can do that, I guess."

"Something like an old Browning Hi-Power, nine millimeter. Not one of those plastic jobs. And a shoulder holster."

"We'll do our best."

"Like when?"

"I'll make some calls."

Dawn was well along by the time they had signed for their rooms at the FBI's Quantico facility. As the clerk led them to their rooms, which were side by side, Modin held tightly to Carmellini's hand.

Tommy thanked the man, who left after unlocking Anna's room and handing them the keys. She pulled him into the room behind her.

After the door closed, Carmellini swept her into his arms and held her. "Hell of a first date," he said.

Clutching his chest, she could hear his heart beating slowly, lazily, thudding along like an old, slow clock.

"Why were those men trying to kill you last night?" Tommy Carmellini asked Anna Modin. They had awakened in the same bed around noon, made love again, then he made two cups of instant coffee from a jar of the stuff he found in the kitchenette cupboard. Now she was seated in bed with the sheet pulled around her, sipping the hot drink, while he sat in the only chair in the bedroom with a towel around his waist.

Carmellini normally refused instant coffee, but at noon after the night he had had, he decided it wasn't bad.

"Revenge, I suppose," she said. "There was another woman, Nooreem Habib, who loaded the computer files of Walney's Bank onto disks for Janos Ilin. I was her courier." She went on, telling him about the bank that financed terrorists, about Janos Ilin . . . everything. She told all of it. "Ilin wanted Jake Grafton to have the CDs, so I brought them to him."

Then she fell silent, slightly shocked by what she had done. To share information with people without a need to know was truly Russian roulette. People had a nasty habit of chatting, telling other people interesting tidbits, for a whole grab bag of reasons, not the least of which was to sell you out for their own advantage. Every Russian child learned that hard fact in grammar school. She knew all that and spilled it anyway.

Carmellini drank half his coffee and decided he didn't want the rest. He put the cup on the nightstand.

"Those guys last night weren't very good assassins," he observed.

"Almost good enough," she observed.

He shrugged. "Maybe they're in Paradise in the arms of the virgins right this very minute, enjoying the start of an eternity of sexual delight. Isn't that what they're promised?"

"So I've heard."

"Talk about sexually repressed! *Playboy* should give the holy warriors free copies, tell them a little of that is available right here on Earth while you are alive to enjoy it, and you don't have to be a martyr to get it. But those guys last night were all bound up. I did them a favor sending them on their way. On the other hand, I hope Norv and Arch are shoveling coal in the hottest corner of hell."

"Those were the men who tried to kill you in the airplane?"

"Yeah. Hell of a world, ain't it?"

"Who *are* you, Tommy Carmellini?"

He shrugged. "I'm a thief. Joined the CIA to avoid prosecution for burglary. Another guy and I stole some diamonds. He got caught with the ice and finked on me. Now the agency has me working for Jake Grafton."

He rarely told anyone the truth about himself. Certainly no women. But Anna Modin was special, he sensed. Only the truth would do with her.

She prompted him with personal questions, so he ended up telling her the story of his life. It was nothing special—he was just a kid who wasn't like all the others, and had been smart or lucky enough not to get caught . . . most of the time, anyway.

When he ran down they sat in silence, listening to the muffled street sounds coming through the closed window.

"Are you ready to go find something to eat?" he asked.

"Later," she said, pulled the sheet aside, and held out her arms.

Afterward, lying with her head on his shoulder and her hair brushing his cheek, he asked, "Where do you go from here?"

"I don't know. Until those men in Cairo are dead . . ." She left it hanging.

"When will you know it is safe?"

"Janos Ilin will tell me."

"The FBI is going to change your name and hide you. You'll wind up answering the telephone for some dentist in Peoria or flying a cash register at a supermarket."

"Ilin will find me," she said simply. "When he needs me."

"For what?"

"For something that needs to be done."

CHAPTER SEVENTEEN

The days passed swiftly as spring brought more rain and warm weather to the Washington area. The cherry blossoms came and went, the crowds filled the tourist attractions, the trees leafed out, and the grass grew mightily. The sight and sound of lawn mowers became part and parcel of the Washington scene.

Jake Grafton saw little of it. It seemed he only got home to sleep. Eating was a breakfast sandwich or burrito at a fast-food joint on the way to work or a sandwich at his desk. Occasionally he made his way to the CIA cafeteria, only to bolt his food and run when his cell phone or pager summoned him.

A lot seemed to be happening, but it was difficult to make sense of it.

Toad Tarkington called from New York on a secure telephone located in the offices of the joint terrorism task force. "You ain't gonna believe this, boss, but we found another of the goddamn things."

"Where?"

"Seems to be under a new apartment building in midtown Manhattan." He gave Jake the address. "There are not many new buildings in this section, but the old one on this site was condemned by the city about ten years ago when the landlord didn't do repairs after a fire. From what I can learn, a developer acquired the property, tore the old building down, and built a new, taller one in its place. Four floors of parking under the thing. We drove the rig to the lowest level. No shit, we've got a hot spot under the floor."

"Same indications as you found at Hains Point?"

"Yep. Harley is pretty sure. He can talk your leg off about various kinds of radiation, which particles can penetrate dirt and which can't, but the bottom line is it looks about the same to me."

"When did they erect this building?"

"I talked to the super, visiting in a low-key, bullshit way, trying to get info without sending the guy to general quarters. Told him we were an independent contractor looking for leaking sewer gas. He bought it, I think. Says the city issued the occupancy permit for the building six years ago. The thing filled up immediately even though the apartments are pricey. You know how living space is in this town."

Jake played with the telephone cord while Toad talked. The damn thing was knotting up again. "How long do you think it will take to cover the major avenues in the city, up and down the rivers, both sides of the harbor?"

"A week to do it right, I think."

"Do it right."

"Yes, sir."

He passed this info on to General Alt and Sal Molina, who would, Jake knew, pass it on to the president and the National Security Council.

"So what do you think we should do about this one, Admiral?" Molina said when Jake had finished his recitation.

"My recommendation is do nothing right now. Whatever is down there has been there for six years. A few more weeks or months isn't going to make any difference."

"I'll pass that along. Needless to say, the National Security Council is tied up in knots over the first one. Everyone has a different opinion. We're trying to keep the circle of knowledge small, but you know how these things are. If we are sitting on bombs, it's eventually going to leak. When it does, oh boy!"

"If you don't mind my asking, sir, how are you and Butch Lanham getting along?"

Sal Molina sighed. "You know, he's the epitome of the Washington type, an educated idiot, amoral, with no scruples that anyone has ever noticed. He goes through life with a wet finger permanently aloft to catch any change in the breeze. His only god is Ambition. Talks a good line, too."

"I got the picture."

"Where next?"

"I thought I'd send the van to Boston since it's just up the road. We need a week to do New York first, though."

"The Council is arguing about that, too. Lanham wants to take charge, pull the strings."

"He's welcome to it, for all I care. I'm not getting much sleep and my stomach's a wreck."

"Tell me about it. But the president isn't buying Lanham's spiel just now. He says you found the first one, let's see what else you turn up. That could change."

Like the weather, Jake thought. "Uh-huh."

"Talk to you later."

Coast Guard Captain Joe Zogby made a multimedia presentation to Jake and Gil Pascal. The view was side-looking radar shots of the Mediterranean in the hours after the staff suspected that *Olympic Voyager* left Port Said. What it all boiled down to was a disappearing blip. Moving, then stationary, then gone.

"Sunk," Zogby said. "We have no way of verifying that that blip was *Olympic Voyager*, but as you see, she disappeared quickly. She hasn't been seen or heard from since."

"Someone sank her," Jake said bitterly.

"That means the weapons were no longer aboard," Pascal added.

"Is there any way we can get a list of the ships in Port Said from the moment it arrived until, say, a week later?" Jake asked. "Names and destinations?"

"The FBI is working on it, sir," Zogby replied. "They've sprinkled money all over that corner of Egypt, we've gotten the Egyptian government involved, and we have names of ships to show for it. But if one ship was left off the list . . ."

Jake studied his toes, then turned to Gil. "When is the next Corrigan unit being delivered?"

"This weekend if everything goes well. Monday or Tuesday if it doesn't."

"We're running out of time," Jake muttered to no one in particular.

The Delta Force augmented Customs offices up and down the East Coast. Armed with every conventional Geiger counter that could be purchased, borrowed, or scrounged, the soldiers were helping Customs officers search every ship before it entered port. The operation was huge. Jake and two flag officers from the Pentagon met daily, going over deployment options, looking at the percentage of ships searched, reviewing efforts to find more Geiger counters—generally solving problems and making policy decisions. This effort took several hours out of Jake's day, every day.

More time was spent reviewing material provided by Zelda Hudson. The cells in Florida seemed to be static. It was infuriating—the more Jake read about the cells, the more convinced he became that some or all of them were waiting for the bombs to arrive. The navy, Coast Guard, and Customs Service were using Geiger counters and dogs to search every ship coming into Florida. They were finding a lot of drugs and aliens being smuggled in, but no bombs.

There weren't enough assets to search every ship coming to America, or even the East Coast. Was he fixated upon Florida because of the presence of the suspected cells? Were the cells red herrings? Hell, were these little knots of Middle Eastern men even cells?

Doyle's death or disappearance—how did that fit? Was that event even part of this puzzle, or totally unrelated?

The bombs buried in the cities—terrorists, or . . . who?

The harder Jake pressed the more information Zelda's staff produced. Yet there was no structure; the data came as piles of printouts.

"All we're doing is killing trees," he complained as he leafed through a huge file on Coke Twilley. "I can't make sense of this. There might be a gold nugget in all this treacle, but how would anyone know?"

"We need people to analyze the data," was Zelda's reply. "Get me some more people, competent ones for a change."

"Wrong answer," Jake said curtly. "There aren't any more people for me to get, competent or incompetent. You get this unscrewed. There must be a way to correlate disparate facts and figures to construct a picture. Find the facts that don't fit."

"I'm up to my eyeballs in this shit, Admiral. There are only so many hours in the damn day."

"Don't cuss at me, goddammit!" Jake roared. "I do the fucking cussing around here. You know what the stakes are. For the love of Christ, you're sitting smack-dab on the center of the bull's-eye at ground zero! What will it take to make you jerk your head out of your ass?"

Zelda wasn't intimidated. There wasn't a man on earth who could accomplish that. "You have us wasting time on these five men. I don't think there's anything to find."

"That's my call," Jake snarled. When he got angry the bullet scar on his temple turned red. Right now it was livid. "One of these guys is dirty." He picked up Twilley's file and tossed it onto the desk in front of her. "All this drivel won't change my mind. Get back in your hole and find the guilty son of a bitch."

On her way out of the office Zelda passed by a secretary's desk. "I heard him shouting through the closed door," the woman said, glancing at the admiral's door to see if the monster was going to come charging out breathing fire. "What was *that* all about?"

"He fanged the shit outta me," Zelda said as she went by. She was in no mood for a wet-hankie session with a horrified civil servant.

Alas, Grafton was right. Some way had to be found to separate the one gold nugget from all this mud.

If there was one.

Tommy Carmellini had been in Quantico two days when he finally got his pistol—a Browning Hi-Power—a shoulder holster, and ten rounds of nine-millimeter ammunition. The FBI agent who delivered it to him in Anna Modin's room wanted him to sign a receipt.

"We took it off a drug dealer we arrested in Washington last week," he said. "It isn't listed in the computer as hot. So far we haven't been able to trace it."

"Man in that line of work needs a good gun," Carmellini remarked as he popped the empty magazine into his hand, pulled the slide back, and checked the chamber. "He going to want it back?"

"Not unless he beats the rap," the agent said dryly.

Carmellini checked the safety—these old automatics only had one, a thumb safety that locked the hammer in the cocked position. He tried the trigger, then flipped the safety off and pulled the trigger again. The hammer fell with a crisp sound. "Nice shooter," he said. "Let's hope they convict him."

With the signed receipt in his pocket, the agent left. Carmellini inspected each of the shiny brass cylinders and carefully loaded them into the magazine, then snapped it into the handle of the pistol and chambered a round. Using both hands, he lowered the hammer to the safety notch and pushed on it with a thumb to make sure. Since the pistol lacked a grip safety, he felt uncomfortable carrying it cocked and locked. He would just have to remember to ear the hammer back for the first shot.

A pistol wouldn't make him or Anna bulletproof, but it would let him worry them some. Assuming he saw them in time.

He had talked to Harry Estep earlier that morning. The FBI had been unable to identify the bodies.

When he got off the telephone with Harry, he called Jake Grafton. Didn't get him, but an hour later, after he got his pistol, Grafton returned the call.

"I feel like a wart on an elephant's ass sitting here in Quantico."

"How's Anna?"

"She's fine. My feet are fine, and so's the rest of me."

"Your job is to guard her," Jake said. "You two don't have to stay in Quantico, but I want you with her or in earshot twenty-four hours a day. The FBI will get her into the Federal Witness Protection Program in a couple weeks. The paper is going from desk to desk. Until then, you're her life ring."

"Okay, boss." Tarkington called the admiral "boss," and Tommy had picked up on it.

"And, use your cell phone to help Zelda. The CIA has a couple of specialty teams wiring up outside databases and what not, yet we still need your friends the independent contractors for sensitive jobs." The CIA teams were nominally working for the FBI, so as to avoid the prohibition against domestic operations by that agency.

"Scout and Earlene?"

"That's right. Coordinate all that by phone. Make it happen. Stop in and see Scout and Earlene if you have to. What I don't want you to do is take Anna to Langley, the Hoover Building, or my apartment. Someone may be watching." Carmellini couldn't get Anna in either of the government facilities, but he understood what Grafton meant: don't leave her in a car in the parking lot while he went inside.

"I talked to Harry a while ago," Tommy said. "He said they can't identify those two Baltimore dudes."

"John Doe One and Two. They use Roman numerals for the numbers."

"I saw a newspaper this morning. Sounds like I am in deep and serious shit in Baltimore." The first remark had been a warm-up for this unstated question. Carmellini pressed the telephone against his ear.

"The assistant D.A. in charge of the case is an ambitious young woman with an agenda," Jake Grafton told him. "She's a little peeved that you reloaded and shot those guys again. They were each dead after the first bullet hit them. An inappropriate use of force, she says. 'Grotesque' was her word."

"Uh-huh."

"There was a comment or two about you being out of control."

"Uh-huh."

"How much more of this do you want?"

"That's enough, I guess."

"You might as well wallow in it. You're a savage beast, she said, turned loose by the federal government to rend and mutilate the corpses of your victims."

"Uh-huh."

"It's a racial thing, according to her. You kept shooting them after they were dead because they weren't white."

"I kept shooting them because I wanted to be damn sure they were dead."

"That's what I told her. She didn't buy it."

"And because they shot the waiter and scared the living shit outta me and I was really pissed. Tell the D.A. bitch I enjoyed it."

"I'll call her as soon as we get off the phone. They take racial politics seriously in Baltimore. She's having her day in the newspapers and thumping the gun control drum. The reality is these goons were armed killers who had just gunned an innocent Baltimore native—a black one, by the way—in an attempt to get Anna. This D.A. will sober up when she realizes no one is saluting the bloody rag she ran up the pole."

"What's the penalty in Maryland for mutilating two corpses?"

"We're still researching that. Maximum looks like a thousand bucks' fine and ten days in jail or castration for each count. 'Course they only do the castration once."

"That's comforting."

"Don't wander too far," Jake Grafton said. "I may need you back here."

Tommy Carmellini promptly forgot about the bitch in Baltimore. He was one of those rare people who didn't fret about things they couldn't do anything about. This quirk was a gift or curse, depending on your belief in the beneficial efficacy of guilt, but whichever, through the years it allowed him to be free from the burdens of worry that made the lives of most transgressors miserable. It wasn't as if he had no conscience—because he did—it was just that he didn't ponder his karma or the fate of the universe. As he explained one day to Toad Tarkington, "Shit happens, and when it does you deal with it. If it doesn't, go on down the road."

After that conversation with Jake Grafton, Tommy Carmellini put in a call to his buddy Scout. Left a message on the answering machine.

Scout and Earlene were out doing something nefarious for the CIA, apparently.

Carmellini stood in the doorway of the bathroom watching a totally nude Anna Modin brush her hair. The sight stirred him to his toenails. He did some mental calculations concerning the state of his finances—bank balances, room on his credit cards, and time remaining before payday—and came to a quick decision.

"What say we go to the Homestead for a few days? I hear it's gorgeous this time of year."

"The Homestead? What is that?"

"It's a resort in the mountains. West of here, not too far . . . four or five hours' drive. Golf, hot springs, gourmet meals, big beds to romp in . . ."

"I do not have many clothes."

FBI agents had brought her clothes from Grafton's and packed a suitcase at Carmellini's apartment. One of them had also driven Carmellini's old red Mercedes from Baltimore. Tommy Carmellini had a willing woman, wheels, a pistol, and plastic on his hip. What more do you need in America?

"We'll rough it," he declared bravely.

"Do you want to make love before we leave or save it until we arrive?"

"Never wait," he answered. "Life is short."

On Monday afternoon Jake Grafton visited the basement at Zelda's request. She had a telephone conversation to play for him. Without explanation from her, she handed him a set of earphones and worked on her keyboard as he put them on. In seconds he heard voices.

". . . Friend at the White House." Butch Lanham's voice.

"How're things going over there?" Jake Grafton recognized that voice too. Jack Yocke.

"There have been some developments that I'd like to share."

"Izzaright?"

"Can't do it over the telephone, of course. Perhaps a meet?"

They discussed it. Decided on a little restaurant Yocke knew about. Jake had never heard of it.

When the two men ended the conversation, Jake took off the headphones. "When did this conversation occur?"

"An hour ago."

"May I have a tape of it, please?"

Zelda nodded and stroked the keyboard. In three minutes she handed him a cassette.

"What are you going to do with it?" she asked.

"I don't know," he answered truthfully. The president might not look kindly on his national security adviser doing some leaking—unless, of course, he put him up to it. And just what was he going to leak about? Afghanistan, the Middle East, our trade relationship with Lower Slobovia? Or nuclear weapons buried in Washington and New York?

Jake held the cassette in his hand, then pocketed it. He sat back in the chair and crossed his legs. "Sunday a week ago I gave you and the FBI two disks that contained copies of the computer records of Walney's Bank in Cairo, Egypt. The FBI wizards say the disks show who is contributing money to finance terrorism and how the money is shuffled around. And loaned or doled out to terrorists."

Zelda nodded. Her eyes were bright, alert.

"The head guy at the bank is named Abdul Abn Saad. He's a pillar of Egyptian society and a secret Islamic militant. I want you to make him a lot richer than he is."

"Explain that."

Jake Grafton stood and stretched. He walked around a little—the place was packed with people, computers, monitors, servers, power packs, and what not, and had wires running everywhere—so he soon gave up on walking. He made sure there was no one in earshot, then came back to Zelda. He perched with one hip on the corner of her desk and looked down at her. "The National Security Council is tied in a knot. Egypt is a valuable ally. Saad has seriously powerful friends in very high places in Cairo and throughout the Arab world. And our people don't want to diddle with foreign banks on the theory that if we don't diddle with theirs, they won't diddle with ours. In the age of terrorism this attitude makes no sense, but there it is.

"So we are going to go where the authorities fear to tread. I want you to hack into Walney's Bank and embezzle a lot of money and give it to Abdul Abn Saad. I want you to cover your tracks so it looks like an inside job."

"You want to make him richer?"

"That's right. Eventually someone there will figure it out and Mr. Saad will be in trouble up to his eyeballs. If his bank also fails, that would be the icing on the cake."

Zelda caressed the keyboard of her computer, then used a hand to brush her hair back from her eyes. Then she looked up at Grafton.

"Up to now I haven't touched anybody's money. Looking at files I am not authorized to see is one thing, but money is something else. This could put me back in prison."

"I've asked you to do it. I'll take the responsibility. You're just doing what you are told."

"With nothing in writing, nothing to prove it went down that way. You drop dead of a heart attack or get cold feet and leave me hanging, I'm screwed. Regardless, I'm probably going back to prison when this is over. Isn't that true, Admiral?"

"I don't run the universe, Zelda. If the people at the White House want you back in the can, you're going. That's always been the case."

She looked at her hands, then put them in her lap. "You're putting me in an impossible position," she said.

"Horseshit!" said Jake Grafton. "Don't haggle with me! I'm asking you to do something for your country. If you do it right, no one but you and I will ever know you did it. There will be no medals, no money, no ceremonies, no pardons, none of that happy crap. For once in your life you'll have taken a big risk with nothing in it for you. For what it's worth, there's a name for people who do things like that—we call them patriots."

He stood, patted the computer monitor, and headed for the door.

After he was gone Zelda sat staring at the monitor.

Naguib went out every evening to meet the blond woman at the Oasis. Ali, Yousef, and Mohammed knew he was going. He made no secret of it. As they watched television and showered, he would nod and leave. If one or two or all of them stood in the seashell parking lot, they could watch him walk through parking lots the entire two hundred yards to the Oasis Bar and Grill.

Mohammed didn't know what to do. If he killed Naguib, Ali and Yousef might freak and desert him. On the other hand, if Naguib didn't want to do his part, Mohammed would be a fool to try to force him into it. And of course he could be telling everything he knew to an American undercover policewoman. Yes, Mohammed knew that the American police used women to trap criminals.

This evening after Naguib left, Mohammed asked his colleagues, "What if Naguib's woman is an American spy?"

They thought about it.

"We wage *jihad*," Mohammed pointed out. "We are on a holy mission. Naguib volunteered, as did the three of us. We knew the mission, what was required of us, what we would have to do. We swore on the beard of the prophet that we would do what must be done to strike this glorious blow. And now Naguib drinks beer and talks to this woman late at night."

"Naguib is a good man," Yousef said stoutly. "He is weak, yes, as all men are weak, and if the slut gives him her body, he will take it. But he will not betray God. He will not betray us."

"FBI agents are very clever," Ali said thoughtfully. He glanced at Mohammed and Yousef, trying to read their faces. Mohammed was also clever, he thought, but not Yousef. Nor Naguib.

"He doesn't know when the weapons will arrive, or where," Yousef pointed out. "Only Mohammed knows."

"He knows us," Ali replied. "He knows our names, our histories, who sent us, where we get our money, what we intend to do."

And so they argued while Mohammed listened, saying nothing. The drift was plain. Yousef wanted to kick Naguib out of the group, rely on him to maintain his silence. Ali saw the dangers of that approach but could not bring himself to say what he thought should be done. Finally they talked themselves out. They turned to him.

"He must not be allowed to endanger our mission," Mohammed said slowly. "It is bigger and more important than we are."

Their faces were stony.

"We are going to die as martyrs for the glory of Allah. We will slay the infidels as it has never been done before in the history of the world. The entire earth will tremble at the mention of Allah's name when it sees our determination. Everyone on earth will convert to Islam, just as the prophet wished. And for this great service, we will be in Paradise."

Yes, they understood all this. The mission was fantastic, glorious beyond description, a service to the prophet that would change the history of the world.

"We must kill Naguib," Mohammed said. "We cannot take the chance that he might betray us, endanger our holy mission."

"Allah is watching," Yousef declared with simple faith. "If Allah wishes us to succeed, we will succeed. Killing Naguib would be a murder of the faithful, which is forbidden by the holy Koran. Certainly you don't intend to ask Allah to aid us with the blood of the faithful on your hands?"

"Sometimes the faithful must die. The faithful died to destroy the trade towers in New York. The three of us will die when the weapon explodes. Naguib has already pledged his life to our *jihad*. The truth of it is that he must give his life now to protect us."

The logic was irrefutable. They chewed at the problem for another twenty minutes, then Ali and Yousef came around. They went to the car and watched Mohammed open the trunk with the key. Four pistols and ammunition were hidden under the spare tire.

With loaded pistols in their pockets, they waited in the darkness outside the motel for Naguib. No one seemed to be watching. The last car had come in hours before, and the office lights were now off. An occasional car or pickup went past on the highway. Only two cars were left in the parking lot of the beer joint next door when Naguib came walking across the parking lots smelling of beer, humming to himself.

"Into the car," Mohammed said.

"I am tired. I want to sleep."

"Things are happening," Mohammed said. "Now is the hour."

Yousef and Ali climbed in the backseat of the sedan and Mohammed got behind the wheel. Naguib had no choice but to get in the right-front passenger seat.

He was half-drunk. He hummed as he rode, thinking of Suzanne.

The silence of the other three finally soaked through the beer haze. They were usually very talkative with each other; their fellow countrymen and coconspirators were their only social outlet.

"Where are we going?" Naguib asked.

"You'll see."

"Has the weapon arrived?"

"Soon," Mohammed said. "Very soon. We must be ready."

"Yes," Naguib agreed sleepily. "Yes."

Mohammed turned off the paved county road he was on and steered the car down a dirt road alongside a deep drainage ditch. The ditch and the dirt road beside it ran straight ahead into the darkness, seemed to go on forever. In the rearview mirror Mohammed could see the lights of the highway and the houses growing smaller.

Well away from the county road, he brought the car to a stop. "This is the place, I think." He looked at a tiny sign illuminated by the headlights and scanned the darkness in all directions, as if he were trying to identify something. "This is it," he said, and turned off the headlights and engine and opened his door.

Everyone got out.

"What is out here?" Naguib asked, looking around himself and seeing nothing at all in the darkness.

He felt something press against his side, then Ali shot him.

There was no pain, just a numbing shock. The report was muffled and he barely heard it.

"No," Naguib shouted, trying to push at Ali, who pulled the trigger again three more times as fast as he could.

Yousef fired once.

With Naguib on the ground, Mohammed turned on a small pocket flashlight. He was still alive, so Mohammed put his pistol against the side of Naguib's head and shot him once more.

"Take everything from his pockets," Mohammed told Ali and Yousef. "If they find him, they will not know who he is."

It was a distasteful task, but they did it.

"Good-bye, Naguib," Mohammed said, and pushed his body over the edge of the road into the ditch. They had to go down into the ditch to throw the corpse into the water, a task that covered the three of them with dirt and mud.

Satisfied at last, Mohammed led the way up the bank to the car. They climbed in and drove away.

An illegal Mexican farmworker found Naguib's body the following day. He saw the tracks along the dirt road and assumed someone had driven there during the night. When he stopped the tractor to pee and eat his lunch, he wandered to the place with the tracks to see if perhaps the people had left anything, like a few inches of whiskey or beer in the bottom of a bottle. That's when he saw Naguib's body in the ditch.

It was late in the afternoon when FBI agent Suzanne Ostrowski saw the body. Local police had pulled it from the ditch; it was lying in the dirt.

Another agent lifted the sheet covering the face. The eyes were wide-open and bulged out from the pressure of the bullet in the brain, almost as if he had been horribly surprised.

Yes, it was Naguib.

The big lunk. So gentle and naive, so trusting . . .

So they killed him. Left him like garbage at the bottom of a drainage ditch.

She was a tough woman, but a sense of profound sadness swept over her. And resolve. If they would kill Naguib, one of their own, they would murder others with as much remorse as if they were squashing bugs.

Tommy Carmellini was in love. He didn't want to get in that condition and certainly wasn't trying, but after two days at the Homestead, he was pretty sure he had arrived. It was the first time for him, and it felt wonderful. Anna Modin was *the* woman.

Unfortunately he wasn't sure she was in love with him. Oh, she looked happy enough, made love like a goddess, liked to play with the hair on his chest, and found moments when no one was apparently watching to kiss him. The experience was heavenly. Yet did she love him?

They soaked in the pool fed by the hot springs, went on short hikes—strolls, really—played several rounds of golf... Anna had never played before and was terrible. She had trouble learning to swing the club properly and sprayed the ball everywhere. And she laughed; oh, how she laughed when the ball went squirting away willy-nilly. She marched over, wiggled her fanny, mugged at him, and whacked it again, laughing all the time.

They also spent a lot of time naked in bed.

The birds sang, puffy clouds with flat gray bottoms floated along in the blue sky, and everything that grew was in bloom this spring.

Did she love him? Tommy Carmellini wondered and worried.

What if she did? She said she was leaving when Janos Ilin sent for her. Would she change her mind? *Could* she change her mind?

Evenings were delicious. A fine meal, wine, watching dusk settle from rocking chairs on the old porch, reviewing the day and laughing some more. And more kisses.

What if, he wondered, she had been lying about being a Russian agent? What if she really were an agent for the SVR?

Oh, Christ, his superiors at the CIA would lay eggs. Jake Grafton would come unglued. Tommy Carmellini would be an unemployed civilian so quick it would take your breath away. Alas, he only had two civilian skills, law and burglary—both equally disreputable. As he mused on it, he wondered if he could find a way to combine them.

When he first arrived at the Homestead and looked around, Carmellini concluded that brown Islamic assassins would stand out like nudes in church, so he had stopped sweating that program. He wore his pistol under his sports coat or windbreaker. When he was on the golf course he put it in his golf bag. At the pool he left it beside his chair inside a small backpack he purchased at the gift shop. Sometimes he just hung the backpack over one shoulder by a strap. Sitting on the porch holding Anna's hand watching the light fade, he put the backpack on the floor beside his chair.

He had checked in with Jake Grafton four times the first day, three the second, found that Scout and Earlene were doing whatever Zelda asked of them, so he was soon down to one telephone call a day. Sometimes he just left a message for Grafton saying he called.

He liked her eyes. The way they crinkled when she laughed, the fact that she laughed easily and often, the fact that she seemed to find him fascinating. Yet was she in Love? Love with a capital L. Or just in lust, enjoying a relaxing vacation complete with the room-service sex package?

Like every lover since the dawn of time, he pondered these things. Fretted them. Found himself hanging on every smile, every touch, every kiss, reading things into every glance or move she made or word she spoke. Or didn't speak. Even her silences were laden with import.

When he could stand it no longer, the evening of the fourth day, he waited until the after-dinner liqueur had been served, then he took the bull by the horns.

"I'm in love with you," he said softly as he held her hand and looked straight into her eyes.

"I love you too," she replied . . . and Tommy Carmellini felt so light that he had to grasp the arm of his chair to keep from floating.

She took his hand in both of hers and turned it over carefully and inspected it, ran a finger along the lifeline and across his palm. Never had he felt anything so exquisite.

"I never thought I would, you know," she continued in her wonderfully accented English, which he never tired of hearing. "Oh, I tried to fall in love. I think every woman does. We all want someone to love us and to give love to. Perhaps it is the human condition. But for me, until now . . ."

She was looking into his eyes again, both her hands squeezing his. "I wish every person on Earth could know this feeling at least once." She released his hand, rose from her chair, and took two steps around the table toward him. Bent and kissed him on the lips, a long, tender, gentle kiss. Then she took her seat again. Her eyes glistened.

The people at the next table applauded politely, and Tommy Carmellini nodded and smiled at them. Anna Modin kept her eyes on him.

He was going to say more, then decided against it. A little voice told him, Don't take a chance. Savor this moment. Treasure it. Remember every nuance of it so that you can keep it in your heart forever. So he reached for her hand and grasped it and sat looking into her shining eyes.

CHAPTER EIGHTEEN

The second Corrigan unit arrived in Washington on a Wednesday morning—days late—mounted in an unmarked white van similar to the first one. Jake put it on the street. He rode around in the van himself to familiarize himself with the problems and the results that could be expected. The first evening he had the driver go by Hains Point. The area registered hot on this unit, too.

The following day he went home early—seven in the evening—to find Jack Yocke visiting over a drink with Amy and Callie.

At Jake's suggestion, Callie had invited the reporter for dinner. This time he didn't bring his girlfriend, Jake noted, and he asked Callie about it when the two were alone in the kitchen. "Did you suggest Jack come alone?"

"No," she said. "I invited him to dinner and said he could bring his attorney if he wished. He showed up alone."

Dinner went well, meat loaf, mashed potatoes, and peas, Jake's favorite. He complimented Callie three times before he finished his second helping. Amy chattered with Yocke—she liked him and he wasn't intimidated by her youth, so that went well. When dinner was finished Amy asked Callie's help with a translation, so Jake and the reporter cleared the dishes.

Alone in the kitchen with the dishwasher humming, Jack Yocke said, "I'm sorta curious about what you're up to these days. I haven't found a soul who will even drop a hint."

Jake Grafton smiled. "It's classified."

"Funny thing, your name did come up in a conversation I had with a White House source. This person is very high up, perhaps said a wee bit more than he should. He did suggest what you are doing."

"Must be nice, having sources like that. They can make a journalist's career, I suppose, maybe even get him nominated for a Pulitzer."

"He was talking about abuse of power."

"Such as?"

"Illegal searches, illegal wiretaps, illegal surveillance, violation of the privacy laws and government regulations on the use of personal information, things like that."

"Serious accusations," Jake murmured, and poured himself a cup of coffee. He held out the pot for Yocke, who snagged a cup from the cupboard and held it out. Jake poured. They got milk from the refrigerator and whitened up the brew.

"A story like that would have to be verified very carefully before I could run it. I'd need to get verifiable facts from at least two impeccable sources, maybe three or four if my editors insist."

"A scandal like that would really embarrass the administration, I suppose."

"That it would. If the people at the top knew about it. If they didn't, there are rogues somewhere that need to be weeded out. Regardless, if there is activity like that going on, the scandal would wreck careers, perhaps lead to prosecutions. The public takes these things seriously."

"I suppose when people tell you dirt on other people, you wonder about their motivation."

"Of course. People tattle for a million reasons, most of them not very nice. On the other hand, if the press waited for saints to bare their souls, newspapers wouldn't have much news in them. Police must listen to snitches, and so do we."

"I suppose."

"News is where you find it."

"Lanham ever talked out of school before?"

Yocke took another sip of coffee while the dishwasher sang and he decided how to handle that remark.

"What if I say yes?"

"Bring your coffee and let's take a ride. Your car is downstairs on the street, isn't it?"

"Yes. Where are we going?"

"To look at the republic."

Jake told Callie that he and Yocke were going for a ride, and Yocke thanked her for the meal. Callie, wise as ever, didn't ask where they were going or when Jake would return.

When Yocke had the car in motion Jake produced a cassette from his shirt pocket and examined the controls on Yocke's dashboard.

"You want to play that?" Yocke asked.

"Please. You do it." He passed the cassette to the reporter and latched his seat belt. Yocke popped the thing in the receptacle on the dashboard and pushed the buttons.

They were waiting at a stoplight when Lanham's voice came over the speaker, then Yocke's. The light changed, and Yocke fed gas. He listened to the recorded telephone conversation in silence. When the conversation was over the tape continued to run. Jake pushed the eject button and snagged the cassette. He returned it to his pocket.

"Where'd you get that?" the reporter asked.

Jake merely looked thoughtful. He finished his coffee, put the cup on the floor between his feet so it wouldn't roll around.

"Is my telephone tapped?"

"No."

"Lanham's?"

"It's a little more complicated than that. The way they explained it to me, each human voice is distinct—not as distinct as fingerprints, but close—and a computer can be programmed to pick out that voice in any conversation from any telephone calls going through the switching equipment being monitored. Then it records that conversation."

"I see."

"Tens of thousands of calls, hundreds of thousands, go through the switching equipment, and computers sample them for voices they are looking for, or words, phrases, whatever. When a computer gets a hit, bingo. Be impossible for a human to do, but computers can do hundreds of calls at the same time—they're that fast. Unfortunately, the computer doesn't start recording until it identifies the voice. Presumably you answered the telephone and the computer didn't recognize your voice. It recognized Lanham's, though, and started recording as soon as the positive match was complete."

"Why Lanham?"

Jake just shook his head.

"So what are you going to do with the cassette?"

Grafton shrugged. "I just did it."

"You going to send it over to the White House?"

"I know what you're thinking. I hear the president gets real pissy about leaks. Regards the leaker as disloyal and all that. This wouldn't be good for Lanham, but no, I'm not going to do that. I'm going to put it in my desk drawer and lock the drawer."

"That sounds like a threat, Admiral."

"Maybe I should be more explicit. In the unlikely event anything classified that Lanham might have discussed with you gets in the newspaper, then I'll reevaluate."

"Surely you aren't the administration's plumber."

"Plumber?"

"The guy who looks for leaks."

"I'm looking for a traitor."

"Are leakers traitors?"

"They could be, I guess, but not in this case. Lay off, Jack. Don't go near Lanham. I don't know what is going on over at the White House, and I don't want to get into the middle of it. I'm a sailor with a classified job. If the president and Sal Molina can't handle Lanham, they're out of their league and unfit for their jobs."

Yocke snorted. "The guy who is out of his league is Lanham. That poor schnook thinks he's got a handle on this shit."

Jake Grafton shrugged.

"So you know Lanham is leaking. Is he telling the truth? Abuse of power is a serious charge."

"Let's go to the Lincoln Memorial," Jake suggested. "That's my favorite place in Washington. I feel like a visit."

Yocke glanced at his watch, then made the next left turn, which took them in the proper direction. At ten in the evening they had no trouble finding a parking place. With the car locked, they set off afoot for the Memorial.

As usual, the marble temple was well lit, with uniformed park rangers and several dozen tourists, who were busy snapping photos of the statue of Lincoln, each other, and the view of the Washington Monument from the main entrance. The flashes of light and warm voices echoing in the building made it seem more like a high school gymnasium than a memorial.

After wandering through the place with Yocke tagging along, Jake Grafton found a vacant spot on the front steps away from the tourists and seated himself. In front of him the white, spotlighted obelisk of the Washington Monument reached upward into the black sky.

"When Lincoln was president the nation tried to rip itself apart,"

Jake said. "Various people argued in good faith that under the constitution the president lacked the power to violate the laws. No one is above the law. In effect, the argument went, the president and the government had to obey the laws even if the republic fell. Lincoln looked at the issue a little differently. He argued that the duly elected, lawful government had the inherent power to do whatever was necessary to save itself. He jailed people without charges or trials, suspended the writ of habeus corpus so judges couldn't let them out, shut down newspapers, declared blockades of American ports, admitted states into the union without going through the constitutional or statutory hoops, issued bonds to finance the war without statutory authority. . . . You know all this, of course."

"I remember my history," Yocke said dryly.

"Some people called him a dictator. King Lincoln."

"And he saved the union."

"He saved the constitutional government, this system of checks and balances. He forced the American people to solve their problems in the Capitol Building, not on the battlefield. Oh, I know, a lot of the people we elect to Congress are shits of the first water. Saints don't get into politics. The politicians wrestle with the issues. They argue, rant, and compromise—which is what they are supposed to do. Some issues they duck, none is resolved for all time. Then they go home to face the voters. That's our system, and it's a damned good one. That is the system that Lincoln said he had the inherent power to defend. I guarantee you, every American is better off today than he or she would have been if the republic had been torn in half because Lincoln obeyed the statutes."

"We're not in a civil war."

"We're in a war against people who wish to destroy America. The best way to do it is to attack the government's ability to protect its citizens. That is the most basic function of government. Any government that can't accomplish that feat forfeits its legitimacy. Our enemies won't attack with a conventional armed force because they don't have one. But it's war nonetheless, war to the very last man, war to the knife, the knife to the hilt."

"If the government becomes a dictatorship to save itself," Yocke argued, "then it is no longer the government most Americans want to live under."

"Precisely. That was Lincoln's dilemma and it's ours."

"If you are arguing that the government has a right to do whatever it wants in secret, you lose. Lincoln acted publicly. That's the difference. Nobody gave the president or you or anyone else a mandate to break the law."

Jake Grafton considered his answer before he spoke. "When I was a very young man I took an oath to support and defend the Constitution of the United States against all enemies, foreign and domestic, and to obey the orders of the officers appointed over me. That is precisely what I am doing. Just that and nothing more." He pointed down the Mall at the unseen Capitol. "If we lose this war, that building down there will become a ruin like the forum in Rome or the Parthenon in Athens."

"Perhaps a better system will come along."

"Bullshit. Every decision that government makes—all of them—involves a balancing of competing interests. City and county councils do it, state legislatures do it, Congress does it. Taxes, budgets, schools, roads, welfare, social legislation, criminal codes, the environment—everything is a compromise balancing the push-pull of competing interests. Humans have tried every other conceivable arrangement to get these decisions made—tribal chiefs, warlords, kings, dictators, oligarchies . . . our system is democracy, and nothing better has been discovered. It's inefficient and messy as hell, but if democracy goes, the world is headed for a new dark age.

"I don't know about you, but those fallible humans in the Capitol Building are the only people on the planet that I trust with my liberty, within the boundaries of the U.S. Constitution. I want them there playing politics, which is twisting arms, trading votes, lying to the voters and themselves and each other and weighing the various shades of gray. I want the president in the White House trying to herd the cats. I want the Supreme Court watching them. I want the press watching everybody. I want that for me, my daughter, her kids, and all the Americans yet to come."

Yocke looked skeptical. "People trying to save the world have a damn poor record. The danger is you'll destroy what you're trying to protect."

Jake sighed. "I don't know why I'm sitting here arguing with a man of words. You're right, absolutely right. What I promise you is this—everything the government does now will someday come out. Every secret will ultimately be revealed. When that day comes the citizens of the republic will decide if the threat warranted the reaction, if power was abused or the law perverted. What we must do is have faith in our elected officials and the patience to wait."

"For a man of action, you talk mighty slick," Jack Yocke said. "I hope to God you know what you are doing."

"So do I, Jack."

That night after Yocke dropped the admiral back at his building, Jake and Callie had a private moment, of which there had been few this spring.

"What's going on, Jake?"

"Someone told Yocke something I don't want him to follow up on or print."

"Did he agree to cooperate?"

"Not in so many words, but I think so."

He sighed, ran his fingers through his hair. "I'm so tired. I'm going to hit the hay."

"You haven't been getting enough sleep."

"We're running out of time, Callie. I don't know what to do about it. We need a break, and, goddammit, I can't buy or steal one."

On the morning of the sixth day at the Homestead Tommy Carmellini decided to face fiscal reality. He called Jake Grafton and got him on the first ring.

"How is the FBI coming on getting Anna set up in a new identity?"

"They are working on it, they tell me," the admiral said. "Everything going okay?"

"Haven't shot anybody yet." Carmellini explained about the money.

"We'll pay you the usual travel per diem," Jake said. "Don't go to your place or mine—they might be watched. You could use my place at the beach, but there's the same problem."

"Uh-huh. What are we doing about that asshole in Egypt?"

"Working on that. It'll take a while for the fruit to ripen."

"Terrific."

"Stay in touch."

At the front desk, Carmellini asked to see the tab, did some quick mental arithmetic, and swallowed hard. Time to drift. He and Anna checked out, loaded his old Mercedes, and headed for Virginia Beach.

They were doing a lot of talking these days. As the miles rolled by she told him of growing up in Russia, of her parents and the stories they told of Stalin and the great terror, told him about school, about working in Switzerland and Cairo.

Tommy Carmellini told Anna the truth about himself. She was the first and only woman to whom he had ever admitted his fondness for sneaking into places where he wasn't supposed to be, his addiction to the challenge of stealing and fencing the loot and planning the jobs, what he thought about his job and Jake Grafton and the other people who ruled his life—he told her all of it, except for the classified stuff. He steered clear of that, and when he couldn't, he evaded politely. She seemed to understand.

That evening they signed into a small efficiency on the north end of the beach. The season had yet to start—the spring wind still had a nip to it and the water was cold—so the price on the condo was right and the beach was relatively empty.

Tommy Carmellini and Anna Modin strolled the sand and felt the chilly wind in their hair and the sand between their toes and watched the seabirds looking for food in the surf runout. Now and then they passed someone jogging with a dog.

On the horizon Carmellini saw ships, probably headed into or out of the Chesapeake, the mouth of which was just a few miles north. The sight of the occasional ship made Carmellini think about nuclear weapons; the thought made him shiver. He wondered if Grafton had found them yet. Obviously that was something they couldn't talk about over a cell phone, nor did Tommy have a need to know.

Was Anna SVR?

She denied it. Was her denial truth or lie?

When he stopped walking she snuggled against him with an arm around his waist and pressed her head against his chest. He could smell the salt in her hair, feel the strands against his cheek, feel the sensuous warmth and firmness of her body.

SVR or not, he loved her.

He had her now, but for how long?

Irritated, he tried to push that thought away. He had lived his entire life from day to day, refusing to worry what tomorrow might bring, and now he found himself concerned about the future. Love does that to you, he decided. It's insidious. Next I'll be thinking about marriage, a little cracker-box house on a postage-stamp lot in a Virginia suburb, furniture on credit, vacation schedules, dreading out-of-town trips, sweating the daily commute. . . .

Ye gods! Was that where life led? To stop-and-go traffic on the eternal voyage to and from the endless suburbs? Was that what happened when you really, honestly and truly, fell madly and hopelessly in love?

"I love you," he whispered in her ear.

"I love you, too, Tommy Carmellini," she said, and tightened the pressure of her arm around his waist.

All things considered, sharing a tract house in the suburbs with Anna Modin wouldn't be half-bad, he thought.

Around the table were seated a scientist from Sandia Labs, three electrical engineers, two physicists, and a vice president of Baltimore Electric with a Ph.D., enough brainpower, Jake Grafton reflected, to launch another Manhattan Project. Leavening this scientific brainpower were Jake Grafton, history major, and Sal Molina, political operator and career insider.

The brains had impeccable security clearances and long histories of consulting with the CIA on technical and scientific matters. They could be relied upon to keep their mouths firmly shut about what they learned here, if anyone could. Jake Grafton thought the secret too hot; it would come out soon. Someone would talk. Perhaps Butch Lanham, perhaps someone at Corrigan Engineering, someone . . .

They were running out of time. He could feel it leaking away, and with every passing day he became more and more irritable. He was having anxiety nightmares when he tried to sleep—being chased and unable to escape. The monsters were right behind him.

He tried to forget the monsters and pay attention to what was being said.

After an hour, the Ph.D. vice president from the power company said, "Let's do it. Cut the antenna lead and sever the power connections to these weapons. Then they can sit there until doomsday."

A poor choice of words. Every face in the room registered that fact.

"Is that safe?" Sal Molina asked again. Safety was his mantra. He wanted oaths signed in blood from every one of these people that the weapons would not detonate when the power supply was interrupted.

"Of course it's safe," one of the brains shot back. "We've been all over that. Power interruptions are rare but inevitable. If those weapons were going to explode when the load was lost, they would already have done so long ago."

"What if each weapon contains a battery to maintain power when the net is down? The battery might last for a while after the power is permanently severed, then detonate the weapon before it loses its ability to do so. Is that a possibility?"

The weapons people didn't think much of that scenario. Grid

power could be permanently lost for any one of a number of perfectly ordinary, legitimate reasons. It would be in no one's interest to have the city vaporized a few days later.

The president's man was obviously uncomfortable. He also feels the sands of time running through the glass, Jake thought. He watched Molina make an obvious effort to maintain his legendary cool. When he thought he had his face back on, he turned to Jake.

"What do you think, Admiral?"

"Let's do it. Cut the power and antenna leads, then we'll dig them up when the EPA makes us."

The scientists made polite noises at that attempt at humor. Sal Molina signaled that the meeting was over. As the brains filed out he stayed seated at the table and signaled for Jake to remain.

When the two men were alone, before Molina could speak, Jake said, "Tarkington called from Boston two hours ago. There's one there, too. It went into the fill for that new cross-harbor tunnel they're digging through the city. It's wired up to a nearby office building."

"For the love of Christ! How in the name of God can people do this crap under our very noses?"

"This isn't the time to swarm all over those contractors asking questions. We'll sic the FBI on them when we think we've found all the bombs and disabled them."

Molina eyed Grafton without enthusiasm. "Where are the Corrigan detectors? All I've heard are promises."

"Corrigan's way behind. We've got exactly two. From what I hear we're lucky to have them. Corrigan intended to farm out the manufacturing. When he found that wasn't going to fly he had his engineers start hand-building the things. I don't know what he's telling the president—"

"Blowing smoke up his ass," Molina said sourly.

"—His engineers tell me they are doing everything they can, and we'll get the detectors as soon as they're ready. And not before."

Molina made a rude noise. "No detectors! Buried bombs! The president is going to ask how many of these sons of bitches we're walking around on. What's your guess?"

Jake shook his head from side to side. "Don't want to guess."

"Looks like we outsmarted ourselves on Star Wars, doesn't it?"

"Yes," said Jake Grafton. "It does."

Watching Harley Bennett find the bomb buried in the fill for the new cross-harbor tunnel in Boston convinced Sonny Tran that he was operating in the dark. The four Russian bombs purchased by the Sword of Islam were due to arrive in the United States on ships the day after tomorrow . . . and yet there was a nuclear weapon buried in every major East Coast city the team had visited, Washington, New York, and Boston.

Right now he thought it probable there were bombs in Philadelphia, Chicago, San Francisco, and Los Angeles . . . perhaps Miami, Atlanta, and Seattle, maybe even St. Louis or Kansas City. Dallas, certainly, Houston . . .

Did Corrigan know about the buried weapons when he sold the government the detectors? If he knew they were there, why did he fund the Sword of Islam's purchase?

Or was finding them pure serendipity, the kind that would make Corrigan America's most beloved industrialist and entice a grateful Congress to give him a medal?

Sonny concluded that it would be impossible to determine the true course of events from the facts he had, so he stopped trying. The important thing was the bomb that Nguyen went to Florida to steal.

Sonny wished he knew what the FBI knew about the cells waiting to receive the things. He needed an entry to Grafton's inner circle, and he hadn't been able to find one. Here he sat, driving a van through Boston.

Everything hinged on Nguyen. If he were good enough, they had a chance. If he weren't . . .

Sonny took a deep breath and sifted through the situation again.

His pager went off. He removed it from his belt and looked. Karl Luck.

Nguyen Duc Tran was sitting in the last booth in the back of the bar, watching the door, when he saw Red Citrix come in. There were only five other customers in the place—three stringy men in dirty jeans and T-shirts, and two equally worn women. They were all nursing beers at the bar, smoking, and talking desultorily, while a professional basketball game played on the television behind the bar. Red ignored the sitters, nodded at the bartender, walked back to Nguyen's booth, and took a seat.

"Hey," Red said.

"Hey."

"What'll it be?" the bartender called.

"Gimme a Bud," Red said loudly. His thinning hair was white, his skin ruddy and splotchy. His hands had a slight tremor, as if he had been seriously ill in the not-too-distant past.

"I didn't think you'd really show up," Red said softly to Nguyen.

"Hey, I put it together. There's money to be made."

"The fucking feds are looking under every rock for terrorists. Shit, I check under my bed every night to see if I've got an FBI dude under there. A lot of guys are taking a vacation until things cool down."

"There's money to be made," Nguyen Duc Tran said again. He lit a cigarette.

Red Citrix worked for a freight forwarder. He was the man with the manifests who brought containers through customs, paid the duty, and sent the steel boxes on their way. Nguyen had done business with him twice before. Each time he had paid Citrix $10,000 cash to redirect a container. The containers were laden with European manufactured goods, which he stole and fenced, but he had led Citrix to believe they contained illegal narcotics. A thief was no one special, but in south Florida, dope dealers were serious people. Crossing one was extremely perilous to your health.

"Don't want to tell you your business," Red Citrix said now, "but since I like you, I want to give you a friendly warning. There's some heavy people that will get damned pissed if they find out you're doing business in their territory."

"How they gonna find out?"

"Well, I dunno." Red Citrix fell silent while the bartender placed the tall draft on the table and walked back toward the bar.

"We're businessmen," Nguyen said lightly, exhaling smoke. "You and I have done business before and probably will again. My associates know the arrangements." He shrugged. "People have tried to fuck with us before. Hey, man, you know how it is—gotta protect your business or you won't have one."

Nguyen thought it a safe bet that Red would sell him out the minute he thought he could profit by doing so and get away with it. He wanted to ensure that thought never crossed the man's mind.

"I never fucked over anybody," Red declared fiercely, and sipped his beer. "That's why I'm still alive. This is a goddamn tough place down here, don't you forget it."

"There's a gym bag on the floor. The money's in it."

"Okay."

"Pick up the bag, take it to the men's and count it. I want you happy as a pig in shit when I walk out of here."

Red took a long pull on his beer, then picked up the gym bag and headed down the hallway. Four minutes passed before he returned. He was smiling. He tossed the gym bag back on the floor and took another healthy swig of beer, then wiped his mouth on the back of his hand. "It's all there," he said, and grinned.

"Lot of money," Nguyen said, his face deadpan. "Tell me how things are going down there at the port."

Red Citrix crossed his arms on the table and began. "Feds crawlin' all over, and that's a fact. They're using Geiger counters, waving them friggin' wands everywhere. They even search ships at random before they enter the bay. Every ship is searched in the harbor before it can come into the piers. Customs and Coast Guard everywhere." He continued for five minutes, talking personalities and numbers, what was searched and what ignored. Nguyen let him talk.

When the man ran down, Nguyen put one arm on the table and said, "I thought Geiger counters were for finding uranium and stuff?"

"Yeah. They're looking for bombs, we figger. Won't admit a damn thing, but with those Geiger counters, it's sorta gotta be that. They ain't looking for dope—don't even have dope-sniffing dogs—I know all those dogs by sight. These are new dogs, bomb-sniffers I think. Unless you guys advertise or something you'll not have any trouble."

"Pray that I don't," Nguyen Duc Tran said very distinctly. "You and I got a deal. This is business."

"Don't get all sweaty," Red said, squinting through the cigarette smoke at the man across the table. "Like I said, the port is crawling with feds—Customs, FBI, Coast Guard, even army guys—all looking for bombs and weapons and such-like. This is a bad time. They may pop your box. I got zero control of that. They do, it's down the shitter and that's that. They can't touch me and they can't touch you. We're clean. Life goes on. Tomorrow's a new day. You can't live with that, keep your fuckin' dough."

"Don't cross me, Red."

"Hey, I'm honest. That's why people do business with me. I've been helping guys get stuff into the country for damn near ten years now. Occasionally Customs pops a box—that's your risk, not mine. I do what you pay me for. I'm going to be right here six months from now, next year, the year after. I ain't goin' no place 'cause I got no place else to go."

Nguyen produced an envelope from a pocket and pushed it across the table. In it was a sheet of paper with the container number, the shipper, consignee, and the address to which he wanted it shipped. He had cut the numbers and words from a newspaper and taped them to the paper. He had worn gloves when he did it.

Red Citrix opened the envelope, took out the paper, and glanced at it. "What's in the box?"

"Office furniture."

"For Corrigan Engineering?"

"Right."

"Okay," Red said, and pocketed the paper. He pushed the envelope across to Nguyen, who pocketed it.

"We need to talk about this love thing," Tommy Carmellini said to Anna Modin as they walked hand in hand upon a deserted beach in the rain. A raw wind whipped at their legs and windbreakers, not too chilly, as gray clouds scudded swiftly overhead on their way out to sea. Even the seabirds were struggling today; when they weren't probing the wet sand for food, they stood with their heads pointed into the wind.

The couple had found the windbreakers on sale this morning in a beachwear store, and were now trying them out. She adjusted the hood of hers so that she could see him yet still keep the stinging raindrops from her face. A strand of dark wet hair was visible on her cheek. "The spy thing is bothering you, isn't it?"

"Ah, that's no big deal," he scoffed. After a glance at her expression, he admitted, "Yes, it's bothering me a little."

"I thought it might be. You are thinking, she said she didn't work for the SVR, but was she telling the truth or lying? And there is no way to know. To really know. Is there?"

"No," he admitted.

"It's one of those things you must take on faith. If it matters to you."

"Well, to tell you the truth, it matters."

"Why?"

"It just does."

"Can you articulate the reason?"

He thought as he walked. "Love's one of the important things in life, and there are others. I'm an American. It isn't cool to say it, but

I love my country. I haven't always obeyed every jot and comma in the statute books, but I care about these people. White, black, brown, yellow, it doesn't matter, they're *my* people. We're all in this American thing together. That sounds sorta cornball, but that's the way it is."

"So there are things in your life more important than love?"

"As important," he admitted. "I suppose that's a fair statement. If you were a spy stealing secrets or servicing a network or corrupting folks, yeah, it would matter."

She wrapped her arm around his waist and matched her steps with his. "I feel the same way," she said. "I am a Russian woman. I do not work for the SVR. I never have. I work with—and for—a man who is fighting evil. There is a lot of it in this world to fight. You already know his name, which is a precious secret—Janos Ilin.

"Ilin is indeed an officer in the SVR, a very high one as a matter of fact, but he does not serve that organization, which is a criminal conspiracy, by the way, that under its old name functioned primarily to keep the Communist Party in power. The bureaucracy lives on today in Russia with many of the same people, and it continues as it always has to function as the strong right arm of the ruling oligarchy. The aristocrats have foresworn communist ideology, they say. No more garbage about labor heroes or the new socialist man. Little else has changed. Kings and dictators and small oligarchies have ruled Russia as far back as we have written records. Always there have been secret police to control the masses, to manipulate them, to confound and destroy organized opposition, to maintain the social and power structure.

"Ilin has no budget, no gadgets, no bosses, no one to answer to except his own conscience, and I am his army. Me—Anna Modin. There are probably others—I do not know about them nor do I wish to. A fact or name I do not know I can never betray, even inadvertently. I have met only one of Ilin's soldiers, Nooreem Habib, and I saw the men who killed her. She gave her life in the fight against evil. Do you understand?"

"Yes."

"I thought you would. That is one reason I love you. You are the first man I have ever gotten to know who would understand. Most men want a woman's body for sex and her social standing to boost theirs. They want her to applaud as they wield power and thereby acquire money. That is the way it is in Russia and Europe and Egypt. Is it like that here?"

"A lot of women think so," he admitted.

She nodded. "Although you have stolen, money is not the god you serve."

"I suppose not," Tommy Carmellini muttered. "I certainly don't have much of it."

"Nor power."

He shook his head, even though she was looking at the sand and couldn't see the response.

"You enjoy sex, yet almost any woman could provide that, and you don't seem to have a harem."

Carmellini cleared his throat. In the service of truth, perhaps he should admit that getting laid once or twice a week was pretty darn high on his priority list. He had had his share of bedmates and girlfriends through the years; he enjoyed feminine companionship. The truth of the matter was that he liked women, liked everything about them, including their bodies. He started to tell her that but she had motored on.

"You seem to have a good sense of who you are," she continued. "You aren't dogmatic or a braggart; you listen—many men don't—and you are genuinely interested in other people. I like you a lot, Tommy Carmellini. And I love you. There is a difference, you know."

He didn't want to go there. After a few more steps he stopped and turned to face her. "Was all that intended to inform me why you won't marry me?"

"I was hoping you wouldn't ask, then I wouldn't have to say no."

She had tears leaking from her eyes. That was when he realized that he knew the truth—she wasn't a spy.

He kissed her gently on the lips, both eyes, and the tip of her nose, then wrapped an arm around her shoulder and led her on as the rain pelted their bare legs and feet. Their feet left little impression on the hard sand.

CHAPTER NINETEEN

Star Transport Corporation's *Evening Star* was intercepted fifty miles off the coast of Florida by a Coast Guard helicopter. She was a large, modern containership displacing sixty thousand tons. As the helo hovered, a team of four inspectors went down one by one on the winch. When they were safely on deck the crewman lowered their gear to them, then the helo flew back to the coast for refueling while the team went to work.

Carrying Geiger counters on straps over their shoulders, team members walked beside, over, and around every stack of containers on the ship. They went down into the holds, the engine rooms and machinery spaces, crew compartments, galley, the heads, the ship's office, the fantail—they inspected the entire ship from stem to stern. The ship's crew and officers assisted, opening and closing hatches, turning lights on and off, producing manifests and ship's papers, answering questions. The team leader stayed in contact with Coast Guard headquarters and the pilot of the helicopter, when it was in range, using a handheld radio and satellite telephone.

Not a single Geiger counter registered anything more than normal background radiation during this preliminary inspection. The team had not opened any container and some were buried too deep in the stack to get near, but every container would be wanded individually as it was off-loaded at Port Everglades.

Two hours after they boarded, the team members were winched

back aboard the helo, which flew them on to another ship barely making steerageway five miles away.

Evening Star worked back up to fifteen knots and continued toward Port Everglades.

The sun had slipped below the horizon when *Evening Star* anchored near the entrance to the harbor. The following morning she was boarded by another team of inspectors. Twenty-four hours later she moved against a pier and the process of off-loading her cargo of containers with giant cranes began. More inspectors were on hand, and this time they wanded every container as it was readied for lifting to the pier.

The containers were sorted and moved to giant stacks to await Customs inspection. It was then that Red Citrix first saw the container carrying the numbers that Nguyen Duc Tran had given him. In his stack of paperwork was a multicopy manifest he had prepared showing the shipper, cargo in the box, the consignee, and its final destination. The manifest looked like every other computer-generated document in his stack.

As a soldier in army fatigues walked a bomb-sniffing dog by the box and another walked around it one more time with a Geiger counter, a Customs officer looked at the manifest, scanned the numbers on the box, then wrote on the form, "No duty owed."

"Okay," he said, taking one copy of the form for his records and handing the other copies back to Red.

It was that easy.

Although Red didn't know it, the container contained one of the four bombs that General Petrov sold to Frouq al-Zuair. The original manifest, which Red had trashed, would have caused the container to be delivered to the food shipment warehouse where Mohammed Mohammed and his friends worked.

The warriors of the Sword of Islam had not anticipated that one of their weapons would be stolen, but they had thought it likely that the Americans might inspect one or more of the containers and find the bombs, so they took the precaution of sending the four containers to four different consignees, through four different ports.

All the bombs were now on American soil.

Red Citrix was not the only person at Port Everglades to take note of the container of office furniture from *Evening Star*. Mahfuz Saleh was a data entry clerk who spent his days keeping track of containers on the computer database. He had been waiting for this container for weeks, so when he saw the number, he removed a piece of paper from his wallet and checked it against the number on the paper digit by digit.

Suddenly his palms were sweaty. He looked around guiltily to see if anyone was watching. Apparently not. He took a head break.

He didn't know what was in the container or why it was special, but he knew it was. He had speculated endlessly about what might be in it and had concluded that it probably contained weapons—rifles and ammo and perhaps plastique explosive.

Mahfuz Saleh had no desire to be a martyr. He enjoyed life and even America—he was earning good money and sending much of it home, money the family desperately needed—but the ties of blood and religion were strong within him. A man at his mosque had approached him a year ago and asked for his help. He had agreed, and was given money to purchase a computer and encryption software, the RSP software that the American government had tried to suppress for years. It lost the battle, of course, so this powerful encryption tool was made available to narcocriminals, terrorists, and Third World dictators in the name of privacy.

From time to time Saleh received encrypted messages. He normally used public telephones to pass the messages on to the parties to whom they were addressed. One such message several weeks ago gave him the number of the container and a telephone number to call when it arrived.

"Memorize the container number and the telephone number, then delete this message. When the container comes, call the telephone number from a public telephone. Then wipe your fingerprints from the telephone, so no one can prove you used it."

Mahfuz Saleh had not followed directions precisely. He had not destroyed the paper containing the telephone number and the number of the container—he knew all too well that he might forget them and shame himself before Allah and the holy warriors.

Nor did he intend to use a public telephone. Last week the telephone company removed the nearest public telephone, the one at the filling station a block from Saleh's office. So many people used cell phones now that the revenues from the pay phone didn't justify its maintenance.

As he walked the hallway toward the men's room Mahfuz Saleh nervously fingered the cell phone in his pocket. The rest room was empty. He went into the stall and removed the paper from his pocket. He turned on the cell phone and waited for it to log onto the net. When the symbol in the little window indicated the device was ready, he carefully dialed the number, checking it digit by digit before he pushed each button.

Finally he pushed the send button and held the small phone to his ear.

One ring, two, three, four—what if no one answered?—five, six . . .

"Yes." The word in Arabic.

"It's here," Mahfuz Saleh said.

"Allah Akbar!" the voice proclaimed in his ear, and the connection broke.

Mohammed Mohammed stood with his cell phone in hand, momentarily overcome by the moment. It was here! The great moment was approaching!

He put the phone in his pocket and went looking for Ali and Yousef. After Naguib's death, Yousef had applied for the empty warehouse job and got it, which was fortunate.

Patsy Smoot had asked them where the big man had gone, and Mohammed told her he had gone to live with other friends.

No policeman had ever interviewed Mohammed, Ali, or Yousef about Naguib's death. Mohammed didn't even know if the authorities had found the body. He had been very nervous for days after the killing, but it had to be done and all three of them knew it. Even, he told himself, Naguib.

Yousef said that Allah was protecting them from the authorities. Mohammed felt Allah's power and might and knew it to be true.

There were three hours left in the shift; Mohammed felt it was too dangerous to leave early. He watched the clock as he stacked boxes, thinking of what must be done.

The telephone call from Mahfuz Saleh to Mohammed Mohammed should have been intercepted by the FBI, which had indeed applied for and received court authorization to tap Mohammed's cell phone number. Unfortunately the agents monitoring cell phones and hardwired telephones for the joint task force were so overwhelmed with work that they had yet to enter Mohammed's number into the system.

Yet things were happening at the task force. Some of the suspected seventeen cells were showing signs of activity. Cryptic telephone calls to two of them had been intercepted. Both these cells had checked out of the rooming houses where they resided and set forth upon the highway.

A call from Baltimore sent another cell driving north up the interstate in a two-year-old flower-delivery van. After the initial calls, two of the cells called members of other cells. Before long nine of the suspected seventeen cells were in motion.

Hob Tulik called FBI director Myron Emerick in Washington and told him what was happening. Both men sensed that the waiting period was over.

"Three calls," Emerick mused.

"From Baltimore, Boston, and Savannah," Tulik repeated.

"Nothing from Florida?"

"Not yet."

"And not a peep from Customs," Emerick gloated. "After Corrigan units and Geiger counters and mobilizing the army and navy, they still didn't find those damned bombs!"

"Apparently not, sir."

"Stay on these guys with a full-court press, Hob. This is *it*! Use as many assets as necessary. Everything else in the country can wait. These people are going to lead us to those things."

"Yes, sir," Tulik replied.

"Remember what we talked about. When the on-scene commander is sure the weapon is present, move in fast. Shoot anyonc that doesn't surrender quick enough. Under no circumstance are those people to be given a chance to detonate one of those things."

"I've briefed every office on the East Coast," Hob Tulik assured his boss, then said good-bye.

He stood staring at the telephone for several seconds, tugging at his lip, troubled by the fact that there had been only three initial telephone calls. If there were four bombs, why not four calls? Were there cells the FBI didn't know about? Or had one of the bombs gone elsewhere? Europe, perhaps, or Los Angeles. Maybe San Francisco.

Oh, well, he thought, worrying about the West Coast and Europe and undetected cells was Emerick's job, not his. He picked up the phone and called FBI offices in other cities to tell them what was happening and what assets he needed.

Tulik was quickly inundated with requests for manpower. It was then that he made a serious mistake. Since eight of the suspected cells had received no telephone calls and seemed to be continuing with their normal routine, he called off the agents who were following or monitoring them and gave them other assignments. After all, no one had ever suggested that all seventeen of these groups were terrorists. Had he thought about it he would have probably left an agent to watch Cell Eleven, the members of which were suspected of killing one of their own, but he was thinking about nuclear weapons and extremely busy, and he forgot.

Neither Tulik nor Emerick called Jake Grafton. The FBI could handle it, thank you very much.

After their shift in the citrus packing house was over at midnight, Mohammed Mohammed and his two colleagues drove to a personal storage facility that Mohammed had rented under another name. There they retrieved three 9-mm submachine guns, two thousand rounds of ammunition, binoculars, and night-vision goggles. There was another submachine gun in the storage unit—Naguib's—but they left it there.

They then drove to the Port Everglades shipping terminal and parked along the fence. They sat in the car looking at the thousands of containers stacked within and, above the tops of the buildings, the superstructures and cranes of container ships.

It was an awesome sight. The river of world trade flowed through Port Everglades. In those containers were riches beyond the wildest dreams of the American Indians and Spanish explorers who walked this land just a few centuries ago.

The three Arabs were unimpressed. They were interested in people. Was the container with the weapon being watched? Had American Customs or the FBI learned what it contained?

Naturally Mohammed didn't know which container was his, so he scanned everything in sight, the entire scene, with his binoculars. He knew that surveillance would be sophisticated, but assumed that if it were there, he would see something. A plane overhead, perhaps, or a van with antennas. He looked in vain for vans, even opened his car door and scanned the sky with the binoculars. He saw a passenger jet that quickly flew beyond his range of vision.

He could see no one atop the buildings, no one walking around with nothing to do.

"No guards in sight," he said aloud, then passed the binoculars to Ali.

If the FBI indeed had the container that held the weapon under surveillance, it was lost to Mohammed Mohammed, and he well knew it. He also knew that under American law, until he approached the container there was no way for the prosecutors to link him to it.

He had thought about this moment for many a night this past six weeks, lying on the floor or the bed at Smoot's Motel. He needed to get to a point where he could see the containers as they left the shipping depot. If the FBI knew about his container, he would probably see agents. If so, he could drive back to Smoot's Motel and await the arrival of another bomb in three months, or six, or a year. Whatever.

He had scouted this area before, so he knew the place he wanted to watch from. He started the car engine, drove there, then parked.

After another careful scan of this area, he gave the binoculars to Ali. "Watch for FBI. They will be difficult to spot, yet if they know about the bomb, there will be many of them. And police."

A Freightliner cab pulled out of the yard towing a container on a truck chassis. The driver blew through the stop sign, turned right, and accelerated away down the street.

A locomotive whistle blew, a long, a short, then a long. Through the fence they could see it, a long, sinuous snake laden with containers. It began to move.

"How long are we going to wait?" Yousef asked.

"As long as it takes," Mohammed said curtly.

The words were no more out of his mouth than another truck came thundering down the boulevard toward the gate and turned in. The corner Mohammed had picked was going to be a busy place.

Nguyen Duc Tran had the same problem that Mohammed Mohammed had—he also needed to know if the container was being watched by federal officers. Unlike Mohammed, he had no intention of sitting outside the Port Everglades gate in plain sight waiting for someone to become suspicious and call the police or FBI.

He was waiting at the location where Red would have the container delivered, a building site of a new golf course in Jupiter, Florida. He had arrived earlier that afternoon, before the construction crew knocked off. With his Corrigan credentials and tractor cab, he fit right in. He actually told the site manager the truth: He was waiting for a container to be delivered that had to go to another Corrigan site.

"I don't know why in hell they decided to send it here, but that's what the dispatcher told me."

The manager merely nodded. Nguyen wandered off to find a shady spot to sit. Being from Texas, he wasn't bothered much by the heat, humidity, and bugs.

After the construction crew left, he went to eat dinner, then came back to the site. The container would arrive during working hours, of course, when there was someone there to sign for it. But if the police or FBI discovered what was in the container, they would probably stake out the area before it was delivered. If that happened, the game would be over for Nguyen, and he would merely climb in his tractor and drive away.

The crazy thing was that he didn't know if the container was even in the country. He didn't want any further contact with Red Citrix, and he certainly didn't want Red calling him. If it were in America and the FBI hadn't found the weapon inside, some local hauler would deliver it sooner or later.

At dusk Nguyen found a large earthmover and spread a blanket under it. He lay down on the blanket. From behind the giant tires he could see the two mobile homes about two hundred yards away that were being used as offices for the engineers and foremen. That was the place the truck driver would probably drop the container, he assumed. A light mounted on a pole in front of the newer mobile home lit the area fairly well. He scanned the area with his binoculars.

Nguyen had a rifle lying on the blanket beside him, a Remington Model 700 in .308 with a four-power scope. He used a night-vision scope he had ordered over the Internet from a sporting goods company to glass the vast area unilluminated by the solitary pole light.

Nothing.

Time passed slowly. He napped, drank water from a bottle, scanned periodically with the night-vision scope and the binoculars, then napped some more. Twice he crawled out from under the earthmover to take a pee.

The waiting was difficult. He had spent his life anticipating the opportunity to kick these American bastards in the nuts, and it was finally coming. He shivered as he thought about it. His mind wandered to the pricks he had known through the years, the bastards who had harassed him unmercifully when he was growing up, the teachers he had loathed who loathed him.

Someone once said that revenge is overrated. Whoever that fool was had obviously never drunk very much of it, Nguyen thought. Getting even is one of life's great thrills. Revenge is the only pure emotion, he decided, unleavened by any of the others. Its purity makes it sweet.

Well, perhaps it is not absolutely pure. Hatred is always part of the desire for revenge. And God knows, Nguyen thought, *I hate these bastards, hate everything they stand for, from their sanctimonious preaching about human rights to their hypocritical tut-tutting over the poverty of the non-white world and their crusade to turn the Earth into a wilderness park for the idle rich to hike in. Americans are truly perfect assholes: the better you know them, the less you like them.*

Sonny Tran was tired. At two in the morning he was piloting the van carrying the original Corrigan detector through the mean streets of Boston. Toad Tarkington and Harley Bennett were in the back of the van wearing headsets and watching the needles. With narrow streets lined with parked cars, hills everywhere, and old brick buildings crowding the sidewalks, Boston looked as old as it was.

Sonny's opportunity came suddenly, unexpectedly. He was slowing for a red light when he heard a truck roaring down the hill from his left toward the intersection. The truck had the green light.

Now he saw it, a large garbage truck. The driver was off the brakes, letting it roll.

Sonny waited a heartbeat, then floored the accelerator of the van. It shot into the intersection. For an instant he thought he had judged it wrong, that the garbage truck was going to impact the driver's door.

But no—the van was going just fast enough to escape that fate. The impact was three feet behind the driver's door, a smashing thunk that tore the wheel from his hand and twisted the cab in against the left front wheel of the truck, which continued across the intersection as it began turning sideways. With tires squalling amid the shriek of tortured metal, the truck's momentum carried it completely across the intersection before it rolled over onto its right side. It impacted several parked vehicles, then jolted to a stop.

Dazed by the impact and skid, Sonny saw that every piece of glass in the van was gone. Glass bits lay everywhere. He unbuckled his seat belt and fought his way across the cab to the right-side door and tried to open it. It was jammed. Carefully, trying not to cut himself, he crawled out the hole where the passenger's window glass had been.

Standing on the pavement, he saw that the truck driver was alive, although his face was bloody. That's when Sonny felt something wet on his own face. He wiped at it and found that it was blood.

He heard a groan from the back of the van. The rear doors were sprung and he could see into the twisted, crushed interior. He saw somebody wedged between one of the seats and the floor. Toad Tarkington. Toad groaned again.

Sonny grasped Toad's arm, tried to work him out of the wreckage. Tugging, pushing, swearing, he slid the moaning man from the van and laid him in the street. Vaguely he was aware that someone was watching from the sidewalk, someone using a cell phone.

Toad was only half-conscious. He was breathing and had a good pulse, although his eyes wouldn't focus.

Sonny crawled into the wreckage to check on Harley Bennett. The engineer was obviously dead, crushed and pinned by twisted metal. Sonny could just reach an arm . . . without a pulse. He went back to Toad.

He was trying to make him comfortable when a police car came roaring up with lights flashing. Seconds later a fire truck with siren moaning slammed to a stop and firemen bailed off.

Karl Luck was worried. He had been trying to contact Sonny Tran and had yet to hear from him. The bombs should be in the country. He stayed glued to the television, waiting for the government to announce they had found the bombs and arrested a clandestine army of suicidal raghead fanatics, and that hadn't happened either.

He was waiting in front of the television in the library of the Corrigan mansion when the industrialist came home at three in the morning. He had attended a reception at the White House and flown back to Boston on his private jet. The maid told him Luck was waiting, so he sent his wife on to bed and joined Luck in the library.

"Don't you ever go to bed?" Corrigan asked as he crossed the library and opened the door to his private office. "Come on in. Let's fix ourselves a drink." Corrigan led the way to a wet bar in the far corner of the room.

Luck waited silently, watched Corrigan pour the cognac into snifters, and accepted one. He sipped politely and waited.

"President told me they're closing in. The FBI knows who these people are. He expects arrests tonight or tomorrow—make that today. Public announcement within twenty-four hours of the arrests."

Luck felt the weight of the world lift off his shoulders. He sank into the nearest chair and took a healthy swig of cognac.

Corrigan opened a drawer and selected a cigar. He didn't offer Luck one. He guillotined the butt end and fired it up with a silver cigar lighter.

"The president wants us to sell the government a thousand detectors on a cost-plus basis," he said, eyeing Luck through the smoke. "The Europeans and Japanese will probably buy another thousand. We'll build a factory to make 'em. After we get them delivered we'll upgrade the things and sell parts and get service contracts—we're talking serious money; I estimate a couple billion over the next five years. At least half that will be pure profit. Naturally I said yes. And he talked again about naming me to the London embassy."

Luck raised his glass in silent tribute, then took another healthy swig. It was at that point that he realized he loathed Thayer Michael Corrigan.

"He's also talking about announcing a worldwide war against the Islamic fanatics after we recover the bombs," Corrigan continued thoughtfully. "Wipe the bastards out wherever we can find 'em. When the country learns about the bombs, the Congress and the public will demand it."

Karl Luck drained the last of the cognac from his glass, then rose from his chair and walked to the bar. He poured himself another and sipped on it. Corrigan seemed lost in thought, puffing slowly on his cigar.

" 'He that troubleth his own house shall inherit the wind,' " Luck muttered into his glass.

"What's that?" Corrigan said.

"Nothing," said Karl Luck. "Just an extraneous thought." The truth was that he had always known Corrigan was a shit. Yet he was in a position to make serious money with little risk, so he had become his trusted lieutenant. He was as dirty as Corrigan and the thought didn't make him happy. Okay, the big scam was about over, and he was a triple millionaire. Time to go fishing permanently and stop fretting the fact that the world belongs to the Corrigans.

"Good night," Karl Luck said distinctly. He left the empty glass on the wooden bar.

Corrigan watched him go through the tobacco smoke.

U.S. ambassador to Great Britain! He'd come a long, long way, by God, and he was wise enough to realize how lucky he'd been. Fought and scratched and taken huge risks. Used his head every minute. Was bathed in luck, a lot of which he manufactured for himself. Sure, he'd done some things that he didn't want to read about in the public press or even think about. Who the hell hadn't?

That was the way the game was played in America. All these big houses around here, out on the Cape, in the Hamptons, Newport . . . new money, old money, the people all did the same thing—used their brains to play the system and make their fortune, and used their lawyers to keep it.

Those ignorant fanatics are going to make me filthy rich, he thought, not for the first time. The irony was exquisite.

The only man alive who could put him in prison was Karl Luck.

He thought about that. The man wasn't given to idle chatter, and he was far too smart to incriminate himself or anyone else as a sop to his conscience. He liked money and the good life it would buy. Unless, of course, he was looking at a lot of years in prison. If the prosecutors gave him immunity in return for his cooperation, he'd tell them everything he knew, Corrigan reflected. Karl Luck would do a deal like that. Most men would.

Thayer Michael Corrigan was going to be an ambassador. He'd put his Corrigan Engineering stock in a blind trust for three or four years, let the engineers run the company until money was piled to the rafters, then he'd sell out for five or six billion. Laugh all the way to the bank.

He didn't need liabilities like Karl Luck.

Corrigan took a good pull on the cigar and exhaled slowly, savoring the taste and smell of the smoke. He remembered the White House this evening, the president, the beautiful ladies and the lights of Washington. . . . A smile crossed his face. He was at the very top.

London was going to be fantastic. Meeting the queen, the P.M., dinners at the embassy . . .

He'd mention Luck to the Russian. Why take a chance?

The hospital in Boston called Jake Grafton at home. The ringing telephone woke him. Still three-quarters asleep, he got it off the hook and up to his ear. "Grafton."

"Sir, this is Memorial Hospital in Boston. One of our patients, a Mr. Tran, asked us to call you."

He was awake now. "Sonny Tran?"

"I'm looking at the admission form. . . . His first name is Khanh—I hope I'm saying that right. There has been a traffic accident. He and

Mr. Tarkington were brought here. There was another passenger in their vehicle, a Mr. Bennett I believe; he was dead on arrival."

"Can I talk to Tran or Tarkington?"

"They are both still in the emergency room. Mr. Tarkington is unconscious."

"Have Tran call me as soon as possible."

Callie was wide awake. Jake cradled the telephone and turned on the light. "There's been a wreck in Boston," he told her. "Toad is unconscious. One of the other men with him is dead—fellow named Bennett."

"What are you going to do?"

"Get a plane and go to Boston. Would you call Rita on your cell"—Rita Moravia was Toad's wife—"and ask her if she would like to go? I'll have more info for her when I get it."

While Callie was making that call, Jake used the landline to call his chief of staff, Gil Pascal.

The night had been long and tiresome for Mohammed Mohammed. He had stayed awake to check the numbers on every container that left Port Everglades. Ali and Yousef periodically walked to the McDonald's a block away for coffee or soft drinks, but he had stayed in the car.

It was still dark that Friday morning when the container he was waiting for came through the gate. The driver even made an attempt at a legal stop before he cranked the steering wheel and turned left, passing right by the rental car where Mohammed Mohammed sat at the wheel, with Yousef asleep in the passenger seat and Ali asleep in the back.

That was the container! Those numbers on the side. . . . that was it!

No one following the truck. That was plain. The driver had been alone in the cab.

But why did he turn left? The container was to be delivered to the citrus warehouse, and he should have turned right to get there.

The truck was fast disappearing in Mohammed's driver's door mirror. He made a quick decision to follow it rather than go to the citrus warehouse and await its arrival.

The engine started with the first crank. Mohammed pulled the transmission into gear, cranked the wheel over for a U-turn, and fed gas.

Ali and Yousef awoke as the car lurched through the turn and accelerated with tires squealing.

"Is that it?" Yousef pointed at the truck, now a hundred yards ahead of them.

"Yes, and the driver is going the wrong way."

CHAPTER TWENTY

Dawn had arrived but the sun was not yet up when the tractor hauling the container from Port Everglades pulled up to the mobile-home office at the golf course construction site. The driver got out of the truck and stretched, casually scanning the other rig parked there, the 'dozers and backhoes and piles of pipe. He walked over to the office, rattled the locked door, checked his watch, looked around. Nguyen Duc Tran watched him through binoculars. The driver was wearing a faded Harley T-shirt, worn jeans, and cowboy boots.

The driver peed in the dirt, then took a seat on the single wooden step of the office and lit a cigarette.

Nguyen lowered the binoculars and carefully peered around the huge black tires of the earthmover he was lying under, looking for other people or cars or airplanes. He saw the sedan carrying Mohammed Mohammed and his two confederates drift to a stop on the street near the turn-in to the site.

Nguygen used a finger to focus the binoculars. Three men in the car. Not FBI or police—they would have been in place before the container arrived; they would have learned its destination. Construction workers, perhaps, a few minutes early for work. Or Arab terrorists.

Mohammed Mohammed was also using binoculars. He didn't see Nguyen Duc Tran lying under the distant earthmover, but he saw the driver plainly enough, sitting on the office step smoking and occasionally glancing at his watch. He studied the container again. At this distance with eight-power binoculars, he could just read the number on the side of the container. He studied it, repeated every number to himself.

Yes, that was the one.

He lowered the binoculars and wondered what he should do.

Mohammed removed his cell phone from his pocket and flipped it open. He fingered it idly while he considered his options.

There was the weapon he had been waiting for, and it wasn't where it was supposed to be. He had not forgotten the container number nor had he gotten it twisted. *That* was the container. Perhaps there had been some mistake with the delivery manifest. Or someone was stealing it.

He looked at the keyboard of the telephone and dialed a number he had committed to memory. After the third ring a male voice answered. "Akram, this is Mohammed. *Allah Akbar!*"

The FBI was not monitoring Mohammed's telephone, but it was monitoring Akram, who led the cell the FBI had designated as Number Fourteen. Unfortunately the man who normally listened to the conversations on monitored numbers was busy just then arranging communications between the police agencies and FBI agents who were shadowing the cells that Tulik thought were hot. This call was automatically recorded and would be listened to whenever the technician had time. He was busy now, and he was going to get a lot busier.

The driver got tired of waiting, so he fired up his tractor and began preparations to unhook the truck chassis that carried the container.

Nguyen divided his attention between the driver, the car parked on the street, and scanning in all the other directions. A sliver of sun peeped over the earth's rim and bathed the scene in a golden light, but he didn't notice.

The driver moved the tractor away from the chassis and left the engine idling. He walked behind it, tied up brake lines and electrical cords, then took a clipboard from the cab of the tractor and resumed his seat on the step of the office. He lit another cigarette.

Well, by God, there it was, Nguyen thought. All he had to do was go down there, sign the clipboard, hook up, and drive off.

The driver wasn't going to let him sign for the load unless he had a key to the office, and he didn't. He could always shoot the driver, of course, and throw his body into the container, but the people in the car on the street would see him do it. In any event, someone would start looking for the missing driver before long. And if those three watching from the street were indeed terrorists, they might get pissy when he tried to hook up and drive away.

Anxious as he was, Nguyen could only wait.

Mohammed Mohammed was feeling the burden of each passing minute. There sat the weapon, misdelivered or stolen. If he and his men drove over there and shot the driver, they could hook up the chassis to the tractor and drive off. Mohammed knew how to drive a truck—he had planned to drive the delivery truck to New York.

But what if this were a setup? What if there was a squad of heavily armed FBI agents clad in body armor hiding in the construction office or the weapon container?

He scanned the whole area again with his binoculars, looking for someone, something, anything. Another glance at his watch. Twelve minutes since he telephoned.

Akram should be here soon with three other men, all armed. With seven men, they would go get the weapon. If there were police or FBI agents hidden and waiting, they would kill them.

"We shouldn't wait," Yousef said, seeming to read his thoughts. "The construction workers will arrive soon, and they will call the police. We can't kill all of them."

Mohammed was torn. Would Akram arrive before the construction workers? Should he wait for Akram or go now?

Even as he weighed it, his eye registered a gleam of reflected light from one of the distant earthmovers. He aimed the binoculars, held them steady as possible, and sweetened up the focus. He could see the head and shoulders of a man lying beside a massive wheel. He, too, was holding binoculars. The flash had been the reflection of the rising sun in one of the lenses.

So they *were* waiting!

Myron A. Emerick was in his element. He sat in the command chair in the FBI operations center at the Hoover building in Washington and listened to the reports of FBI agents, police SWAT units, and surveillance helicopters as they came in. A video feed from an airborne helicopter played on a giant screen.

The crew in the operations center was running simultaneous surveillances on nine cells of suspected terrorists in south Florida, all of whom were in cars or vans and driving north. Already the operation had tied up two hundred agents and local police, and more would soon be needed. The surveillances were as loose as possible, so the suspects wouldn't know they were being followed.

One of the problems with using local police was their proclivity for whispering to local television crews that something was going down. It hadn't happened yet this morning, but it might. It was a risk Emerick had to take. He had no choice; he had to let the terrorists lead him to the weapons. Every other option would take a lot more time. Once they knew the government was on to them the terrorists would either try to escape or stop dead, right where they were, and he wouldn't find the weapons without a massive search.

Hob Tulik was in Florida, running things out of the antiterrorism task force offices; every now and then Emerick heard his voice on the circuit. Emerick's deputy, Robert Pobowski, was standing by the duty officer, listening and making an occasional remark.

Emerick stretched his legs, then stood. In tense moments he found it difficult to sit.

As he paced he thought about the three telephone calls that had started the suspects in motion. If there were four weapons, why not four telephone calls?

Were there cells the FBI didn't know about? That was the most likely answer. In all probability one of those unknown cells received a call and was at this moment on its way to take delivery of a nuclear warhead.

But where?

Emerick stared at the map.

How could he cut through the knot, find the missing cells? The only thing he could think of was to inspect those weapons they could find, see why they weren't found in customs and port inspections, and go from there. Everyone wants a magic bullet, but sometimes there aren't any. Good, solid police work had turned up these three—that was what would be required to find the fourth.

When the president called in a few minutes, he would tell him that. Solid, competent, thorough, honest-to-God police work did the job every time. There was no substitute for it. Not now, not ever.

"Ten minutes, *Inshallah,"* Akram told Mohammed over the cell phone. "If you are where we think you are, it will take us ten minutes. If you are somewhere else, I do not know. Why was the weapon delivered there?"

Mohammed slammed the cover of the telephone closed, terminating the conversation. The fool! If the FBI were listening, he was telling them everything!

Well, Akram and his men might be here in ten minutes or they might not. *Inshallah!*

"We should shoot the driver and take the weapon," Ali insisted. "I see only one man lying under that earthmover."

"You see only one! But how many are there?" Yousef demanded. "Do you know?"

"Allah Akbar!" Ali roared. "We must trust to Allah and fight the *kafirs*! Allah is with *us*! There is the weapon!" He pointed at the container.

Mohammed was beside himself, unable to reach a decision. He was ready to give his life to smite the wicked Americans a mighty blow, not to die stupidly.

He was reaching for the ignition key, about to start the car and go for it, when a pickup passed the parked sedan and turned into the dirt road leading to the construction office. The man driving parked right beside the building and got out. He was about sixty, balding, with a magnificent gut hanging over his belt.

Mohammed used his binoculars. The delivery driver pointed to the container and offered some papers. The man from the pickup laid the papers on the hood of his truck, looked them over, then signed with a pen offered by the delivery driver.

After a handshake, the delivery driver walked toward his truck.

Another pickup entered the yard. A man got out carrying coffee in a styrofoam cup. As the delivery driver climbed in the cab of his tractor two more vehicles arrived, one behind the other.

"They will get on with the day's work," Mohammed told Ali and Yousef. "We will give them fifteen minutes to disburse, then get that tractor and hook it to the chassis with the container." A huge risk, and they would probably have to shoot some of these people, but they needed the weapon. They would shoot the watching man, too.

They were watching other vehicles arrive, counting people, when they realized that the parked tractor was now moving, backing up to the chassis. Ali saw the tractor move first.

As he pointed, Mohammed focused the binoculars. The driver was backing smartly, using the mirrors. A professional, obviously.

Where had he come from?

"When the chassis is on the rig, we drive in. Yousef, shoot the driver. Ali, watch for anyone who might have a weapon, like that man under the earthmover"—Mohammed had lost track of him—"and I'll get in the cab. Yousef will ride with me. Ali will follow in the car."

They checked their weapons, made sure they were loaded and the safeties were engaged.

"Allah Akbar," Yousef whispered.

"Where is Akram?" Ali asked.

Mohammed watched the driver. He seemed to have all the connections attached between the container and the tractor. Now he was wiping his hands on his jeans, now he was walking around the rig one last time, checking. . . .

"Let's go." He started the engine, engaged the transmission, and rolled around the corner, along the dirt road toward the buildings. Some people turned to look.

He braked in front of the trailer and Yousef opened the door and leaped out, an Uzi in his hand.

The man beside the rig shot Yousef twice before he could point his weapon. He collapsed in the dirt.

Mohammed Mohammed slammed the transmission into reverse and backed up with the accelerator on the floor, the engine screaming and dirt flying. A shot shattered the windshield.

Ali leaned out an open window and hosed a burst as Mohammed cranked the wheel to slew the rear of the car ninety degrees and jammed on the brakes. The open passenger door yawed wide. He pulled the transmission into drive as he spun the wheel, then he jammed the accelerator to the floor and fishtailed toward the boulevard. The passenger door slammed shut.

When he reached the street, Mohammed made a right turn and skidded the car to a stop. He and Ali bailed out with submachine guns in their hands. Mohammed ran across the street, took up a position directly across from the construction site entrance. The tractor-trailer rig was already in motion toward the street, accelerating, its engine winding at full throttle before every shift.

On the other side of the street, Ali stepped into the middle of the dirt driveway, brought the submachine gun to his shoulder, and aimed carefully.

Nguyen Duc Tran didn't wait to find out if his windshield was bulletproof. He stuck Miguel Tejada's Glock out his side window and, using his left hand, began squeezing off shots in Ali's general direction. He didn't expect to hit him, merely give him something else to think about.

Ali ignored the bullets whipping around him. Shooting the driver wouldn't stop the truck—he realized that now. Paralyzed by indecision, he froze for a few critical seconds.

He was trying to jump aside when the front bumper of the massive tractor hit him and knocked him backward six feet, then the tractor ran over him. Nguyen Tran cranked the wheel over to make the turn onto the street and stayed on the gas. He didn't even feel the thump as the right rear wheels of the tractor ran over Ali, killing him instantly.

Mohammed didn't shoot. He, too, realized that killing the driver would cause the truck to crash, which would not help the cause.

As he stood watching the container carrying the nuclear weapon speed away down the wide street, a flower-delivery van skidded to a halt beside him. Akram was at the wheel.

Mohammed ran around the front of the vehicle and threw himself through the open door. "Follow that truck," he shouted. "Someone's stealing the weapon!"

"What about your men?" Akram demanded, looking at Ali's corpse.

"They are already in Paradise. Follow that truck!"

Jake Grafton caught an executive jet at Andrews Air Force Base. Rita Moravia, Toad Tarkington's wife, was waiting in the terminal. The two of them climbed aboard as Jake told Rita everything he had learned about the crash, which wasn't much. "Toad was in back when the crash occurred. The guy with him, Harley Bennett, was killed. The driver was Sonny Tran. He called me from the hospital." He told her what Sonny had relayed about Toad's condition.

Rita took it well, he thought. She was a career naval officer, too, and she had been through her share of emergencies, been to her share of funerals and memorial services. Still, when it's your husband, the father of your son, it's not business as usual.

When the jet leveled at altitude, she tried to make conversation.

After they had discussed what Callie and Amy were up to these days, Jake asked about Rita. "Callie and I don't see you often enough," he said. "What are you doing these days?"

"Planning for Fleet Week in New York, the last week in May. With the mood of the country like it is, the administration wants to make a big deal out of it. And the New Yorkers need it." She went on, explaining how many aircraft carriers and surface warships were going to be there. "The Canadians, Brits, French, and Germans are sending squadrons. The Israelis are sending a destroyer. Several ships from South America will come, even a couple from Japan."

She welcomed the chance to stop speculating about her husband's possible injuries and talked with some enthusiasm. Jake let her talk.

He had forgotten about Fleet Week. He had seen articles in the newspaper and heard people at the Pentagon talking, but none of it registered. He had his mind on other things.

"Tell me about security," he prompted Rita.

"It's going to be heavy. Fleet Week is obviously a terror target." She went on, telling him how the warship anchorages would be sanitized. "No one wants a repeat of the USS *Cole* incident, especially in New York Harbor."

A somber Jake Grafton sat staring at the bulkhead of the little plane.

A helicopter was waiting at Logan Airport to fly them to the hospital. Gil Pascal had been on the telephone, apparently. Sonny Tran was waiting beside the pad when the helo landed. He was whacked up, too, with a bandage on his forehead. "Ten stitches," he told them. "Some glass they had to take out. I was damned lucky."

He led them through the corridors, telling them about the accident and Toad's condition. "He has four bruised ribs and a mild concussion. Some cuts, twenty or so stitches. He'll make a full recovery, the doctor said."

"What about the van and the Corrigan detector."

"Totaled. The whole thing is junk."

Jake stopped to talk to the doctor outside the ICU while Rita went in to see Toad. The doctor repeated Sonny's report in more detail.

Sonny stayed in the corridor when Jake entered the ICU. He saw Rita bent over a bed, kissing Toad, who was hooked to an IV and heart monitor. She straightened as Jake approached, yet held tightly to her husband's hand. He was conscious and alert. His face was badly swollen, and he had some stitches over his right eye. On the monitor his heartbeat and blood pressure looked steady and normal.

"Hey, boss," Toad said. "Fate sorta reached out and whacked the ol' Horny Toad."

"So I hear. How you doing, shipmate?"

"Sore as hell. Woke up a little bit ago, just in time to get a kiss from the greatest woman on the planet."

Jake leaned over the bed, as close to Toad as he could get. "Tell me about the accident."

"I don't remember much. We were in back, Harley and I, watching needles when the world caved in. Knocked me out. I must have regained conciousness at some point because I remember someone saying a garbage truck hit us."

"Uh-huh."

"Sorta funny, though. I kinda remember Sonny goosing the thing just before the impact. He might have been trying to avoid the collision. I fell off the stool and was on the floor when the side of the thing just came smashing in on us. Harley was sitting on his stool."

"Uh-huh."

"How is he?"

"Harley?"

"Yeah."

"He's dead. Didn't they tell you?"

"Maybe they did. I've been out of it. I don't remember."

"He's dead. Sonny got a cut on the head."

"Oh, Jesus!"

"It was an accident. Just concentrate on getting well. I need you back at the office."

When he went out in the hallway Sonny was still there, sitting beside the nurses' station with his head in his hands.

"Sorry, Admiral. I feel really bad about the accident. It's hell, Bennett dying like that. That garbage truck came blowing down that hill and there was nothing I could do."

"Toad said he felt you jam on the gas."

"Well, yeah. I tried to get through the intersection ahead of the truck, but . . ." He shrugged.

"I understand."

"Hell of a thing, I know. How about some time off? I'm not going to be able to keep my mind on business for a while."

"Sure. A few days off will be good for you."

"I need to chill."

"You've been working pretty hard," Jake said. "Take a couple weeks. Check in occasionally, tell me how you are doing."

"Okay." Sonny shook hands and wandered off.

Jake watched him go. He had no grounds to have him arrested, and that would be the only way to hold him. If he used his cell phone or credit cards, Zelda could track him. That would have to do.

He probably should get a copy of the police accident report, but that could wait. The hard fact was that he was down to precisely one Corrigan unit, and there were still four Sword of Islam bombs headed this way. And Fleet Week was coming! How in hell did he forget that?

He took the cell phone from his pocket and dialed Gil Pascal.

The nurse at the desk leaned toward him and spoke in a stage whisper. "Sir, would you take your phone to the visitors' waiting room. The transmissions affect our telemetry."

"Right," Jake said.

She pointed, and he went.

Mohammed Mohammed and Akram conferred. They were in the van a hundred yards behind the truck with the bomb. The little parade was on a two-lane state highway headed north.

They discussed their options. If they drove alongside the tractor and shot the driver, the truck would crash. Could the five of them lift the bomb into the van before the police arrived? What if the weapon were damaged in the crash?

"If he stays on roads like this, he will come to a stoplight sooner or later," Akram pointed out. "When he stops, we can drive up beside the cab and shoot him. The truck will be stopped, you can climb up and drive."

"On an interstate highway he would have to stop at a weight station eventually," Mohammed mused. "I don't know where he is going, but if it is a long way he will have to stop for fuel."

At the mention of the word "fuel," Akram looked at the van's gauge. Half a tank. "We will probably run out of fuel before he does," he said gloomily. "If we stop he will drive on and escape us."

None of the options looked good. The men in the back of the van had opinions, too, so the discussion grew heated as the miles rolled by. With all the uncertainties, the consensus was that they should wait.

Something good would happen. The truck would stop for some reason. *Allah Akbar!*

In the cab of the tractor, Nguyen Duc Tran regularly checked his rearview mirrors. The flower-delivery van was back there a hundred yards or so, following faithfully. Where it had come from he had no idea, but he didn't waste time fretting bad luck.

The police were undoubtedly investigating the shooting at the construction site. Thank heavens he had taken all the copies of the manifests with him. Someone might have gotten the number on the license plates of the tractor or trailer, but he doubted it. The construction workers were diving for cover when he last saw them, probably convinced they were trapped at a drug shootout. He hoped they kept that thought firmly in mind. Those guys undoubtedly knew that people in south Florida who ratted on drug dealers had short life expectancies. They probably wouldn't volunteer information to the police.

He again checked the van in the rearview mirror. As he drove he put a fresh magazine in the Glock, then laid the pistol on his lap. He reached behind his seat and brought up the Uzi. He had two magazines taped together, so after he emptied the first one he merely had to jerk it out and flip it over to insert a fresh one. He put the Uzi on the seat beside him.

He had bottled water to drink, a full tank of diesel fuel, and on these back roads he could avoid the weight stations.

If the ragheads were waiting for him to stop, they were going to wait quite a while.

He thought about what they might do. They wanted the container intact—that would limit their options.

After a half hour of this Akram and Mohammed reached a decision. Once they did Mohammed began making telephone calls on his cell phone. If they could get people ahead of this rig, they could ambush it, shoot out the tires of the tractor. That would be dangerous, but there was no help for it. With the rig stopped, the chassis carrying the container could be hooked to another tractor and driven away. They needed people to move fast to make it happen because the runaway nuclear weapon was proceeding north at sixty miles per hour.

Fahah Saqib, twenty-two years of age, believed in *jihad* against the *kafirs,* the infidels. He grew up in a small village on the edge of the desert, a son of tribesmen with the mark of the desert still on them. He wasn't sure precisely what the American infidels had done to Islam, but all his life he had been told by uneducated, bearded holy men who had never been far from their village that the infidels were the enemy, and he had never questioned it. It was a fact of life, like the desert and the presence of Allah.

Nor did he question it these past six months, which he had spent in America enduring the worst kind of cultural shock. He knew nothing about the country, couldn't speak the language, didn't like the food, hated the music, and was horrified by the women, who were everywhere, in every public place and private shop. There was nowhere to escape them. They paraded their charms, wore revealing clothes, painted their faces and nails, tried to tempt men into sin. They were brazen sluts of the worst sort. And he had been forced to eat with them, deal with them, sit beside them, watch them tempt men they did not know . . . *tempt him.* . . .

Fahah Saqib felt as if he were visiting the country of the devil where evil prevailed, where the greatness of Allah and the words of the prophet were despised. He had seen the children and girls smiling, snickering, pointing at him and his friends. He felt their amusement, their contempt. And he hated them. *Kafirs!*

This morning as he rode in the back of a van on its way somewhere—he didn't know where and the leader hadn't told him and it never occurred to him to ask—he thought about the weapon. He knew only what people said, that it was a superbomb that could wipe out a city and everyone in it. He had no idea how it worked or why. Naturally the *kafirs* made it, although they lacked the courage to use it.

The men of the Sword of Islam would show the world they had the courage and the power, Fahah Saqib thought. The *kafirs* who survived would know the fury of *jihad* and the power of Islam. Embrace Allah or be destroyed—that was the prophet's message to the unbelievers, and it was Islam's message now.

As the sun rose this Friday morning the leader, Saeed, briefed the men. The weapon would arrive this morning at a Wal-Mart in suburban Atlanta. They would be waiting for it when it arrived.

When it arrived, the men in this van would surround the container and prevent anyone from getting close, such as police or warehouse workers. They would be given weapons before the bomb arrived.

While they were defending the bomb, Mohmad Salaah, the leader from the other van, would unload enough of the container's contents to get to the weapon. He would hook the weapon to a series of automobile batteries, and trigger the capacitor. A few seconds later the weapon would detonate, destroying much of Atlanta. Naturally they would all die, too—a regrettable sacrifice, yet necessary—and proceed straight to Paradise.

Fahah Saqib was ready. He had lived as best he could and was ready for the eternal pleasures. *Allah Akbar!*

On the outskirts of Atlanta the van stopped for a few minutes. Salaah went to another vehicle and returned a few moments later. Weapons were passed out. Fahah Saqib was given a submachine gun and several magazines of ammunition. With the weapon in his hand he felt like a warrior, a warrior for Allah, and was almost overcome by emotion. He had to turn his head to keep the others from seeing the dampness of his eyes.

Soon the van was rolling again, each man cradling his weapon in his lap.

The Wal-Mart parking lot was practically empty when they arrived. A few vehicles were parked near the employees' entrance and several abandoned or broken-down cars speckled the lot, but that was about it.

As directed, Fahah Saqib took up a post behind the Wal-Mart, near a large Dumpster. He lay down amid the weeds and trash beside the Dumpster and put his spare magazine on the ground beside him. He had already inserted one in the weapon. Now he chambered a round and put the safety on.

It had rained during the night, he noted. The asphalt was damp, with puddles here and there. The smell of garbage from the Dumpster was heavy in the moist air. Fahah Saqib had not eaten this morning, but the smell of rotting garbage made him lose his desire for food. There would be plenty in Paradise, he thought. However, after some reflection, he wondered if there were any food there at all. Pondering the question, he decided there probably was, because Allah knew men liked food.

The minutes ticked by slowly. Fahah Saqib looked repeatedly at his watch.

There were no other people in sight. Several times he heard airplanes, and once a helicopter a long way off. He didn't look for them.

"Three of the cells are in Atlanta," Hob Tulik told his boss, Myron Emerick, over the encrypted line. Emerick was in the FBI's crisis management center in the Hoover Building in Washington, monitoring the situation. Tulik was still in Florida. "They are in a Wal-Mart parking lot, armed to the teeth, waiting for something. Perhaps waiting for a weapon to arrive."

"Is it there now?"

"I don't think so. They parked two of the vans in the center of the parking lot in front of the store and stationed men around the building and on the edge of the lot. They have made no attempt to enter the store or parked trucks or vehicles. Looks to me as if they are waiting. There's a total of a dozen suspects, we believe, nine on guard and three by the vans."

"All armed?"

"Yes, sir. Apparently so."

"If the weapon is there, I want you to send the men in now."

"I don't think it's there."

"Why not move in now, arrest these men, then wait for the weapon?"

"Sir, I have no way of knowing what these suspects are waiting for."

"Okay," Emerick said. Sometimes you had to go with gut instincts because those were all you had. His brain told him Tulik was right and his gut told him the Atlanta suspects were waiting for a weapon.

He called the White House and got Sal Molina. He relayed what he knew.

"Where are the other weapons?" Molina wanted to know.

"We are not sure. We've got terrorists running around willy-nilly right now. Got people on 'em . . . if they get within rifle shot of a nuke, we'll bust 'em."

"Keep me advised. The president has asked me to keep him informed minute by minute."

"Right," said Myron Emerick, and hung up. He sat staring at the giant computer-generated map display that covered the far wall, and wondered aloud, "Where the devil are the other weapons?"

A few minutes before eight in the morning a tractor pulled onto the Wal-Mart property towing a chassis with a container on it. The driver raced his rig across the empty parking lot and only applied his brakes to slow for the turn down the narrow place beside the building. Fahah Saqib heard the vehicle coming and tightened his grip on his weapon.

The driver came into sight behind the building. With the tractor snorting diesel exhaust, it backed smartly to the loading dock. Leaving his rig running, the driver strolled inside to find someone to sign for his load.

That's when two of the militants came walking around the building. They climbed into the tractor cab and put it in gear. They drove it slowly around the building and parked it next to their vehicles in the center of the lot.

Fahah Saqib saw the rig disappear around the building with Saleem and another man in the cab. He waited where he was. Fifteen seconds later the original driver of the tractor-trailer came out of the building, saw his rig was gone, and began running after it. Fahah Saqib stood up then, leveled the submachine gun with the butt against one hip, and triggered a burst at the man.

Missed him, of course.

He triggered another burst, which went so far over the man's head that he didn't see the bullets strike.

The driver turned and ran for his life back toward the loading dock. Saqib tried two more bursts, one of which made a hail of sparks against the concrete loading dock. The driver threw himself up on the dock with surprising agility, rose instantly to his feet, and lunged for the door.

When he disappeared, Fahah Saqib lowered his weapon and thoughtfully removed the magazine. He inspected it, then replaced it with a full one. Well, he had only fired a submachine gun once before, one magazine, about a year ago.

He was leaning against the container, watching the loading dock, when an FBI sniper shot him from three hundred yards away. He didn't hear the shot. The bullet went through both lungs and his heart. He collapsed, wondering what had happened. Ten seconds later his heart stopped.

Two helicopters swooped down across the roof, headed for the main parking lot. In less than thirty seconds five of the militants were dead, four more were wounded, and the remainder had thrown down their weapons. One ran. Local police arrested him a half mile away in the middle of an overgrown vacant lot.

The agent in charge of the operation, George Ekimov, opened the container. It was packed with light office furniture, cheap stuff made of soft wood. His men began unloading the furniture while an agent with a powerful spotlight and a video camera recorded everything.

Halfway through the load they came to beanbag chairs. The first ones that the agents unloaded seemed unremarkable, but then they tried to pick up one that was too heavy for two men to lift. It took four men to scoot the thing out of the trailer.

Ekimov used a knife on the fake leather covering. He reached into the cut and pulled out a handful of the pellets. They were made of soft metal, blown with air to give them bulk. He used his pocketknife on one of them.

Lead.

More chairs were removed, revealing a mound of canvas bags taped into position with an extraordinary amount of duct tape. Ekimov used his knife to cut away a bag. He examined it under the video camera's spotlight. The bag contained twenty-five pounds of #8 lead birdshot.

When the bags of birdshot were completely removed, there sat the warhead, bolted to the floor of the container. It was smaller than Ekimov thought it would be. Between the warhead and the container floor was a half-inch-thick sheet of lead. Each of the four or so dozen high-explosive detonators that surrounded the round warhead was wired to a black box—a sea of yellow wires. Ekimov assumed the box was a complex capacitor designed to send electrical impulses to all the detonators at the appropriate nanosecond. There didn't appear to be a battery or source of electrical power, although there were wires protruding from the box that one might use as a connection point.

One of the agents told him there were a dozen car batteries in one of the vans. "Maybe they were going to detonate it right here," the agent said to Ekimov.

"Perhaps," he said. "Start questioning the survivors. Where are the other weapons? Find one that speaks English and get it out of him."

"Miranda warnings?"

"No. This is war. They're enemy soldiers until somebody in Washington says different. Where are the other bombs? Find out, Goddammit!"

"Yes, sir."

While the photographer circled the weapon and continued taking video from every angle, Ekimov got on the encrypted telephone to Hob Tulik. When he finished that call, he made another, to the Explosive Ordnance Disposal (EOD) team that was standing by at Naval Air Station Jacksonville. While he was talking he heard a rumble of thunder.

Holy . . . ! A lightning bolt in this vicinity might set this thing off, he thought.

"Better hurry," he told the EOD team leader.

The parking lot shooting in Atlanta was soon on local television stations. A traffic helicopter in the vicinity got footage of the FBI agents unloading the container. No one in law enforcement whispered the word "nuclear," and several hinted at drugs, so that became the story—FBI and local cops had seized a container full of drugs. Soon the video from the helicopter was on the broadcast and cable networks.

Jake Grafton was in the executive terminal at the Boston airport when he got a call from Gil Pascal alerting him to the story. As it happened a television in the pilot's lounge was tuned to MSNBC, which was running the helicopter video. The container was an ominous presence. Although the voice-over commentator was rambling about drugs, Jake Grafton wasn't fooled.

His cell phone rang again. Harry Estep from the FBI this time, with news. The FBI had a nuke—it was in that shipping container that was on television.

"It was sitting on a lead plate, surrounded with lead birdshot and blown lead pellets. That's probably how it came into the country."

Jake Grafton grunted. He had suspected something like that, but why say so?

"Emerick thinks all the weapons are in the country. He hopes to get them in the next twenty-four hours, he says."

"By God, I hope he does," Jake said fervently.

"We're running complex surveillances on a couple of groups that are going somewhere in a big hurry right now. Perhaps to collect bombs. I'll keep you advised."

"Right."

It must have been Jake's tone, because Estep continued earnestly, "Soon as I know something, I'll call you."

"Right," Jake said, and flipped the mouthpiece shut.

Fleet Week, he thought as he stood watching the video from the helicopter circling the Georgia Wal-Mart parking lot. If a nuke went off in New York Harbor amid a hundred warships, the public would think it had been an accidental explosion of an American weapon aboard a U.S. Navy ship. There would be no one left alive to tell a different story. The blast in New York Harbor and the subsequent radioactive and political fallout would deal the American economy a devastating blow. U.S. Navy warships would be banned from most of the world's ports, including, probably, those in California and Puget Sound. America's ability to protect her interests around the world would be paralyzed, perhaps fatally so. Since America was the foremost defender of liberal civilization, that, too, would be in jeopardy.

One bomb . . . and the era of Pax Americana would end in a mushroom cloud.

CHAPTER TWENTY-ONE

The two-lane highway ran north through central Florida through scrub pine and swamps and past occasional mobile homes sitting on naked scars in the red earth. The May sky was clear and blue. The asphalt was steeply crowned with berms of crushed coquina.

Nguyen Duc Tran kept the tractor-trailer rig at sixty miles per hour. The van was still behind him, a hundred yards or so back.

The first town they came to had a bypass around it, so he took it. One stoplight, and he began slowing. The light turned green by the time he was down to forty, so he jammed on the accelerator and went on through.

He wouldn't be so lucky every time.

If the Arabs in the van decided to shoot out the rig's tires, they would have him. The fact that the rig might crash was the only thing that had kept them from doing that already, he thought.

They were committed men who would stop at nothing. They would do it before long.

Perhaps, he thought, they were using their cell phones to get another carload of terrorists into position ahead of him.

He began looking for roads leading off into the swamps to the left and right.

Akram and Mohammed Mohammed argued over the best course of action. Crashing the truck might damage the weapon—if that happened they were defeated. And yet, failure to stop the truck was certain defeat. Unless they intercepted it farther north when the driver stopped for fuel. Fortunately the road was very straight, a ribbon of asphalt running through the hinterland.

One of the men in the back of the van was on a cell phone to the leader of the third cell assigned to their group. Alas, the cell was only now leaving Broward County, two hours behind them. It would never catch up.

Akram and Mohammed were going to have to make a decision and take their chances.

They came to a decision. "We will shoot out the tires," they agreed. "Shooting out the rear tires will slow the rig, and it will be forced to stop. Then we will kill the driver and transfer the weapon to the van."

All they needed was a place along this road with no witnesses to telephone the authorities. Or few witnesses.

While they consulted a road map, they heard a siren, faintly at first, then growing in intensity. Then they saw the police car in the rearview mirror. It overtook them with flashing overhead lights, the headlights blinking . . . coming quickly at eighty or ninety miles per hour, eating up the road.

In the passenger seat Mohammed checked his submachine gun. If the policeman wanted the van to stop, he would kill him.

But the police car didn't slow. It moved into the passing lane and didn't slacken its pace. It roared by on the left and stayed in that lane, passed the tractor-trailer, and moved into the right lane and raced on toward the horizon.

Although Akram and Mohammed didn't know it, the policeman in the cruiser was being summoned by the joint antiterrorism task force to man a roadblock on an interstate highway near the Florida–Georgia state line. Washington had issued orders for the establishment of roadblocks. Since even the police lacked the manpower to block every road, the interstates were the first priority.

Nguyen Tran suspected that he would find roadblocks on the major highways, so he had no intention of driving on one. He watched the police cruiser until it was out of sight, then checked the van in the rearview mirrors. Still back there. And time was running out.

He reached behind him and pulled the Remington from its resting place. He laid it on his lap, the barrel pointing toward the driver's door.

Ahead on the left he saw an unpaved road leading away at a ninety-degree angle into the swamp, with its tangled brush and undergrowth. That would have to do.

He pushed in the clutch and downshifted, used the engine to scrub off some speed. He couldn't get too slow in the turn or the terrorists would be out and shooting before he could do anything. He had to time this perfectly.

And he did. The truck was still going at a good clip when he braked heavily, causing the trailer to fishtail, then released the brakes and jammed the accelerator down as he cranked the wheel to the left.

The tractor turned, the trailer tilted, the left side wheels left the ground . . . and he just made the turn amid a spray of gravel. He spun the wheel to straighten out and kept the accelerator down. The rig stabilized and began accelerating down the narrow coquina road. The vegetation closed in on both sides.

When the rig began slowing, Mohammed leaned out the passenger window with the submachine gun. Now was the time to shoot out the rear tires!

Akram braked the van too quickly, and the range didn't close sufficiently before the tractor began turning.

Mohammed thought the trailer was going over. It went around the turn with its left wheels off the ground, smoke pouring from the right-side tires.

The turn was so unexpected that Akram swerved to avoid the truck. He was well past the truck before he got it together and slammed on the van's brakes.

"Back up," Mohammed urged. "Follow him. This is our chance."

Akram slammed the transmission into reverse, squealed the tires backing up, then pulled the lever back into drive and cranked the wheel over.

The delay hadn't been long, but now the tractor-trailer was several hundred yards ahead, accelerating into the piney woods.

The van could go faster down this road than the rig could, Nguyen knew, and would catch him soon. He had little time. Now or never.

He jammed the clutch to the floor and locked the brakes. The big rig slewed as it decelerated and he fought the wheel, trying to keep it on the narrow, rutted road. It came to rest in a shower of gravel and dust. The van was still a hundred yards behind. He turned off the engine and pulled the key out of the ignition switch. Grabbing the Remington and the Uzi, Nguyen bailed.

With his feet on the ground, he paused. Dropping the Remington beside him, he lifted the Uzi and aimed carefully at the oncoming van. When it reached forty yards he opened fire.

Akram had just gotten the van stopped and the transmission into park when the hailstorm of 9-mm slugs arrived. They punctured the radiator and the windshield, causing it to craze into an opaque mess. The bullets kept punching holes in it, so chunks of glass began flying out.

Akram was killed by a bullet in the head. A slug hit Mohammed in the neck, incapacitating him.

Behind him the men in back got the door open and threw themselves through it. One caught a slug in the ribs as he got up off the road, then two more in the legs and one in the arm. He fell to the ground and didn't move again.

By this time Nguyen had fired the entire magazine, thirty rounds, in three ten-shot bursts. He stepped to his right to get a better view of the van as he jerked the empty magazine out, turned it around, and shoved home the fresh magazine that had been taped to it. He glimpsed one of the men bounding for the brush. The other man managed to get to his feet and begin shooting his Uzi from the hip at Nguyen. He should have aimed.

Nguyen fired an aimed, ten-shot burst at the shooter. Five slugs hit him, knocking him backward. Nguyen emptied his submachine gun at the van and the two bodies lying beside it. Then he dropped the weapon, grabbed the Remington, and threw himself to his right, into the waist-high brush. He began crawling away from the tractor and the road.

Mohmad Adeel hid behind a tree and listened to the silence. The shooting had stopped.

One moment they had been sitting in the van, talking about stopping the tractor-trailer, and the next moment they had been trapped in a rain of bullets. He had seen Akram's head snap back when the slug hit him and knew he was dead. He saw blood pour from Mohammed's neck. He remembered Alaeddin falling—he didn't know what had happened to Omar. Both were also dead, probably.

Mohmad Adeel's hands were shaking violently. As he pressed himself against the tree he felt the wetness in his trousers and realized he had lost control of his bladder.

That *kafir* was out there with his weapon. Mohmad Adeel's duty was to kill him to avenge Akram and Mohammed and Omar and Alaeddin.

Mohmad Adeel looked carefully around his tree, which wasn't large. He could see the container and most of the tractor. Looking the other way he could see the van, see Omar and Alaeddin lying beside it covered with blood.

It wasn't supposed to be like this. They were holy warriors on *jihad*. Allah was supposed to protect them.

He pushed that thought away as unworthy.

Where was the infidel? Close to the tractor, probably. No doubt he would try to get back in the tractor cab and drive it away. Drive away with the warhead belonging to the Sword of Islam.

Trying to make as little noise as possible, Mohmad Adeel moved toward the standing rig. He stayed in the brush, moving slowly. If he could get in a place where he could watch the tractor, he could kill the infidel when he tried to get back in it.

When he was abeam the tractor he hunched down so he could see under it. *This is good,* he thought. *I will shoot him in the legs and kill him after he falls.*

He moved a little sideways, crouched behind a bush, brought his weapon to his shoulder, and thumbed off the safety.

Nguyen Tran sat in the brush listening. All he could hear were insects buzzing and, high overhead, a jet. The jet sound faded, leaving only the insects. One landed on his face. He gingerly reached and crushed it.

He didn't know if there were any more Arabs alive. He thought he had seen someone running away from the van on the other side of the road, but perhaps he hadn't. With the recoil and noise of his weapon and his fierce concentration on the man shooting at him, he might have been mistaken. Even if someone did manage to escape, he might have stopped a bullet. He might be dead or dying.

The tractor was tempting. If he could get in it, he could leave these Arab sons of bitches here to rot.

If I were one of those Arabs, he thought, *I would be hoping that my enemy tried to get into that cab.*

Holding the Remington with both hands, he began moving, staying as low as possible. He would get in front of the tractor, where he could see across the road.

From his hiding place behind his bush Mohmad Adeel could see only the tractor. The brush was thick on both sides of him. If he raised his head a little he could see the shot-up van back along the road.

Mosquitoes landed on his face and neck and began chewing on him. He wasn't used to mosquitoes. Flies, yes, but not bloodsuckers. He tried to shoo them away.

Time passed.

He thought about Akram and Omar and Alaeddin, the men he had lived with for months. This morning they had been so alive and now they were dead. Killed by an infidel. It was horrifying, when you thought about it, the triumph of evil.

He knew why there was evil in the world, to test the faith and strength of the men of Islam. But there were so many enemies, so much evil. . . .

Where was that cursed *kafir*?

He swatted at the mosquitoes. What a place!

What was he going to do after he killed this man? He didn't know how to drive a truck.

He would use the cell phone, he decided, call the leader of the other cell in his group, tell him where he was. With the help of the other holy warriors, they could get the warhead into a van. That is what he would do.

Mohmad Adeel was swatting mosquitoes and looking under the tractor when the bullet from the Remington sledgehammered him off his feet.

At first he didn't understand what had happened. He tried to rise, to find his weapon, then stared at that red stuff gushing from his side. The second bullet killed him instantly.

Five minutes passed before Nguyen Duc Tran came sneaking up. One look at Mohmad was enough. His mouth was open, his eyes staring fixedly at infinity.

Nguyen continued along parallel to the road, back toward the van.

There might be another man out here, and if there were and he saw Nguyen first, he would get the first shot.

When he got to a position where he could see the right side of the van, he could see four bodies. Mohmad made five.

That was right. He had seen five of them in the van.

Nguyen moved over to the van, staying ready. The Arabs were quite dead.

He paused and lit a cigarette. Should he pull the bodies over in the brush out of sight, push the van off the road? He would not be able to hide the van, just get it out of the center of the road.

Whatever he did, he was going to have to get on with it. Someone would be along this road before long and he had to be gone.

After three deep drags, he flipped away the cigarette. He put the Remington on the ground out of the way, then grabbed the nearest body by the ankles. When he had it out of sight he pulled the next one over beside him. The two in the vehicle took some time to extract. They hadn't bled much because they had died so quickly. He pulled the driver off into the brush to the left, the passenger off to the right. Then he put the van in neutral, cranked the wheel slightly left, and got in front of it.

The front of the van was perforated with bullet holes and only shards of windshield remained. Antifreeze leaked from the radiator and made a puddle on the road. The tires were still intact. With a mighty shove he got it rolling. The crown of the coquina road helped. He managed to get it rolling fast enough so that it went down off the road before the brush stopped it. Good enough. He used his shirttail to wipe away his fingerprints on the steering wheel and the front of the vehicle, then wiped the perspiration from his face.

He kicked the weapons in the road into the brush.

Nguyen retrieved the Remington and walked to where his submachine gun lay. He put both weapons in the cab of the tractor, lit another cigarette, and wiped his hands and face with a rag from behind the seat. He checked his reflection in the mirror, making sure he had no blood on his shirt. Satisfied, he climbed behind the wheel. The diesel roared into life, spewing smoke from the chromed stacks. When the engine was running smoothly, he slipped the tractor into gear and fed gas.

The rumor that the shipping container in the Wal-Mart parking lot in suburban Atlanta contained a nuclear weapon, not drugs, spread quickly. A policeman used his cell phone to tell his wife; she called her best friend, who called her husband, a reporter at an Atlanta television station. In minutes the rumor was on the air. Within an hour the White House was forced to admit that the rumor was true.

Trading at the New York Stock Exchange and the NASDAQ were suspended at noon. In Washington nonessential government workers were sent home by nervous cabinet officials in early afternoon. The president decided to address the nation via television from the Oval Office that evening, and the networks agreed to broadcast it.

The White House press spokesman went in front of the national media to answer questions about the FBI's arrest of a terrorist group and answer questions about the nuclear warhead. One of the very first ones was, "Is this a stolen American weapon?"

"No," the spokesman replied.

He refused to amplify that remark or answer additional questions on the warhead's origin, so talking heads all over the nation began speculating.

Tommy Carmellini and Anna Modin walked into a café in Virginia Beach for a late lunch and found the staff huddled around a television. He and Anna watched over their shoulders. After ten minutes he steered her to a table.

"I have to go back to Washington," he said. "It's hit the fan. Vacation's over. They may need me."

She nodded. She hadn't discussed the four Russian warheads with Carmellini, but she certainly had with Jake Grafton, and she knew Carmellini worked for him.

They ate in silence, each of them lost in their own thoughts. When they were walking back to the motel to pack and check out, she told him about General Petrov and Frouq al-Zuair.

"How do you know all this?" Carmellini asked.

"I was there when Petrov sold the warheads and Zuair took delivery. I told Janos Ilin. He came to America and told Jake Grafton."

Carmellini nodded. He had wondered how it went down but never asked Grafton or Tarkington, and of course neither of them would volunteer a fact like that, which could cost Ilin his life if it got out. Carmellini had no need to know. "You shouldn't be telling me this stuff," he said.

She reached for his hand and held it. "It's nice to have one person in this world that I can tell everything. Sometimes the load gets very heavy."

He wrapped his arm around her shoulder, turned her around, and kissed her.

The cabinet room at the White House was crowded that evening. Jake Grafton found a seat against the wall. Cabinet officers sat around the table, the heads of various agencies behind them, and interspersed here and there, key members of both houses of Congress. These people were talking to each other in earnest, whispered conversations.

The president's address was an hour away. Jake knew he planned to show the nation the videotape of the weapon the FBI had made that morning.

The White House photographer took a few candid shots after the president came in, and Jake managed to stay out of those. The president stopped on his way in for a few private words with a knot of senior members of Congress. The president looked tired. Jake noticed that Myron Emerick managed to be talking to the attorney general when the photographer aimed the camera at the people around the table.

When the photographer left the room, the president got down to business.

"As everyone in America knows, the FBI confiscated a nuclear weapon from a group of Islamic terrorists this morning in Atlanta. Regardless of the speculation on television, the warhead was not American. We believe the terrorists had four of them."

The Senate majority leader, who was not of the president's party, spoke up. "Why weren't we briefed about this sooner? Four nuclear weapons imported by terrorists? How the hell do we know that?"

"I'm not going to stand here and discuss intelligence sources," the president snapped.

"I was briefed about nuclear threats. And biological and chemical and so on, all very theoretical. Nobody told me there were four goddamn bombs being delivered to Wal-Mart. What in hell is going on here, anyway?"

The president was not apologetic. "This administration has kept you as informed as the needs of national security would allow. The intelligence oversight committees were briefed in more detail."

"We weren't told enough, sir," the senator said hotly. "Not by a long shot."

The meeting went downhill from there. The president was at the center of a firestorm, an inevitable one, Jake thought. Regardless of what the man did or failed to do, the critics were going to be after him. Jake wouldn't have traded jobs with him for all the money on Wall Street.

"We've heard all about these damned Corrigan detectors," one congressman said loudly, "and we've been asked to provide money to buy hundreds more. Where are they and why didn't they work?"

After a few heated exchanges, the president demanded silence and got it. "We are trying with every means at our disposal to find the weapons," he said, "and arrest terrorists. What we can't do is shut the country down and stop the economy dead while we hunt for them. If we do that, the terrorists have won. That is what they are trying to make happen. Our way of life is at stake. This is a war we cannot afford to lose."

"If a bomb goes off, we've lost it," a congressman shot back.

"We all know that," the president retorted. "And we lose if the public panics—"

"I got news for you," another congressman said hotly. "They've panicked." He waved hugely. "You've got 250 million frightened people out there. They wake up on a Thursday morning in May to another ordinary day, and by the time the sun goes down they are on the brink of being victims in a nuclear war. They want to know what the hell happened."

Before the president could respond, another congressman thundered at his colleague, "Last week you were on every network saying the administration was too focused on terrorism and ignoring the economy."

The president was icily calm. "*Enough!* We're doing our best to keep the country running and find the bombs. We've found one warhead. We'll find the others. We'll tell the public everything we can, when we can. Someone around here has to have some faith in the good sense and resiliency of the American people. I do! They've survived civil war, world wars, depressions and recessions, and September eleventh. They can weather this crisis, too."

That ended it. The cabinet officials stayed behind, but everyone else was asked to leave the room.

Sal Molina was waiting for Jake Grafton outside the room. He led him along the corridor to his office. Before he could close the door the president joined them.

"Talk to me," the president said.

"All four warheads are probably in the country," Jake said, meeting the president's gaze. "The FBI has been tracking seventeen suspected terrorist cells in south Florida; last night they began moving. Two of the cells rendezvoused at that parking lot in Atlanta, and soon thereafter a truck drove up to deliver a container to that Wal-Mart store. The weapon was in the container packed in lead, which is why all our search efforts with Geiger counters didn't find them. I hope and pray the Corrigan detector will do better."

"Detector? I thought we had two of them."

"One was hit by a garbage truck last night in Boston. We have one operational detector, and it's in Washington, which is, in my opinion, the most likely target."

"Emerick thinks that some of these groups will lead him to the other weapons," the president said. "He promised me they would."

"I hope he's right, but I doubt it. I think the terrorists thought the FBI might know of these groups, so they were sacrificed as a diversion."

The president rubbed his face. He looked ten years older than he did the last time Jake saw him.

"I've damn near kissed Corrigan's ass to get more detectors. Promised him everything but sainthood, and if I had ten detectors right now, I'd put in a personal call to the pope."

"His engineers are hand-building the things and having their troubles. It's a complex piece of gear. Corrigan was never in a position to manufacture them."

"Shit!" said the president of the United States, and dropped into Molina's desk chair. Jake sat on the desk with his legs dangling. Molina sat behind the desk.

Jake continued: "The CDs Anna Modin brought from the bank in Egypt lead us to believe that the money the Sword of Islam used to purchase the weapons came from the United States. It's a tenuous trail and wouldn't hold up in court. As far as I know, the FBI has done nothing to try to find that trail in this country."

The president grunted.

"One of the possibilities is that Corrigan provided the dough."

That comment rocked the president and Molina. They sat stunned. "T.M.?" the president said. "Blowing up a city?"

"Oh, no. Selling the government a hundred Corrigan detectors. Being named ambassador to Great Britain—oh, yes, I've heard the rumors. Money, prestige, power, position. He's the man of the hour, so he's my prime suspect."

"I told you he's a suspicious bastard," Molina remarked to his boss.

"You're wrong," the president said fervently, directing that remark at Grafton.

"Let's hope I'm not. If I'm right, I'm on the trail of a bomb. If I'm not . . ."

The president was thoroughly confused. "But you said Corrigan doesn't want to blow up a city."

"He may not, but apparently the possibility that someone might double-cross him never crossed his mind. His number two man is a guy named Karl Luck; he likes to ride around Washington and Boston in Corrigan's limo. He's been meeting with a CIA employee named Sonny Tran. Tran works for me. Tran could be the man behind the disappearance of another CIA agent, a man named Richard Doyle."

"Got any evidence?"

"Of the meetings, yes. Zelda Hudson has tapes of Corrigan's limo driving around Washington. She has Sonny Tran on two of them getting into that limo. One shot of him getting out." He explained about the police traffic cameras at intersections, how he was stealing a video feed from police headquarters. "And last night Sonny Tran was behind the wheel of the van carrying Corrigan Unit One when it was hit by the garbage truck in Boston. The fact that he was there was a mistake on my part—I thought I should keep him away from Washington." He threw up his hands. "We're monitoring Tran's and Karl Luck's cell phones, we've got a beeper on the limo, we're digging into both men's backgrounds, trying to find leads that will take us somewhere."

The president looked at his watch, then at Grafton. "What about the buried bombs? Who put them there?"

"We won't know for sure until we dig one up and inspect it. I think we'll find the Russians buried it when they realized Star Wars was going ahead regardless. There's a faction in the Russian government that refuses to give up a nuclear deterrent."

"Secret weapons don't deter anything if your enemies don't know about them."

"Ah, they know they have them, so the weapons are political chips in Moscow."

The president knew all about power politics in a nation's capital. He accepted that assessment without further comment. "Who sent Ilin to us?" he asked.

"No one in Moscow. Ilin came on his own hook. If you need a conundrum to ponder when you go to bed tonight, ask yourself if Ilin knew about the buried weapons. Did Ilin arrange for Petrov to sell warheads to the Sword of Islam so that we would look for weapons, thereby finding the buried Russian bombs, or was that a coincidence?"

"Jesus Christ, who is this fucking guy?"

Jake Grafton took a deep breath before he spoke. "Assuming we can find these terror warheads before they pop, he's a guy who did us a favor."

The president stood, adjusted his trousers and tie. "I've got to talk to the nation. Find those goddamn bombs!"

"Aye aye, sir."

The president reached for the doorknob, then paused. "I may have been the only elected person in that room a while ago who believes in the American people. Even if these things go off, the American people will endure. The survival of our republic isn't in jeopardy. The terrorists believe it is, but they are wrong.

"It's the survival of *their* way of life that will be on the block. If nuclear weapons explode in American cities, we are headed straight for World War Three, and all the words in the world won't be able to stop it. The war won't be fought here—it will be fought *over there*.

"If you thought the public was outraged after Pearl Harbor and September eleventh, you won't believe what will happen in America if Washington goes up in a mushroom cloud. The American people will elect some implacable bastard who will lead a holy war against Islam. The Romans tore Carthage down and sowed the earth with salt—this will be the twenty-first-century equivalent. Think genocide."

With that he opened the door and went out.

CHAPTER TWENTY-TWO

A stunned nation watched and listened to the address that Thursday evening by the president of the United States. One of the people who heard it on the radio was Dr. Hamid Salami Mabruk, who was now back in the country. He had finished his classes for the day at the university and listened in his pickup on the way to Washington.

As he had predicted to his colleagues when this mission was being planned, the authorities had indeed been watching the cells of militants in Florida. One of the two weapons allocated to the cells had been seized by the FBI. Mabruk suspected the second warhead soon would be.

The success or failure of the entire operation now rested on his shoulders. He had thought that development also probable.

He had his work cut out for him tonight, and he knew it. The bomb had been delivered to the Washington Convention Center in the heart of the city. He had selected the Convention Center after weeks of searching and watching, for several reasons. The site was in the heart of the downtown between the White House and the Capitol, near the FBI's Hoover Building, the Treasury. . . . When the warhead detonated, the explosion would cut out the heart of the American government. Even the buildings not flattened by the fireball, like the Pentagon, would be mere shells. Secondly, the Convention Center was relatively deserted at night.

He had sent an encrypted e-mail to his contact in the Sword of

Islam informing him of his choice, so that the container could be shipped there.

Tonight was Thursday, and tomorrow and through the weekend a trade show was being set up. The cover was perfect. He had credentials—he was William Haddad, an electrical equipment manufacturer from Philadelphia, he was an exhibitor, and he was here tonight to set up his exhibit early. He had already met the security staff, sprinkled twenty-dollar bills around. They were expecting him.

He drove slowly by the Convention Center looking for police cruisers and unmarked cars. Seeing none, he turned around and came back, then parked across the street from the loading dock, which sat behind a chain-link fence topped with barbed wire. The container was there, backed in against the dock on a truck chassis. The tractor that had delivered it was long gone. Two other containers were parked beside it.

Mabruk used his binoculars to scan the streets and roofs.

He saw no one. He assumed that if the authorities had discovered the weapon in transit, they would have confiscated it. Still, they could be watching the container to see if someone was going to come for it. Or they could be waiting inside.

It was a risk, one he could not avoid. He didn't have the evening to waste watching. He intended to arm the weapon and put it on a timer. He would be long gone, on his way to arm the second weapon in New York, when this one detonated.

He wasn't going to be in New York either, when that one exploded. Unlike the *jihad* soldiers, Dr. Hamid Salami Mabruk had no intention of heading for Paradise anytime soon. He intended to do a lot more damage to the infidels in the years ahead. God willing, he would live to see the Muslim world united under God's banner.

Had Mabruk heard the American president's private remarks to Jake Grafton and Sal Molina, he would have agreed with his assessment of the aftermath of a successful nuclear attack on America. He, too, thought that these explosions would ignite World War III. Bin Ladin and Dr. Zawahiri were absolutely correct: Nothing less than a world conflagration would force the vast bulk of the Muslim people worldwide to abandon their apathy, to choose sides. The explosions would prove that the infidels were vulnerable, and the wrath of the non-Muslim world would force them to defend themselves.

The possibility that the Muslims might lose the great war to come did not cross his mind. Allah was with them. If the true believers united in *jihad,* the forces of the devil would be defeated in the final war between good and evil. That he knew in the depths of his soul. Even the Christian Bible said so.

He locked the pickup and walked to the exhibitors' entrance of the convention center. The security guard, a black woman wearing a radio in a holster on her belt, looked at his credentials and searched a document on a clipboard for his name. "You have an early setup approved," she said. "Got you right here."

"I have some equipment in my truck," he said. "How can I get it in?"

"I'll open the gate by the loading dock to let you in. Can you get your stuff in from there?"

"Yes. I would appreciate that."

"Ten minutes. Let me get someone to stand here for me." She began talking on her radio. Mabruk walked back to his pickup and drove it to the gate. He turned off the engine and sat waiting. A few people were on the street, but only a few. He heard a far-off siren that wailed for a time and didn't seem to be getting closer. Several jets could be heard, probably flying down the river into Reagan National Airport.

Hamid Mabruk sat calmly, listening and waiting. The tension was extreme, but the payoff was close. As he sat there he prayed.

The guard appeared eleven long minutes later. She unlocked the padlock, swung the gate open, and he drove through. She locked the gate behind him.

He parked next to the container. "I'll unlock this personnel door and you can use that," she said as she took a wad of keys from her belt.

"I really appreciate this," Hamid Mabruk said warmly.

"Glad to help, honey. If there's anything else you need, just ask." She walked back through the cavernous loading area, her footsteps strangely silent, until she disappeared around a turn.

He was alone.

The overhead door was not locked. He pushed the switch beside the door and it rose slowly, whining a little. He stepped out on the dock and opened the door to the container. This one was packed with boxes full of electrical equipment. Hamid Mabruk allowed himself a tight smile—the container looked exactly as it had when he had sealed it aboard *Olympic Voyager*.

He now had a choice to make. Two cables were hidden behind the lower box on the right-hand side, as he stood looking in. Merely moving the box would give him access. If he carried the car batteries in, wired them to these cables using a timer, the whole thing would explode when the timer ran down. Rigging the setup shouldn't take much more than half an hour.

He could set the timer to detonate the weapon in three hours, giving him ample time to get out of the city.

Or he could unload the weapon with a forklift—there were three of them sitting near the door. He could hide it inside the Convention Center behind a pile of boxes, set it to detonate tomorrow, when downtown Washington was full of people. The explosion then would have the largest dramatic impact, might even make it onto television networks around the world. That wouldn't happen if it detonated during the night. Moving the weapon would also protect it if the container were searched tonight or tomorrow morning.

He walked back through the huge storage bay looking for possible places to put the bomb. *It's a risk, of course,* he admitted to himself. *The truth of it is I feel lucky.*

Jake Grafton found Tommy Carmellini and Anna Modin sitting on the couch with Callie watching television when he returned home that evening.

"I thought you were going to keep her out of sight until the FBI had that new identity ready to go," Jake said to Carmellini after the greetings, when they went to the kitchen to fix a pot of coffee.

"Well, yeah, but when we heard the news today, I figured I ought to get back here and see if there is anything I can do. Feel pretty useless strolling up and down the beach. And I've gained five pounds."

"I can see you're porking up. Glad you came back. Callie tell you Toad was in a crash last night in Boston?" Carmellini nodded. Jake continued, "We're down to one Corrigan unit, and it's here in Washington. I just have time for a cup of coffee. They're swinging by in a half hour to pick me up."

"Mind if I tag along? I haven't seen this thing in action yet."

"Anyone outside pay any attention to you when you came into the building?"

"No. Everyone in North America is someplace watching television, even the terrorists."

"Anna should be okay here," Jake said, as the first of the coffee dripped through. "You two getting along okay?"

"Oh, sure," said Tommy Carmellini.

"She hasn't been put off by your disgusting personal habits?"

"She hasn't complained."

"Wonderful. The news here is that Zip Vance has a new girlfriend. He's stepping out with one of the secretaries."

"How's Zelda taking it?"

"Don't think she's noticed yet. She's been pretty busy."

"He needed to get on with his life."

"Don't we all." Jake pulled the pot from the coffeemaker and stuck a cup in its place. When it was full he substituted another cup for it and handed the first one to Carmellini. "There's milk in the fridge."

"Right."

"So are you and Anna going to get married, or is she going to Europe or Russia when this is over?"

Tommy sipped the coffee experimentally before he answered. "Going somewhere," he said, meeting Jake's eyes.

"Umm."

Jake took cups of coffee to the women, then sat with them to drink his. Callie asked how things went that afternoon at the White House, and Jake didn't want to talk about it. The third time he glanced at his watch, she smiled and told him he had better get ready to go. She went with him to the bedroom, where he changed from his uniform into jeans, a sweatshirt, and tennis shoes.

"Anna's going to stay here tonight," he said, "while Tommy comes with me. Should be okay. Keep the doors locked, and if anything sounds or looks suspicious, call nine-one-one, then call me on my cell." He took an old revolver from his sock drawer, loaded it, and stuck it in his hip pocket.

In the living room Carmellini took off his windbreaker and stripped off the shoulder holster. "Put this thing in your bag and keep it handy." He explained how to work the pistol. "Just ear the hammer back, point it, and pull the trigger. It'll go bang."

She held the pistol tightly against her chest with both hands. "These have been the best two weeks of my life," she said.

He pulled her to him in a fierce hug. "Yeah."

"So is this the way our lives are going to be?"

"I'm not the one on a mission from God, woman. I'm not going anywhere. You want to stay, just say so. You want to get married, we'll find us a judge."

She buried her face in his shoulder.

They were standing like that when the Graftons came out of the bedroom.

"Kiss her and let's get outta here," Jake said as he walked by. Carmellini obeyed the order.

Hoss Baker was a retired navy chief petty officer. He had grown up dirt poor on a worn-out tenant farm in Mississippi and joined the navy to get the hell out. Once out, he never went back. His last tour of duty had been in Washington, so he remained here after he retired. The city had a vibrant black community, he found a job at the Convention Center, he and his wife fit right in.

Things happened in Washington. Conventions came one after another, the Wizards played at the MCI Center right down the street, there was music, art, political theater . . . all in all, it was a good town. Beats the living hell out of Mississippi, he thought, and chuckled.

Baker surveyed his little office. He felt pensive tonight, vaguely troubled. No doubt the news on television about the recovered nuclear weapon and the president's address this evening were part of it. He had watched the address before he came to work. God knows America had its troubles—every black man knew it was a damned long way from perfect—but the fact that there were people out there who wished to destroy all of it, the good as well as the bad, seemed somehow obscene.

Tonight his small, well-lit room seemed a safe sanctuary. The desk was oak, given to him by his son, who was a lawyer here in town. He liked the solidity of it, the smooth, grainy feel of the wood, the inherent strength.

On the wall were photos of him with some of the celebrities and politicians whom he had met while working here, as well as a photo of an admiral pinning a Navy Commendation Medal on his shirt. He had been younger then, and skinnier.

He stood, adjusted his trousers and his pistol belt. Then Hoss Baker did something he rarely did—he removed his pistol from the holster and popped the magazine from the handle. He jacked the shell from the chamber and put the pistol on the desk. After thumbing all the cartridges from the magazine onto the desk, he carefully reloaded the magazine. He snapped it back into the pistol, jacked a new shell into the chamber and engaged the safety. Then he lowered the pistol into the holster and carefully put the strap over it, ensured the Velcro catch was engaged.

Hoss Baker left the office and walked the hallway rattling doorknobs, then descended the stairs to the main concourse. Two custodians were polishing the floor there. He strolled through the convention hall, where he found three small crews constructing exhibits for the next convention, one crew taking one down. A man was working on a refrigeration unit in a snack-bar kitchen. One electrician was replacing a faulty circuit breaker in a power distribution room. Hoss knew the electrician, who had served four years in the air force, so he paused to visit for a few minutes.

Mabel Jones was the security officer on the exhibitor's door. Hoss had hired her two years ago. She had ridden the bus north from Georgia as a young woman, looking for a better life. She had two sons, one in the army and one in prison for dealing drugs. Her man, whom she never married, had died of diabetes some years back.

"Who's in here tonight, Mabel?"

"Got the list," she said. "Pretty quiet, all things considered."

Baker scanned the clipboard. "Who's this Haddad guy? I didn't see him."

"Back around the loading dock. Let him in an hour ago. Joe stood by for me." Joe was the outside guard.

"I'll go back that way. Everything okay?"

"Sure. What're you doin' here tonight? Thought this was your day off."

"Watched all that crap on television, couldn't stay home. Had to do something."

He heard the forklift before he saw it, a beeping as it backed up. The ones used inside the building were electric and made little noise except when backing. The sound was coming from a concession supply storage room. Hoss Baker walked that way.

The storage room door was open and the forklift was putting something in there. What the hell? That place was supposed to be locked. And who was driving the forklift?

He approached the forklift as the driver turned his head to back out. He stood watching with his arms crossed. The driver stopped the thing, got off, walked toward Hoss. A man from the Middle East, in his forties, perhaps.

"What the hell you doin'?" Hoss Baker asked, not aggressively.

"Hope you don't mind," the man said, gesturing toward the storage room. "The door was open and I needed someplace to put my supplies until I can set up my booth."

Hoss walked toward the open door, the man following. "You aren't supposed to be driving that thing," he said, gesturing toward the forklift. "Liability. And that room is supposed to be locked up. Thing's full of soda pop and candy bars. People steal—"

The words died in his throat when he saw the warhead resting on its pallet. Small, round, festooned with wires leading from the detonator contacts—after watching the FBI videotape from Atlanta this afternoon on television, Hoss Baker instantly recognized it for what it was.

He started to turn, drawing his pistol, when a bullet from a silenced .22 hit him in the head. He fell to the concrete floor, twitching, breathing raggedly.

Hamid Salami Mabruk stepped over to Hoss Baker and shot him again in the head. That shot killed him. He jabbed the pistol into his waistband and grabbed Hoss by the feet. He dragged him over behind a pallet stacked with cartons of soft drinks. Hoss was a big man; Mabruk was breathing heavily when he got him there.

A bad break. So much for a daylight explosion. He would have to get the batteries rigged and the timer wired up, then give himself perhaps an hour to get out of town.

Oh, bad break!

Mabruk jumped onto the forklift and drove it over to the exterior door. There was a stack of empty pallets there—he placed one on the forks. He would put all the batteries into the storeroom in a single trip, which would save some time.

He had cut the padlock on the storeroom door. Fortunately he had another in his pickup. Even if security personnel came looking for the dead man, they probably wouldn't try to open the lock until they had searched the entire building. They would be dead before they finished that chore.

The bags of birdshot in the container—there was nothing he could do about that. He would padlock the container door, too. The weapon would explode before anyone got around to cutting off the padlock, *Inshallah!*

The technician working the Corrigan unit in the back of the van had rings dangling from his ears and tattoos peeking out the neck of his shirt. Jake Grafton tried not to stare. He hadn't gotten used to the new ways youth had found to declare their independence from convention.

Tommy Carmellini chattered as the van rolled through the streets of downtown Washington and Jake and the technician watched the needles on the meters. After they had circled the Capitol, they drove up Constitution Avenue. "She doesn't work for the SVR—I'm positive about that. Really a great person. You know, I've looked all my life for a woman to share life with, and when I finally meet her, she's got another commitment. Isn't that the way life works?"

"How are you dealing with that?" Jake asked over his shoulder, without taking his eyes off the gauges. The technician was concentrating, too, ignoring Carmellini's recitation of his romantic woes.

"It's a bummer. At least she isn't married to some other Joe. Or Ivan. But it's frustrating as hell, you know? I never really thought love would bite me. Sure, I've jumped into the sack with my share of broads, but that's all they were, broads. Oh yeah, a few nice girls, too, but when the nice ones figured out I was a thief they didn't want any part of my act. Sure as hell weren't going to take me home to introduce me to Mom and Pop. Anna doesn't care. It's me she loves. . . ."

He fell silent, thinking about her, about how she hugged him before he left the Graftons' apartment. Maybe she would change her mind about leaving. He weighed that possibility.

"Do you want to drive over to the Pentagon, check around there?" the driver asked.

"No. Go over to Pennsylvania Avenue, work your way north and east, then west. We'll go all the way around the White House."

The driver acknowledged.

"The D.A. in Baltimore decided not to prosecute," Jake said to Carmellini, to fill the silence.

Carmellini grunted. He didn't want to discuss that subject, which was ancient history. He had more important matters on his mind.

"Uh-oh," the technician said. "We got something hot around here."

Jake was fixated on the gauges.

"Getting hotter. . . . Real hot. Jesus Christ!"

Jake got off the stool and took two steps forward so that he could look out the window. The van was rolling along in front of the Convention Center.

"Fading now," the technician said. His name was LeRoy. "We're going away from it."

"Around the building," Jake said to the driver. "Circle the Convention Center." The driver took the next left.

Jake went back to the gauges. After two trips around the building, LeRoy wiped the perspiration from his face with his shirttail. "It's in there, swear to God."

Jake hunkered down beside the driver as he circled the building one more time. He saw the containers by the loading dock, the gate in the fence that was ajar.

"Stop here," he said. He went back through the van and got out. He examined the padlock on the gate. Someone had cut it with bolt cutters. The lock lay on the ground. He opened the gate enough to get through, walked over, and inspected the containers. Well, it could be, he decided.

He climbed up on the dock. All three containers were padlocked. He went back to the van and spoke to the driver. "I'll open the gate. You back in. Have LeRoy wand the containers for radiation."

This operation took three or four minutes. "This one on the end has had something radioactive in it, but it's not hot. Whatever is setting this thing off is inside the building."

"Tommy, you and the driver help LeRoy rig up the sensor cables. I'll walk around to the vendors' door—it's open, I think—and get someone to unlock these doors. We'll run the sensor cables right through these doors."

"Okay."

As he walked around the building, Jake Grafton used his cell phone to call Zelda, who was at the office. She answered on the third ring. "Grafton here. I'm downtown at the Convention Center, at the loading dock. We got a real hot reading on the Corrigan unit. Get onto the police traffic camera system. See if you can find some footage of a vehicle that might have been here in the last little while. It may still be around."

"Want me to call the police or FBI?" Zelda asked.

"Not yet. I'm on my cell. See what you can come up with while we check things out here. Then call me."

The guard eyed him coldly when he got inside. "May I help you?"

"Name's Grafton." Jake displayed his CIA ID. "We're checking this area for radioactivity and got a hit on the meter. I want in through your loading dock."

"I'll have to call my supervisor," she said. "He's here tonight. I saw him just a little while ago."

"Do that."

She used her handheld radio. "Hoss, this is Mabel. Where are you?"

No answer. She tried again.

"We have a man setting up an exhibit back there," she said to Jake. "My supervisor went to check on him a while ago." Mabel Jones looked at her watch. "It's been over a half hour," she added pensively.

Now she was worried. "Radioactivity, you say?"

"That's right. Let's go see if we can find your supervisor. What's his name?"

"Hoss Baker. I'll go look. You stay right here."

She walked away. Jake let her get ten feet in front of him, then he followed. She didn't seem to notice. She walked quickly.

When they reached the area of the loading dock, she stopped, looked around. If she was surprised Jake was behind her, she didn't show it. "I don't see him," she said. "Or Haddad, the exhibitor. Hoss came to check on him."

"Did you know that someone cut the lock off the gate outside, in the loading area?"

"No," she said, frowning. "Joe is our outside security man, and he hasn't said anything about it."

"Maybe it just happened. Was anyone out there?"

"Haddad, the exhibitor, parked out there, but I locked the gate behind him."

"He's gone now. Why don't you look for your boss. Tell me if you find him. Open this door for me before you go." He gestured at the overhead door nearest the place where he had left the van.

Mabel Jones was plainly worried. The man beside her had a commanding presence, as if he expected her to do as he asked. Yet she was still undecided, unsure of what to do as he punched numbers into his cell phone.

"Me again, Zelda. Call the FBI and the police bomb squad. The Convention Center. Tell them not to waste time. Get Gil Pascal at home and have him go to the office to help you."

That call made up Mabel's mind. She strode to the overhead door control panel and pushed the button to raise it. Then she went looking for Hoss Baker.

Once they got the cable sensors inside, the search didn't take long. In five minutes Jake was looking at the padlock on the door to the concession storeroom.

Tommy Carmellini bent down, retrieved something from the floor, and held it out for Jake's inspection. "Twenty-two casing."

Jake examined the small brass shell. He sniffed it. He could still smell powder residue.

"I want a bolt cutter," Jake said. "There should be one in the van. Hurry."

Mabel Jones came back with two policemen as Jake was cutting the lock off the storeroom door. Carmellini showed the policemen the shell as Mabel announced, "I can't find Mr. Baker, the security officer."

Jake opened the door, used a flashlight to examine the storeroom. When he saw the warhead he said to LeRoy, "There it is, by God."

He found the light switch beside the door and flipped it on. Batteries on a pallet, a timer, the warhead covered with wires. . . . He was inspecting it when he heard Mabel exclaim, "Oh, my God, they killed Hoss!"

One of the policemen stood beside Jake, looking at the warhead. "It's just like the one they found in Atlanta, isn't it?"

"Yep," Jake said, looking at the timer. Seventeen minutes left. Even as he watched the seconds were ticking away. "Get on your radio. We need the bomb squad right fucking now."

The cop made the transmission, talked to the dispatcher. While he was talking Jake turned to look at the body. The second policeman was searching for a pulse. "Is he dead?"

"Yeah."

"Nothing we can do for him. Leave the body. You and your partner take Mabel and go to the exhibitors' door. The FBI and bomb squad are on their way. If you can get them on the radio, have them come into the loading dock area. If they come to the exhibitors' entrance, bring them here the instant they arrive. Go!"

They went. Tommy Carmellini and the technician bent over the timer, which was ticking away.

"Not much time, boss."

"LeRoy, what's going to happen if I cut the leads from the timer to that box"—he pointed—"with the bolt cutter?"

LeRoy looked. "That must be some kind of capacitor, I think. If you cut that wire, the damn thing should be disabled."

"What if the capacitor already has a charge stored?"

"The fucking thing might go."

"Cutting the wire between the capacitor and the junction to the detonator leads?"

"Maybe we ought to operate there."

"Fourteen minutes, boss," Tommy Carmellini said.

Jake picked up the bolt cutter, examined the wires.

His hands were slippery. "Help me with this, Tommy." Jake placed the jaws of the bolt cutter around the wire, Carmellini provided the muscle. He had plenty of it. The jaws sliced the wire as if it were a garden hose.

"Next one." When both the wires were severed, Jake had Carmellini cut the wires from the timer while he watched, then had him sever the battery wires.

All three men moved the pallet that held the batteries away from the weapon, just in case.

The Corrigan technician used his shirttail on his face again. He muttered an oath.

Jake heard sirens. As he listened the sirens swelled in volume.

And he heard his cell phone ring. He took it from his pocket and opened it.

"Yes."

"This is Zelda. We have a shot of the vehicle that was parked by the Convention Center loading dock, a pickup truck with a cab over the bed. I have the license number."

"We found a bomb here. See if you can find where the truck went. And have someone run the plate. I want a name and address. The man who armed the bomb probably drove the truck."

Jake and LeRoy were sitting on the loading dock with their legs dangling over the edge when the bomb squad truck rolled through the gate. Both men were smoking cigarettes. Although Jake hadn't smoked in twenty years, he had gratefully accepted LeRoy's offer of a cancer stick.

"In there," Jake said to the bomb squad sergeant, and jerked a thumb over his shoulder.

Carmellini came out of the building and took a seat on the dock beside Jake. "This thing would have popped if we had gone over to the other side of the river to drive around the Pentagon."

"Yeah."

"Are there any more in Washington?"

That was the question. Jake sat thinking about it. He had precisely one Corrigan unit and it was here. Two of the four warheads had been seized.

He hauled out his cell phone and dialed Zelda again. "Well?"

"The pickup headed north. We saw it make the turn from New York Avenue onto the Baltimore-Washington Parkway headed north."

"Okay."

"The bad news for him is that there has been a wreck on the Beltway on-ramp from the parkway. Traffic is at a standstill."

"Welcome to the city."

"Pennsylvania plates on the pickup. It's registered to a Hamid S.

Mabruk." She gave him the address in a suburb outside of Philadelphia.

"Call Harry Estep. Have the FBI get over to his house and seal it. Harry can get busy on a warrant. Murder One. This guy killed a guard here at the Convention Center. He's armed and dangerous. Give them everything you have."

He broke the connection and sat thinking. Either Mabruk had armed more than one weapon in Washington, or he was on his way to arm others now. Or both.

The safe way to play it was that both possibilities were true. Once Jake had made that decision, the best course of action became plain. He would leave Carmellini and LeRoy to search Washington for more weapons, and he would have Mabruk followed, not arrested, to see if he would go to another bomb.

Jake called Zelda back. Gil Pascal answered the telephone. "I was on my way in anyway. Couldn't sleep."

"I want Mabruk found and followed," Jake told him. "Tell Harry. Give him my cell number. And I'll need a chopper. Get on it, please."

He turned to Carmellini and LeRoy. "Carmellini's in charge. I want the city swept from end to end. LeRoy, you know about the hot spot on Hains Point. Call Gil Pascal immediately if you find anything. Call me at dawn if you don't."

"Aye aye, sir," Tommy said. He wasn't in the military, but that seemed to be the right answer.

"Go," Jake Grafton said. "Now."

CHAPTER TWENTY-THREE

When he saw the brake lights on the vehicles ahead of him, Hamid Salami Mabruk became worried. He had armed the warhead, locked up the storeroom, and gotten out of the Convention Center without meeting anyone. He had had to cut the padlock on the gate to get the pickup out of the loading area, but an investigation of the broken lock wouldn't lead anyone to the storage room for hours. By then it would be too late.

The cars in front of him halted, crept forward, then halted again. The second time they stopped they didn't move.

He looked at his watch. Ten minutes . . . the weapon would explode in ten minutes. If he could get past the Beltway he should be okay, essentially out of the two-hundred-kiloton blast area, although to escape the radiation effects completely one would have to be several hundred miles away.

Yet the Beltway was at least six miles ahead.

He darted into the far right lane. The truck behind him honked, and he pretended not to hear.

Perhaps he should drive in the emergency lane, get around all these cars.

Nine minutes!

The traffic crept forward. Up to three miles per hour, now five . . . and the brake lights came firmly on. Everything came to a dead stop.

Eight minutes.

Sitting here he was going to be on the edge of the blast. The initial concussion would be terrific, would blow out car windows and fill the air with flying glass and debris. A few seconds later the thermal pulse would arrive—the heat would take the paint off cars, fry flesh from bone. . . . As the rising fireball consumed all the air around it, air would rush in from all directions to feed it, creating a hurricane. An explosion that size, two- or three-hundred-mile-per-hour winds could be expected. These winds would cause most of the damage outside ground zero. Buildings weakened and twisted by the initial blast and perhaps set afire by the thermal pulse would be destroyed by the hurricane rushing toward the vortex. The air would become a semi-solid, full of glass fragments, dirt, stone, metal, everything the hurricane could lift. That debris would sandblast structures, shred and abrade anything standing . . . rip flesh from bone.

Radiation . . . at this range the radiation from the initial blast might be lethal, so what did it matter what came after?

Seven minutes.

He should have armed the weapon inside the container. That would have been the safe and logical course. Moving it, trying to time the explosion to create the perfect terror strike, was hubris. He knew that now. What had he been thinking?

Mabruk turned on the radio, jabbed buttons, realized that the buttons were set for Philadelphia stations and began twisting the dial, looking for a radio station that would tell him about traffic delays. Had there been a wreck ahead? Or was this a police roadblock? Perhaps an army unit searching trucks for nuclear warheads?

Music, ads . . . talk, talk, talk. Someone talking terrorism from a telephone . . . more ads. A preacher ranting about hellfire. . . . *They'll see hellfire soon enough.*

He snapped the radio off.

Six minutes.

Why had he picked this route out of the city? Of all the possible ways to exit Washington, why this one?

His hands were shaking. He looked at his watch again. The second hand swept mercilessly on.

Five minutes.

Mabruk cranked the steering wheel to the stop and turned carefully out into the emergency lane. Began creeping forward, accelerating. Someone moved to the right to cut him off, so he jumped the curb and drove up onto the grass to pass, then dropped back onto the pavement. Kept going.

Doing fifteen miles per hour now. Not enough time . . . every mile between him and the weapon increased his chance of surviving the blast. Every car length was a victory.

Ahead of him was an overpass. Nothing unusual about that, but as he approached it an eighteen-wheel rig moved right to occupy half the emergency lane. With the concrete abutments on the right, there was no way to get by.

He stopped, pushed angrily on the horn.

The tractor didn't move.

Four minutes.

Now, at last, the tractor crept forward, still taking up half the emergency lane, yet the bank on the right was too steep for vehicles behind it to get around.

Mabruk jabbed the horn savagely, held it down. He cursed, roared his frustration.

Three minutes.

Another hundred yards farther on.

Two.

The *kafir* bastard . . . he should get out of the pickup and run up there and shoot him, so at least he would die first.

One minute.

The big rig stopped dead.

Hamid Salami Habruk stared at the second hand of his watch. Frozen, unable to think, he watched the tiny black hand march relentlessly around the dial.

At the very last moment Habruk remembered that the blast would smash the windows from the pickup. He lay down in the seat.

And waited . . .

Waited . . .

He held up his wrist, stared at the watch, mesmerized. The second hand continued to swing.

Another minute passed.

The bomb didn't explode!

Oh, it will! It will! The timer was inaccurate—it had never been calibrated—it wasn't a precision instrument. The weapon will detonate at any moment.

But it didn't.

Another minute crept glacially by.

Hamid Salami Mabruk slowly raised himself to the sitting position. The big rig ahead of him inched forward. Automatically he allowed the pickup to creep along after it.

The weapon didn't explode!

The stretch limo slowly entered the parking lot of the Waltham, Massachusetts, nightclub, the Naked Owl, precisely at midnight and crept between the parked cars. When it reached the far end of the lot, the chauffeur turned it expertly and put the car in motion toward the nightclub door.

A man came out of the nightclub, walked around the front of the limo, and opened the right-rear door. The interior was dark, lit only by the glare of the Naked Owl's neon. The limo was moving almost as soon as the door swung closed.

Sonny Tran seated himself diagonally across from Karl Luck, who nodded and muttered something.

The chauffeur turned onto the street and accelerated. Sonny opened his briefcase as Luck said, "You've been watching the news, I presume?"

Sonny nodded. He had the sweep gear in the briefcase. He didn't take it out, merely turned it on. It would have been impossible to use in the dark interior of the limo if the instruments hadn't been backlit.

"One weapon recovered, three still out there somewhere." Actually two had been found, but the news about the second one had yet to be released.

Sonny concentrated on the gauges of his instrument. Sonny turned the knob that changed frequencies.

"To be frank," Luck said to fill the silence, "I'm worried that they might not find the other three bombs before the terrorists explode them."

The needle hit the peg. A jolt of adrenaline shot through Sonny Tran. He refined the freq. The needle pulsated, went from zero to darn near off the scale, then swung back to zero. It did so once every two seconds.

A beacon! There was a beacon in or on the car.

He scanned every freq the device was capable of detecting. He got the hit on only that one frequency. He turned off the gear and sat looking at Karl Luck, who was rambling. "... Corrigan's feeling pretty damn good. He's making money like he owned the mint, the president is going to make him ambassador to Britain, and if a bomb pops, it's the victims' tough luck. He'll drop a check for the relief committee in the collection plate at church. The man has the conscience of a hamster."

Try as he might, Sonny could think of no reason that Luck or

Corrigan would want to track this vehicle. That left the feds. *They were on to Corrigan. And Luck had led them to him.*

Sonny put the briefcase on the seat next to him and moved over beside Luck. Now they were both facing forward. A curtain obscured the view of the driver's compartment, and presumably his view of the passengers.

Luck went on in a conversational voice. "The other night Corrigan talked about hiring a Russian he knows to kill the Arabs who shipped the weapons here. He doesn't want them squealing if they're arrested." Luck's head turned, and he looked at Sonny. "Wouldn't surprise me if he pays Ivan a few extra bucks to get rid of you and me. Maybe not. But maybe yes. Consider this fair warning."

"Thanks."

"You're talkative tonight."

Sonny shrugged. He rested his chin on his right fist and looked out the window, trying to look relaxed as his mind raced. Obviously the feds were tracking this car from a distance. Perhaps they had photographed him getting in, perhaps not.

Grafton! That bastard!

He had been in this limo before, of course, and if the FBI had already checked it for prints, they had him. The chauffeur probably washed it daily. It was a risk, but he could wipe the door handles and seats. That would have to do.

Luck was still talking. ". . . The Arabs killed our man in Cairo, made it look like suicide. Threw him out the window of his apartment. *Olympic Voyager* is missing with all hands, including Vandervelt. They're obviously going to kill everyone in the chain, given enough time."

Sonny Tran reached for the briefcase, put it on his lap, and opened it. He extracted the knife with his right hand, then rammed it up to the hilt in Luck's chest. Luck shuddered once, then collapsed.

Sonny closed the briefcase, put it on the floor. He left the knife in Luck's heart until he was sure he was dead. He picked up his left wrist, felt for a pulse. Nothing. Only then did he extract the knife. It took quite an effort to pull it out. He arranged Luck's tie and coat so the wound wouldn't be obvious.

The limo was driving along a street in an industrial area. This would have to do.

He leaned over the dead man and pushed the intercom button. "Mister Luck has fainted. Perhaps a heart attack. Pull over and help me."

"Certainly, sir."

As the limo came to a stop, Sonny hopped out the right side and walked around behind the vehicle, holding the knife down by his thigh. No pedestrians. A truck passing, going the other way

The chauffeur opened Luck's door, leaned in. Sonny rammed the knife into his back, straight into his heart.

He pushed the man into the car, lifted his legs in, and closed the door.

The engine was still running. Sonny got behind the wheel and drove away.

Should he try to find the beeper? Even if he found it and got it off the limo, how much extra time would that give him?

Not enough, he decided.

Using a knuckle, he opened the glove compartment. Yes, it contained rags—chauffeurs habitually wiped these limos every time they stopped for any length of time.

As he drove he used a rag on the glove compartment and the shift lever and scrubbed the steering wheel, which was covered in leather.

He parked the limo on the top deck of the parking garage at the downtown train station. Not a soul around at this hour of the night. He took the keys, stuck them in his pocket. Working as quickly as he could, he wiped all the door handles and latches, inside and out. The knife was still in the chauffeur's back; he wiped the handle and left it there. Finally he removed the briefcase, did the exterior door handles, then locked the car with the button on the key and walked away.

With the rag around his fingers so that he wouldn't leave prints, he walked along the parked cars trying each door. He found an older sedan that was unlocked. He got in, looked under the mat and in the cup holder and glove compartment for a spare key. No.

Hot-wiring the car took ten long minutes. The car started and ran strongly. Three-quarters of a tank of gas.

The ticket to get out of the garage was over the visor. He had the ticket he had taken from the automatic dispenser when he came in driving the limo, but he would owe no money on it since he had been in the garage less than thirty minutes. If he used it, the man at the booth would have a reason to remember him.

He presented the ticket from the visor and paid forty dollars. The man in the booth saw him, which was unavoidable. A video camera photographed the car's rear license plate as the car sat at the booth; there was no camera pointed at the driver.

Out on the street Sonny Tran fed gas and rolled.

Hamid Salami Mabruk drove northeastward toward Wilmington at ten miles per hour below the speed limit, trying to figure it out. After the weapon failed to explode, he had needed another thirty minutes to creep by the off-ramp wreck. Since the off-ramp to the Beltway was closed, he found himself headed northeast on the Baltimore–Washington Parkway, where it seemed as if every other overpass was being reconstructed. Traffic routinely slowed to twenty miles per hour, formed a single line, and crept by. Sometimes the pace dropped to stop-and-go as people raced forward as far as possible, then cut into the one open lane. He had finally turned off on an east–west road that took him over to I-95. He found himself in another traffic jam going through the Harbor Tunnel in Baltimore. At two in the morning. He pounded the steering wheel in frustration.

He would never get to New York before dawn to arm the warhead. Impossible to do it during the day, so that meant he couldn't arm it until tomorrow night, at the earliest. And the president talked about using the military to search. Someone might find the weapon between now and then.

Why didn't the warhead in the Convention Center explode? It couldn't be a problem with the batteries—they were new, and he had tested them repeatedly before he loaded them in the pickup. Not the timer, which he also tested repeatedly. Perhaps the capacitor was bad. Yes, that must be it, the capacitor. He had mated it to the weapon in the Red Sea weeks ago; no doubt the contacts inside had corroded in the salt-laden air.

He dismissed the possibility that the weapon had been found and disarmed before the timer ran down. Not that, surely. Once the security personnel determined the guard was missing—and it would take a while for them to reach that conclusion—then the search would begin. Even if someone unlocked the storeroom and found the body and the weapon, they wouldn't disarm it—not Convention Center guards. They would have called the police bomb disposal squad, and it would take a while for them to arrive.

No, the problem had to be the capacitor.

Where could he get another? He should have a new one with him to install in the circuit when he armed the weapon in New York. The possibility of another failure was too bitter to contemplate.

The ringing telephone awoke Myron Emerick, the director of the FBI. Robert Pobowski, the deputy director, was on the line. He broke the news—Grafton had found a nuke in the Washington Convention Center.

Emerick took it hard. Ignoring his half-awake wife, he said a few dirty words.

Pobowski continued his narration. The man that apparently armed the warhead was proceeding northeast up I-95. "He's either going home or to arm another bomb. Grafton wants us to set up surveillance on his house. Grafton's on his way to New York City right now in a Pentagon helicopter." Pobowski told Emerick Mabruk's name, where he lived.

"He wants us to follow this guy?" Emerick demanded.

"No. He thinks if he goes to New York the techno wizards in the Langley basement can track him on traffic cameras. He wants us to stay off him so that he'll lead Grafton to another bomb."

"That son of a bitch!" Emerick muttered. He wasn't referring to the suspect, but Grafton. "He's making us look like county Mounties, ordering us around so he gets the collar and the glory."

"Yes, sir."

"I got a call yesterday from a friend of ours on the White House staff. You won't believe this, but Grafton's people have hacked into our computer system. They've been reading every file entry on the Florida cell suspects. He knows as much about them as we do."

Pobowski remained silent. He was also a veteran of Washington's political maneuvering. Everyone was on the team, yet the promotions and budget dollars went to the people who produced results, not to role players. Like Emerick, he believed the future of the FBI was on the line. They couldn't afford to let Grafton steal the spotlight.

"That explains a lot," Pobowski said cautiously.

"Damn right," his boss grumped. "From now on I want the files kept with paper. No more computer entries. I don't want him stealing our work."

"There's been another development in Boston," Pobowski reported. "Grafton asked us to put a beacon on Corrigan's limo—he didn't want Corrigan to know about it, for obvious reasons. An hour ago the limo was parked on the top level of the Boston train station. No one around it, apparently. Dark windows, but our man shined a flashlight in. Two bodies in there."

"Nothing on the computers," Emerick repeated. "Let's see if we can keep this to ourselves and make something of it. Be sure and tell Harry Estep that he is not to volunteer FBI information to Grafton. If he asks a question, Estep is to answer it, but that's it."

"I understand, sir."

Emerick hung up the telephone and rolled over, trying to get comfortable. He found that impossible.

Another nuke, in Washington, for Christ's sake. And Grafton found it! That fact would play right into the hands of the people in Congress who wanted to reorganize federal law enforcement, put everything under one cabinet secretary. Damnation!

Emerick rolled out of bed, went downstairs to the kitchen to make a pot of coffee. When it had dripped through he sat sipping a cup and ruminating on the situation. He couldn't afford, he decided, to play second fiddle to Grafton. He called Pobowski back.

"If that suspect goes home, arrest him. Interrogate him on the spot. If he knows where another nuke or two are, get it out of him."

"What if he wants a lawyer?"

The rules of criminal procedure, which the Supreme Court decided in the 1950s and '60s were mandated by the United States Constitution, were not designed for the age of terror, as Emerick well knew. He wasn't going to let New York or Philly go up in a mushroom cloud because Habruk chose to exercise his right to remain silent. To hell with the lawyers!

"Trying to flatten an American city with a nuke isn't a crime, it's an act of war. Regardless of his nationality, this man is an enemy soldier—he doesn't have a right to a lawyer. Do what you have to do, Bob."

"Yes, sir."

It was four in the morning when Nguyen Tran drove his rig into the yard of an old tobacco warehouse in rural South Carolina. A regular semitrailer sat backed up to the loading dock, which was only large enough for two trailers. Nguyen put his rig into reverse and expertly backed the container into the empty spot.

A key on his ring opened the padlock. The interior of the warehouse was dirty, with opaque, fly-specked windows mounted high up.

The glass in one of the windows was completely gone, so bird droppings were scattered liberally throughout. Nguyen used his flashlight to ensure there was no one in the building, then he opened the overhead doors of the loading dock with hand cranks. The wheels squealed in protest as the doors rose.

A bird disturbed on its nest overhead fluttered and squawked.

Nguyen unlocked the door to the container and began unpacking. The furniture he stacked out of the way. When he got to the soft chairs loaded with blown lead pellets, he walked back to one corner of the warehouse and started the forklift that sat there. After it warmed up, he used it to off-load the chairs, one by one.

He had to cut loose the duct tape that held the bags of birdshot in place and carry the bags from the container one by one. He stacked them neatly by the door.

When he got to the warhead he inspected it carefully with the flashlight. From the cab of the tractor he got a socket set, which he used to run out the bolts that secured the pallet holding the warhead to the container floor.

Satisfied at last, he opened the door to the regular cargo trailer and climbed back on the idling forklift. In three minutes he had the warhead positioned in the other trailer. Instead of bolts, he used adjustable cargo straps to secure it in place. Then the job of repacking the birdshot around the warhead began. He used two rolls of duct tape to secure the bags, then moved the chairs in. When all that was done, he carried in the light furniture to fill up the rest of the space between the warhead and the trailer door.

He parked the empty container under the trees behind the warehouse, where it would be partially hidden from the road. Then he unhooked the tractor from the chassis that held the container and maneuvered the tractor to pick up the trailer that now held the weapon.

After he had the air brakes and electrical connections hooked up, Nguyen wiped his hands on a rag from the tractor's tool bin and carefully stowed his tools and flashlight.

He checked the warehouse one more time, then lowered the overhead doors and replaced the padlock on the personnel door.

The sky was growing light in the east when he drove out of the yard and headed northeast on the two-lane ribbon of asphalt.

The streets of the Bronx were quiet at five o'clock in the morning when Sonny Tran parked the stolen sedan under an elevated rail line and jerked the ignition wires apart. He got out of the car and walked to the back, where he took the license plate off with a screwdriver he had acquired earlier that evening at an interstate filling station.

No one was out and about in this neighborhood of burned-out tenements and blighted lives. Even the street-corner crack salesmen were in bed at this hour.

Sonny used the chauffeur's rag to wipe his prints from the steering wheel, gearshift, and door handles. He was especially careful wiping the area around the ignition switch and pulling the dangling wires through the rag. When he had rubbed every surface he might have touched, he got out of the car. He left it unlocked. With a little luck, the car would be stripped by this time tomorrow.

Carrying his briefcase, he walked the three blocks to the stairs that led up to the subway station. After wiping the license plate, he bent it double and dropped it in a trash can on the platform. He only had to wait five minutes before a train came rumbling in.

Hamid Salami Mabruk lived in a quiet neighborhood just ten minutes' walking distance from the university where he taught. He owned a typical older urban bungalow with an unattached garage on the back of the lot that one reached by driving down an alley. Large maples shaded most of the yard and brushed against the roof of the house. Six-foot-high board fences ran the length of the property on both sides and gave Habruk and his adjoining householders the illusion of privacy.

It was five-thirty in the morning when Habruk drove down the alley and used his remote to open his garage door. He eased the pickup through the narrow opening, killed the engine, and lowered the overhead door with the remote.

He sat with his head on the steering wheel, trying to think.

What a night this had been! The weapon had failed to explode, he had been in every construction traffic jam between here and Washington. A drive that should have taken two and a half hours had taken six.

Tonight! He would get some sleep, then go to New York and arm the weapon there tonight. He would get another capacitor from the hardware store this afternoon, just in case. The weapon would destroy New York City and alter the course of human history. Tonight!

He made a great effort to rouse himself and get out of the pickup. The garage was not large—he had to close the vehicle door to go forward to the door that led to the backyard. It was locked, of course—to keep neighborhood children and dope addicts out—so he fumbled with his key ring until he found the right one. Unlocked it and opened it and stepped through.

Three men stood there with pistols leveled. "*Freeze!* FBI—you're under arrest!"

He stepped backward and slammed the garage door.

Without thinking he pulled the .22 automatic from his belt. The silencer was still attached to the muzzle.

He would get back in the pickup, drive out of here! Even as this thought went through his head he heard a vehicle come roaring down the alley and brake to a stop outside the garage door, blocking it.

Someone pounded on the door.

"You're surrounded, Mabruk. Open this door and come out with your hands up!"

He fired the pistol though the door. The report was just a mild pop. He heard a groan.

He was trapped!

Enraged, he fired two more shots through the door, then placed the blunt round silencer against his head above the right ear and pulled the trigger.

CHAPTER TWENTY-FOUR

Jake Grafton was standing on top of the Met-Life Building in New York City when the sun peeped through the clouds to the east. He was leaning on a rail, out of the way, holding his cell phone in his right hand. The chilly spring breeze whipped at his light jacket and jeans and made him shiver a little. It had rained during the night, and the air was still cold.

The sun's appearance was spectacular, with the whole of the city at his feet. He was facing south. In the distance he could see the harbor and the bridges to Brooklyn and the Statue of Liberty. Behind him commuter helicopters came and went. The chopper that Jake had arrived in was parked on the helo pad farthest from the passenger terminal exit.

It was here that he learned from Gil Pascal that Hamid Mabruk had driven home. And it was here that he learned that Mabruk had shot himself when FBI agents attempted to arrest him. "They took him to the hospital in critical condition," Pascal reported. "He shot himself in the head with a twenty-two about thirty minutes ago. I'm getting this on the other line from Harry Estep in the FBI command center."

He called Harry. "I asked Zelda to tell you people to follow him, not attempt an arrest."

"Admiral, I don't mean to sound disrespectful," Harry said, "but the FBI doesn't take orders from you."

Jake thought about that for a moment. "I suppose someone in the Hoover Building gave the green light for an arrest."

"Yes, sir."

"Someone really senior."

"That's a good guess."

"Emerick, I suppose."

"I can't confirm that. But I have no doubt that the order to arrest Mabruk came from the top."

"Terrific. I hope Emerick knows where the other two bombs are and grabs them this morning. That would save all of us a lot of wear and tear on our stomach linings."

He snapped the phone closed.

He shouldn't have made that last crack, but . . . Jesus H. Christ, he felt so goddamn frustrated!

The streets below were dark canyons. The rising sun reflecting off buildings and acres of window glass chased away the gloom. As he stood looking, a commuter helicopter came in to land amid a hurricane of noise and rotor wash. Grafton leaned on the rail until the buffeting air subsided.

New York!

When the helo shut down, he used his cell phone to call Sal Molina. He had the number memorized.

"It's Grafton."

"Good work you did last night. Where are the other two?"

"That's what I called to talk about. The FBI just screwed up an attempted arrest of the guy who armed that one last night. He managed to shoot himself in the head. Still alive, but even if he lives, he isn't going to tell us anything."

"Okay," Molina said, sounding as tired and frustrated as Grafton felt.

"I've got our one Corrigan unit cruising Washington. Nothing so far. What I want to do is bring the thing to New York. I have a feeling that this is the most likely target for the others."

"Evidence to support that?"

"None. Just a gut feeling. Atlanta, Washington—they gotta have New York on their list. The Corrigan unit is the only thing that will find one of those warheads if it's packed in lead."

"The White House is releasing the news about the warhead you found last night. If you thought the warhead in Atlanta got Congress and the public stirred up, wait until you see what happens today. I'll talk to the president, but I suspect he will want the Corrigan unit to stay in Washington. This city is the seat of our government. An attack in New York would be devastating, but one here would be catastrophic."

"Yes, sir," Jake Grafton said. He had spent his adult life taking orders, even if he didn't agree with them.

"Could you be available to talk to the press later this morning?"

"Not unless I receive a direct order to make myself available."

The helo behind him came to life; Jake rammed a finger in his ear to hear Molina's reply. It sounded like "I'll get back to you," but it might have been something else. Jake snapped the telephone shut and leaned on the rail.

After the helo departed Jake called Gil Pascal again. "What is going on with the FBI?"

"Zelda isn't having much luck. They aren't putting anything about those terror cells on their computer system. There's been an interesting development on the wire services about a shooting involving some Arabs at a golf course construction site in south Florida. Two of them are dead. One was run over by a tractor pulling a container off the site. Apparently the container had just been delivered by a local hauler. The driver shot the other one. The rig kept on going."

"You don't say?"

"All this happened just after sunrise yesterday morning. The police are trying to get more information on the dead men from INS. They're probably talking to the FBI, too. Of course, no one got the plate numbers on the truck. The witnesses can't even agree on the brand of tractor."

"Uh-huh."

"Yesterday afternoon there was another shooting involving Arabs in north Florida, west of Jacksonville. Place is a piney woods, I take it, on a dirt road off a state highway. Five Arabs dead in that one. No suspects. Again, local police are e-mailing details on the dead men to the INS."

"What does Zelda think of all this?"

"She thinks the decedents may have been members of the terror cells the FBI was tracking. I thought of calling Harry Estep and asking, but I thought I should mention it to you first."

"Don't call Harry. I think he's got orders from headquarters."

"He's probably pretty busy," Gil said. "The Boston police have two corpses on their hands, Corrigan's right-hand man, guy named Karl Luck, and his chauffeur. Both stabbed around midnight."

"In Boston?"

"Yep. They were left in the limo at the train station."

"How's Carmellini doing?"

"Called in about an hour ago. Everything is quiet. He wants someone to relieve him, LeRoy, and the driver so they can get some sleep. I'm working on it."

"That Corrigan unit is gold," Jake replied. "I want armed guards in an unmarked car following it everywhere it goes. No more wrecks."

"I'll make it happen, Admiral."

"Where is Sonny Tran?"

"New Jersey. A security camera got him boarding a subway in the Bronx at dawn. He changed trains at Penn Station and rode out to Newark. We lost him there."

"Cell phone?"

"It's not radiating. It's apparently off."

"Keep me advised."

Jimmy Doolin had had his truck-driving job for three weeks; if he wasn't careful, he was going to lose it. He was running late with this load, which should have been delivered yesterday.

Yesterday! Ha! He parked the rig with the load on it so that he and Luellen could sign that contract on the condo. When he got back in the rig, he had a fender-bender with some old lady who wasn't sure what state she lived in, got a traffic citation—Oh, man! He was going to have to talk really fast to explain that to the boss.

That cigar-chomping fatty would probably fire him on the spot. If the boss canned him, the condo people were going to be all over him like stink on shit. They wouldn't let him out of the deal. And Luellen—what would she say?

The roads were still slick from the rain last night, and already traffic was loading up. Jimmy Doolin had his mind on things other than driving when he took the expressway off-ramp in the Bronx. The grade was steeper than he thought and the light at the bottom was red. He slammed on the brakes.

The truck chassis behind him fishtailed, the tractor slid through the light. The container on the chassis slid out to the right and wrapped itself around a steel power pole. The walls of the container split like a ripe melon, its contents gushed forth.

One of the things that came squirting out was a nuclear warhead packed in birdshot. The duct tape holding the bags of birdshot in place tore loose. Bags fell off as the warhead—which was really heavy with all that lead wrapped around it—caromed off a parked car and rolled a little ways down the street like an oversize bocci ball.

Jimmy Doolin was wearing his seat belt and wasn't hurt. He turned off the ignition and got out of the cab, cursing mightily. The container was ruined, the contents spread from hell to breakfast. He had a cell phone in his pocket. He dialed 911 to get the police started this way, then called Luellen to break the news to her. The condo was history.

The army officer in charge of the troops searching New York was Brigadier General Tom Zehner. The helo carrying Jake Grafton landed fifty yards from Zehner's mobile command post in Battery Park and shut down. Grafton walked across the grass and showed his Pentagon pass to the uniformed guard at the temporary fence that kept the curious away, and was admitted.

Zehner was a medium-sized man who exuded an air of perpetual calm. He knew who Jake Grafton was, even if he was wearing jeans and a ratty light jacket. Three other officers were in the command post conferring with the general.

After the greetings, they got down to it. "What are your orders?" Jake asked Zehner.

"Search every container coming into the city. We're using Geiger counters. I'm having my men open every third one."

"You are not searching every trailer and truck?"

"No, sir. There is no way. I've got three thousand men. The police are helping direct traffic, but my men are doing the searching. All the traffic crossing onto Long Island, Manhattan, and Staten Island has to cross tunnels, bridges or ferries. We're working them all. I've shut down all ferry traffic to the eastern end of Long Island. The people out there are bitching, but I did it anyway."

Zehner went to the map on the wall. "I gave up on the Bronx. I don't have enough troops. We stop the traffic when it crosses into Manhattan." Zehner looked Grafton in the eyes. "Right now the delay at the checkpoints is three hours. We're strangling the city. If we searched every vehicle, traffic would essentially cease to flow. The city would be isolated. Kept up long enough, the people in the city would starve."

"Railroads?"

Zehner showed him on the map.

"Airports?"

"No, sir. They have their own security."

Jake parked his butt on a desk. Most of the chairs were stacked with office supplies. "How long you been doing this?"

"Two days, sir."

"The warhead the FBI snagged in Atlanta was packed in lead shot and blown lead pellets. It's enough to fool a Geiger counter."

Zehner threw up his hands.

"What if a nuke is already in the city?" Jake pressed.

"Admiral, I only have so many troops. They must eat and sleep. Unloading every truck coming into the city to inspect it would be the equivalent of putting up roadblocks and denying all access."

"How would you use more people if you had them?"

Ten minutes later Jake's cell phone rang. Sal Molina was on the line. "The president wants you here for another meeting."

"Yes, sir," Jake said. "I'm on my way." He turned to a major who was standing against the wall. "Tell the chopper crew to start the engines. I'll be out in three minutes."

The White House meeting was crowded with senior military officers and the heads of federal agencies. Butch Lanham, the national security adviser, was the chair. Sal Molina sat in the corner cleaning his fingernails. Emerick belligerently acknowledged giving the order to arrest Mabruk. He insisted the Florida terrorist cells might still lead the FBI to the bombs, although that possibility became less likely with every passing hour.

The politicians in Congress were reacting to the army's stranglehold on traffic going in and out of New York, and that had to be dealt with.

Everyone wanted more Corrigan detection units, which weren't forthcoming. Corrigan Engineering was doing its level best, but another operational unit was at least two weeks away.

They were arguing about using troops to search tractor-trailers and about the Coast Guard's prohibition of pleasure boat traffic along the East Coast when someone came in to inform them that a warhead had been discovered at a truck crash in the Bronx. A sigh of relief swept the room.

"That's three," Molina said fervently.

"One explosion would be more than enough," General Alt snapped in reply.

Jake knew how Molina felt. He, too, felt a huge sense of relief, as if a great weight had been lifted from his back. Finding one was a labor for Hercules—finding two out of the question.

When the meeting broke up, Alt buttonholed Grafton. Sal Molina appeared at Jake's elbow. "Good work last night," the chairman said.

"Thank you, sir."

"Where's the other warhead?"

"God only knows. I'd bet a paycheck, if anyone wants to bet, that it's in New York or on the way there."

"This crowd hasn't a clue," Alt said sourly. "How are you going to find it?"

"We can't search the whole country," Sal Molina said while Jake considered his answer. "Atlanta surprised me. It could be anywhere, Chicago, L.A., San Fran, Dallas. . . ."

"Do you have a plan?" Alt snapped at Grafton. He was in a snapping mood.

"Keep doing what I'm doing, General, which is looking for the bad guys and trying to anticipate their targets. And praying we get a break. Last night was pure luck. If we had gotten there seventeen minutes later than we did, we'd be having this discussion in hell."

"There's one still out there," Alt said heavily.

Jake spoke slowly, feeling his way along. "We didn't find these warheads when they came into the country because they were packed in lead. They're here now. Let's stop searching the ships and redeploy our people."

"I agree that searching ships now is futile," Molina said. "I'll talk to the president about shuffling the troops."

Jake continued, "We've got to stop searching trucks going into New York—we're strangling the city. We'll search them in the city with roadblocks at random places. I want to use everybody we can lay hands on to search Washington and New York, and every other big city in the country."

"You're looking for a needle in a haystack. We'll never find it that way."

"Probably not, but we'll show the public we're looking, and we'll show the terrorists, too. Whatever plans they had for that last weapon are going to be reconsidered." He gestured with his hands. "We need to make them do what we want them to do, then be ready when they do it."

Alt looked around. The three men were the only ones left in the room. "Let's hear what you think."

"Fleet Week. If I were a terrorist, I'd find a way to detonate that warhead in New York Harbor during Fleet Week, which starts eight days from now. Ships from navies all over the world will start arriving any day. If there is a nuclear explosion in the harbor during Fleet

Week, half the people on earth will assume that a U.S. Navy weapon detonated. The other half will assume the terrorists did it. Either way they win."

Jake ran his fingers through his hair. "If I were a terrorist and I had one bomb left, that's what I'd do with it." It sounded lame, and in truth it was.

"We could cancel Fleet Week," Molina pointed out.

Alt looked askance at Grafton. "You still feel lucky?"

"This is our best shot, General."

"General Alt?" Molina asked the chairman.

"Don't cancel it."

"I am never going to play poker with you two," Molina said. "You'd bet the ranch without even a pair in your hand."

Jake Grafton was so tired his eyes burned, yet there was something he had to do before he went home. When he arrived at his office in Langley, he called Gil and Zelda into his office and closed the door. As they brought him up to date on the weapon that had been discovered that morning in New York and filled in more details about the bodies in the limo in Boston, Jake rummaged through the piles of files on the floor behind his desk.

He pulled one out and opened it on his desk. He hunted for the paragraph he wanted. "Ah-ha! I thought I remembered seeing this." He motioned to Zelda and Gil to come around the desk. They read over his shoulder.

"Sonny Tran had a brother, Nguyen Duc Tran. Trouble with the law as a youngster, fighting, drinking, dropped out of school at the age of sixteen. Diagnosed as a passive-aggressive personality. Got a GED when he was twenty. Is now a long-distance truck driver."

Zelda took a step back. "That incident yesterday at the golf course could have been a hijacking," she mused. "Did I tell you?—Corrigan Engineering is the contractor building the course—the container was addressed to them."

Jake Grafton smiled. It was his first smile in weeks, and it felt good. "I think I see a light at the end of this tunnel. It's a mighty small glow, but it's there."

He closed the file and carefully inserted it in his desk.

"Don't breathe a word of this to anyone," he said. "I want the fourth warhead, not suspects in jail."

They nodded.

"Corrigan," he said to Zelda. "Cell and landline telephone conversations, e-mail, everything you can get on him."

She nodded her understanding.

"Now if you good people will excuse me, I'm been up for nearly thirty hours; I've got to go home and get some sleep. See you this evening before you go home."

With that Jake Grafton walked out of the office, whistling softly.

The Corrigan van dropped Tommy Carmellini in front of the Graftons' apartment building. He rode the elevator up and knocked on the door. Callie opened it. "Come in, Tommy," she said, and pulled the door wide.

He looked around for Anna.

"Jake isn't home yet," Callie said. "Anna left an hour ago with two U.S. marshals. The FBI is putting her in the witness protection program."

"She coming back?"

"I don't think so."

"She leave a phone number or anything?"

"No. Just this note." Callie handed him an envelope, then went to the kitchen to give him some privacy while he read it.

Carmellini sat down on the couch and carefully tore the envelope. Inside was a piece of notepaper, folded once. She had written in ink, "Tommy, I'll be back someday. I love you, Anna." That was it.

He crushed the note in his hand, wadded it into a tiny ball.

He sat frozen, breathing in and out, in and out, listening to the thudding of his heart. After several minutes he opened his hand, looked at the wadded-up piece of paper, and carefully smoothed it out. He read the words again, then folded the paper until it would fit in his wallet. He stowed it behind his driver's license.

Callie Grafton came out of the kitchen carrying Carmellini's pistol and shoulder holster and two glasses of water. Tommy accepted a glass of water and sipped at it.

She sat down. "Jake called a while ago," she said. "He said you two found thc warhead in the Convention Center last night."

"Yeah," he said. "It was a long night."

"I heard on the news that one was found at a truck crash in the Bronx this morning."

"I heard that, too. Good news, huh."

He finished the water and put on the shoulder holster. "Thanks for the water."

"Come by and see us, Tommy."

"Yeah," he said. "I'll do that."

Jake was in a good mood when he arrived home less than a half hour after Carmellini departed. He kissed his wife, gave her a huge hug, then said, "I'm hungry."

"We've got some leftover chicken."

"Terrific. How about a chicken sandwich?"

While he ate she told him about Anna Modin's departure and Carmellini's visit. "He's in love with her, Jake."

"Renews your faith in humanity, doesn't it?" her husband said with his mouth full. "Here we are on the brink of Armageddon and people are still falling in love. Maybe the species will survive after all."

"So there is one warhead still out there?"

"Yeah."

"Where is it?"

"I think it was hijacked. That's good and bad. The terrorist cells in Florida were made up of suicidal warriors—they would have popped the thing pretty quick. Mabruk didn't want to die in the explosion—he set the weapon to blow after he cleared town, which was damned lucky for us, by the way. We arrived seventeen minutes before it exploded." He snorted. "Maybe I should buy a lottery ticket today. I'm shot with luck."

He drank some milk, then said, "The hijackers have something planned. I don't think they'll blow it the minute they lay hands on it."

"How could anyone hijack a bomb? How would they know where it is to steal it?"

"They knew the plan. Someone who knew it had to tell them."

"So who are the hijackers?"

"I've got an idea, but I tell you, Callie, the evidence is thin enough to read a newspaper through. Still . . ." He took another bite and munched slowly, savoring the food. When he swallowed he said, "Corrigan probably put up the money to buy the weapons, figured on double-crossing them, making sure we found them. The terrorists double-crossed him. Yet someone in the terrorist organization knew where the weapons were to be shipped, and that person sold or gave away the information. My guess is it was someone involved in the transportation of the weapons. Could have been any one of the people who knew—doesn't matter who—the point is the hijackers learned where the weapons were being delivered. Maybe they had one delivered to a destination they picked, maybe they were there to meet it at the terrorists' destination. What is indisputable is that we have seven dead terrorists and a missing weapon."

He finished the sandwich and stood. "I feel better."

"Toad's coming home today," she said. "Rita called from Boston."

"Shouldn't have had Toad and Bennett riding around with that asshole," Jake grumped. "Should have known better."

Callie was going to ask him to explain that remark, but Jake headed for the shower. Fifteen minutes later he collapsed in bed.

The news that Karl Luck had been murdered shook Thayer Michael Corrigan badly. He had been watching the continuous news coverage of the discovery of the warheads on television when the police arrived to give him the news, and to ask questions. Who had Luck met, when, where, why? Corrigan didn't know any of the answers. The fact that he didn't know was the thing that shook him, not Luck's death.

After the police left he sat trying to figure out what in the hell was going on. He hadn't a clue, and he knew it.

Who killed him? Not muggers or thieves—the police said both Luck and the chauffeur still had their wallets on them. A prostitute? Corrigan didn't think Luck went in for that sort of thing, and if he did, he certainly wouldn't want the chauffeur along as a witness. And then there were the wallets.

Sonny Tran? That was a possibility.

Or Arab terrorists?

One of the two, surely.

A knife. Not a gun, but a knife. Corrigan thought about that, too. He had never killed anyone, but if he were going to, he would use a pistol. Perhaps poison. A knife was too personal, too messy; you had to get so close, and you had to have a lot of strength. The police said Luck was stabbed through the heart and the knife was jammed to the hilt in the chauffeur's back. There was something . . . brutal . . . about the knife.

Was the killer after him, too?

Ah, that was really the issue, wasn't it? Being stalked by an assassin was one thing, but one who got so close he could ram a knife into your heart and watch your face as you died—that was a man to be feared.

Although it was only two hours after breakfast, the sun was shining outside, and the room was pleasantly warm, Corrigan felt a chill. He opened his desk and found the automatic he kept there. He took it out, looked at it. Rust spots in several places. He hadn't had it out of this drawer in years.

He checked to make sure it was loaded and the safety was on, then slipped it into his jacket pocket. The weight of it pulling on his tailored wool suit jacket made him feel silly.

A popgun like that wouldn't stop a suicidal assassin on a mission from God. Holy damn, those people used submachine guns and car bombs in Egypt. And knives. Hacking up tourists was one of their tactics.

He sat down before the computer on his desk and turned it on. While it was booting up, he opened his safe and removed a small leather-bound address book. He had used a code—it took him several minutes to decode the computer address he wanted and the public key.

He spent ten minutes composing the e-mail message, correcting it several times before he was satisfied. Then he encoded it on the RPS software and hit the send button.

Zelda Hudson had Corrigan's encrypted e-mail within minutes after he had sent it. Unfortunately, she couldn't decode it—she had neither Corrigan's public key nor the recipient's private key. She printed it out and put it on Jake Grafton's desk. When he came in that afternoon, he found it there and went to the techno-wizards' basement computer center.

"What's this?" he asked Zelda.

"Corrigan sent it to someone."

"Can you decode it?"

"No."

"NSA?" NSA was the National Security Agency, the government's cryptographers.

"Nope. It's an RPS code—there is no known way to decode it without one of the two keys."

"Terrific," he said, and went back upstairs to his office.

Toad Tarkington and Rita Moravia were waiting when he got there. They had just flown in from Boston.

"You look like you were run over by a garbage truck," Jake said.

"That's supposed to be funny," Toad said to Rita, who didn't grin.

"Sorry," Jake said. "Bad joke. I owe you an apology, Toad. I shouldn't have let Sonny Tran wander around with you and Bennett. He probably maneuvered that van into the path of the garbage truck on purpose." He passed the police report of the accident to Toad. "The driver of the garbage truck said the van accelerated to get in front of him. There was no way to stop. The police didn't cite either driver because they had two conflicting stories."

"You think he wanted to destroy the Corrigan detector?"

"It's junk. And Sonny has disappeared. He didn't go home, and he isn't answering his cell phone. In fact, Zelda tells me he doesn't have it on. She can't track it through the cell network."

"Wow," Rita said. "If that crash was intentional, that was a gutsy move. He could have been killed, too."

"Sonny Tran is one cool customer," Jake acknowledged. "I—well, hell, I screwed up. I apologize."

Toad waved it away. "Forget it, CAG. We're all doing the best we can."

Jake looked at Rita. "I need your help. I want to know everything there is to know about Fleet Week in New York. I'll call your boss in the morning and get you transferred over here."

An hour later, when Toad and Rita were on the way home, Rita remarked, "He looked a little more upbeat than he has the last few times I saw him."

Toad agreed. "That garbage truck crack was the first funny he's tried in a month. He thinks he's on to something."

"Amen to that," Rita said fervently.

The following afternoon Zelda intercepted an encrypted e-mail to Corrigan. It was from a sender in France. She printed it out and was studying it when her computer began flashing. She had an e-mail! Someone had sent her one at the CIA! Sarah.Houston was the addressee.

Who in the world?

She called it up. This one was from the same person in France who had e-mailed Corrigan. She studied it, then realized she was looking at an encryption key. Actually, two keys.

Fifteen minutes later she had Corrigan's outgoing and incoming e-mail decoded. She printed them out and carried them upstairs to Jake Grafton's office. The admiral was in conference with Rita Moravia. The secretary took the e-mails in and handed them to Jake Grafton.

Sixty seconds later he was in the outer office. "How'd you get these?"

"Someone sent us the keys." She handed him the message she had received. He dropped into a chair, glanced at the keys, then carefully read the decoded messages.

"Zelda, I thank you. Your country thanks you." He popped out of the chair and kissed her on the cheek, then scrambled back into his office with the messages in his hand. He slammed the door closed behind him.

Zelda Hudson, rubbing her cheek, stood in front of an amazed secretary. "But I didn't do anything," she protested, then wandered off to get a soda pop.

In midafternoon the tractor-trailer rig pulled into a small warehouse facility in Newark. Nguyen Duc Tran backed the trailer up to a loading dock, killed the engine, got out of the cab, and stretched.

He looked around casually, then climbed the stairs to the loading dock and went in the large open door.

His brother, Sonny, was sitting at a desk against a sidewall. He was the only man in the place. Nguyen pulled the nearby folding chair around and sat in it. He lit a cigarette, took a puff, and grinned.

"I've been wondering where you were," Sonny said.

"I had an adventure. The Arabs did not part with their toy willingly."

"There have been some articles in the newspaper about dead Arabs scattered around Florida."

"It was fun," Nguyen said expansively. "I truly enjoyed it." He jerked a thumb toward the rig at the dock, and laughed.

"You are a nihilist, I think," Sonny said thoughtfully.

"And you aren't?" Nguyen waved the hand that held the cigarette in a large sweeping gesture—"Smashing those bastards was . . . perfect. Just perfect! Damn, I feel good."

"We won't survive this adventure," Sonny said, his eye on his brother.

"Hey, everyone has to die. When it's over there's nothing, nothing at all. No paradise and no hell. All you get is the juice you make before you go." Nguyen dropped the half-smoked cigarette and stepped on it. "You want to look at it? It's a helluva piece of work."

"In a minute. There's no hurry. A helicopter will take it to the job site Monday morning."

"I wondered how you were going to get it by the troops. I heard on the radio that they're searching every truck going into the city."

"Helicopter. We'll go over them."

Nguyen Duc Tran laughed raucously. He leaned back in the chair and shouted his glee at the heavens. Despite himself, Sonny Tran laughed, too.

Yes, smashing this rotten, misbegotten society and the bastards who built it was indeed sublime.

At midnight Jake Grafton boarded an executive jet at Andrews Air Force Base. He was the only passenger.

He settled into a window seat on the left side and reclined it as soon as the pilot lifted the landing gear. The plane took off to the south and banked into a climbing left turn. Soon the lights of Washington were visible stretching to the horizon. Traffic delineated the Beltway, he could see the Washington Monument and the Capitol . . . a sea of lights, millions of people.

He tossed and turned, trying to get comfortable as the lights of Baltimore passed off the left wing. There was a cloud deck over the ocean, so he didn't see New York, which was almost a hundred miles northwest of the plane's course. Boston went under the nose a while later. He drifted off to sleep with the jet on course for the North Atlantic.

Paris was as it always was, a magic city, a city of youth and dreams, today under a high, clear, pale May sky. Jake Grafton was wearing jeans, tennis shoes, and his ratty windbreaker as he sat on a bench in front of Notre-Dame. Above him the gargoyles watched the human parade as they had for centuries.

He bought a bag of seed for the pigeons and dribbled it out parsimoniously until he tired of it, then he threw them the last handful and emptied the bag. They ate it at his feet.

He was early, of course. He would be early at his own funeral, or so Callie had said many times through the years when he urged her to hurry up. Maybe it was the navy, all those years of being at the appointed place before the appointed time, just in case.

He saw the limo pull up and Thayer Michael Corrigan get out. The limo got under way and disappeared in traffic. Corrigan was well dressed in a dark suit. He looked around, didn't see who he was looking for, so he took a bench across the plaza from Jake, facing the street, with a young tree behind him. Jake watched his profile. Corrigan ignored the birds and tourists and lovers, glanced at his watch, then crossed his legs.

Corrigan had been sitting there for five minutes when Janos Ilin came walking along the sidewalk that led from the bridge across the Seine to the Left Bank. Jake Grafton saw him first. Ilin glanced his way but gave no sign he recognized him. The Russian walked over to the bench where Corrigan was and sat down beside him.

After they had been talking a moment or two, Jake rose to his feet and walked toward them. There was an empty bench at right angles behind Corrigan and Ilin, so he made for that and seated himself.

". . . I need some help from you," Corrigan was saying. "We've done a lot of business in the past, and I know you are a trustworthy man of utmost discretion."

"How may I be of service?" Ilin asked in nearly flawless English.

"There are some men in Cairo who must be eliminated. I am willing to pay, of course, a reasonable fee and all expenses. It must be done soon. They killed one of my colleagues, and I am worried that they will try to murder me."

"What have you done to them?"

"It was a business deal. I can say no more than that. We live in difficult times."

"Indeed," said Ilin. "Of course, I would have to know more. Names, addresses if you have them. And it will take some time. These things cannot be arranged overnight."

"I understand, but there is a time constraint. As I said, they killed my colleague the night before last in Boston." He forgot to mention the chauffeur, Grafton noted. Corrigan wasn't a man who paid much attention to chauffeurs.

Ilin remarked, "They sound quite determined, and several jumps ahead of you. You may well be too late. I suggest you go to some remote island, hire good men as bodyguards, stay there. Live quietly and they may not find you. Even if they do, you will have fair warning when they come and can defend yourself. Your money will buy you that, which is more than most men get."

"That's ridiculous," Corrigan said derisively. "I thought you were a man of the world who could make things happen."

"Things, yes, but not miracles."

"For Christ's sake, you have the resources of the SVR at your beck and call. Surely you—"

"Mr. Corrigan, you have been misinformed. I am here as a private citizen. I represent no one but myself."

Corrigan didn't understand. "Perhaps we should discuss money. I am willing to pay a large fee. A very large fee. There are three of them, Abdul Abn Saad—he's a banker, Walney's Bank in Cairo—a man called Ashruf, and one called Hoq—he's associated with them, I'm not sure how."

"I know of these men. They have come to my attention in my professional capacity, you understand—governments share information. They are Islamic extremists, holy warriors . . . terrorists. Killing them will not be easy."

"Of course not. That's why I came to you. Name a price."

"You're getting ahead of yourself. I have agreed to nothing. Your job would be an expensive undertaking. People would have to be hired, equipped, and put in place, covers created, bribes paid. . . . Are these men in Egypt?"

"Saad is, and Hoq. I have no idea where Ashruf might be found."

Ilin sighed heavily. "A difficult, laborious, high-risk undertaking, at best. A million American for each of them, at least."

"Done. Half in advance, half when the job is done."

"That would be for expenses. The fee would be another million each, if I agree to undertake it."

Corrigan's head bobbed up and down several times. "Done. Half in advance, half when the job is finished."

"How do I know you will be able to pay when the job is finished? Aren't the Americans investigating these men?"

"Everyone is, I would imagine."

"Then you see my difficulty. If by some chance some investigating authority established a link between you and these men, you might be . . . shall we say, detained. Arrested, perhaps. Indicted. Forced to defend yourself. Surely, Mr. Corrigan, you see how difficult it would be for me to collect if you were incarcerated somewhere and refused to pay after I completed my contract."

"I am not going to be arrested. The authorities know nothing, and I have an impeccable reputation."

"It is unfortunate that reputations are not bulletproof, is it not? By chance, are you aware of the name of the man that the American president appointed, ad hoc if you will, to find the warheads the group known as the Sword of Islam purchased in Russia and imported into the United States? He may know that the men you named are part of that group."

"I—no, I might have heard his name, but—"

"Grafton. He's a rear admiral in the United States Navy. Two stars, rank equivalent to a major general in your army or air force. Sometimes he wears a uniform, sometimes he doesn't."

"I've heard the name. Never met the man." He had forgotten meeting Jake at the White House.

"Well, allow me to introduce you." Ilin half turned and gestured. "Thayer Michael Corrigan, Rear Admiral Jacob Lee Grafton."

Corrigan turned slowly, looked into the cold gray eyes of Jake Grafton, who was staring at him. Corrigan looked back at Ilin, said bitterly, "I thought you were an honorable man."

Before Ilin could reply, Corrigan arose from the bench and walked away. He disappeared into the crowd in the direction of the Left Bank.

Jake walked around and sat down beside Ilin. "Thanks for inviting me to your little meeting. It's not often I get to sit close to a billionaire."

"They are a rare breed. Did you get enough?"

"To ruin Corrigan? I think so. No doubt he thinks I recorded it."

"Hmm."

"We've still got one of those goddamn terrorist warheads rolling around loose. Any idea where I might find it?"

"None. I have faith in you, though."

Grafton snorted. "If you hear a big bang from America, don't bother sending flowers."

"How many buried bombs have you found?"

"Three so far. How many are there?"

"I have no idea. The leaders of the SVR are industrious and don't do things by halves."

"You could have just told me, you know."

"No, I couldn't. Then they would have smelled a leak. Corrigan provided a perfect cover—the money and the terrorists and the warheads Petrov sold them are real. Moscow doesn't suspect me, and they won't."

"I'm not going to thank you until we find the last warhead."

"I suppose not."

"In a couple weeks we're going to start digging up the buried bombs. Any danger of those damn fools in Moscow popping them when we do?"

"I think not. They were assets to fight the political battles in the Kremlin. The ultranationalists took comfort from them. The people responsible were promoted to very high positions. You understand these things."

"I have a favor to ask of you," Jake said. "Unlike Corrigan, I can pay nothing." He told Ilin what it was.

"I'll see what I can do," Ilin said.

The admiral nodded. "Well, thanks for the e-mails. Now that you have our address, send us a Christmas card."

Jake Grafton stuck out his hand. Janos Ilin shook it, then got up and walked away, scattering the pigeons.

CHAPTER TWENTY-FIVE

On Monday morning Sonny Tran stood looking up at the Statue of Liberty. The pedestal and the statue were covered with scaffolding. "Are you going to be able to get all that scaffolding off in the next five days?" Sonny asked.

The man he directed the question to was Hoyt Wilson, the chief engineer on the statue refurbishment project.

"Oh, yes," Hoyt said, "but let me tell you, I've been damn worried about your gadget. We're right up to the wire, man, with my neck on the line." He was referring to the deadline made necessary by the Fleet Week schedule. The refurbishment project had to be finished and the scaffolding removed from the Statue of Liberty by Saturday, the first day of Fleet Week.

"The Park Service engineers have been all over this project," Hoyt continued. "They've tested the new light, worked out all the bugs. It's going to be officially turned on and dedicated at the opening ceremony the first evening of Fleet Week, Saturday night. With the fireworks and ships all lit up, this will be a once-in-a-lifetime sight."

"Oh, yes," Sonny said. "Still, we live in troubled times, and Pulpit has priority over light shows and fireworks."

Pulpit was a classified project. Hoyt Wilson had a security clearance, as did the handful of workmen who were going to help install Pulpit. Yet Wilson didn't know what it was. He asked now. "Just between us, Gudarian, what the hell is this thing you're putting up there?" Sonny's badge proclaimed that he was Harold P. Gudarian ("I was adopted after the Vietnam War"), an employee of the department of defense.

"Man, I don't want to go to prison," the fake Gudarian said smoothly, "and I'll bet you'd rather not."

Wilson nodded curtly and bit his lip. "Forget I asked."

Sonny looked around, then said in a low voice, "Why do you think Corrigan Engineering got this job? The company wasn't the low bidder." Indeed, Corrigan *was* the low bidder, but Sonny doubted if Wilson knew that. In fact, Corrigan won this project three years ago—that the firm's radiation research had led to hardware and the age of terrorism had arrived almost simultaneously was purely coincidence. And a horse Sonny could ride.

Wilson stared as Sonny continued, "Surely you know about the firm's work with radiation detectors?"

"Oh!" The light dawned for Hoyt Wilson. His eyebrows went up toward his hairline. He had heard the news of the warheads being discovered in Atlanta, Washington, and the Bronx.

"You never heard it here, amigo. Officially Pulpit is a system that keeps track of ships in an anchorage. The mechanics are classified."

"I appreciate your confidence—not another word," Wilson said abruptly. "The chopper is going to set your gadget on the balcony. As you know, it wouldn't fit inside—things are damn tight up there. I want you up there supervising when the chopper brings it. There shouldn't be a problem. When it's in place we'll start tearing down the scaffolding."

"After we get it up there, I'm going to seal the statue, put locks on the doors. I'll be up there through Fleet Week. We don't want any unauthorized persons in the statue until after Fleet Week."

"That might be a problem," Wilson said, frowning. "There's a television crew that wants to film from inside the crown when the torch light comes on. The Park Service gave them permission."

"We'll see how it goes. Don't cancel. I'll be talking to you. Believe me, my superiors at D.O.D. have the authority to overrule the Park Service on national security grounds."

"I understand."

"One of my colleagues is going to be along later today. I'll let him in."

"Sure."

They entered the structure through the visitors' entrance, an opening in the mid-nineteenth-century star-shaped Fort Wood, which once guarded New York Harbor. Although the architects who designed the fort would have never believed it, the granite fort made a perfect base for the colossus. Above the old fort rose the base of the pedestal, then the pedestal itself, the foundation upon which the 225-ton weight of the statue rested. Both the base and the pedestal were poured concrete structures faced with granite.

As Wilson and Tran rode the elevator to the observation level, Wilson said, "We could have lifted your toy up there with the crane if we'd had it in time."

"Saved time doing it with the chopper," Tran explained. "Then there is the security angle. The fewer people who see it, the better. And absolutely no photos. We'll cover the thing so all the planes and helicopters flying around next week don't breach security."

"Let me know if we can help," Wilson said.

When the elevator reached the observation deck, they walked outside onto the viewing platform, or balcony. At this point they were roughly halfway up the 302-foot total height of the statue. From here they rode a tiny elevator up the side of the scaffolding.

The elevator had no sides, no rails, nothing—each passenger donned a safety harness at the bottom and snapped a carabiner ring onto a metal piece, so they couldn't fall off. Sonny Tran held on grimly as the open elevator rose. The wind tugged at his hard hat. He wanted to close his eyes as the elevator rose and rose, and the island below shrank dramatically. Finally, he could resist no longer—he slammed his eyes shut and didn't open them until the elevator jerked to a stop. He found that the elevator had stopped at the level of the goddess's chin. Wilson hopped off the elevator as if they were on the fifth floor of a department store, motioned for Sonny to join him, then jogged up a short ladder to the lady's right ear. From here a longer ladder went above her arm to the torch balcony.

Sonny steeled himself and followed. He didn't look down, just concentrated on Wilson's shoes in front of his face as the wind whipped at his clothes and hat—it seemed as if the wind could effortlessly pluck him off the ladder and hurl him into space. Teeth gritted, eyes on Wilson's shoes and ankles, he climbed rung by rung.

He was shocked when he saw how tiny the torch balcony was. Actually it was about nine feet in diameter. Perhaps the fact the torch was suspended here on the very apex of the statue—a hundred yards above the island below—made it seem smaller than it was. A piece of the railing had been removed so that people could enter via the ladder.

"I hope I don't pee my pants," he told Hoyt Wilson when he had snapped his carabiner ring onto balcony metalwork. Wilson didn't bother with a safety line. No doubt he had been up here so often that he was no longer impressed with the view, which was sublime. He glanced at his watch impatiently, then removed two pages of blueprints from his pocket. He kept them folded so they wouldn't blow away and began pointing out the attachment points and electrical connections to Sonny.

Tran tried to ignore the altitude and wind and concentrate on what Wilson was saying. The gentle, subtle motion of the torch as it responded to the wind didn't help.

Two laborers came up on the elevator. One climbed the ladder to the torch and strapped himself to the scaffolding. The other waited until Sonny's tools came up on the elevator before he climbed up, carrying the toolbox in one hand in apparent total disregard of the height and the breeze. He went back down and waited for Sonny's duffel bag to come up on the elevator, then carried it to the balcony.

Sonny turned from looking outward to an inspection of the light assembly. The new torch light was smaller than the old one, yet the box housing the warhead would have to go on the balcony. The warhead would have fit inside if Sonny could have removed it from its housing, which was merely camouflage. Unfortunately there was no way to do that—he and Nguyen had used a chain hoist to get it into the box.

"I'm amazed the Park Service approved Pulpit's installation, out in the open like this," Wilson remarked.

"The Park Service wasn't asked," Sonny snapped. "Anyone bitches, tell him to take a good look at Ground Zero."

The helicopter was ten minutes late. Sonny was feeling more comfortable about being up so high in such a small place when he spotted it coming from the northwest, with a load suspended under it. Seconds later he heard it.

Yes!

He forgot all about the height. He had his warhead! This Saturday night, with this harbor full of gray warships and dignitaries, he and Nguyen were going to deliver a blow from which America would never recover. They were going to change the course of world history.

Two determined men. Only two.

The noise and downwash from the rotors of the chopper as it hovered over the torch was astounding, a sensory overload that made it hard to move or think or breathe. Wilson and the laborers seemed to have no problem, although Sonny could not force himself to release his hold on a piece of angle iron. The warhead, batteries, and capacitor in their housing were lowered straight into the balcony. In less than thirty seconds the workmen had the hoist straps loose.

As the helicopter flew away the noise level dropped. Sonny leaned in, put his hand on the box.

Yes!

Commander Rita Moravia brought a giant aerial shot of New York Harbor with her when she reported to Jake's office in the Langley complex that morning. Toad helped her tape it to a wall in an office near Jake's—the only one with enough wall space. The shot was annotated with open lanes and anchorage positions for the warships.

When Jake arrived, the wall was completely decorated. Rita took him into the empty office to look. "We've been using this blowup to assign anchorage positions, work out liberty boat routes, VIP tours, garbage runs, everything. . . . The Fleet Week staff had another, so I swiped this one."

"This is just what we needed," Jake muttered, tapping the photo. "Have you met Zelda?"

"No, sir. Heard a lot about her from Toad."

"Today's your lucky day—you're about to meet a twisted genius in the flesh, the great Zelda Hudson. In the meantime, help me carry some chairs and stuff into this office. I just moved. We'll have the morning staff meeting in here."

When she arrived, Zelda said a tight hello to Rita, nodded at everyone else, and took a seat.

Rita opened the meeting by passing out the Fleet Week schedule. The opening ceremony on the evening of the first day drew Jake's attention. The president was going to be there, ten other heads of state, six prime ministers, five vice presidents, and half the ambassadors to the United Nations—the ones from countries that liked America this week. The senior members of Congress, New York and New Jersey's congressional delegations—Jake ran his eye on down the guest list—celebrities, singers, sports stars, the mayor of New York, admirals from everywhere, the list ran on for pages. Even Thayer Michael Corrigan's name was on the list. "Holy cow," Jake muttered.

"They've been putting this thing together for a year," Rita said in way of explanation. "It's the navy's week in the spotlight, our chance to win a few friends, which we will need desperately for the budget wars."

"Giving everyone a short boat ride and a ton of fireworks oughta do it," Jake agreed. "Where is the opening ceremony?"

"Aboard USS *Ronald Reagan*." The *Reagan* was the navy's newest carrier, just commissioned. "The CNO wanted to show her off before she transits Cape Horn to the West Coast."

"Where are you going to put her?" Jake asked.

Rita used a pointer on the chart. "Here in front of Liberty Island. The scaffolding from the refurbishment will start coming down today, so Lady Liberty will be the backdrop. After the refurbishment she's all polished and shiny. The president will use a radio switch to turn on her new torch light, which is twice as powerful as the old one. The television types wanted Liberty alone in the background, rather than against the Manhattan skyline—they don't want people staring at the spot where the World Trade Center towers used to be."

She spent another five minutes running through the logistics and size of the operation. When she finished, Rita sat down.

Jake glanced at every face in his small audience before he began speaking. "As you know, the Sword of Islam purchased four warheads in Russia and shipped them here. We have recovered three of them. Those are the facts—now for the theory: I think Sonny Tran and his brother Nguyen hijacked the fourth weapon in Florida and are planning to explode it somewhere. New York, Fleet Week"—he picked up the schedule and flipped to the first page that listed the opening ceremonies guests—"are perhaps the place and time. You must admit, this is a juicy list of bigwigs."

He paused, looked from face to face again. "I need you people to verify or refute that theory, the sooner the better."

Nods from everyone. No questions about how he arrived at that theory, just nods. This was, after all, the military.

"Let's talk about how we're going to do it," Jake said, and went on from there.

Late that afternoon Nguyen Duc Tran rode one of the work boats over to Liberty Island from Manhattan. He had credentials from Corrigan Engineering, so there was no problem. He walked along with a backpack over his shoulder and a toolbox in his hand watching a swarm of men on the statue piling scaffolding on a platform suspended from the crane. When the platform was full, the crane operator lowered it to the ground, where another group of workmen unfastened that platform and quickly rigged an empty one to the crane hook. Back up the new platform went for another load of scaffolding.

Holding his hard hat on, Nguyen tilted his head back and looked up at the statue against the sky. He felt so good he wanted to laugh and shout. *Hey, all you rich American bastards. Sonny and I are going to fuck you good. Fuck you straight into hell!*

He entered the edifice at the tourist entrance. After a glance at his badge, the guard allowed him into the elevator, which lifted him to the balcony level. The door to the stairs that led upward was closed and locked. No one was there, not even a Park Service inspector.

Nguyen took a handheld two-way radio from his backpack and turned it on. He checked the frequency, then keyed the mike.

"Sonny?"

The reply was a while in coming. "Yo."

"I'm at the door."

The minutes dragged. Nguyen used them to inspect the exit door. There were, he knew, two staircases, an up and a down. The door to the down staircase was padlocked. He added a padlock of his own to the hasp, then went back to the door that led to the up staircase.

Eight minutes after he made the radio call, the door opened. Sonny grinned at him. When he was inside, they closed the door and used a portable electric drill from Nguyen's toolbox to install an interior hasp and padlock. Then they rigged an alarm that would sound if the door were opened.

With that job accomplished, they went around to the exit door and installed a hasp, padlock, and alarm on it.

With Sonny leading, they went back up the stairs. Sonny carried the toolbox and Nguyen his backpack. It was a long climb. The new steel girders wore fresh paint. Even the stairs had a new coat of paint and new nonskid applied. They could hear the noise made by the workmen removing the scaffolding just beyond the lady's copper skin—only 3/32nds of an inch thick. They could even hear their voices, although they couldn't make out individual words.

When Sonny reached the door to the ladder inside the statue's arm that led to the torch, he opened it carefully. Normally, he knew, this door was padlocked to prevent tourists from gaining access to the torch. Of course now there were no tourists. They padlocked this door from the inside and installed another alarm. The noise it made would be loud enough for them to hear it, they thought, although they didn't really expect to hear the alarms on the doors far below. They were designed to panic intruders, not warn them in the torch.

The arm was small, the fit tight. Sonny and Nguyen had to make two trips to get the toolbox and backpack up to the torch.

They entered the torch where Lady Liberty's hand held it, under the balcony that surrounded the flame. Sonny grinned at Nguyen. "What do you think?"

"I think we're going to fuck these sons of bitches good."

"You should have been up here when they delivered the thing. What a trip! They started tearing down the scaffolding as soon as the workmen climbed down."

Nguyen climbed up the ladder beside the structure that held the new light. Its massive circular Fresnel lens was inside the flame of the torch. From the ladder, he carefully stepped out onto the balcony. There sat the weapon in the aluminum box that he and Sonny had installed it in last night.

A dozen ships were in sight, coming and going, a few anchored awaiting a pier up the Hudson or East River. There was an overcast this evening, visibility about seven miles. The buildings of Manhattan were quite prominent to Liberty's left. The Brooklyn shoreline and Staten Island were farther away. Just visible as an outline in the haze was the Verrazano Bridge across the narrows, off to the right.

Sonny joined him on the platform.

"We're high up, aren't we?"

"Three hundred feet," Sonny replied. "You should have come up the scaffolding and outside ladder! I almost lost my cookies a dozen times." He stood with both hands on the railing, looking down at the scaffold workers. He was getting more comfortable with the height.

"You got the thing wired to the batteries?" Nguyen asked.

"Not yet. I wired it to the regular power supply just in case. You and I need to wire it to the batteries now and test the capacitor. Then we'll wire the capacitor to the detonators."

"Think somebody will figure something out before the opening ceremony?"

Sonny grinned again. "Doesn't matter. We can pop this thing anytime we want—tomorrow, the day after, next week. . . . When it goes, most of New York is going to be a radioactive smoking hole. We did it, Nguyen! *We've won!*"

Sonny used a screwdriver to open the access panel to the warhead's housing. He giggled from time to time.

"Checkmate," he muttered, "checkmate," and laughed aloud, a high-pitched keening noise.

Of course it was Zelda who first produced solid results. When Jake came to work Tuesday she was waiting.

"Do you ever sleep?" he asked.

"Can't. Nguyen D. Tran has a Texas commercial driver's license and owns an over-the-road tractor registered in Texas." She passed Jake printouts of the information from the Texas Department of Motor Vehicles. "He paid road-use taxes on that tractor in thirty-four states last year, and twenty-two so far this year. Sometimes he uses a credit card to buy fuel." She passed him a printout of the credit card company's computer records.

"Using that you can construct a history of his trips. It's tenuous because he only fills the tractor once a day and sometimes he pays cash.

"He often hauls for Corrigan Engineering as an independent contractor. Corrigan issued him an ID card so he can get into Corrigan job sites." She handed the admiral a printout of the Corrigan data on Nguyen Tran. There was even a photo.

"Would a truck driver need an ID card?" Jake asked. "I guess I sorta thought truckers would be admitted only if they had invoiced material to deliver."

"One suspects so, so the ID card means that something is going on with Corrigan. The Trans have an 'in.' I surfed the Corrigan photo library and came up with this." She gave Jake a sheet showing a photo of another Vietnamese man, one Harold P. Gudarian.

"Sonny Tran," Jake muttered, and tossed the sheet on the growing pile.

"As you know, Corrigan Engineering does major projects all over the world. Here's a list of the projects they have going in the New York area."

Jake looked at the list. There were only four projects. Two of them were sewage system expansions on Long Island, one was a bridge job in Hoboken . . . and one was the refurbishment of the Statue of Liberty.

"Sweet Jesus!" Jake Grafton whispered.

Zelda wasn't finished. "Corrigan project managers update the home office on their progress every evening via e-mail. Here is a printout of the Statue of Liberty daily progress reports for the last three months."

It was a serious pile of paper. As Jake thumbed through it, Zelda said, "Yesterday's report is on the top page."

Jake turned to it. Read about delivery of "Pulpit," and initiation of scaffolding tear-down. There was more, a lot more, about rest room final inspections and electrical problems and site cleanup, but the word "helicopter" leaped from the page at him.

"A helicopter."

"It could fly a bomb right over all those inspection teams."

"Oh, yes." He ran his fingers through his hair and pulled at his nose. "Pulpit," he said, trying out the word. "Whatever that is. Good work, Zelda. Has Gil come in yet?"

"I saw him at the coffeepot a moment ago."

"Send him in, please."

Gil had a copy of the morning paper with him when he came in. Jake was studying the wall photo of New York Harbor.

"Did you see this, Admiral?" He held the paper out. Thayer Michael Corrigan had made the front page below the fold. Died yesterday afternoon of an apparent heart attack. Found in his study at dinnertime by a maid. Captain of industry, prominent philanthropist, friend of presidents, and so on.

"Darn," Jake said, and glanced at the other headlines.

"Just got off the telephone with Harry Estep," Gil continued. "He says the local police found an empty bottle of sleeping pills on the desk beside Corrigan's body. The wife doesn't want any talk of suicide. She's already had a pet doctor sign the death certificate certifying a heart attack. Harry thinks the local prosecutor is going to let him be buried without an inquest or autopsy."

"Below the fold," Jake mused. "He wouldn't have liked that. And he's going to miss Fleet Week."

He tossed the paper into the unclassified wastebasket and pointed to Liberty Island in the photo on the wall. "Here it is, maybe," he said.

"Do you think it's already there?"

"That's the problem—it might be. We go charging in with Geiger counters or Corrigan units and the Tran brothers might push the button."

He looked at his watch. He was just flat running out of time. He walked out into the main office. Tommy Carmellini, Toad Tarkington, and Rita Moravia were there. Tommy was casually dressed, ready for another day riding around in the van with the Corrigan unit. Toad and Rita were wearing khaki uniforms. He pointed at Rita and raised his voice. "Go home and change into jeans and work shoes or flying boots, something leather. Gil, get Rita a helicopter. Tommy, get her a Geiger counter and backpack. I want her on Liberty Island by the noon hour."

He clapped his hands. "Go, people. Now!"

At eleven-forty-five that morning Rita Moravia boarded the crew boat in lower Manhattan for the ride to Liberty Island. She was wearing jeans, leather hiking boots, and a hard hat. Around her neck was a National Park Service ID. In her backpack was a Geiger counter.

Jake Grafton talked to her on her cell phone as she drove to the Pentagon to catch a helo. "If they brought the warhead in by helicopter, it isn't packed in lead anymore. The Geiger counter should pick up the radiation. Check the whole island."

She also had a clipboard. She would walk around the island making notes, trying to look like a typical government inspector out to fill up a form with cogent observations.

During the night the first of the foreign warships had arrived in New York Harbor, two destroyers from Italy. They were anchored adjacent to each other. As she watched, a liberty boat departed from the side of one of them, jammed to the gunwales with sailors in whites.

Three gulls flew alongside the crew boat, eyeing the passengers one by one to see if anyone was interested in making a food donation. Apparently not. They rode the wind wave off the boat all the way to Liberty Island anyway.

Halfway to the island Rita turned and looked back at Manhattan. Then Brooklyn, Staten Island. . . . Millions of people lived and worked within ten miles of this island, all busy with life.

The head, arm, and torch of the Statue of Liberty were clean of scaffolding, which was almost down to Liberty's waist. Even as the boat approached, the large construction crane lowered another pile of scaffolding to the ground. Rita could see the men high up, taking the scaffolding apart.

When the boat docked, she queued up and took her turn getting off. She didn't expect to recognize anyone, and she didn't.

Out of the stream of workers and members of the press, who were also taking a tour today, Rita paused and took off her backpack. She unzipped it to gain access to the Geiger counter and donned the headset so that she could listen to the audio.

She checked the readings on the gear, then set out for the old fortress. If the Trans knew anything about nuclear weapons, they would try to get the warhead as high as possible to maximize the blast effect of the detonation. That meant the statue and the construction crane were the most likely places.

She got some buzzing as she walked around the outside of the old fort. She went in, took the stairs to the base of the pedestal. On the lower observation deck, which was really the top of the old fort, the Geiger counter squealed in her headset.

It was here! She walked completely around the base. The tone increased in intensity and volume the closer she got to the pedestal, and dropped as she walked away, to the edge of the old fort wall.

She circled the statue again, walked away, came back, left in another direction, and so on, until she was sure. The radiation seemed to be centered on the statue, not the construction crane, which sat beside the star-shaped fort. The crane's main tower rose to a fantastic height, then the arm stuck straight out across the gap between the crane and the statue. Cables led down from the end of the crane to the hoist platform the steelworkers were loading with scaffolding components. The weapon could be on the arm of the crane, she thought, but she doubted it.

Most of the island was behind the colossal statue, which faced east. Rita walked around, looking at everything, then went back inside.

She took the elevator to the upper observation level. She inspected the closed door that led to the "up" staircase, but didn't try to open it. She noted that the door marked "down" wore two padlocks.

She went out onto the observation balcony. The Geiger counter audio was louder. She had to turn down the volume. It was above her, then.

She went back inside, rode the elevator down, then walked out of the old fort. She went west across the island, past the construction trailers, piles of sand and scaffolding material, closed concession stands, public rest rooms, and the museum. When she was as far from the statue as she could get, she removed a cell phone from her pocket and draped the earphones around her neck. She dialed Jake Grafton's private line at Langley.

He picked up the telephone after the second ring. "Grafton."

"It's here, Admiral, just as you thought. It's in the statue."

When Jake finished his conversation with Rita Moravia, he stood mesmerized by the aerial photo that covered the wall. He sighed, then picked up the telephone and dialed Sal Molina at the White House.

"Jake Grafton. We need to talk as soon as possible."

"This evening?"

"How about within the next half hour?"

"I have a meeting."

"Cancel it."

"Come on over to the White House."

"Okay."

The subway was crowded. Jake Grafton stood and casually examined his fellow passengers. They were all sizes and shapes, ages and colors. A lot of tourists, apparently, here to see Washington before the heat and humidity of summer became oppressive. Kids wriggled, adults chattered or read or watched the walls of the tunnel flashing past.

Sal Molina was waiting for him at the security station. "We found it," Jake said as soon as he got through the metal detector.

"Where?"

"New York Harbor—the Statue of Liberty."

Molina stopped, stared into Grafton's eyes. "Sure?"

"It's there."

"Corrigan do it?"

"No."

"We'd better go see the president. He's twisting Senate arms just now." Molina led the way.

The president left the senators to listen to Jake's recitation.

"Good God," he said when Jake paused for air. "We're living in the age of maniacs." He sat silently for several seconds, trying to digest it.

"We'd be irresponsible if we didn't cancel Fleet Week," he said. "Maybe we should start evacuating New York City."

"We can't do either of those things," Jake said sourly. It was obvious that the president didn't understand the situation, which was a reflection on Grafton himself. He should have explained it better. "Those two homicidal idiots have the bomb in the statue. Wiring it to batteries and a capacitor is pretty simple. We must assume the weapon is hot—it's armed now. They haven't blown it yet, so they must be waiting for something. I suspect they are waiting for the Fleet Week opening ceremonies. They're waiting for the ships to arrive so they can sink them, and for you to arrive, Mr. President, so they can kill you."

"And if they are discovered or the party is canceled," the president said bitterly, "they'll just detonate the thing."

"That's about the size of it."

Jake's cell phone rang. He hauled it out of his pocket without apology and opened the mouthpiece cover. "Yes."

"Rita. Sonny's brother Nguyen just came out of the men's john. He's getting something to eat at the snack wagon." Fortunately neither man had ever laid eyes on Rita, yet she had studied their photos.

"Sonny must be around," Jake said. "Stay put, see if Nguyen goes up and Sonny comes down. Don't let either man spot you watching."

"Okay," Rita said, and broke the connection.

So they weren't holed up in the statue. Didn't need to be. It only took one man to push the button.

"You're still in charge," the president said pointedly, as Jake returned his cell phone to his pocket.

"They're maniacs, and we're running out of time," Jake said. "I'm going to New York as quickly as I can get there. We'll need the cooperation of the FBI and the Coast Guard. It's critical that we don't let these men suspect we're on to them—it's got to be business as usual on that island until we're ready to move."

CHAPTER TWENTY-SIX

Late Tuesday afternoon U.S. Coast Guard cutter *Whidbey Island* dropped her hook a half mile east of Liberty Island and backed down. Then she dropped another from the stern and tightened the cables so that she was moored between the two. Anchored bow and stern, she wouldn't swing when the tide changed.

On her closed bridge, Jake Grafton studied the Statue of Liberty with binoculars. There was someone on the balcony of the torch. A man. The warhead was probably there. The FBI had questioned Hoyt Wilson in his office on Liberty Island a few minutes ago and telephoned Jake. Wilson said the chopper delivered a box, "Pulpit," which was placed on the balcony since it was too large to go in the torch.

The agent who talked to Jake said, "We had to threaten this guy with arrest as a material witness, but he finally said that Gudarian told him the Pulpit device was a Corrigan radiation detection unit. I think he's afraid of going to jail for having classified information."

"Keep him there," Jake had said. "I want to talk to him."

It must still be on the balcony of the torch, Jake thought, and lowered the glasses. He rubbed his eyes.

The statue was in the ship's forward port quarter, about twenty degrees left of the ship's centerline. Beside Jake a sailor used a laser range finder to compute the exact distance. "Nine hundred and forty yards, Admiral."

"Very well."

The captain of the cutter was a lieutenant in rank, Schuyler Coleridge. With the anchors out, he ordered the bridge cleared so that he could be alone with Grafton. The admiral repeated the range to him.

"Think you can do it if necessary?"

Coleridge used his binoculars to glass the background behind the statue, then turned to the chart of the harbor. "Got a great shot from this position, but if we miss the shells are going into New Jersey."

"That's why you're here. You have a twenty-five-millimeter gun. If we use a five- or eight-inch gun, we'll blow up refineries, and we would have no guarantee that the contact fuses in the shells would detonate when they passed through the torch."

"Yes, sir." Lieutenant Coleridge couldn't have been over twenty-eight years old. He looks about Amy's age, Jake thought. *Ah me, his own ship. The lucky dog!*

"I think this is the best angle," Jake said, turning back to the business at hand.

"I agree," Coleridge said, and raised his binoculars again.

Jake continued, "The warhead is probably on the torch balcony. The renovation superintendent says the box it was in was too large to go inside the torch, and the warhead's probably too heavy for two guys to move, even if they took it out of the box."

"I see two men on the torch balcony."

Jake looked. He saw them, too.

"We're going to try to verify the weapon's location," Jake continued, "give you its exact position within the structure. I'll use the radio to give you the information. I want your Bushmaster manned and ready at all times. Don't aim it until I tell you; if the bad guys see that gun pointing at them, they'll smell a rat." The Bushmaster cannon was a 25-mm chain gun with a 400-rounds-per-minute cyclic rate. It had a 150-round magazine.

Coleridge lowered his binoculars and looked Jake square in the eyes.

"If I tell you to fire," the admiral said, "I want you to open immediately at the torch, right above Liberty's fingers. I want to shoot the torch off the statue."

"Sir, our gun is electro-optically aimed and unstabilized. I can't guarantee hits with the first rounds out of the tube."

"Got a good shooter?"

Coleridge grinned. "My gunner is an artist."

"Okay. Shoot until I tell you to cease fire or you run out of ammo. The skin is copper plating—the shells will go right through. There is a steel framework, and that is what we have to cut. The gunner will have to work his fire from side to side across the torch. I just hope to hell a hundred and fifty rounds is enough. Be ready to load a second magazine."

"If the warhead is armed, it may explode when it hits the ground," the lieutenant objected. "Or if one of the twenty-five-millimeter slugs hits the electric triggering mechanism."

Grafton nodded. "Indeed it might. I guarantee you that if it's armed and one of those maniacs pushes the button, it'll go nuclear. If it does, you and I will learn about it from St. Peter."

"Yes, sir."

"The more likely outcome is a conventional explosion—some of the high explosives in the warhead might go off and spew plutonium around the island and harbor if a shell hits the warhead or it smashes into the ground. That happens, we'll have a hell of a mess on our hands. But I'd prefer that to a nuclear blast."

Schuyler Coleridge took a deep breath.

"You're my last card, Mr. Coleridge. I won't ask you to shoot unless all else fails."

"Do I have permission to tell my crew what they are shooting at, sir?"

"No. This matter is classified top secret. You may tell your executive officer and your gunner. No one else."

"Aye aye, sir."

"By the way, liberty is canceled. Button up the ship. No visitors. No mail, e-mail, or telephone calls."

"I've already given the order."

Jake and the Coast Guard officer discussed radio frequencies and he used his handheld radio to talk to the cutter's radio operator. Finally he shook Coleridge's hand. "Good shooting," he said.

Fifteen minutes later a Coast Guard launch came alongside to take Jake off. It came up on the starboard side so that a watcher with binoculars on Liberty Island, if there was one, wouldn't see who boarded the launch.

Jake took the launch to Battery Park and walked to the dock that Corrigan Engineering was using for their crew boats. He displayed a Park Service badge and boarded the boat. No one he knew was aboard, he noted with relief. Not that he expected anyone. He had been talking to Rita via cell phone. Both the Trans were in the statue this evening. After Nguyen went to the rest room, ate, and returned to the statue, Sonny came down. He also used the rest room, then got something to eat from the snack wagon just before the operator closed for the night. After he had eaten he too returned to the statue.

When Grafton got to the island an FBI agent in work clothes and hard hat was waiting for him. He had an extra hat in his hand and handed it to Jake, who put it on. The agent led the way to the administration building and went upstairs to the second floor. A man in dirty jeans and T-shirt sat on the stairs with a backpack between his knees. He was also FBI, and there was a weapon in the backpack. He flashed a smile at Jake as he went by.

Sonny and Nguyen had checked the capacitor last night. It worked precisely as it should. The car batteries put out twelve volts each. They tightened all the connections, inspected the detonator terminals, wired everything up. Sonny put two firing switches in the circuit, either of which was capable of triggering the warhead. One he put right on the box that held the warhead. The other he put in the little work area where the goddess's hand grasped the torch. He checked each of the switches before he completed the final connection from the capacitor to the detonators.

This afternoon he checked all the connections again, looked everything over, then he and Nguyen sat on the balcony and kept an eye on things with binoculars. He kept down, under the level of the top rail, and looked out through the gaps.

"Either one," Sonny told Nguyen, gesturing to the switch on the box. "The one here or the one in the hole." He laughed. He was laughing a lot now. It was all so funny—checkmate! The bastards didn't even know they were doomed. Perhaps he should tell them, somehow. How would he do that?

He asked Nguyen about that.

"Why tell them?" his younger brother sneered. "They think they're so goddamn smart, with all the money and power. When this thing explodes they'll learn different. Learn that life's a dangerous journey and it doesn't always go the way you want."

"Through no fault of your own," Sonny added.

"Yeah," said Nguyen. He wished he had something to drink. A beer or whiskey or something. He lit a cigarette and savored the smoke as he watched the crane lower another load of aluminum scaffolding. Idly he focused his binoculars on the Coast Guard cutter.

Someone was swabbing the deck, another sailor was using a hose on the upper works, two guys were working on the gun forward of the superstructure. They had the cover off the gun and were doing something—he couldn't see what. He lowered the binoculars and sat thinking about things.

So it was about over. The end of the trail was in sight.

"We tell them we're going to do it," Sonny said, "they'll know that a nuke aboard a Navy ship didn't blow."

Nguyen didn't reply. He was thinking about wasting those ragheads in Florida, watching the little bastards die. That had been fun. He sat thinking about how it had been. When his cigarette burned down to the filter, he lit another and threw the butt over the rail.

"Don't do that," Sonny grunted. "Bastards will come up here."

"So? We'll blow 'em all to hell. Maybe shoot a few." Nguyen removed his pistol from his toolbox and put it on the deck beside him.

"Not yet." Sonny pointed to the *Ronald Reagan,* which was maneuvering into her assigned anchorage with the help of two tugs. She was three or four hundred yards farther east than the Coast Guard cutter that had anchored earlier. "When the big honchos are aboard and the television cameras are broadcasting the signal all over the world, then we do it."

Nguyen nodded. Too bad he couldn't watch New York go up in a mushroom cloud on television. The fall of the American empire, and he and Sonny would be the dudes who shoved it off the cliff.

He felt damned good.

No wonder Timothy McVeigh didn't apologize. Fuck 'em all.

"You know," he told his brother, "there's something to be said for giving the world the finger." He jabbed his aloft.

Sonny Tran laughed and laughed.

Hoyt Wilson was chewing a fingernail when Jake Grafton came into the room. Two FBI agents were with him, a man and a woman, and a tape recorder sat between them.

"Mr. Wilson has been very cooperative," one agent said.

"Terrific," Jake said, and dropped into a chair behind the desk. He pulled out the bottom drawer and propped his feet up on it. "Hope you don't mind," he said to Wilson.

"Not my office," Wilson replied.

"This man who called himself Gudarian—did he say he was spending the night on the island?"

"Yes. Said he and a colleague were going to stay in the statue through Fleet Week."

"Did you see a colleague?"

"No. Anyone could have come over on a work boat if they had the right credentials. He said he was going to lock it up, keep unauthorized people out."

"When did you leave last night?"

"Around six on one of the boats. Didn't see Gudarian after I left him." He shrugged.

"Seen him today?"

"No."

The man was plainly nervous. There was no way Wilson could pretend everything was normal if Sonny Tran dropped in for a chat. Jake asked one of the agents to find Rita Moravia.

"Do you have a guard on the statue?"

"We had one, construction security, a rent-a-cop. I didn't want workers sneaking up there on company time. I laid the man off. Maybe I shouldn't have with the Pulpit project and all, but it didn't seem—"

"What work remains to be accomplished inside the statue?" he asked Wilson.

"Everything is done except for a thorough cleaning. The best time to clean any construction site is after the construction debris is removed."

"Sure." He led Wilson on, chatting about the renovation of the statue, what had been done, how close to budget they were.

"Did Gudarian say he was expecting anyone else?"

"No. I told him about the television crew that has permission to film from the crown during the opening ceremony on Saturday, and he said we might have to cancel. Said he'd let me know."

"Okay."

"I want you to know that I thought this was a legit thing, Department of Defense approved. We had messages on it. Gudarian had a D.O.D. pass. He looked okay to me. I don't want to get in trouble over . . ."

When Rita came in, Jake introduced her to Wilson. "This is your new assistant. She's going to sit in your office in case Gudarian wants to talk to you. You need to get off the island, go home. Stay there."

"But the scaffolding, the cleanup . . . the job! We've got a contract to fulfill!"

"I take full responsibility. Believe me, the people in Boston have their hands full burying Mr. Corrigan. You'll catch no grief from them."

"Who *is* Gudarian, anyway?"

Jake rose from the chair and came around the desk. He put a hand on Wilson's shoulder. "Go home and stay there. Turn on a ball game. Tell anyone who calls that you are running a fever. No statements to the press. Nothing to the neighbors."

"This is my job," Wilson said, shaking off Jake's hand.

Grafton's tone changed. "You're smack in the middle of a classified matter involving national security. If you reveal it to anyone without a security clearance, you'll be arrested and prosecuted. Do you understand?"

"Who the hell are you?"

"You don't need to know that either. What will it be—home with the mouth shut or jail as a material witness, without bail?"

"Hey," Hoyt Wilson said. "Let's not go off the deep end here. I haven't done a damn thing wrong and I've been cooperative. I want to go home—I'll keep my trap shut."

Jake turned to Rita Moravia. "Take a tour and be seen with him. Shut down the scaffold crew and the crane. Have them come back in the morning at the usual time."

"Yes, sir," she said, and, taking Wilson by the elbow, steered him out.

Harry Estep, Tommy Carmellini, and Toad Tarkington arrived on Liberty Island after dark. Together with Rita Moravia and another half dozen FBI agents, they met in a small conference room in the National Park Service's admin building. Through the window the floodlit back of Lady Liberty was visible.

The FBI had brought pizza, sandwiches, and sleeping bags for their troops. When he saw Estep, Jake said, "Thanks for doing the witness protection thing for Anna Modin."

"Sorry it's taking so long. We'll have everything in place next week."

"Next week?"

"Yeah. She's staying at your place, isn't she?"

Jake realized that Carmellini was standing beside him, staring at Estep as if he'd seen a ghost.

"Let's talk about it next week," Jake said.

Tommy Carmellini took a seat in the corner and stared at his toes.

Over pizza Jake explained the situation. "There's an armed nuclear warhead on the torch balcony. Two homicidal maniacs are baby-sitting it. I think their plan is to blow it Saturday night during Fleet Week opening ceremonies, but they may panic and pop the thing anytime. In fact, the longer we wait, the more likely it is that they will sense the presence of law enforcement and push the button. I propose to take them down tomorrow morning."

Dead silence. It was broken when Harry Estep asked if anyone had thought about evacuating the people from the area around the harbor. "There must be eight or ten million people around this harbor who will be killed or maimed or poisoned with radiation if those criminals detonate that thing."

"How much time will an evacuation take?" Jake asked. "Can we keep it off radio and television? I don't know that Sonny and Nguyen have a portable radio or TV up there, but they might. What if we're evacuating and they blow the thing tomorrow night?"

"I'll be blunt, Admiral. Was the decision to take these people down in the morning made in the White House?"

Before Jake could reply, Toad Tarkington jumped into the fray. "I don't know how you do things in the FBI, but when an admiral in the United States Navy says we're going to fight, we're going to fight." He opened his mouth to say more, but a look from Grafton stoppered him.

Jake was deadly calm. "You've been ordered to cooperate, Harry. If it goes wrong tomorrow we'll all be dead and it won't matter who did or didn't sprinkle holy water on the grand plan."

Estep wasn't intimidated. "Input from a variety of sources might increase our chances of success."

"This is a military operation, not law enforcement," Grafton shot back. "I've been placed in command. Like everyone in this room, I obey the orders of my superiors. If you are unable to perform your professional duties for any reason under the sun, say so now so that I can get someone else."

Estep surrendered. "I withdraw my objection," he said.

"Fine," the admiral replied coldly. "There are several unknowns, and they complicate our problem. We don't know if the warhead detonator is radio-controlled. Nor do we know if the stairs and arm are booby-trapped. In any event, I suspect they could detonate the weapon with ten or fifteen seconds warning.

"We have a Coast Guard cutter anchored nine hundred forty yards in front of the statue. If worse comes to worst, I propose to order the captain to use his deck cannon to shoot the torch off the statue. The risks are obvious."

Dead silence followed that remark.

"I propose to put an FBI sniper on the crane. The problem is the location of the crane, to the north. It is not in the optimum location, and there's nothing we can do about that. Still, a sniper there would have a shot at anyone on the northern half of the balcony at a reasonable distance."

He certainly had their attention. His audience didn't seem to be breathing.

"The door from the torch to the balcony is on the west, or back, side of the torch. I intend to put four snipers on the west side, on top of the admin building or in trees, wherever. They'll have longer shots than the man on the crane, but with four of them, we increase our chances of a fatal hit."

"We don't have that many snipers here in New York available right now," Estep said.

"We'll use marine riflemen from the *Reagan,*" Jake said without missing a beat.

He continued, "Once we get the two men, we need to get someone to the weapon as quickly as possible. A properly equipped man on top of the crown, maybe up the arm, might be able to get to the torch, bypassing any booby traps or triggers on the stairs."

"What about a helicopter?" Estep asked.

"These guys came down from the torch yesterday evening one by one, went to the rest room and got food," Jake said thoughtfully. "They may have a timer set to detonate the weapon if they don't return within a certain period of time. The nearest places we can base a helo are Battery Park or the *Reagan*. It'll take time for a chopper to fly over, hover, and lower someone. It might take more time than we have."

"This isn't much of a plan," Estep observed sourly.

"I thought about having a cruiser use an eight-inch gun to shoot the torch off. I doubt that the shell would explode, but a hit would probably wipe the torch right off Liberty's arm. The problem is the weapon is undoubtedly armed. I'm afraid that course of action would simply mean that we pulled the trigger ourselves."

In the silence that followed, Jake directed his gaze at Carmellini. "Will you climb the statue? There won't be ropes, and we can't drill holes for safety anchors. You may fall off. If the enemy sees you too soon, I'm going to have the snipers and Bushmaster open up, but they may shoot you off that thing. Will you try it?"

Carmellini took a deep breath and exhaled completely before he nodded yes.

Jake looked from face to face. "Whatever we're going to do has to be done before the scaffold removal crew comes to work. We don't need an audience to gawk and point. And we can't afford to change the routine around here and make these guys suspicious. Whatever we do, it must be quick and deadly."

"You don't really have a plan," Estep said again.

"If you have a better idea, trot it out."

"One option is to wait for them to make a mistake."

"Time works against us. Every minute that passes with us on this island looking at them is a minute in which something can go wrong."

No one had any more objections. They discussed details for an hour.

As the meeting broke up, Carmellini buttonholed Jake. "Who were those guys who came for Anna?"

"Either assassins or Ilin's men. We'll sort it out next week. She's alive or she isn't."

Jake walked on out. There was much to do, and he didn't have time to fret about Anna Modin.

The Explosive Ordnance Disposal expert was an army warrant officer—Jake asked how much experience he had—who had been working with explosives for twenty-five years. The name tag on his uniform shirt said "Dillingham."

"I got a good look at the one you found in Washington, Admiral, so I shouldn't have any trouble disarming this one."

"Is there any way to rig it so that it will blow if someone tries to disarm the thing?"

"Yes and no, sir. If the cables to the detonators are severed downstream of the capacitors, then it can't go off. Of course, you can put a loop circuit on the thing with a sensor that will fire it if it senses a voltage drop, like someone cutting a wire. But they have to be cutting the wire on the loop circuit."

"Can you tell by inspection if it's rigged that way?"

"Yes, sir. If I have enough time."

"You're implying that they may rig a timer of some sort."

"Just like the fellow did in Washington."

"Umph," Jake muttered, and commenced chewing on his lower lip. Well, hell, this was going to be damned dicey—he knew that going in. "You stay out of sight and out of the way, Mr. Dillingham, until we need you. When we need you, the need will be urgent."

During the night a visitor arrived, Sal Molina. He found Jake watching the technicians set up the communications equipment in the conference room, the same room Jake had used to brief everyone.

They stared out the window at the floodlit statue as Jake briefed Molina, who grunted occasionally. He had no suggestions. When he had heard everything Jake had to say, he went into a private office, shut the door, and called the president.

When the darkness of night faded, low, dirty gray clouds could be seen scudding across the sky. The dark water of the harbor was frothy with whitecaps. Three more warships had anchored during the night. Ferries were steaming on their usual routes, airplanes were coming and going from Newark and JFK, whips of smoke rose from the stacks of the refineries in Bayonne and Jersey City. The day promised warmth and rain.

Jake Grafton glanced up at the torch of the statue, visible above the foliage of the trees outside the admin building, and wondered what those two up there were thinking this morning.

He didn't wonder long. He had decided sometime ago that they were both crazy, hate-filled killers. He just hoped that they weren't going to do the dirty deed in the next few hours.

He went back into the admin building. The FBI had set up a command post in the second-floor conference room. A technician in earphones was sitting there turning the pages of a morning newspaper someone had brought over from Manhattan during the wee hours. He shook his head at Jake, who put on the second headset anyway and sat on the edge of the table.

Nothing. The technician continued to turn the pages of the newspaper, read selective articles. His name was Salmeron.

The headset cord was just long enough to allow Jake to get to the coffeepot and box of doughnuts without taking it off. He helped himself and sat back down on the table.

"Looks like rain." That wasn't Sonny. Must be Nguyen.

"Yeah. Wind kept me awake."

"Sleeping on a steel floor kept me awake," Nguyen said. "And the way this damn arm thing moves in the wind. It's a wonder it hasn't broke clean off."

Sonny muttered something. Jake pressed his earphones to his ears, trying to catch the words. Nope, all he heard was noise.

He and Salmeron were listening to three parabolic microphones aimed at the torch. Each of them caught some of the sound, and the computer put the tracks together and played them for the listeners in real time.

One of the mikes was under the trees to the northwest of the statue, another was east, in front of it looking up, and the third was to the south, on the lady's right hand. The parabolic dishes of the east and south mikes were both visible from the torch, if either man had looked. So far they hadn't. The trick, Jake well knew, was not to listen too long.

"Have the technicians break down the parabolic mikes and get them out of there," he told Salmeron. "I don't want them spotted."

He glanced at his watch. It was two minutes after six. Around seven-thirty the steelworkers were going to be back at it.

There was a small replica of the Statue of Liberty on the desk nearby. He picked it up, ran his fingers over it, then placed it so he could reach it.

He used the handheld radio to call the cutter *Whidbey Island*. "You guys ready this morning?"

"That's affirmative."

"The target is the base of the torch, above the fingers. The thing is on the outside balcony, south side."

"Roger that."

"Repeat it to me."

"The base of the torch."

"Out."

At the next desk over, another FBI technician was monitoring a tactical communications network. Jake asked him, "Is the sniper doing okay?"

"Yes, sir. He reported a moment ago that he saw both men. One's on the balcony, one's inside. He can just see the head of the man on the balcony."

"What's the range?"

"Sixty-seven yards. Like shooting a fish in a barrel."

The sniper had climbed the crane during the hours before dawn. Just now he was in the operator's cab, sitting so that he could see the torch. He was actually about twenty feet above the top of the torch, sixty-seven yards away, so he was actually looking a bit down at the balcony. He was sitting on the floor of the cab looking through one of the operator's lower windows.

The sniper's name was Brendan McDonald. Jake had talked to him before he climbed the crane. "You ever shoot anyone with that rig?" Jake asked, nodding at the scoped bolt-action .308 rifle McDonald carried.

"No, sir. Never had to."

"If you have to shoot, I want your target really dead really quick. I don't know where the trigger for the weapon is, maybe on the weapon, maybe somewhere else. We need a one-shot kill."

"Yes, sir."

McDonald thought about that conversation as he sat in the cab on top of the crane. What a trip it had been climbing up here in the dark, carrying rifle and radio and a backpack full of water, crackers, and an empty bottle to pee in, plus ammo and laser range finder and binoculars.

The crane actually sat slightly east of north of the torch. McDonald could see into the balcony, but the weapon on the south side was out of sight. Nothing could be done about that. The crane could not be moved until it was disassembled.

Climbing up here had been an exercise in terror. At least it had been dark, so he wasn't tempted to look down. Now that the day had come McDonald couldn't believe he had done it.

He tried to put the view from the perch out of his mind and concentrate on the problem, which was that he didn't have a shooting position. He was inside the cab. Where he really needed to be was on top of it.

It wasn't a large structure, maybe six feet long by four feet wide. He could use carabiner rings to fasten his safety harness to the structure, so he wouldn't fall off. He hoped. Still, the risk was high. If he did slip and ended up dangling off this crane, one of the Trans would surely see him.

Regardless, he had to get to a place where he could aim the rifle for that one-shot kill that Grafton demanded, or he was going to have to hide here useless until the show was over or the world ended.

Brendan McDonald grew up in Cleveland, went to school in Michigan, and had worked out of the FBI's New York office for years. He had dozens of friends in New York, hundreds of acquaintances, a girlfriend and an ex-wife. He thought of those people as he adjusted his gear, slung his rifle over his shoulder, hooked a carabiner ring on one end of the ten-foot safety strap to a piece of structural steel inside the cab and hooked the other onto his safety harness. The earpiece and throat mike that allowed him to communicate on the tactical net were taped in place, so they wouldn't fall off. He inspected the run of the safety strap, trying to decide if the line might be cut by something if he fell and put a strain on it. Looks okay, he thought.

Still no one in sight on the torch balcony.

The ladder came up to the door in the back of the cab. He would have to get out on the ladder and scramble on up.

He tried not to look down. Holy Mother . . .

Brendan McDonald grasped the ladder, stepped out, and forced his muscles to move.

Last night before they knocked off, the scaffolding crew had torn the scaffold down to just one course above the observation balcony on top of the pedestal. Tommy Carmellini scrambled up onto the scaffolding and examined the small pile of gear that the two FBI agents had helped him carry up here. He was on the north side of the statue, out of view of anyone on the torch balcony. This was the side of the statue he was going to have to climb.

He looked up, trying to see how it was going to go.

He would have to traverse under Liberty's chin, then gain her right arm and climb up to the torch. If he could get that far, he could shoot through the air and water vents in the balcony floor. Or try to climb up on it.

The skin of the statue was composed of copper sheeting, which was riveted to the frame of the statue. That frame was now steel, though originally it had been iron.

He was wearing a safety harness and had a rope coiled over his shoulder, but this was a free climb—if he fell, he was dead.

He was going to have to climb quietly, and that meant suction cups. The FBI had spent most of the night acquiring the equipment Carmellini asked for. He assumed they had gotten it from climb shops in New York, but he didn't ask.

That Grafton! Nuclear weapons, terrorists, and he was Joe Cool. Toad said that when the admiral was young his squadron mates called him "Cool Hand," after the Paul Newman character in the movie.

Grafton hadn't turned a hair when the FBI dude said no FBI agents had come for Anna. Well, someone did. Carmellini thought about that as he checked his gear, cinched his backpack straps tight, made sure the laces on his climbing shoes were properly tied.

Grafton was right, of course: she was alive or she was dead. That was the reality. And there was nothing on God's green earth he could do about it.

As the morning breeze tugged at him in the gray light, he installed the first suction cup, pumped the handle to force the air out and create a seal, then tested it with his weight. It held. He did another one about waist high. It didn't hold, so he had to reset it. Standing on the first one, he placed the third one about shoulder height. Now he moved up to the second, using arm and leg strength, and broke the seal of the lowest cup using a string. He hauled it up, then straightened and installed it higher.

The statue was 151 feet tall. Call it 150. If he installed a cup every thirty seconds two feet above the last, he would need fifteen minutes to climb this thing. If he did a cup a minute he would need a half hour. Forty-five minutes to an hour was more likely—this was damned strenuous exercise—so that was the estimate he gave to Grafton.

Up the side of the statue he went, being careful to avoid thinking of Anna. Anything but that! Fortunately Tommy Carmellini had always had a good head for heights. He didn't bother to look down, but if he had it wouldn't have bothered him much. Climbing was great sport with him and good practice for burglary.

Standing on the observation balcony level in the top of the pedestal, Rita Moravia placed a stethoscope she had borrowed that morning from the construction first-aid office against the door to the crown stairs and listened.

Toad Tarkington was there with a submachine gun, one with a short barrel decorated with a long, sausage-shaped silencer. The weapon had no sights. He wore it on a strap over his shoulder.

Rita went out on the observation balcony and looked up, trying to see how Carmellini was doing. The scaffolding obscured her view. She returned to the door, applied the stethoscope, and stood listening.

Toad took the elevator down to the base of the pedestal. When he got into the position he wanted, he too checked in with Jake Grafton on the tac net.

"Toad's in position."

"Rita's in position."

"Tommy's halfway up. Another fifteen minutes, at least."

"McDonald's ready." The sniper's voice was distorted somewhat, barely recognizable.

"Estep's ready." Harry Estep and a squad of heavily armed FBI agents were inside a construction trailer near the main entrance to the statue. They wore body armor and were armed with submachine guns and satchel charges. If necessary, they were to blow the doors and fight their way to the torch.

In the admin building, Jake closed his eyes, concentrating on the situation. He was betting that the warhead was armed, the two men were in radio contact with each other, and they probably had some kind of alarm on the staircase. Then there was the door to the torch, three-quarters of the way up—it was probably alarmed and locked, too.

The safest course was to wait until one of them came down. They would eventually, but when? How long could he wait? What if Sonny or Nguyen saw the sniper or Tommy climbing the statue?

What if they pushed the button? What if a shell from *Whidbey Island* detonated the warhead?

Unable to stand still, he paced behind Salmeron and the other radio operator. Over in the corner, Sal Molina sipped coffee. Jake wondered how in the world he could keep it down.

Nguyen had spent the night on the balcony. He had one blanket under him and one on top, so he had slept reasonably well. He slept on the east side of the torch, sheltered slightly from the wind.

Now he sat on the blankets and played with the Glock. He took the magazine out of the pistol, emptied the shell from the chamber, and dry-fired it at this and that while he thought about wasting the drug dealers in Kansas and the Arabs in Florida.

He enjoyed killing people. Came to that realization a little late in life, he thought, and chuckled. He leaned forward and looked to his right. Sonny had a blanket draped over the weapon.

He reloaded the Glock and jacked a shell into the chamber, then engaged the safety.

"I need to take a piss," Nguyen called to Sonny, who was curled up under the light machinery.

"Drink the rest of the water in one of your bottles and pee in it. That's what we brought them for."

"I want to stretch my legs. I'm tired of sitting here."

"Lie down then."

"Sonny—"

"And when you do go, leave the fucking pistol, man. You look like you're itching to shoot someone."

"Anyone," Nguyen agreed.

"Pee in the bottle, then get busy with the binoculars. Crawl around the balcony and take a squint in all directions. Keep alert."

"Right." Nguyen reached for his backpack and hauled out the submachine gun. He cradled it in his lap, lit a cigarette, and studied the mechanism. Even a cup of coffee would be good.

Petty Officer Second Class Joe Shack wiped the morning dew and sea spray from his Bushmaster for the fifteenth time. He was wearing a sound-powered headset and listening to the skipper on the bridge. The old man—Coleridge—had just given him the range again, 940 yards.

A nuclear warhead! God in heaven! Who in hell would have believed it? Joe Shack, standing here ready to cut loose with a 25-mm cannon at a nuke?

He was nervous. He had tried to get some food down this morning before dawn and promptly vomited it back up.

Shoot at the base of the torch, the old man said, right above her fingertips. Saw that thing clean off the statue.

A good breeze was blowing and the cutter was taut on her mooring lines. Still, she was moving a little in the swell, and that worried him. With an unstablized gun, every shell didn't go where the gunner wanted it—that's a fact. The new Bushmasters were stabilized, of course, but the friggin' Congress hadn't given the friggin' Coast Guard the money to buy the new mounts. Low priority, he had heard. Nobody cared about the problems of shooting back at drug runners or pirates who were shooting at Coasties.

He stopped thinking about money and what he didn't have, and eyed the statue again. Ooh boy! Used the clean end of the rag to carefully wipe the moisture from the lens of the optical sight. Didn't want that puppy fogged up if and when.

Well, if that thing exploded he and all the guys on this tub were going to be radioactive ash. No two ways about it.

Hell, everyone in the harbor would probably go together.

He was thinking about that when he eyed the statue again, and saw something moving up the side of it. He had a good set of young eyes, but at a half mile in this light. . . .

"Skipper, guns. What's that on the north side of the statue, there by the tablet?" The skipper had binoculars.

"It's a man. Climbing the thing, looks like."

"Holy . . . !"

"Just stay cool, Shack. You can do this if you have to."

"Yes, sir."

"The admiral won't ask you to shoot unless it's absolutely necessary. If it is and he gives the order, just do the best you can."

Fuckin' A, man. Talk about balls, Coleridge had a set! He was going to sit up there on the bridge and watch ol' Joe Shack terminate life as we know it in the Big Apple. Goddamn steel *cojones*.

He was wiping furiously on the barrel of the cannon when the first drops of rain splattered on his face.

The marine detachment officer in charge aboard the *Reagan,* Captain BoBo Joachim, had brought his four most senior enlisted marines with him. He left them behind the admin building, out of sight of the statue, when he reported during the small hours of the morning. Now he had them positioned so that each had a good view of the torch. Each man had a shot of about three hundred yards. The steep angle allowed each rifle to be placed on a rest, in this case a rolled-up marine blanket. Over each man was a camouflage net or burlap bag, whatever seemed to best break up his outline and make him blend into the landscape.

Two of the marines were trained snipers, and Joachim had given them the two scoped sniper rifles from the ship's armory. The other two, both expert riflemen, were using issue M-16s with peep sights.

All the marines wore headsets that allowed them to listen on the tactical net, yet not transmit. If and when Admiral Grafton gave the order to fire, they would hear it as the words were spoken.

When BoBo Joachim returned from checking on his men, he stationed himself in the window near Grafton and focused his binoculars on the torch. His job was to call Carmellini's and the Tran brothers' position for Grafton.

He was scanning with the binoculars when he saw Tommy Carmellini, a tiny figure, move up onto the tablet in the statue's left arm. He told Grafton he was there.

Tommy Carmellini was resting where the tablet and Liberty's arm made a flat spot when a handful of rain drops hit him. Uh-oh. Rain would make this copper slick as snot.

"Tommy," he whispered. "I'm on the tablet."

He had no time to lose. It would probably be quicker if he free-climbed the rest of the way. He looked up, searching the folds of Lady Liberty's robe for hand- and footholds, then stood to his full height and reached. The wind buffeted him and more raindrops hit his cheeks and hands. He got a good hold with his left hand and hoisted himself up.

Jake Grafton fingered the small statue, studied the tablet that bore the date "July 4, 1776" in Roman numerals.

"It's raining," he heard Rita say. "Just a few drops, so far."

He looked at his watch. 6:25.

The raindrops didn't bother Brendan McDonald on his perch on top of the crane's control cab. He had his neutral camo blanket rigged over him to break up his shape and silhouette, and that kept the rain off. The wind pulled at the blanket and threatened to tear it off before he got it secured, but he had it now.

It was a miracle he hadn't fallen off this friggin' thing when he was getting up here and wrestling with the blanket and getting into position under it.

The real benefit of the blanket was that it functioned like a set of blinders on a horse—it forced him to concentrate on the only thing he could see, the view through the telescopic sight on the rifle. No one on the torch had seen him when he was getting into position and rigging the blanket, which was damned lucky. At this range they could have shot him right off this crane. Or pushed the button on the bomb.

The torch was about twenty feet below him, so his view was slightly down. Staring through the sight now, he could see the legs and lap of a man on the balcony. The man had a submachine gun in his lap and was smoking a cigarette. He fondles that weapon like it was a rosary, McDonald thought. The other man wasn't in sight.

He told Jake Grafton about the man on the balcony and received an acknowledgment.

His parents had wanted him to go into accounting, which was their profession. Perched 350 feet above the ground sweating a bullet or nuclear incineration, Brendan McDonald realized that he should have listened to his parents.

Tommy Carmellini felt as if he were scaling an Alp, a damn steep, slick one. He crossed under Liberty's chin and gained her right shoulder. Standing on it with his back to her neck, he looked up, trying to catch his breath. He was tired; two weeks of soft living without exercise had taken their toll.

He was about thirty feet under the torch. He had another ten feet of robe to cross, then the smooth plates of the goddess's arm rising up to the torch. He readjusted his gear, drained a small plastic water bottle and restowed it.

"Tommy. I'm ready for the arm," he said over the net.

"One man on the balcony, Tommy, east side, sitting." Jake Grafton's voice. "Go."

Carmellini scrambled upward. When he gained the top of her robe, he readied the suction cups and attached the first two. The copper was wet; he found the cups had to be as tight as he could get them to hold. A light misty rain blew on his face.

Inadvertently he glanced downward. God, he was high!

He paused and removed the coil of rope from his shoulder. Holding one end, he tossed it around the arm with his right, trying to make it come back to his left.

And missed.

He pulled the rope in and tried again. This time he got it. He snapped the hooks on the end of the rope to the carabiner ring on his safety harness. Just in case. Then he started upward using the suction cups.

Sitting in the little area at the top of the ladder inside the torch, Sonny Tran heard the slap of the rope on the arm twenty feet below him. It was a single sound that echoed inside the arm.

A moment later he heard it again.

He listened carefully. Something was down there.

"Nguyen," he called, "you see anything?"

"No."

"Get off your ass and look."

Up on the balcony, Nguyen picked up the binoculars and sat erect. He looked over the edge of the balcony rail, looked at the *Reagan* and the cutter, looked at the ground far below. And saw nothing that piqued his interest. He moved to the north side of the balcony, staying low, and looked again.

He examined the crane with binoculars. No one in the control cab yet. Man, how would you like to have the job of operating that damned thing, climbing up and spending the day there, then climbing down every evening? If that crane ever collapsed, the operator was a dead man.

He moved on around the balcony to the west side, right in front of the open door. He studied the admin buildings, the boat dock—there was a boat arriving now and people getting off—glassed the piles of construction material and the walks and buildings.

He moved on over to the south side, right beside the weapon. He patted it, then glassed the south side of the island.

"Looks okay to me," he told his brother, who was seated below him, inside the door.

"Well, I heard something. I'm going to set the timer for fifteen minutes, then I'm going downstairs for a look. Check your watch."

Nguyen did so. It was 6:47 A.M.

"Okay," Nguyen said. "I'll turn my radio on."

After setting the timer, Sonny turned and went backward down the ladder inside the arm.

With his head literally against the arm, Tommy Carmellini heard the noises of Sonny descending. He didn't have a free hand. He had his tac net earpiece in his left ear, so he turned his head and pressed his right ear against the copper skin. He could hear someone in there, which meant they could also hear him. He froze.

Sonny descended the ladder to the door that blocked public access to the arm. He and Nguyen had installed a padlock on the inside last night—he unlocked it now, and with pistol in hand, gently pushed the door open.

Not a soul in sight. He gingerly looked around, pistol in hand, ready for anything.

Christ, he had heard something!

Maybe a bird that accidentally flew into the structure, or a skin plate cooling.

He used the radio. "All clear. I'm going on down for a look. Stay alert."

"Right."

The words came over a scanner that the FBI technicians had set up to monitor the civilian two-way radio frequencies. Jake Grafton heard it and recognized Sonny's voice.

He keyed the mike for the tactical net. "Rita and Toad, Sonny's coming down. You snipers, be alert."

Sal Molina sat erect in his chair. His eyes were closed, but he was listening, Jake knew, visualizing the people and what was happening.

Jake Grafton picked up the miniature statue, turned it over in his hand, rubbed it with his fingers.

Sonny Tran descended the steps slowly, stopping frequently to listen. Whatever that noise was, he had not heard it again.

Down, down, down, the steps went on and on. He descended slowly, making no noise, the pistol at the ready.

If they got him they wouldn't win. Nguyen would hear the shot, would set off the warhead. And send all these fucking bastards straight to hell.

Carmellini stayed frozen until he heard Jake's voice in his left ear.

Still misting rain. The water coursing down the side of the arm had soaked him. He moved upward and, holding his weight with his left arm, used his right to remove a suction cup and attach it higher.

Running out of strength. He should not have agreed to do this. He was out of shape, too old for this shit, and he damn well knew it.

He pulled himself up with his right hand and used his left to detach that cup. Hc had it off and was moving it when the right cup slipped.

He grabbed with both hands, but there was nothing to hold on to. Off the arm he went, falling toward the earth far below.

Brendan McDonald saw Carmellini fall. "Tommy fell. He's hanging on the end of the safety line."

Jake Grafton heard the words and snapped over the net, "Where's the man on the balcony? Watch him!"

Carmellini hung from the safety line adjacent to Liberty's right armpit, three or four feet below the arm. He still had a suction cup in each hand.

His heart was hammering, his chest was heaving, . . . He paused for ten seconds to gather his strength, then stowed the cups and began pulling himself up the line toward the arm. Using every ounce of strength he possessed, fighting the water dripping off the structure, he attached a suction cup with his right hand and heaved himself up.

Sonny listened at the door at the foot of the stairs for half a minute before he unlocked it. He pushed it open. No one in sight. He put the pistol in his waistband under his windbreaker and stepped out into the area in front of the ticket booths.

Satisfied, he jabbed the button to call the elevator. Funny that it should be down. He had ridden it up and left it here when he went up.

Perhaps a watchman had ridden up and looked around, then ridden down. That would explain it. Or perhaps the elevator was on a timer.

When the door opened he entered. Jabbed the down button.

The door closed and the elevator descended the shaft toward ground level.

He stood to one side as the door opened, moved carefully.

Damn place was empty as a pharaoh's tomb.

He walked out and turned the corner.

Toad Tarkington was standing there with the submachine gun leveled. Even as Sonny realized who it was, Toad pulled the trigger.

The silenced submachine gun buzzed loudly, and shells kicked out as Toad held the trigger down. The bullets marched up Sonny's chest and neck and smashed his head back, jackhammering him off his feet.

He was dead when he hit the ground.

"Sonny's down," Toad said on the tac net.

"Get up there," Jake Grafton told him. "Nguyen's alive and well and Tommy's dangling off the arm."

Toad took the time to check Sonny's pockets. He pulled out the two-way radio and put it in his own pocket. No radio-control unit, he noted, that might be used to detonate the warhead remotely.

He took the elevator up and met Rita at the door. She also had a submachine gun—she had been waiting out on the observation deck in the event Sonny went out there first.

Together they began climbing the stairs.

Scrambling back up onto the arm, Tommy Carmellini was making noise, noise that even the wind couldn't muffle. Nguyen Tran heard it. Staying low, he moved around to the north side of the balcony and looked down. And saw Carmellini.

He didn't know who he was—he had never seen him before—but it was obvious that the authorities were up to something. People don't scale the Statue of Liberty on a lark.

Nguyen and Sonny had agreed months ago what they would do if the authorities got on to them. They would detonate the weapon then and there. And win!

Nguyen keyed the mike on the radio. "Sonny? Sonny?"

No answer.

Well, hell, why not?

He straightened up, grasped the Glock in both hands, leaned over the rail, and took careful aim at Tommy Carmellini.

"Hey, asshole!" he called. "Look up here! Look up and see what I'm going to give you!"

Brendan McDonald saw it happening. He didn't even have time to say anything on the tac net. He centered the crosshairs of his rifle on Nguyen Tran and pulled the trigger.

The shot knocked Nguyen back against the core of the torch. He looked down at his chest at the spreading red stain, so stunned and amazed that he didn't realize he had dropped the pistol.

I've been shot, he thought.

The fact that the bullet had penetrated his right lung—had gone completely through his body—didn't register. Now he remembered the warhead.

Gotta push the button. Blow it!

He staggered to the west, going around the balcony toward the weapon. The switch was there, right there, and all he had to do was reach it.

Jake Grafton was watching through binoculars. He saw Nguyen, holding himself erect with one hand on the railing and one on the side of the torch, fighting grimly to put one foot in front of the other.

"Snipers, kill him! Now!"

The reports of the four marine rifles sounded as one. People getting off the work boat and buying coffee and doughnuts at the snack wagon heard it and looked up, startled.

Three of the bullets hit Nguyen Tran, smashing him against the torch. By some miracle he stayed erect, staggering, trying to reach the warhead.

Then he fell outward, against the railing. In his determination to stay erect he stiffened his legs—soaked up another bullet from Brendan McDonald—and went over.

Jake saw the body falling. He dropped the binoculars.

"Come on," he roared at Sal Molina. "Come on!" He raced from the room, took the stairs three at a time, and burst from the building on a dead run.

Harry Estep, two of his men, and Dillingham, the bomb disposal expert, followed Toad and Rita up the stairs. They didn't run. It was just possible the place was booby trapped—after all, Sonny and Nguyen had all night. How paranoid were they?

Toad inspected the ladder leading to the torch with a flashlight before he began climbing.

Rita was right behind, with Dillingham behind her.

The timer was at the top of the ladder. It was a mechanical unit with a dial one twisted to set the time. Less than a minute to go.

Toad wiped his fingers, looked at the faceplate of the timer. Beside it was a switch, just a simple dollar switch from an automotive parts store.

He was breathing heavily from the climb and his ribs hurt like hell.

He wiped his hands again on his trousers. The bomb expert was way back there—and there wasn't enough room for him unless Toad went all the way up to the balcony. He had to make a decision.

He twisted the dial to the stop and released it. Now they had thirty minutes.

"This is the timer and trigger switch," he muttered at Rita. Then he went on by, on up to the balcony.

The steel plates there had blood on them. Toad ignored the red splotches, looked over the railing. Carmellini was coming up the goddess's thumb.

"Hey, shipmate," said Toad. "Toss me a rope."

"I don't have one to toss," Carmellini hissed, and set the next cup.

Jake Grafton climbed the ladder inside Liberty's arm and found no one in the base of the torch. He continued upward to the balcony.

Dillingham had the access plate off the box the warhead was in and was inspecting it with a flashlight when Jake arrived. He reached in with a set of wire cutters. When he backed out, he saw Grafton.

"It's safe, Admiral."

As Jake helped Toad and Rita haul an exhausted Tommy Carmellini over the railing, he heard Harry Estep on his cell phone. "We've got it, Mr. Emerick. The weapon is safe."

Carmellini flopped down on the balcony, gasping for air.

"Thanks, Tommy," Jake said, bending over. "You gave us our chance."

"Next time . . ." Carmellini rasped out between breaths, "I want . . . a desk job. Promise me!"

Rita hooted with laughter, and Toad joined in.

Aboard *Whidbey Island,* Lieutenant Coleridge told Joe Shack on the sound-powered telephone, "Stop polishing that damn gun and put the cover on it." Then he picked up the mike for the public address system, which had a loudspeaker in every compartment of the small ship.

"Liberty call for everyone except the duty section. If you have the hots to see New York in the rain, now's your chance. Bosun, get the launch in the water."

Joe Shack threw his rag on the deck and ran for the railing. When his stomach settled down, he stood looking at the Statue of Liberty. He drew himself to attention and saluted. She didn't salute back—merely stood there against the gray sky with her torch held aloft.

Shack got out the cover for the gun and began the process of installing it.

Grafton, Carmellini, and the Tarkingtons were sitting with their backs to the torch facing Manhattan a half hour later when Jake's cell phone rang. He dug it out of his pocket. It was Callie, calling from Washington.

"Where are you?" she demanded.

"Sitting on the balcony of the Statue of Liberty watching the clouds over Manhattan. It's a gorgeous day, misting rain. The Empire State Building is fading in and out."

"Emerick is on television. He just announced that the FBI found a warhead in the statue. Do you know anything about it?"

Jake began laughing and couldn't stop. He passed the cell phone to Rita, who listened to Callie, said something, and also dissolved into laughter.

When he got the phone back, Jake told his wife, "I'll tell you all about it this evening. Thought I might take the train home with Carmellini and the Tarkingtons this afternoon. Could you meet us at Union Station? I'll call you later, tell you when we're getting in. Bring Amy and we can get some dinner somewhere."

"I love you, Jake."

"I love you, too, Callie."

CHAPTER TWENTY-SEVEN

In the weeks following Fleet Week, Jake Grafton's ad hoc computer staff was transferred in toto, people and equipment, to the joint antiterrorism task force. Their labors had begun to bear fruit. The tangled skein of money transfers throughout the world was being untangled, the identities of those people and governments around the world who put up the money for terrorism were being established, and terrorist cells in America and Europe were being uncovered, cells that were made targets of traditional law enforcement investigations.

Tommy Carmellini went back to his regular job at Langley, only to find that the paper on his desk had accumulated dramatically in his absence. Rita Moravia went back to the Fleet Week staff, which was in the midst of its own postevent wrap-up and planning for the event the following year.

Gil Pascal left for a Pentagon billet, and Toad Tarkington received orders to the staff of Atlantic Fleet. Toad had to find a new job because Jake submitted his retirement papers, as he said he would, and scheduled himself for terminal leave.

Zip Vance married one of the secretaries after a whirlwind courtship and found himself assigned to the CIA's permanent technical staff. He stopped in to shake Jake's hand, muttered something about Zelda that Jake didn't catch, and said good-bye.

Zelda Hudson's future was very much up in the air. She stayed at the remnants of the bank of computers in the basement and finished her self-assigned project, which she titled "A Day in the Life of a Drug Dealer." The video tracked a drug dealer through the streets of Washington using traffic surveillance cameras, video cameras at convenience stores and those that monitored pay telephones, cameras in malls, department stores, and the public housing projects. The video ran for twenty-two minutes.

Jake sent it to the Justice Department for a screening. The legal eagles were horrified, apparently, because three days later an assistant attorney general telephoned Jake and demanded that he personally destroy the tape and delete the computer file.

"Outrageous!" the lawyer thundered. "Never in my career have I seen a more egregious violation of the civil liberties of an American citizen."

"What did you think of that doper driving around the nation's capital peddling poison?"

"The amazing thing," the lawyer said, "is that you made the tape in direct violation of the statute that prohibits the CIA from spying on Americans."

"I was thinking of sending copies to CNN and CNBC," Jake said lightly. "Think they'd air it?"

"I am referring this matter to the attorney general with a recommendation that you be court-martialed."

"Better hang on to your copy of that tape, then," Jake retorted. "You're going to need it as evidence." He hung up on the assistant attorney general.

Three days later he was summoned to the White House by Sal Molina. The president wasn't in town just then, so the White House lacked its usual charged energy, that center of the universe feeling. Jake found Molina in his cubbyhole office a few yards down the hallway from the Oval Office.

"So you're retiring," Molina said with amusement.

"Yep. Gonna become a civilian and get rich in corporate America. Get an accounting job with some stock options."

"Sure. You'll fit right in at America Incorporated. By the way, I got a call yesterday from an assistant attorney general. He wants your head on a platter. Demanded that you be court-martialed. What in hell was that all about?"

Jake told Molina about the tape, about how Zelda Hudson cobbled it together from various video feeds.

"You let her do it, of course."

"Of course."

Molina removed a classified file from his desk, took out the document and tossed it across his desk. "Page three," he said.

The document was the daily intelligence brief for senior White House and National Security Council executives. Jake found a paragraph that had been circled. Walney's Bank in Cairo collapsed three days ago, the item noted. Then last night, Cairo time, the president of the bank, one Abdul Abn Saad, was murdered with a car bomb.

"Saad, his wife, and their chauffeur—boom!" Molina said when Jake handed the document back. "You know anything about this?"

"I might be able to throw a little light in that corner," Jake admitted. "I asked Zelda to loot the bank, bleed money from Sword of Islam accounts into some accounts Saad had in Switzerland. She told me she covered her tracks pretty well."

Molina grinned. "Won't be the same without you around here."

Jake smiled.

"What are we going to do about Zelda?"

"I suggest you send her over to NSA." NSA was the National Security Agency. "They're tearing their hair out over there trying to decrypt these public key codes that every software store in the world is selling. Zelda is a certified genius. Maybe she can help."

Molina thought about it, sighed, then said, "I'll talk to the president about it."

They chatted for a few more minutes, then Jake shook hands and left.

Molina was as good as his word. The Monday following the White House visit, Zelda stopped by Jake's office. She was going to NSA. "Thanks, Admiral, for everything. You've saved my life twice now."

A smile and a handshake, and she was gone. Jake pulled out the bottom drawer of his desk, propped his feet up, and was deep into a copy of *Trade-A-Plane* when he heard another knock on his door. "Yo."

Tommy Carmellini came in and dropped into a chair. "I hear you're retiring."

"That's right. Terminal leave starts in ten days."

"So what are you going to do now?"

Jake held up *Trade-A-Plane*. "Going to buy a Cessna 170 and go flying with Callie. Been thinking about it for years. We're going to do the whole lower forty-eight before the snow comes."

"And after that?"

"Well, I don't know. Might do it again next summer. And the summer after that. Might even take up fishing."

Carmellini nodded. From his coat pocket he produced a postcard. "Got something I thought you might be interested in, Admiral. Arrived at my apartment in yesterday's mail."

The picture was of a riverboat on the Seine.

"Didn't you meet Ilin in Paris?" Carmellini asked.

"Yes, I did."

Jake turned the card over. It carried a French stamp and an illegible postmark. The message was in English. "I'll be back someday. Love, Anna."

"That her handwriting?" Jake asked as he passed the card back.

"I think so."

"Looks like life isn't over for you after all."

Carmellini got out of his chair and stretched. A smile crept across his face, then he grinned broadly.

Jake Grafton slammed his lower desk drawer, grabbed his hat and the copy of *Trade-A-Plane,* and said, "Let's give ourselves a meritorious day off. There's a plane in Frederick the owner wants me to fly—he thinks I'm a sizzling hot prospect. Let's go do it."

As he walked out of his office with Carmellini trailing in his wake, Jake shouted, "Tarkington! Lock up and turn out the lights. Let's go fly."

POSTSCRIPT

Snow driven by a bitter wind swept across the vast, barren steppes of central Asia. It was a dry snow, accumulating on top of the frozen earth and the existing crusted snow patches at a rate of less than a quarter inch per hour because the temperature was ten degrees below zero. It streaked horizontally through the headlights of the truck and reduced visibility to yards.

The driver fought the wheel with both his gloved hands as the wind pushed against the side of the truck. "Not too much farther, I think," he said to the man in the right seat, Frouq al-Zuair, who huddled deeper into his heavy coat. The truck's heater was incapable of raising the temperature inside the cab above the freezing level. Drafts coming around the edges of the ill-fitting doors and through rusted holes in the floorboards didn't help.

"Is the van still following?" Zuair asked the driver.

"It's back there."

Both men felt relieved when they spotted a gleam of light in the snowy darkness ahead. Sure enough, it proved to be a naked bulb mounted high on a pole beside a gate. On each side of the gate a high wire fence ran away into the darkness.

The driver turned off the road and pulled to a stop beside the guard shack, in front of the barrier. Frouq al-Zuair steeled himself and opened the truck door. The icy wind was vicious. He hustled around the front of the truck and jerked open the door to the guard shack. The soldiers inside were huddled around a heater. Several had their backs to it.

"I am Ashruf," Zuair said in Russian. "I came to see General Petrov."

Two of the soldiers went outside to inspect the trucks while one of the others made a telephone call. When he hung up he nodded at the remaining Russians, who went outside to raise the gate. Zuair got back in the truck.

The inspection took another two minutes to complete, then the gate opened and one of the guards waved the truck and van through.

The wind seemed to become fiercer as the truck and the van that followed it left the guard shack behind. The vehicles bumped and jostled over the frozen ruts in the road, occasionally sliding, as they crossed a low ridge and descended toward a lit compound, the only light in that black universe.

There was another gate on the compound. An armed guard waved them through.

They passed two idling tanks, then stopped in front of a well-lit single-story building. Zuair went inside. General Petrov and two officers were there, as well as the long-haired woman he had seen the last time he was here. She was wearing an ankle-length fur coat and a fur hat.

"We want four warheads, Petrov." He glanced around the room. "Where is the sample?"

"The weapons are still in the magazine. They told you the price? Four million American?"

"We brought three million. We will not pay four."

"For that price you get three warheads. Your friends in Saudi Arabia are rich and can afford to pay us for the large risk we are taking."

Zuair was obstinate. "Then I have come all this way for nothing."

They haggled while the woman lit a cigarette, seemingly bored. At last Petrov capitulated. "This time I will give you four bombs for three million. But if you come again, the price is a million each. Not a penny less. It takes money to play this game."

The Arab went to the door, motioned to the men in the van that sat behind the truck. Five of them brought in dark green duffel bags.

They remained in the room while one of the army officers emptied the bags upon the table. The woman got out her equipment and began inspecting random bills as the army officers counted the bundles.

When they finished that task, they began counting the bills in random bundles. They arranged the bundles in stacks.

"It's real currency," Anna Modin said finally, after ten minutes of inspection.

After huddling with the army officers, who compared their tallies, Petrov announced, "We are satisfied. Three million."

He led the way out into the snow and climbed into the cab of a truck full of troops. The truck got under way, leading Zuair and his friends in their own vehicles.

The snow and wind had not eased. If anything, it was worse. The little caravan passed twenty or so magazines before it stopped in front of one.

As Zuair climbed out of the truck cab, a series of floodlights atop the magazine and on the opposite side illuminated, temporarily blinding him.

He heard the ripping of a machine gun, felt something hammering into the truck door. Then something slammed into his legs, knocking him to the frozen earth.

Someone screaming. . . . He heard someone screaming.

He reached into his coat, tried to pull his pistol free as the first machine gun was joined by others. He was lying on his side and the weapon was under him. He struggled to roll over but he couldn't feel his legs. Then something hit him in the arm and he lost feeling in it.

The shooting continued, long bursts from multiple weapons. How long it continued Zuair didn't know, but finally all the shooting stopped.

He was lying on his side, feeling the warmth of his own blood soaking his clothes and coat when a foot rolled him over. General Petrov stood there, a pistol in his hand. He grinned at Frouq al-Zuair, pointed the pistol at his head.

The Russian bent down. He placed the muzzle of the pistol against Zuair's forehead, then reached into his coat and tugged at the Arab's pistol. When he pulled it out, he straightened.

"Put them all in the truck, then back it into the magazine," Petrov shouted. "The van, too."

Rough hands seized Zuair, lifted him bodily and carried him around behind the truck. The cargo door was open, and the soldiers—there were now four of them holding him—tossed him into the empty bay. The shock of hitting the hard floor drew a groan of agony from Zuair. Other bodies were tossed into the truck. At least one other man was still alive, because he, too, groaned.

Finally the door closed. A minute or so later the truck started and began to move.

When the motion stopped and the truck engine was turned off, Zuair struggled to move with his good arm. A body lay across his injured legs. The shock of the bullets was beginning to wear off.

Fighting intense pain, Frouq al-Zuair managed to lift his head from the bed of the truck. He could see nothing in the darkness.

Then he heard the fireproof steel door of the magazine slam shut.

His strength failed him. He collapsed and lay still. He listened to the moans of the other man who still lived, but they stopped after a bit.

Cold. The blood from his wounds had soaked his clothes, and now the cold attacked the wetness.

He tried to crawl but lacked the strength. Murdered by infidel Russians! He was cursing them when he passed out from loss of blood.

Sometime later that night his heart stopped.

When General Petrov returned to the compound, he went straight into the single-story building. The stacks of money were still on the table. Anna Modin was seated where he had left her, but another man, a tall, lean man wearing a blue suit under an open coat stood relaxed, with his feet apart, at the far end of the room.

Petrov faced the stranger. "Who are you?" he demanded.

The man's hand swept up. There was a pistol in it, one wearing a large silencer. The gun had been hidden by the folds of the coat. "Doesn't matter," he said.

Petrov glanced at Anna Modin, who was lighting a cigarette. Their eyes met as she lowered the lighter.

"Where are my men?" the general demanded in a hollow voice.

"They suddenly realized that they wanted to be somewhere else," the stranger said. "Are the Arabs dead?"

"Yes."

"What did you do with the truck and van?"

Petrov licked his lips. "They're in an empty magazine with the bodies."

"Why did you kill them?"

"The risk was too great. Someone was bound to talk eventually, and the whispers would get to Moscow. Whispers always do, don't they?" Petrov shrugged, then dived sideways and grabbed for the pistol in his belt holster.

Janos Ilin's first bullet missed Petrov, but his second didn't. Nor did the third.

When Petrov ceased moving, Ilin walked toward him. Petrov's eyes followed him.

"Why?" said Petrov.

"An American naval officer asked a favor of me. This was it."

With that comment Ilin aimed the pistol at the center of Petrov's forehead and pulled the trigger again. Petrov's head jerked under the impact of the bullet, then his eyes ceased to focus and he stared fixedly at nothing.

"What are we going to do with the money?" Anna Modin asked Ilin.

"Someone has to pay for the war against terrorism," Ilin said. "It might as well be the terrorists."